Nine to One
A New Generation

Book 1

By: Peter Evan Fatouros

Peter Evan Fatouros

First paperback edition January 2024

Paperback ISBN: 978-1-0689095-1-1

Other works published by the author:

Clockwork Bread

1965

March 21st, 1965
Bellevue Hospital

Nurse Lilah Banks was walking through the maternity ward with a pile of fluffy, pink baby blankets in her arms when she almost ran into Dr. Henry Cornish.

"Sorry Doctor, I didn't see you there."

"Yes, well. Close call, but no harm done. Where are you off to in such a hurry?"

"The nursery sir. They've run out of pink blankets for the little girls. Third time in as many days."

"What do you mean?"

"For the last few days, the nursery has been full of girls, sir. Barely any boys at all."

"How unusual. I think that I'd like to see this for myself."

The doctor gestured with his hand that the nurse should lead the way. He then followed behind her until they reached the maternity ward where head nurse Mercy Monroe was waiting for the new pink blankets.

"Sorry it took me so long to get here. I almost ran into Doctor Cornish in the hall."

"Yes, well, you're just in time. We're going to be needing those blankets soon. We have four more women in labor & I'll bet you that at least three of them will be girls."

"Should I get more blankets?"

"I'm not even sure if we have more. Do me a favor, head down to the laundry & tell them that we'll need some more pink baby blankets from them as soon as we can have them."

"Yes mam."

Nurse Banks then headed off on her way to the laundry while Nurse Monroe went to speak with Doctor Cornish.

"Is something the matter doctor?"

"I shouldn't think so. They all appear to be healthy. Have there been an unusual number of newborn boys in distress?"

"No Doctor. It's just that most of the babies that have come through here in the last few days have been girls."

"When did this start?"

"I'm not certain. I remember that two or three days ago, I noticed that we were running low on pink blankets."

"How many boys have been born here in the last three days?"

"I'm not sure Doctor, maybe seven or eight."

"How many girls have been born in that time?"

"I can't be certain, but I'd say somewhere around sixty or seventy. We're seeing about as many births here as we normally do Doctor, it's just that almost all of them have been girls for the last few days. Should we be worried?"

"I don't know. I've never heard of anything like this."

March 28th, 1965
Oval Office

"What do you mean 90%?"

Lyndon Johnson sat behind his desk in the oval office in disbelief. When his Secretary of Health, Education & Welfare had requested an emergency meeting on a Sunday afternoon, he had been expecting that it would be something to do with the civil rights marches of Martin Luther King jr., or perhaps something to do with health issues of soldiers returning from Vietnam. He wasn't expecting the secretary to tell him this.

"That's right Lyndon, reports started flying around a few days ago from concerned doctors. When I first heard about it, I asked the governor's office of every state if they could get confirmation. I just got the last confirmation this morning. It seems that every hospital in the country is reporting the same anomaly. Over the last seven to ten days, 90% of all newborns in the country have been girls as opposed to the normal 50%."

"Has something like this ever happened before?"

"No sir. On occasion, there are minor deviations from the norm, a day or two where boys or girls are 60% of newborns in a hospital, but nothing like this. Nothing that has hit the entire country at once, across every demographic, for over a week. It's unheard of."

"I see. Is this new anomaly happening anywhere else Anthony?"

"It seems to be. I've called up my counterpart in Canada, Judy LaMarsh, the Minister of National Health, and Welfare. She's been getting very similar reports from across the Canadian provinces & territories. It's the same with Kenneth Robinson, the Minister of Health in the UK & with Raymond Marcellin, the French Minister of Health. I've currently got several members of my team contacting governments all over the world. It seems to be happening everywhere."

President Johnson was stunned. His mind immediately started trying to think of the potential ramifications of what was happening. If this was happening to the Soviets, they might see it as some sort of an attack. He quickly jotted down a note to contact Leonid Brezhnev, the new First Secretary of the Soviet Union.

"Anthony, before I have to start making some important & delicate phone calls, I need to know if this is a long-term problem, or just some sort of a blip that will only go on for a week or two."

"I understand sir, I'll see if I can get hospitals to start submitting anonymous ultrasound information, which should at least tell us if this will go on for weeks or months. I'll try to have something for you in the next few hours."

"Ultrasound? I'm not sure that I've heard of that one Anthony."

"It's a medical device that was invented a few years ago. It's sort of like sonar for the womb. It sends ultrasonic sound waves into the uterus & the reflection of those soundwaves allows us to construct a picture of what's happening in there."

"Impressive. Is it safe for the child?"

"Perfectly safe sir. It's not a common procedure just yet, but a number of hospitals have started implementing it for the purpose of detecting medical issues before the child is born. I believe that we should be able to use this to determine the gender of children up to 15 or 20 weeks before birth. That should give us an indication of the next few months."

"Get to it Anthony. I've got a war, a civil rights movement & a space race to deal with. The last thing this country needs right now is some sort of long-term... lack of sons."

March 30th, 1965
Audience room in Buckingham Palace

Harold Wilson walked into the audience room for his weekly meeting with the Queen. He had known that when he became Prime Minister almost six months earlier, that there would be times when he would have to present the Queen with some distressing news. However, this was not the kind of thing that he had thought that he would have to report. Once the royal guard introduced him, he bowed his head from the neck as was custom.

"Your Majesty."

He then took a seat opposite her as she indicated for him to do each week.

"Hello Mr. Wilson, I must say, I was rather surprised when your office called & asked to hold our meeting a day early. Is something the miss with Gambia?"

"Ah, no Ma'am. All seems well with the Gambia since they gained their independence in February. This early meeting was requested for a more... unusual situation that has developed. We've been learning about this as a result of unusual reports from various hospitals & conversations with the American Secretary of Health, Education & Welfare."

"This sounds rather serious. Has there been some sort of an outbreak?"

"No Ma'am, there seems to be an issue coming from maternity wards all over the country."

At the mention of maternity wards, the Queen seemed to almost reach for her abdomen unconsciously before pulling her hand back. Having given birth to her fourth child just a year ago, the news of a nationwide maternity issue had her attention as her Prime Minister kept talking.

"Apparently, over the course of the last two weeks or so, nine out of ten newborn children have been girls as opposed to the normal one out of two."

"I see. Have the doctors given any indication of what might be causing this?"

"None. Our physicians, as well as the physicians of America, Canada, France & West Germany are completely baffled by this. To make matters worse, the limited ultrasound data from America & our own hospitals indicates that this phenomenon will continue for at least the next few months."

"I see. Are there any groups that are being more heavily affected by this anomaly?"

"None that we can see Ma'am. While we do not yet have all of the information, it seems that this is affecting every person & group to the same degree."

"I see. Is there anything that we can do about this?"

"Medically, Ma'am, no. We don't even know what's causing it. We're pretty much limited to making sure this news doesn't leak to the media until we've got at least a few answers for them in order to avoid a panic. Other than that, the only real thing that we can do is to create a specialized team of medical researchers to investigate this anomaly."

"I see. You mentioned several other countries earlier, is this phenomenon affecting the entire globe?"

"I can't give you a definitive answer on that just yet, but preliminary indications show that it is indeed happening everywhere."

April 5th, 1965
CBS news desk

Tens of millions of Americans watched from their homes as the six o'clock news came on. Those who were watching CBS, watched as Walter Cronkite looked over a set of papers as he was introduced by the voice over naming the reporters that would be covering the nation's news. He then put his papers down, looked into the camera, & brought the news of a strange phenomenon to America.

"Good evening. Tonight, we have a news report of an unusual & unexpected phenomenon occurring in the United States & around the world. This report comes from the Secretary of Health, Education & Welfare, & it concerns maternity wards in every corner of the world. Normally, as we all know, baby boys & baby girls are born at about the same rate. Roughly one girl is born for every boy. This is why there are approximately the same number of men & women in almost all parts of the world. Sometimes there are minor deviations in one hospital or another, a situation where there are a few more girls born or a few more boys for a short time. However, it always seems to balance out & return to normal very quickly."

Cronkite then took a second to doublecheck the figures on his paper in order to ensure he gave everyone the right information.

"However, starting sometime around the middle of March, a little over two weeks ago, the normal ratio of girls to boys changed rather drastically. Instead of the normal one to one ratio, it has changed to a nine to one ratio. What this means is that for every nine girls that are born, there is only one boy coming into the world. According to doctors & officials, there has been no change in the number of babies being born, nor has there been any sort of problem with pregnancies carrying boys. It is simply that 90% of all newborns for the last two weeks have been girls."

He took a second to allow those numbers to sink in for the viewers.

"While several people may have heard in local news stories & newspapers about this on the smaller scale of individual hospitals, we can now confirm that this is not by any means a local phenomenon. This appears to be happening in every maternity ward in the country. Additionally, it is not just happening to Americans. Reports from several government agencies indicate that this is happening in all of our allied countries as well. Incomplete reports from neutral countries indicates this seems to be happening there as well, & what few reports we can get from behind the iron curtain indicate that something very similar & possibly the same thing is happening in the communist world as well."

As countless Americans watched the news, not entirely sure what to make of it, Walter checked his notes once more.

"While we do not yet know what has caused this event, we do know that it will continue for at least the next four to five months. A relatively new procedure known as an ultrasound is now more & more being performed on pregnant women to get a peek at the developing child to make sure that all is well. The noninvasive procedure uses soundwaves from a device placed on the belly to form a picture of the interior of the body, similar to how the Navy uses sonar to see what's happening underwater. Approximately halfway through pregnancy, this procedure can be used to determine the sex of the newborn to be. Data collected from all over the country indicates that 90% of the children that will be born in the coming months are female."

All over the country, pregnant women that had never heard of an ultrasound found themselves staring at or gently rubbing their swelling bellies as they considered asking their family doctors if they could get an ultrasound.

"As we speak, doctors all across the country are gathering as much data as they can on this phenomenon. President Lyndon Johnston has instructed Congress to set up a special commission of the country's best doctors & medical researchers to study the issue & determine a cause &, if need be, a solution. Several members of the budgetary committee are looking for emergency funding for the commission."

Cronkite then took his glasses off & looked into the camera.

"It is important that we do not panic or lose our heads in any sort of hysteria. For all we know, this anomaly could just be temporary, like an outbreak of a disease that appears, infects several people, & then vanishes. The best doctors that humanity has to offer are working on this & even if they cannot find a solution, we will have many years to adapt to & compensate for these changes."

April 9th, 1965
National Institute of Health, Bethesda, Maryland

Dr. Edward Swanson looked at the director of the National Institute of Health in total disbelief. Rumors of a government program to investigate the cause of the birth ratio anomaly had been circulating at the institute for almost a week. He had definitely been intrigued by the idea of being a part of the project. But this was not what he had been expecting.

"I'm sorry sir, you want me to… lead… the whole national commission… as its director?"

"Yes Ed. That's the direction we've decided to go with."

"But… what about Doctor Harris?"

"Doctor Harris is a fine doctor, but quite frankly, he's less than four years from retiring. In the event that this is a long-term program, we don't want to lose public confidence by needing to change the leadership after just a few years."

"But won't he be upset that he was turned over for such an important project?"

"I doubt it. Between you & me Ed, Doctor Harris is already a bit overwhelmed with the projects under his belt. The last thing that he needs right now is to be put in charge of a nationwide research project with global concerns. Besides, didn't you attend a lecture just last year from that French zoologist? What was her name?"

"Madeleine Charnier, she was describing her paper on the action of testosterone on females of the agama species."

"Exactly, you have experience with the most recent discoveries in the field of gender & sex selection. You also know some of the world's leading experts. You'll be perfect for the job."

Edward took a moment to collect his thoughts.

"While I appreciate your confidence in my abilities, how exactly am I supposed to figure out why all of a sudden, 90% of newborns are girls? We're not even sure exactly how sex is determined in the womb, let alone what could possibly affect it."

"I explained that to the government & they have agreed to give us a massive boost in funding. You'll be able to hire as large a team as you'll need from all over the country. Whatever equipment or facilities you need, just put in the request."

"That's great & all, but I don't know if the equipment or facilities that we would need even exist."

"The equipment to get to the moon doesn't exist yet either, but the US & the USSR plan to be there within the next five years. If it doesn't exist, set up a team to invent it. Spare no expense. The faster we can get this issue fixed, the smaller the disruption to the American way of life we'll have to deal with in twenty or thirty years."

"How much money are they giving us?"

"A lot. Not quite NASA money, but once the secretary of defense told the President that he was setting up a study to figure out how long-term gender imbalances might affect our military..."

"This commission became a national priority."

"Exactly Ed. Indications are that we're going to have full bipartisan support for what essentially amounts to a blank cheque. Whatever you need, just file a request for it."

As the Director of the Institute got up to leave, Edward Swanson sat back in his chair & began to imagine the sheer scale of the project that had just been dropped in his lap.

April 19th, 1965
Oval Office

"I could really use some good news Dean. I'm trying to win a war & it doesn't help that twenty thousand students were protesting the war in the streets over the weekend. I've got NASA telling me that it took them a month to figure out that astronauts will need to bathe on long term missions & I've got a briefing in an hour about how a communist party looks like it'll be making gains in the French election in a few days. So, give me some good news."

Dean Rusk, the secretary of state sat down across from the President & opened the folder that he had just carried into the room.

"Well, I have some good news on the gender ratio commission that will be very helpful to us sir."

"Right, that problem, what's the news."

"Well, the first bit of news is that the Soviet Union also seems to be affected by this phenomenon. We don't know if it's to the same extent, but we know that they are being affected by it."

"Well, that's good. Last thing that we want is for the American people to get whipped up into a frenzy because of something to do with the Soviets."

"Hopefully, the CIA will be able to get us some proper estimates, tell us if it's nine to one for them as well. In other good news, we've been working to get some cooperation between our commission & other countries programs & we are getting some success."

"Other countries are willing to work with us on this?"

"Some of them. Canada, England & France are going to share both their results & their data with us as long as we share ours with them."

"Sounds fair, anything else?"

"Yes, all of the other members of NATO have agreed to share the results of their efforts, although not their data. So, as they make discoveries, they'll tell us what they find."

"That's good. Now we just have to hope that we find a solution before the Soviets."

Dean closed his folder & leaned forward, taking a nervous breath before asking the question that was burning in his mind.

"Sir, if we do find a solution before the Soviets or the communists do, are we going to share it with them?"

Johnson leaned back in his chair & contemplated it. If this gender imbalance wasn't solved within a year or two, it could cause major social disruptions & military issues. The issues would be even greater if one side found a solution & the other didn't. If they found a solution & kept it from the communists, that could destabilize the communist countries. Many of those countries were already struggling. If they had an unending deficit of sons & the west didn't, that might just break communism permanently.

Then again, if the Soviets found a solution & kept it to themselves, it would be extraordinarily difficult to keep proving that communism needed to be stopped.

"Once we can convince them to admit that they are being affected as well, we need to sign a deal with them promising to share solutions."

"What if they don't admit to the problem or refuse to share any solutions?"

"Then pray that we solve it first, otherwise our grandchildren will be an all-woman's chorus singing the Soviet national anthem."

May 15th, 1965
National Institute of Health, Bethesda, Maryland

Doctor Swanson looked at the stack of boxes sitting on the desk. It looked as if he would need a sherpa if it got any higher. The piles of birth records & medical examinations were a mess of pure chaos. The small team that he had already hired was hard at work, struggling to sort it all out & in some cases, to translate it.

So far, all that they had managed to gather from the records was that the same thing that was hitting the United States was also hitting England, France & Canada in just the same way. Starting in mid to late March, ninety percent of all newborns were female with no measurable change in the amount of birth defects & complications.

"I see that the storm is upon us."

Dr. Swanson turned around to see a tall man with the thickest mustache that he had ever seen talking to him in a Hungarian accent.

"Dr. Todor Fekete I presume. Glad that you could start with us so soon. Please, follow me to my office where we can talk without being buried alive."

Dr. Fekete followed close behind Dr. Swanson. He had been surprised to get the call to come to work on the commission. Sure, there weren't many genetics experts in the world on account of the fact that it was a fairly new field, but he was certain that there were others that would have been called upon long before his name came up. Once in the office, they both took seats opposite each other at Swanson's desk.

"Can I be honest with you Dr. Fekete?"

"I would hope so since I'll be working for you."

"I haven't exactly kept up with all of the latest research on genetics. One of my researchers mentioned that we should consider hiring on a specialist in the field, but I can't see exactly how it'll be useful."

"Well, the first thing that I'll determine is if these children are genetically female."

"You can do that with DNA?"

"Yes, we discovered which genes are primarily responsible for gender in 1959. Since then, we've discovered that almost all men have one set of gender chromosomes & almost all women have a different set. The handful of exceptions that we have found so far all seem to come from individuals who are unable to reproduce."

"That's interesting, what exactly will we be able to determine with this information?"

"Well, if all of the newborn girls are genetically female, that would indicate the problem lies with the source of their genes, their parents. If half of them are genetically male, then it must be a problem in the womb."

Swanson's eyes opened wide as Dr. Fekete spoke.

"My apologies for underestimating what you can contribute to the project. Finding out where the problem is would be an incredibly helpful piece of information."

"It might also help us to understand when the problem began. If they are genetically female, then the problem would have begun around conception, or possibly slightly earlier if one of the parents were exposed to something."

"I'm going to have to remember to catch up on genetics research. At the moment, all that we can confirm from the ultrasounds is that this issue affected fetuses before week twenty of pregnancy."

"Hopefully, in the coming weeks, I'll be able to narrow it down to before or after conception."

"Well, if you need anything, just let me know."

"Thank you, Dr. Swanson. For now, I just need to know where I can set up my laboratory equipment."

"I'll show you the way."

Dr. Fekete stood up & followed Dr. Swanson to the lab that was being set up for him. Most of the equipment hadn't shown up yet as genetics equipment wasn't yet easy to come across. As he imagined himself working endless hours in this lab trying to extract useful genetic information from infants, he also wondered what other genetic secrets might be revealed. Secrets like why a small percentage of people didn't seem to physically match the gender chromosomes they possessed.

As he was contemplating this, someone knocked on the door of the room the two men were standing in. As the two doctors turned around, they saw one of the secretaries standing there holding a box with Spanish writing on it. She looked towards Dr. Swanson.

"Sir, the files from Cuba are here."

"Excellent, store that & the rest of them with..."

"Sorry sir, this is all that we received, just this one box."

"That's all they sent?"

"Yes sir."

"Wow. Okay, they weren't kidding when they said they would only share limited data. Put it in my office for now."

Before the secretary left, Dr. Fekete stared at the box with intense interest.

"How did we manage to get Cuba to share data with us?"

"Ask the secretary of state. I think it has something to do with easing tensions after the Cuban Missile Crisis. You know, making it look like they're willing to be friendly neighbors so that the nukes don't fly."

"Ah, so they send us a bit of a data & we send them a bit so that we can all say we're cooperating with our neighbors."

"Exactly, which is why this is probably all we'll get from them until relations need more improvement in their eyes."

June 3rd, 1965
Robinson Home, Queens, New York

Mary Robinson leaned back on the pale green couch & put her feet up on the coffee table in front of her. Normally her husband wasn't too fond of people that did that. But since she was eight months pregnant with their first child, he didn't bother her about it. Instead, he handed her the tall glass of apple juice that she had been craving with the sandwich that he had prepared just the way that she had painstakingly instructed him to make it. It had been complicated but seeing her smile for the first time this week had been worth it.

"It's good to see you smiling again Mary. It's been a while since the room lit up like that."

"I'm sorry. It's just, I really thought we were going to have a boy. I mean, look how pregnant I am, my belly is half my body now. I wouldn't have been surprised if twin boys had cartwheeled out."

"I know that we were expecting a boy, but as long our little girl is alright, I'm perfectly happy."

"You're perfectly fine being the first Robinson man to father a daughter in nine generations?"

"Yes. I'm perfectly happy."

David wrapped his arm around his wife's shoulders & held her close as they watched the news. As Cronkite talked about how astronaut Ed White had become the first American to conduct a spacewalk just a few hours earlier, he thought back to that doctor's visit a week ago.

He remembered the doctor offering the new ultrasound test for free. He had been excited about seeing the son that would make ten generations in a row of his family only giving birth to boys. There hadn't been a question about the matter. Mary's mother had even told them that with a belly that big, she would be giving birth to a massive baby boy.

Then the doctor pointed to the sonogram & told them the news. They were having a girl. As far back as his family tree had gone, the only women to be found were the ones that married into the family. When Mary had looked disappointed, he stowed what he had been going through & comforted her.

The truth was, he really was happy that his daughter was going to be born healthy. A part of him even looked forward to raising her. But another part of him felt like his entire family tree was getting the business end of a raw deal.

Mary put her hand on her massive belly. The doctor had very quickly figured out that they weren't happy about having a girl. He had tried to help by telling her about how the latest research showed that it was nothing to do with her womb or her as a person. He said it was something about something called genetics & that it had nothing to do with her.

She still felt like she had failed her husband & his long line of fathers. Feeling a hard kick from within her, she didn't care when the doctor said that whatever was causing it had started a year ago, before their child was conceived. She had felt like the wind had been knocked out of her. She had spent the last eight months preparing for a boy, knowing it was going to be a boy.

Now the baby was due within the next few weeks & she had to restart the process of finding a name for her.

Jul 28th, 1965
Oval Office

The sounds of horns honking & people screaming had been deafening. Time Square had been brought to a standstill by protestors. What had started out as a small protest to the Vietnam war was quickly ballooning as police tried to surround the angry crowd.

Behind police lines, reporters were describing the event that was unfolding. One young photographer slipped past the police & started taking pictures of the crowd of angry people.

Among the pictures that he took were three men burning their draft notices, a young mother holding up a sign that read We have no more sons to give, & a picture of a veteran from the Korean war quietly holding up a sign that read War Is Hell, that's why I only have 1 foot.

Most worrying to the president were the images in the newspapers of teenage boys holding up signs that read We're the last draft, 1983. In picture after picture, the president saw the number 1983 over & over again. Putting down his newspaper, he turned to his aide in the oval office.

"What the hell is this 1983 business?"

"Apparently, they're calling it the 1983 movement. It's a new political theory coming out of liberal universities. They're saying that if we can't fix the birth ratios within the next few years, we'll have to end the draft in 1983."

"1983... Because that's the year that children currently being born will turn 18 & become eligible for the draft."

"Exactly sir. If eligible men only make up a tenth of the population, we're going to have a real difficult time convincing the people that it's a good idea to send them off to war."

"Let me guess, some of them think that we should jump the gun & end the draft now."

"Among the more centrist of the protestors, that is the sentiment. Among the far left, they're saying that this is a sign from God, or Mother Earth or whatever that all war needs to come to an end by 1983."

"So, in other words, we have 18 years to stamp out the spread of communism. That's what they're saying."

"Yes sir. You should know that there's an opposing view to this sentiment."

"Dare I ask."

"It would seem that a state senator from Alabama decided to comment on the 1983 movement after hearing about it for the first time this afternoon."

"Dear God, what did he say?"

"He said that if we don't have enough men to draft into fighting the reds, we'll have to start drafting women into war."

"Jesus Christ."

"Uhm, Mr. President, can I ask you something, unofficially?"

"Sure. What's on your mind?"

"Well sir, if we can't fix the baby boy problem, are we going to start drafting girls? I only ask because my girls would be in college around 1983."

"If we can't fix the issue, I honestly don't know what we'll do. Hopefully, it never comes to the US drafting women. Hopefully, we'll figure out a way to wage war with only small numbers of men. Maybe we'll get lucky & the 1983 movement will convince the reds to stop waging war."

"Here's hoping sir."

August 22nd, 1965
Church of the Lord's Son, Fort Worth, Texas

"Seven Hundred Thousand sons born as daughters!"

The summer heat was beating down on the church & the congregation inside was feeling the heat. Fanning themselves with paper fans that had been imprinted with an image of Jesus on the Cross, they listened to the words of the Reverend Thomas Edwards.

"Seven Hundred Thousand Sons! It's been five months since this devilish imbalance began. In that time, in this country, Seven Hundred thousand children that should have been born as sons were instead born as daughters. Why is God depriving the good people of the world of so many sons? I'll tell you why. Sin!"

To the faithful in his flock, his copper hair almost seemed to burn with righteous fire. His blue eyes seemed to pierce the souls of those who caught his gaze as he preached on the woes of the world.

"Now, some of you may say that we have not sinned. We have been faithful to the word of the Lord, the Lord who sent his Son to lead us to righteousness. So why are we, the faithful, being punished with the sinners & the heathens & the godless & the sodomites?!"

Most of the congregation leaned forward, eager for his answer.

"My children, we are being punished for our tolerance of sinners! We sit here & we praise ourselves for being virtuous. Yet we do nothing as heretics & blasphemers march in the streets, preaching that women are greater than men!"

Several people in the front row cheered him on.

"The Lord tells us that a woman's place is in service to her man. Yet these... witch women... they parade down roads & shout that they are equals to the men the Lord has commanded them to serve. You see these... Liberal women & the foolhardy men they have seduced from righteousness, shouting for equality. What have we done to save these foolish women from the Devil's grasp? What have we done? Nothing!"

Several congregants shouted & cheered him on with a growing fervor & zealotry.

"We have allowed these women to begin deluding the world into thinking that women are equal to men & as punishment, God is taking our sons from us. This is the Lord's message! If you think a woman can take the place of a man, then you have no need for men! This is why some Forty Thousand sons in the great state of Texas have been born as daughters. We have allowed these liberals & communists to say that a woman is equal to a man & so the Lord will show us that this is false."

Shouts of heathens & heretics could be heard as several members of the congregation stood up to shout with the preacher.

"We must be more than righteous! We must be vigilant! We must tell these godless fools that they have strayed from the Lord's path! As the societies of the blasphemous crumbles with no men to lead them, we, the righteous, we shall thrive! Our faith shall sustain us & the Lord shall forgive us & return the bounty of sons to us when we show him our faith & our vigilance!"

As the crowd roared, a pregnant woman stepped forward, the crowd parting to let her walk through to the pulpit. There, she dropped to her knees before Reverent Edwards & spoke the Lord's prayer.

"You see my children. See the natural way of things! She kneels before the Lord, repentant & pleading for his mercy & he shall hear her cries! He shall hear his daughter's calls for forgiveness & he shall show his great mercy by giving onto them sons to bear into this world!"

Many of the women in the church fell to their knees & followed the mother to be in prayer as the reverend continued.

"Our righteous virtue will earn the Lord's mercy as we do what we must to stay true to the word of the Holy Son!"

September 14th, 1965
Oval Office

US Secretary of State Dean Rusk handed the folder over to President Johnson.

"I'm sorry sir, they're not willing to budge."

"Don't worry about it, Rusk. We knew it was a long shot asking the USSR to share data. Are they at least admitting that they're being affected by this?"

"Sort of sir."

"Sort of?"

"They've admitted that they are having an issue with the birth ratios, but their official position is that the Soviet Union's birth ratios are four girls to every boy as opposed to everyone else's nine to one."

"That's why they're not sharing data. If they gave us what we asked for, it would prove they're lying."

"Which means we're not going to be able to get anything out of them until their willing to admit that they're fairing no better than we are."

"It was a good effort Rusk, but I think it's safe to say that we're not getting anything out of the communists. In fact, it's pretty safe to say that the one box of files we got from Cuba is all we're getting. China, North Korea, the Viet Cong, they're probably all going to follow Russia's example & pretend that it's better for them then it is for us."

Dean Rusk sat on the couch opposite the President.

"Sir, I hate to sound like a broken record, but if we find a solution, will we be sharing it with them?"

"We'll see."

October 4th, 1965
CBS news desk

Walter Cronkite looked up as the news came back from its commercial break. As the producer signaled 3, 2, 1 with his fingers, the studio quieted down as the camera lights indicating that they were broadcasting came back on.

"Welcome back to the night's news, continuing from earlier, Pope Paul the VI was in Yankee Stadium today as part of the first ever papal visit by a pope to the United States. There, he led mass in front of an estimated ninety thousand people. After conducting mass, he offered up a special prayer on behalf of the world & the people of the United States for God to bring a swift end to the deficit of sons as more than six months into this phenomenon, there is no apparent end in sight to the unusual ratios of newborn boys to girls affecting the world."

"Tomorrow, it will have been six months since news of the unusual birth gender ratios was announced to the world. In the six months since this anomaly became known to us, there has been little to no progress in finding a cause. Multiple reports coming out of the commission studying this event can only confirm that this anomaly seems to be occurring at conception."

"With a lack of answers or even an ability to narrow down the potential causes, accusations are flying across the country. From semi-plausible accusations, such as those leveled against communist countries, to the far reaching & illogical, such as groups blaming NASA, lesbian radicals & even President Johnson. Law enforcement agencies are now concerned that such confusion & questions may lead to radical groups or individuals that may, in time, endanger the safety of the public."

"Already, we're beginning to see both radical far left & right groups using this anomaly as an excuse to justify calls to action. As such, the White House has issued a statement today to remind the people to remain calm in these trying times. In a public address,

President Johnson reminded the nation that all the peoples of the world are being equally affected & that the best scientists & researchers from around the world are working to solve this issue., & that this is not a time for baseless accusations."

December 13th, 1965
Robinson Home, Queens, New York

David walked into the house expecting the same kind of mess that had been greeting him for the last few months. Mary had tried to keep the house as clean as she had used to, but it was a real challenge when you could only get fifteen or twenty minutes of sleep at a time. Young Elizabeth had been keeping them both up, letting them get just enough sleep so that they didn't keel over.

David counted himself lucky. He could escape to work five days a week. Mary couldn't. So, when he walked in the door to find a relatively clean home & he didn't hear any crying, he was a bit perplexed.

"Mary? Is everything alright?"

Mary walked into the living room from the kitchen with a smile the likes of which David hadn't seen in months.

"Everything is great."

"Why isn't Elizabeth crying?"

"Because Martha from across the street is a saint."

David looked at his wife confused.

"She came over this morning so that I could have a bit of grownup time. She brought over the new Beatles record that everyone is apparently going absolutely crazy over & she helped me with Elizabeth & the house while we listened to it."

"How did Elizabeth like the Beatles?"

"She absolutely loved them. She lay there smiling & jerking her feet as they sang."

"That's good to hear. Because when I came in & I didn't hear crying, I got concerned."

"I know. It's weird not to hear her screaming."

David grinned & wrapped his arms around his wife.

"Well, I can't say that I was ever a fan of their music, but if it makes you & Elizabeth happy, then they're one of the greatest bands I've ever heard of."

Mary smiled as she hugged her husband. David just stood there with her, enjoying their first peaceful & happy moment in what seemed like an eternity.

"I think that on my way home from work tomorrow, I'll stop by a music store & pick up a copy of the new album."

"If you can find one, that'll be nice. Apparently, their flying off of the shelves, everyone is looking to get a copy."

"They're that good?"

"They're the Beatles, David. Plus, there's that last song that they added on. Martha said that the customers in the store were going on & on about it."

"What's so interesting about that song?"

"It's a song about women taking over the world. It's called Tomorrow's Queens."

"Ah, so everyone is going wacky over it because girls are actually taking over."

"Exactly."

1966

February 3rd, 1966
Oval Office

James Webb stood there as the President looked over the photos. The images were rather grainy & showed what looked like a rocky slope. President Johnson put the pictures down on his desk & turned to the NASA administrator.

"Is there any possibility at all that these are fake?"

"No sir. Multiple radio telescopes confirm that the signal is coming from the surface of the moon, specifically from somewhere in Oceanus Procellarum, the Ocean of Storms region."

"So, what you're saying is that they've beaten us yet again."

"It would appear that way sir. Yes."

"Tell me James, how long is it going to be until we can land something on the moon & get our own pictures?"

"It should be sometime in May or June sir."

"So, we're four or five months behind them. Once again, we're struggling to catch up to them."

"I wouldn't say that we're struggling sir."

"You wouldn't James. They launched their first satellite three months before we launched ours. They put a man in space a month before we did. They put a woman in space two & a half years ago & we still haven't done it. Now they're landing probes on the moon months ahead of us. It sounds to me like they're winning."

"Sir, it's one thing to land a probe on the moon. It's another thing entirely to land a man there & bring him back alive. Intelligence shows that they aren't even building a super heavy lift rocket yet. We'll beat them to the moon sir."

"Well James, in the meantime, newspapers all over the world are being flooded with images from a Soviet lander & announcements from the Soviet space program."

"They're probably just trying to use all of this to cover up & distract from their snafu with the birth ratios sir."

President Johnson looked up from his desk.

"You think that the reason they're boasting about their success in the space race is to distract from one confused official who said that the Soviet birth ratio is seven to one instead of the official party line of four to one?"

"It's possible sir."

"James, even if they're using it to distract from a minor slipup that most people don't know about, it doesn't change the fact that they are far ahead of us in the space race. We're going to need some wins of our own. Soon. Have we got anything coming up that we'll be able to do before them?"

"In about a month or so, Gemini 8 will be performing the first ever spacecraft docking while in orbit. Nobody has done anything like that before."

"Well make sure that it goes off without a hitch. The last thing that the country needs is to think that we spent tens of billions of dollars to come in second place."

March 16th, 1966
Swanson Home, Maryland

Dr. Edward Swanson crashed on his couch. Another fourteen-hour day had left him exhausted. Having spent the last few weeks looking into potential environmental contaminants like pesticides. He had hoped that it would be easy to go through the list of potential chemical toxins since there were so few that were used universally around the world.

But none of the chemicals that were used by everyone seemed to be causing a change in the birth ratios. After weeks of endless days & overtime, their best possible explanation appeared to be a dead end.

After spending a few minutes contemplating if he was going to have to direct the bulk of the commission's resources to the impossible idea that this was the result of a virus that could hit everywhere on Earth all at once, he gave up thinking about it for the night.

Grabbing the television remote, he was hoping to find some sitcom or news. Instead, he landed on a talk show where a man in a grey suit was talking next to the other two guests.

"You want to speculate on what this phenomenon means when we don't even yet understand what's happening to us? How can we possibly even try to guess the potential meaning of this if we don't even know what this is? We haven't even confirmed that this is a natural phenomenon, it might be manmade, or as one reporter asked the scientists in today's Gemini 8 briefing, it might be made by someone other than man."

The rest of the guests laughed. Edward remembered hearing about that question on the radio this morning. Some excuse for a 'reporter' had somehow managed to acquire clearance to attend the event & had asked them about rumors that this was the work of aliens trying to keep humanity in check now that we were trying to reach for the moon.

The man who was sitting next to him in a brown suit sat forward a bit more so that the microphone could more easily pick up his voice.

"While it's true that we don't know what's causing this, the fact of the matter is that people are speculating about what this could mean for the world. Just two weeks ago, after John Lennon said that the beetles were bigger than Jesus, he went on to make a comment that the new ratio of women to men is a sign that more peaceful times are upon us. If we assume for a moment that this is a natural event & not some malicious actor, human or otherwise, could we be in for more peaceful times?"

Grey suit thought about it for a moment.

"Well, it would certainly be more difficult to wage war. This is part of the basis for the 1983 movement. Unless we become desperate enough to start sending women to war, we may have to pull back our forces form the world stage. If we only have a tenth of the volunteers, then our options would be to either draft a sizeable fraction of a depleted male population or find a way to function with a greatly reduced military capacity."

"So, you're saying that John Lennon was right, an age of peace is upon us."

"I wouldn't say that, would you trust the Soviets & the Communists to not send women into war?"

"That's a good point."

Having sat there, mostly ignored until this point, the third guest, the woman in the green dress finally spoke up.

"While all of you are concerned about war & politics, I think that a much more interesting change will be occurring on the home front. Has anyone given any thought to what will happen to the economy & industry if this phenomenon is not fixed in the next few years?"

The other guests thought about it for a moment as she continued.

"With only a tenth of the men, who's going to keep the power plants running, or the tap water flowing, who's going to drill for oil & turn iron into steel. I don't know how the military will react, but unless we want to enter into a depression that makes the 30s look like the good old days, the bulk of the female population is going to have to pick up the slack."

The man in the brown suit looked as if he had just realized this. The woman then continued.

"In fact, if this isn't fixed within the next say... ten years, it will completely up end our entire civilization. What's going to happen when these girls get old enough to start dating & marrying? What will happen when they need to start having children? There's a myriad of social, industrial, economic, religious, political & military issues that will need to be addressed if we don't find a solution to this crisis soon. Even if it only goes on for three or four years, it will most likely have profound impacts on society."

A silence fell over the audience as the woman's words opened up a lot of eyes to the potential long-term dilemmas that might arise if a solution wasn't found.

In his home, Edward wrote himself a note to remind himself that he needed to request more researchers so that they could study more possibilities of how to adapt to different futures.

April 10th, 1966
Convention center in California

As Doctor Todor Fekete was escorted out the convention center, he was astounded by the circus of people surrounding it. Everyone had been expecting the media to show up in droves. This convention was for all of the commissions & directives & special panels & special councils in all of NATO & a few other western friendly nations. They were congregating to discuss what they had learned after a year of studying the anomaly with the birth ratios.

What hadn't been expected was the hordes of people there for any number of reasons. Security had already been tripled, with local law enforcement getting involved. As Todor, the lead geneticist for the American Commission into the Birth Ratio Anomaly, walked outside, he was immediately caught in a cacophony of noise.

Several people were holding up signs that read Mama or Papa, an indication that this new, mostly female generation was now old enough that they were calling their parents mama & papa. He had to walk between two opposing religious groups. One group was offering blessings & prayers to the scientists & researchers from around the world to help them solve this crisis. The opposing group was cursing them for trying to interfere in God's plans to bring about judgement day. The police had had to intervene in their opposing arguments multiple times.

A small wave of reporters that recognized him fired off a barrage of questions in his direction that he could barely hear. One group, dressed in reflective clothing, was demanding to know why the aliens that the Gemini missions were talking to were doing this. Another group demanded that the government admit that this was either an attack that they messed up or part of some sort of new world order plot to control the population.

By the time he got to the American bus taking some of the American researchers back to their hotel, he was even more exhausted than he had been when he walked out the door. Carefully walking past an exhausted Swanson on the bus, he was glad that he wasn't in charge as he passed some of his colleagues who were also looking exhausted & disheartened.

Nearing the back of the bus, he took a seat next to Doctor Barbara Collins, the only woman that was working as a researcher in the commission. He had never worked next to a lady doctor before in all of his career. Working with her was giving him hope that science would continue into the future, even if there were not so many men left to push it forward. As he slumped into his chair, the very conservatively dressed Doctor Collins looked up from the notes that she had taken during the convention.

"You look like you could pass out Todor."

"You mean I haven't already."

Todor was rather surprised to hear Barbara chuckle. She rarely laughed or even smiled.

"Not yet Todor, you're still awake."

"That's ashamed, I was hoping that the march from front door to the bus was a nightmare of some sort. Hordes of people representing endless millions demanding answers from us."

"That is a nightmare. It certainly doesn't help that after a year of intense study, the only thing that we can tell them is that we've made zero progress. No, wait, there was some progress. Some team in Spain found out that chimps, apes & other primates are not being affected, it's only us humans."

"Well, that's sure to appease the masses. You know Barbara, I hadn't expected that we would have figured everything out by now as this is a rather large problem."

"Nobody did, this is a probably something far beyond our current scientific understanding."

"Yes, but I was expecting that we would have figured out… something. We don't even really know what direction we should be looking in."

"It is frustrating."

"Yes. When we get back to the hotel, I'm heading right for the bar to have a drink with some friends from other commissions, mostly geneticists, if you'd like, you can join us."

"I appreciate the invitation, but I'm not too fond of drinking with a bunch of depressed men. No offense."

"No offense taken, although if you want, the… the… German commission, or possibly the Austrian program, one of them had a female biologist that shares a drink with us before heading off to have a drink on her own each night."

This was the first that Barbara had heard of another woman being involved in this work. Thinking it over, she decided that it might be nice to talk with a female colleague.

"I suppose a drink or two couldn't hurt. It might be a good idea to let the hair down every now & then."

Todor looked at the rather tight bun of brunette hair that rested just above the back of Barbara's neck.

"That bun comes undone?"

She gave him a playful smack as the bus lurched forward. As entertaining as Todor could be, she was looking forward to having a female colleague to talk to, even if just for a few hours at this horrible convention.

May 18th, 1966
BBC Radio News Desk

All over the United Kingdom, countless people were either turning on their radios or waiting for a few advertisements of later programs to hurry up & end. As they all listened to their radios, many of them sitting down to eat a nice supper with their families, the evening presenter came on to begin reading the evening's news. The man's voice was deep & gentle as he spoke about the main news events that had occurred that day.

"This is BBC radio news. It is the 18th of May, & today's top story, her majesty, the Queen of England spoke at the gathering of the commonwealth of nations. This meeting is to discuss the sharing or research data among commonwealth countries on the issue of the birth ratio anomaly that has plagued the world for the last year. While not all nations within the commonwealth have the resources needed to launch massive scientific inquiries into the nature of this anomaly, her majesty encouraged all nations to contribute what they could, even if it is merely national birth statistics. Queen Elizabeth was quoted as saying that in this time when we are presented with an unprecedented situation that will have massive ramifications for all societies across the globe, it is the duty of each of us to contribute what we can to finding a solution to this new threat on our way of life. Shortly after her speech, the leaders & delegates unanimously agreed to share not only their results, but their data with the United Kingdom's Commission to investigate the anomaly. As the United Kingdom & Canada are already sharing their data with the Americans, this means that all twenty-two nations of the commonwealth, & the United States of America, will be sharing results & data with each other in one of the greatest scientific undertakings in human history, comparable to the American effort to put men on the moon by the end of the decade."

July 16th, 1966
Lincoln Park, Chicago

The two cops were laughing hysterically at the crazy woman who was preaching by the waterfront in her white robes. Virginia Green ran her hand through her long, curly blonde hair, & breathed deeply as the cops walked away from her. As more women began passing her by, she performed the sign of the cross & stood tall in the white priest's robes that she was wearing.

"My sisters! Here me now! The end times are descending upon us! God almighty has measured the men of this world & he has found them to be unworthy!"

One of the cops turned around, grabbed his crotch & shouted out that she should measure his. Some of the people walking past chuckled as she continued.

"The time is now coming sisters! The Lord is now depriving us of men because they are wicked & unworthy! Here my words & know that we have but one more generation to prepare for the return of the one man that was true & pure! The Lord's only begotten son himself shall soon return!"

A few people in the park glanced at the woman in passing as she mentioned Christ.

"You will see with your own eyes! When this new generation reaches adulthood in 1983, the world will tremble as he descends from Heaven!"

Smoothing her robes for a moment so that a larger crowd of people could get closer to hear her words, she stood tall, stuck out her chest & spoke boldly.

"Christ will come down to father the warriors of Heaven with those women who are most worthy!"

Several people in the crowd stopped for a moment, unsure if they had heard her right.

"We must keep our wombs & our souls clean of man! Man has had nearly two thousand years to ready himself & he has failed!

These new girls being born today will be nearly unburdened by men, for there will be just enough of them to tempt away those who are not worthy to carry Christ's seed! As our savior was born of a pure woman, so too must we keep ourselves pure, that we may birth the grandchildren of the lord, a generation of saviors who will rise to stand against the coming darkness of the end of days!"

Several people were now standing around her to watch the spectacle & listen to the mad woman preaching about Jesus coming back to impregnate virgins. The cops that had been laughing at her before had returned in order to keep an eye on the growing crowd around her.

"Sisters! Do not let these impure men sully your wombs with their rotten seed! We must keep ourselves clean & pure! We must only bear children for the savior! Do not marry these men who will fall short of their promises of love & fidelity! Do not bear them children! Save yourselves for Jesus! He is the only one worthy to father those who will fight the darkness to come in the next millennium!"

A few people started walking away, having gotten enough of the show they had stopped for.

"If you are a virgin, stay as such! If you are not, then swear off men from this moment on! Control your corrupting urges to lay with men! Tame the urges through force of will & spirit! If you cannot, then take measures into your own hands & satiate yourself! If even that cannot keep the sick urges to lay with men at bay, they lay with each other! Gratify each other's urges so that you do not fall to the temptation of the men & the serpents between their legs!"

The crowd walked away, some laughing, some shaking their heads at the image of the crazy women telling women to masturbate & sleep with other women to keep themselves pure for Christ. The cops turned their backs as the crowd dispersed. Virginia began to feel her righteousness waning. As it appeared that, yet another sermon was to be ignored, she was about to start packing when she saw a young woman walking towards her.

Hope Baker had been walking through the park, trying to think of a way that she could tell her mother that she had broken it off with the guy that she had arranged for her to meet. Hope's mother had been setting her up on blind dates ever since she realized that Hope was putting in zero effort to find a man herself.

As usual, she had gone out on a few dates with whatever bachelor happened to be the son of one of her mother's friends. She sat through the guy's futile attempt to impress her. She let him get handsy & then she had laid on his bed, hoping that this one would feel anything other than just weird.

This last man hadn't been quite as bad as the others. If she squinted a lot & had a few drinks, she could kind of picture Ginger Grant from Gilligan's Island when she looked at him. That made spending time with him easier, but the sex was still just… weird.

She had broken it off with him after an unprecedented five dates. She had been trying to figure out how she was going to break it to her mother that she had not only dropped another very eligible man, but that she had dumped the son of her mother's best friend from high school. On top of that, her mother had already told the entire family that Hope was going to be bringing her new boyfriend to the family reunion that was only a week away. Her mother hated being embarrassed in front of the family.

All of that had been going through her mind when she had been strolling through Lincoln Park. Then she had heard the sound of a woman talking about rejecting men.

Hope couldn't explain it, but as she stood behind the crowd, some of what the crazy woman said was making sense. No man was good enough. They just wanted to pump something sticky inside of her & leave her feeling weird & a little gross.

For as long as she could remember, her mother had been telling her that according to the priest's sermon, God had a plan, even for the lack of men. Maybe what this woman was saying was the plan. Men just weren't worthy.

As the crowd had dispersed, she walked up to the woman. The beautiful, tall woman with such wonderful curves.

"Hi… hi, I'm Hope."

The woman smiled.

"Hello Hope, I'm Virginia."

"Can I ask you a question?"

"Sure. What can I help you with Hope?"

"You said that we have to resist the urges to lay with men. Well… what if… someone… didn't have any urges… to sleep with anyone?"

Virginia smiled. Hope felt safe seeing Virginia smile.

"I'd say that God has revealed to you exactly what I've been trying to preach to all of those fools. We need to keep ourselves pure. You must be pure if none can tempt you away from his calling."

Hope smiled. It was the first time that someone had been happy about her lack of interest in men.

"Say, Hope, if you have nowhere to be, would you like to talk a bit, say over coffee? I'd like to tell you about a church I'd like to open, hopefully with some women that are as pure as you are."

"I'd like that."

September 8th, 1966
Washington Monument

When President Johnson announced that he was going to be sending another forty-nine thousand drafted men to fight in Vietnam, everyone had been expecting a protest. Few had been expecting the Washington Monument to be besieged by tens of thousands of people shouting 1983.

Nobody was quite sure how the entire crowd of over ten thousand protestors had taken up the simple chant. Only a handful of people had been waving 1983 signs. But somehow, the chant had caught on & now a hoard of protestors were shouting about an end to the draft. Just outside the crowd, reporters were describing what was going on into the cameras recording them.

Later that night, as millions of people watched the protests on the news, some saw one young reporter interviewing a soldier who had just returned from the war.

"Mr. Joseph Roberts, I have to say that none of us were expecting a man with your years of distinguished service to be here today. To be clear for our audience, you're a Colonel?"

"I am, very recently retired after thirty years of service."

"That's incredible Mr. Roberts, which begs the question, why is a military man such as yourself here waving a 1983 sign?"

"Because the 1983s need to be heard. As distasteful as I & a number of my colleagues find the idea of the draft, we do recognize its necessity from time to time. That being said, unless we are the kind of nation that intends to march tens of thousands of women off to war, we need to accept that the draft must come to an end."

"You're referring to the birth ratios?"

"Indeed. If no solution is found, then starting in 1983, it will be immoral to conscript young men to war when there are not enough of them here at home to begin with. This will be a major problem for the military & there seems to be no discussion at all about how we're going to have a functioning military when only a tenth of the population is male."

"Some would say that we'll have to start fighting smaller wars."

"That's a lovely idea, but the last several wars have been getting bigger & bigger. We are going to need a solution to the lack of men to fight & we're going to need to have it in place, with the kinks worked out, before 1983."

"You said before that you're not too fond of the draft to begin with, do you think that it should be abolished?"

"I would love for the draft to be abolished. Sadly, that would require that the world stop creating wars that need more soldiers than the countries involved have."

"I'm sorry Mr. Roberts, it seems that the police are instructing us to pull away from the crowd. I'm not sure if the crowd is growing, getting more restless or if the police are going to try something. Either way, we need to move."

"Not a problem miss. I have to get back to the soldiers for 1983."

"Good luck Mr. Roberts!"

People all over the country watched as the reporter & the Colonel were separated as clashes began between police & the protestors.

Dec 31st, 1966
National Institute of Health, Bethesda, Maryland

Dr. Edward Swanson was sitting at his desk as the final hour of the year counted down. While the radio was softly playing Johnny

Carson's New Year's Eve special, he was slowly nursing a glass of brandy & looking over reports from the different departments of his research groups. Every single one ended the same way, no progress in understanding why newborn girls were outnumbering newborn boys nine to one.

He had started the night by looking over the year's reports just in case he had overlooked some miniscule amount of progress that he could show the President in a few days when he would have to provide a summary on the year's progress to Johnson himself. He really didn't like that he was going to have to tell the President that in a year of research with a blank cheque, they had found nothing.

So, he started drinking & reading old newspapers that he had in the office. Damn near every major article seemed to refer back to the birth ratio anomaly that he was trying & failing to solve. From international events to political movements, to activists' groups & election results. Nearly everything seemed to refer in at least some small way to the phenomenon that he was working on. There were even mentions of the birth ratios in Reagan's campaign speeches that were mentioned in some headlines.

Edward laughed at that one.

"What a year. We learned nothing about the birth ratio problem, everyone is racing to get to the moon, miniskirts, race riots, & Bonzo's costar is now the governor of California. Top that 1967."

He then turned off the radio as it started announcing that the ball in New York was about to drop.

"On second thought, don't top it. Just give me an answer to what the hell is causing all of this."

1967

January 15th, 1967
Church of the Lord's Son, Fort Worth, Texas

"Virtue requires vigilance!"

The congregation cheered Reverend Thomas Edwards on as he stood at the pulpit. Next to him, a young woman, no older than twenty was nursing her newborn child. As she stood there, she summoned up every ounce of courage she had to not run away in embarrassment that she was nursing in front of the entire congregation. It didn't help that the reverend stood next to her with his hand on her back.

"Do you see my children, what happens when you are virtuous & vigilant? Like young Amber who stands before me, you must be true to the word of the Lord & you will be blessed with a son!"

The reverend then grabbed the infant boy & held him up high, leaving Amber humiliated as the entire congregation got a glimpse of her bare breast before she could cover it back up. Reverend Thomas held the naked boy up in the air before his flock so that they could see that a boy had been born to them.

"Do you now see! A son! Born to the righteous!"

The congregation erupted into applause. He continued to hold the baby up for a minute of applause & praise & devotion before handing it back to its mother.

"Amber here is what happens when a woman is not just right with the Lord but works to spread his word. She has donated to the church, she spread the word about the correct, God-fearing men that should be elected to government, & she reminded her husband of his duty to God's country when the Lord had him drafted to go to Vietnam & fight the godless communists!"

Amber resisted the overwhelming urge to cry at the mention of her husband who wasn't coming home.

"She could have given in to temptation! She could have ignored the creeping liberalism into our politics, but she stood firm! She could have used her husband's money to buy pretty dresses & makeup, instead she gave it to God! She could have allowed her husband to become a coward in God's war & seek a draft deferment, instead she reminded him of his duty in the great war against the godless communist horde! Amber here has given greatly, & lost, & labored, & now the Lord above us all has witnessed her great virtue & her vigilance & has gifted her with a son!"

The crowd cheered Amber's name & showered her with praise for her virtue as she resisted the urge to break down in tears over the loss of her beloved husband.

"Amber has resisted the temptations of our society that has abandoned the Lord. But greater still, she has resisted the influence of the serpent in our flock!"

The crowd grew silent.

"There is one among us who seeks to corrupt our faith! One who would take the last sons from our congregation! One who would have the Godless & the queers corrupt God's country! The hidden serpent of the radical sodomites & dykes is none other than Elisa Salomon!"

The crowd turned to Elisa, who was standing in the aisle, holding her newborn daughter. Around her, in the pews, were half a dozen more women, holding newborn daughters, glaring at her with hatred in their eyes.

"Elisa has corrupted us! Before the Devil's birth curse was unleashed onto the world, she gave birth to three sons! Now she births a daughter! Our six sisters, who were close to Elisa, have birthed daughters. Only Amber, who kept clear of this serpent in disguise has righteously birthed a son."

The congregation started shouting at Elisa, calling her a traitor, a demon & a witch.

"No longer shall this devil woman defile our faith! Elisa Salomon, I cast thee out of our congregation! Be gone from this place & never return!"

Elisa turned around & walked away in tears from the church that she had been baptized in & had attended since she had been a child. As she left, Reverend Thomas ran his hand through his copper red hair. He had been nervous that banishing one of the women to birth daughters might backfire on him. But when the Latina woman who had already birthed sons suddenly produced a daughter, he had his sacrifice. He now had time before the flock began questioning why only ten percent of their new children were boys.

February 14th, 1967
Robinson Home, Queens, New York

Peace & quite reigned in the Robinson house. Little Elizabeth was off with her grandmother, leaving David & Mary in blissful peace. They had made such plans for Valentine's Day. A Night that would have included dinner, a movie, dancing. With their first real night of freedom, they had intended to paint the town red like a pair of young lovers. Of course, no plan survives contact with reality.

It takes more than a few hours to recover from the exhaustion of running around after a curious child. By the time that David got home from work, his feet already felt like they were made of lead. Walking into the house, he found that his wife had decided to put on a slow roasting supper rather than go out to a restaurant.

He didn't mind trading a night out at a busy restaurant for a night in & she didn't mind missing out on a night of dancing. Lighting an old candle on the table, they sat down & ate together. While it was a far cry from their original plans, they reveled in the peace & quiet that they had not known for two long years.

When the meal had been thoroughly enjoyed, they both got dressed for a trip to the movie theater. By the time they got their shoes on, they both felt like they were about to pass out. With Mary wondering how her mother had handled having three children by this age & David wondering how his parents had handled having a pack of wild boys, they agreed that their trip to the movies should become a simple stroll around the neighborhood.

Even the evening stroll was shorter than they thought that it was going to be. Barely more than a trip around the block & a quick hello with a neighbor that they hadn't seen in ages. Walking back into their house, they kicked their shoes & coats off, made their way to the living room couch & practically fell into it. After a moment, David sat up a bit.

"Are we an old couple now?"

"No David, lots of young couples go for a walk around the block & nearly keel over."

"Good, I was worried that we were old."

"Not yet David, just tired."

David leaned back next to his wife.

"I don't suppose that you want to retire upstairs for something special?"

"God no. I'm not moving from this couch for a while, if you want anything, you'll have to climb on top of me right here."

David laughed.

"No, no. I just wanted to know if I was going to have to pray for a miracle to not pass out in the middle."

Mary laughed.

"You know David, my mother keeps asking when we're going to give her another grandchild."

"Not tonight. We're not having another daughter until the first one is old enough to babysit."

"I like the way that you think David."

A few minutes later, as Mary resigned herself to the knowledge that she was probably going to pass out on the couch next to her husband, a thought occurred to her. She wondered when it was that David had started thinking about their future children as daughters instead of as just children.

April 10th, 1967
National Institute of Health, Bethesda, Maryland

The second annual conference had been rough. While the crowds hadn't been as large as the previous years, thanks to increased security preparations, they had been just as intense in their desire for answers that nobody had.

What little rest he had managed to get on the weekend after getting home from the conference had evaporated. Doctor Todor Fekete walked into his office & sighed at the sight of articles, files & papers sitting on top of his desk. Grabbing the first thing on top of the pile, he saw that it was an article he had been meaning to read. Fine Structure of RNA Codewords Recognized by Bacterial, Amphibian, and Mammalian Transfer RNA. Putting it back down on his desk, he took a seat & sipped at his coffee when his secretary came in.

"Good morning Dr. Fekete. I have your messages from last week & your appointments for this week here."

She then handed him the lists. He put them on top of his pile of things to do & sat back in his chair while stroking his thick mustache.

"Thank you, I'll take a look at all of that in a minute."

"Is everything alright doctor? You look like you've been through the ringer two or three times."

"That conference was a total bust."

"I heard that there were protests, but I didn't think it was that bad."

"It wasn't the protests. Those are understandable, people are struggling to give birth to boys & they want answers. It's perfectly reasonable for them to be angry. The problem is that we had to spend a week basically acknowledging that nobody has made any progress since the convention of last year."

"I see."

"No progress at all in a year. We spent about twenty something million dollars over the last year & we have nothing to show for it."

"I'm sure it's not really that bad doctor."

"It is exactly that bad. It's that bad & it's worse because it was the same situation with everyone else. Seventeen countries were there representing the forty-one countries of NATO & the Commonwealth of Nations & a few other allies & nobody has made any progress over the last year. We don't know what's causing it, we don't why it's happening, we don't even know which questions we should be asking at this point."

His secretary stood there in stunned silence.

"The combined capabilities, insights & brilliance of the western world & we've got nothing."

"Well... we'll just have to keep working."

"Sure, if Congress will let us. Apparently, even before the embarrassment that was the annual convention, there were a few congressmen that were questioning why so much money is getting no results. If it weren't for Vietnam, we'd probably already be standing in front of congress trying to justify ourselves to the people who write the checks."

"Perhaps one of your new studies will shed light on the situation."

"Perhaps, if the problem is genetic, & if I can get some of these studies going. I've got half the geneticists in the country working for me & we don't have enough to run half of our studies. That's the problem with a new field of medicine, nowhere near enough specialists & to many things to discover."

Standing there, she put her hand on Todor's shoulder.

"Don't give up hope. Just because the challenge ahead of you is massive doesn't mean that it's insurmountable."

"That is true. I suppose that it's back to work then."

She smiled as he took the list of messages from the last week. As she left his office, she resigned herself to the idea that all of her grandchildren were most likely going to be girls.

May 2nd, 1967
Expo 67, Montreal

"Sir, we've got a problem at the new exhibit."

Jeremy had just sat down after chasing people around all morning. Looking at the younger security guard, he leaned back in his chair.

"Which new exhibit? There are new ones every day."

"The World of Women exhibit. Apparently, some people are taking issue with some of the displays & it's getting loud."

"Shit, let's move."

Jeremy radioed a few other guards & told them to meet him at the pavilion in question. He had a feeling that morning that a dispute over that display could blow up into an international incident.

Six minutes later, Jeremy, along with three other security guards reached the exhibit where two other guards were trying to hold back a small group of men. As Jeremy arrived, he blew loudly on his whistle to get everyone's attention. As the arguing calmed down, he walked up to the riled-up group.

"I'm head of security for Expo 67. Would one of you be willing to explain to me what the commotion is about?"

One of the men that had been yelling stepped forward. He looked to be in his mid-fifties & he spoke with a thick French accent.

"Officer, you need to shut down this display, it is obscene & there are children present."

The crowd, composed of people & accents from around the world agreed with him.

"I'm afraid that you're going to have to be more specific sir, I can't have an entire exhibit shut down just because a handful of people don't like the content."

"Don't like the content! The content has pornography in it!"

The entire group shouted in agreement as another security guard showed up.

"Sir, I assure you, there is no pornography in this, or any other exhibit."

"It's right there, officer, see for yourself!"

"If you'll agree to calmly show me what you're talking about, I'll be willing to take this seriously. But I'm not going to shut down an exhibit just because a handful of grown men are throwing a temper tantrum."

The man took a deep breath to calm himself down. He had seen the security guards growing in number & decided that the officer's offer would be the best way forward.

"Alright, I'll show you, but when you see that it is obscene, you have to take it down."

"If it is obscene, I'll have the displays & possibly the exhibit shutdown. Please, show me what the problem is."

The man stepped forward as the other security guards let him through. He then led the way for Jeremy into the exhibit called the World of Women.

The exhibit was dedicated to the anomaly in the birth ratios, & what the next century would look like if the anomaly was never corrected. There were copies of scientific & sociological reports that had been written in the last year. Their graphs & charts showing how the population might crash under certain scenarios. But the focus of the exhibit were the large images showing what women of the future might look like.

There were pictures of women dressed up as construction workers & garbage collectors. There were pictures of corporate board meetings being led entirely by women in suits. There were images of the us senate with only ten male senators. There were a bunch of images of women in combat gear from various branches of different armies fighting in wars all over the world & on the moon. There was even an image of a woman planting a flag on Mars. They walked past all of these & got to the end of the exhibit, just before the image of the woman priest leading a congregation of almost all women in Sunday prayer.

"Here! This is the pornography they're allowing children to come up & see!"

The man pointed to a pair of images. One was an image of a man in a suit coming home from work to be greeted at the door by his four wives. The other was an image of two young women on a date, sharing a milkshake & staring lovingly into each other's eyes across the table.

"You see officer! Pornography! A man with four wives! Lesbians! What's next! You have to shut this down!"

Jeremy sighed.

"Sir, I understand that you don't like the ideas depicted in these displays, but these images hardly qualify as being pornographic."

"Just look at them!"

"I am sir, & the fact of the matter is that what I see is some fully clothed people in a future situation that might just happen, which is exactly the point of this exhibit."

"But... What if the children see this? What if they get... how do you say... what if they get ideas?"

"Sir, I doubt that most children would understand what they're seeing in these images, let alone the kind of future that they may imply. I'm afraid that I'm going to have to ask you & your friends to disperse from this exhibit."

"But..."

"Please sir, before we have to have you removed."

He looked at the images & spit on the image of the young girls on a date before turning away & leaving. Jeremy hoped that this crisis would be averted as he wondered if he was actually looking at the future in these pictures.

June 12th, 1967
Oval Office

Robert McNamara walked into the Oval Office for his scheduled meeting with the President. He was not happy about the report that he was going to have to give, but he knew that the future security of the United States of America depended on it. Senator Albert Gore was shaking hands with the president, finishing up their meeting. As he walked out, Robert took a seat & placed his briefcase on the desk.

"Sorry about that Robert, my meeting with Senator Gore went a little long."

"Not a problem Mr. President."

"You brought the report I assume."

"Yes sir, it's all here. Our research over the last two years has been extensive & exhaustive. The report is rather long, but it is thorough."

"I intend to start reading it tonight, Robert. In the meantime, can you cover a few highlights? Are we going to have to start enlisting women in the army?"

"It appears to be that way sir. To what degree we'll have to recruit women depends on how long it takes to find a cure to this phenomenon, but even if a cure were found tomorrow, we would still need to make some changes."

"I was hoping that you were going to say that we had some more time."

"I was hoping for that to Mr. President. Unfortunately, our analysis doesn't show that. Most men who enlist & most who are drafted are between the ages of 18 & 20. Even if the birth ratios are fixed tomorrow, that still means that from March of 1983 to July of 1986, there will be a massive deficit of male recruits for the armed forces."

"That's just over three years, that's a long time to be going with almost no recruits."

"That it is sir."

"What can we do about it?"

"Well sir, in this scenario, assuming that a fix is found before 1970, we'll have two options. Option 1, hope for a temporary world peace from 1983 to 1990. If there is no war in those years, we should be able to maintain national security with temporarily diminished forces."

"Assuming that that's not likely, what's option 2?"

"Option 2 would be to train women for all non-combat roles. Everything from file clerks to drivers to field surgeons to company clerks. Place all the men into combat roles & as long as there isn't a major global conflict, we should be good."

"And if there is a major global conflict? Do we have an option 3?"

"Try to avoid taking part if we can & hope that we don't have to recruit women to fight."

"So, if a cure is found in the next few years, our best option is to hope for peace during a time when the new generation that is starting to work & marry is ninety percent female?"

"Yes sir."

President Johnson got up from his desk, walked over to the couch where Robert was sitting & sat on the one opposite to him."

"Dare I ask what we're supposed to do if a solution is not found before 1970?"

"Well, sir, if there is no solution by 1970, we'll have no choice but to include women in combat roles as the norm."

"That'll be our only option?"

"Yes sir. There are a number of projections & scenarios described & analyzed, they're all in the report. The basic understanding is that if a solution does not come before 1970, the lack of male recruits starting in 1983 will be too severe. By 1990 we would fall below critical personnel numbers. Unless we would be willing to draft uncomfortably large percentages of the available male population, we'll have to open the military up to female recruitment."

"So, in 1983, we'll need to start recruiting women into the armed forces in combat roles."

"Earlier than that sir."

"What do you mean Robert?"

Robert leaned forward to get a glass of water. He knew that the president wasn't going to be happy about this part.

"Well, sir, if we have to start inserting women into combat roles in 1983 to compensate for the lack of men, we're actually going to need to start much earlier."

"When? 1980?"

"More like 1975 sir."

The President sat back.

"Why so soon Robert?"

"Sir, we've never had women in large numbers serving in combat roles. Hell, we haven't had women serving in any number in combat roles. When we begin enlisting women, there's bound to be issues, issues ranging from privacy to fraternization to psychology. We'll need to have all of these issues ironed out before women are needed to replace the men that we'll no longer have."

"It'll take eight years to work out these issues?"

"Unlikely sir, but there are other issues as well."

"Such as?"

"The report does a very though job of explaining them sir."

"I'll read through it later, I need to know the basics now. What other issues are there?"

Robert took another sip of water before continuing.

"Well, there will be the issue of senior personnel. The military psychologists seem to think that it'll be easier for these female heavy units to function if there are women in higher ranks."

"Well that makes sense I suppose. It's actually kind of smart to have people in charge who can actually understand what the recruits are dealing with."

"Yes sir. The other major problem is that it will take a long time to change society."

"Society, Robert?"

"Yes sir. Multiple surveys have been done over the last two years of women aged sixteen to twenty-six. Less than one in twenty thousand had even considered a career in the armed forces & even fewer considered the idea of being part of a combat unit. Hell, most of them haven't even considered the idea of a career. We're going to need to change the mentality of society so that at least one in five hundred women consider a career in the military. Overhauling society like that will take several years. We'll have to start convincing them that women joining the army is perfectly reasonable while they're still in school & impressionable."

President Johnson was silent for a moment. While he sat there, Robert reached into his briefcase to pull out the confidential report & to place the inch thick document on the table.

"So, what you're saying, is that the next person to sit in this chair, might have to authorize posters next to Uncle Sam that say Lady Columbia wants you to join the army?"

"It's very possible sir. In fact, it's highly likely."

July 17th, 1967
McGill University, Montreal

"Janet! Janet!"

Janet Hill pinched the bridge of her nose. No matter how many times she told Rebecca not to draw any attention to them, she kept on doing it. Now she was running down the hall, calling her name. Janet closed her reference book & looked up as Rebecca practically burst through the door to their dorm.

"Janet, have you heard?"

"Heard what? You, running through the hall calling my name? We want as little attention on us as possible, remember?"

"Right, sorry, but have you been listening to the news?"

"No, I've been doing research for my paper. What's got you so worked up that you went around calling my name?"

"Where's your radio?"

Rebecca didn't even wait for an answer. She went over to the bedside table & grabbed the small radio. She fiddled around with the dials for a moment, filling their small dorm room with all kinds of static until she landed on the CBC news station.

"Here, listen to this for a moment."

It took a minute or two for the presenter to get through the other story that they were working on. Just as Janet was starting to get impatient with her girlfriend, Rebecca turned up the volume.

"Coming again to the news of the hour, in a last-minute surprise turn of events, Parliament has passed a diminished version of minister of justice Pierre Trudeau's omnibus bill C-195. The bill narrowly passed through parliament with 125 votes in favor, 120 votes against & 20 absent votes. While the diminished version of the bill only contains 17 of Pierre Trudeau's proposed updates to the Canadian criminal code, one clause of the bill is set to make waves both at home & abroad."

"The clause causing such commotion, included only in the last few weeks, would effectively decriminalize acts of consensual homosexuality in adults over the age of 21."

Janet went wide eyed at what she had just heard. She continued to listen in disbelief.

"When asked why this clause was added in to begin with, minister of justice Pierre Trudeau was quoted as saying there's no place for the state in the bedrooms of the nation. Prime Minister Lester B. Pearson was later asked if the birth ratio phenomenon played any part in the parliament's decision to effectively legalize homosexuality, he commented that while it is slowly becoming apparent that gay rights will have to be addressed in coming years, he believes that this is more to do with the will of the Canadian people to create a country that is truly free of discrimination."

Janet was flabbergasted. She had never thought that what she & Rebecca did would be allowed.

"The changes to the law are expected to go into effect within the next few days. While initial opposition from Catholic & religious institutions was rather fierce, many organizations are backing down as they admit that these changes may be necessary for women at least in the coming decades."

Rebecca turned off the radio.

"Do you know what this means Janet?"

"Yeah. It means that if we get caught, we won't end up in an asylum for confused women."

"Caught? Janet, it means that we don't have to hide!"

Janet looked at her girlfriend in amazed disbelief.

"Rebecca, I love you, but we still have to hide."

"But they just said that it'll be legal."

"Legal & acceptable are two very different things. Just because we can't be sent to jail, or the nuthouse doesn't mean that we can't be kicked out of university."

Rebecca thought about it for a moment before she sat down on the bed in a slump.

"I didn't think of that. I was just so happy that we weren't going to be breaking the law anymore."

"I know. I'm happy about that too. Maybe one day, in a few years, when these kids are old enough to get married & there aren't enough men to go around. Maybe then, we'll be able to tell the world. But for now, our relationship has to stay in this room."

Rebecca nodded her head. Seeing how dejected her lover was, Janet stood up from her desk & began unbuckling her belt.

"Janet? What are you up to?"

"I figured that we could break the law one more time before that bill gets royal ascent."

Rebecca grinned wickedly; she then patted the spot on the bed next to her in invitation.

September 9th, 1967
Chicago, Church of the Wives of Christ

The studio was small. So too was the apartment above it. Hope had come down to the studio to get away from the phone upstairs & it's incessant ringing. She knew that her parents were just worried about her. Afterall, she had made some radical changes. Moving out of her apartment & moving in with the leader of a lesbian doomsday cult so that she could help to support the prophetess. She knew why her parents were worried, but she could only reassure them so many times in a day before she needed a distraction.

As she read through the flyers to make sure that the information about the next day's sermon was accurate for the fourth time, she found herself glad that they were going to have a nice, warm room for Virginia's sermon.

Once she was certain that they were accurate, she sat down in one of the folding chairs that would serve until they could actually get pews. Their sermons never garnered a large crowd, but every week, she hoped that someone would be coming back & that it wouldn't just be a bunch of new faces that she would never see again.

Hope was about to write a note telling Virginia that she was going to head out to distribute flyers for their church. As she was writing the note, she heard the front door open & turned to see Virginia walking in with another woman. Hope had a feeling that this woman was just another housewife that Virginia had picked up from a local lesbian bar where she was pretending that she was just there for a drink.

"Hey there, Hope, what are you up to?"

"I was just about to go & pass out some flyers."

"Good thinking, leave some of those piles & I'll head out a little later to help. But first I've got a very important meeting to get to."

"Sure thing Virginia."

Hope picked up the sports bag that she used to carry the piles of pamphlets & flyers around town as Virginia escorted the shy woman upstairs to her room. Not for the first time, Hope wondered if the church was just an excuse for Virginia to chase pretty women & repressed housewives around. As usual, she shook her head of such nonsense. Just because Virginia had to have women to help her with her urges didn't mean that this was wrong. After all, what they preached just made so much sense.

Hope headed out into the autumn chill to begin spreading flyers for a church that had only two members.

November 5th, 1967
Dr. Edward Swanson's home

Edward was sitting on his couch in his pajamas enjoying the weekend for a change. Deciding that he needed a good weekend, he arranged all of his meetings for the next week, made sure that the commission would be able to get by without him for two days, came home & took the phone off the hook. He figured that if it was really important, they would know where to find him. It was nice to be able to get away from the discussion of the birth ratios.

Turning on his tv, he flipped through the channels until he came across some sort of talk show. Turning up the volume, he sat back on his couch & watched as the grey-haired host reintroduced the show from a commercial.

"We're back from our sponsors & just as before, we're talking about next year's election. We're exactly one year away from election day & we're discussing the main issues that will likely be considered by the people when they cast their ballots."

Zooming out, the camera showed the three guests sitting around the table as the host continued.

"So far tonight, we've discussed a number of major issues. The race riots that have shocked this country, the ongoing war in Vietnam, the supreme court & the Apollo program. Now all that's left for us to talk about in what time we have remaining is the issue everyone has thought about, but some people still aren't really paying attention too, the birth ratios."

Edward threw up his hands in disbelief & frustration. There was no escape. Tempted to change the channel, he instead kept watching, thinking that it might be a good idea to get an insight into what people thought about his work.

"It's now been about two & a half years since girls became ninety percent of all newborns. A year from now, when Americans go to the ballot, it'll have been three & a half years. How do we think that this will affect the election?"

The first guest, a middle-aged man with just a touch of grey in his blonde hair was the first to answer.

"While some of my colleagues may disagree with me on this, I don't think that it'll play much of a role at all in the outcome of the election."

The slightly younger woman who was sitting next to him looked at him in disbelief. Dressed & styled conservatively, Edward was surprised by how passionate she became.

"How can you possibly say that?! The very foundation of our culture is set to be radically overturned by this phenomenon. How is America going to function when these children grow up! How will marriage work, how will employment work, how will the army work?!"

"Yes, I understand that these are important issues that are heading our way faster than some of us would like to admit. But the simple fact is that the polls suggest that Americans are more concerned about current issues than something that's twenty years down the line."

"Not even twenty years! Every study, every analysis, everything has shown us that the very foundations of our society are about to be upended, this should be the most important issue that voters are concerned about!"

"I agree, but they aren't."

Before the woman could scream at him again, the third guest, a young man who looked like he had just graduated twenty minutes ago whistled to get their attention.

"Meredith, we can all agree that the birth anomaly should be the main issue in this election, nobody is disputing that. The problem seems to be that a lot of Americans don't seem to realize the full extent this phenomenon will have on their lives. I think that a large part of the issue might be that the children of this new generation are too young for most people to pay attention to them."

"So, what, nobody is going to care about them until they can vote?"

"No, I think that when the mid-terms come up in 1970, that's when everyone will start paying attention, because by that point, the number of parents affected by this will represent a massive part of the electorate & their will undoubtedly be an endless array of news stories talking about how educational policy & school sports teams are being affected by the fact that the new class of students is ninety percent female. Right now, it's all just hypotheticals about the future for most people."

"So, there's no point in talking about it now?"

"I didn't say that. For new parents, for people concerned about our military readiness, for a number of small groups, this is a major concern that will probably shift a few votes one way or the other. But the simple fact is that most Americans aren't really paying attention yet & it doesn't help that the candidates aren't really talking about this subject a lot just yet. It's hard to know how this will affect the election when the parties haven't even figured out what they want their platforms to be."

Her argument seemed to run out of steam. She could see that he was right. Neither party had taken a real stand on the issue yet because nobody seemed to have any idea about what they should be doing about it.

Seeing that this conversation probably wasn't going to be going anywhere, Edward turned off the television & decided to dive into a good book in order to escape any talk of the birth ratios.

54

1968

January 23rd, 1968
California State Capitol

Assemblyman Connors suddenly burst into assemblyman Markman's office like a storm. Connors looked up from the calendar that he had been double checking.

"Lesbians! How could you Markman? How could you side with the Democrats to allow this?"

"Calm down Jeremy. Have a seat."

"I will not! Not until you tell me what in God's holy name you were thinking. This bill is going to pave the way for lesbianism to take root in this state like a cancer!"

"Jeremy! Calm the fuck down & have a seat."

Jeremy took a deep breath & composed himself before taking a seat across from the man that he had trusted up until half an hour ago.

"Alright, I'm calm. Now Markman, explain this to me."

"I don't see why I should have to explain to you why I voted for this bill. It makes perfect sense. The federal commission on birth ratios isn't getting anywhere, we need to reinforce our state efforts & this bill quadruples the funding for it."

"I understand that part of it. I would have voted for it myself if the bill were just that. But this... study... How can you go along with this queer agenda to destroy the American family & turn the women of our state, of our country, queer?"

Markman took a long breath before answering.

"Look Jeremy. I'm not too happy about the idea that this might signal to the public that we're softening our stance on homosexuality. But the fact of the matter is that there is a very high chance that this phenomenon is not going to go away any time soon. Hell, it's been almost three years & we don't even know what's causing it yet."

"So, what, you're just giving up on what's natural?"

"No, Jeremy. I'm being realistic. There is a chance that this birth ratio thing could go on for years, decades even. What happens if we have entire generations that are only one tenth male?"

"We'll find a way to get through it & still uphold God's laws."

"One man, one woman, no divorce? Those laws Jeremy?"

"Yes. Those laws. We need to protect the sanctity of marriage from the direction that the left seems hell-bent on moving in."

"And believe me Jeremy, I would love to do just that. But in case you haven't been paying attention, in about fifteen years, it's going to become really hard to maintain one man & one woman when the women outnumber the men nine to one. If the birth ratios don't get fixed soon, God's laws & population statistics are going to clash & the statistics are going to win."

"How can you say that?"

"Because it'll be hard to win an election when one man, one woman & no divorce means that eight out of ten women will never be able to marry. Tell me, how would you get them to vote for the party that would be saying that they can't get married because we chose to leave the lack of men up to God?"

"Someone will figure it out."

"I hope so Jeremy, I really do, but we need to be practical here. The election is coming up in ten months & not only do we need to remain united, but we also need to look like we're working on solutions."

"But voting with the democrats to conduct a decade long survey to study how society would work if we allowed lesbian relationships? That can't be the solution."

"Don't forget, the study also includes other alternatives that may work if we don't find a solution."

"Oh yes, lest I forget, polygamy, reproductive infidelity, test tube babies & all the other ungodly things that some people are willing to consider."

"At least they're still man & woman."

"No, they are one man & nine women, or one man & one woman & eight harlots, or one man & one woman & a lab technician."

"Look Jeremy, I get it, I don't like any of these ideas either. I don't like that my granddaughters might have to be part of a harem, or have to find companionship with other women, but the simple fact is that if we stick to our guns about marriage & sexuality for too long, we're going to start losing elections. The world has changed & we might just have to change with it if our party wants to survive."

Jeremy felt as if he were swallowing the most bitter pill of his life. His colleague & the other six that voted with the Democrats were right. If this problem wasn't solved soon, his party would have to choose between stepping to the left or possibly dying on the right.

Feb 8th, 1968
Oval Office

"So, am I going to win or not?"
President Lyndon Johnson closed the folder that contained the endless array of statistics that had been gathered by the polling groups. William Marvin Watson, Johnsons' chief of staff, picked up the folder & fished around inside for a few specific pages.
"Well Lyndon, our party can win, but you can't."
"Explain that to me. Why can we win, but I can't?"
"Over the last few months, more & more people have started talking about the birth ratios. It seems to be the result of a number of factors that we underestimated. The 1983 movement, more religious leaders talking about it, hearing it mentioned on the news all the time. A majority of Americans are starting to get concerned about it or at least are paying attention to it."
"That's a good thing? The commission still doesn't have any answers as to what's happening, let alone how to fix it."
"That's true Lyndon, but they see democrats at every level of government pouring money & resources into finding a solution as well as trying to figure out how we'll get by if we don't find a solution. Meanwhile, large swaths of the republicans have not mentioned it, underplayed it, or have spent the last three years offering prayers that seem to be ineffective."
"So, we look like we're doing something, but they look like they're sticking their head in the sand."

"Exactly. That combined with all of the social progress that we've made has large sections of the population loving us. On top of that, it looks like the American Independent party is going to take at least one or two states in the south, depriving the republicans of at least a dozen electoral votes."

"That all sounds good Marvin."

"It does, there's just one problem."

"Vietnam."

"I'm sorry Lyndon, but it's become an albatross around your neck. Every day, more & more people see our involvement as a mistake. The 1983 movement has been adding a whole lot of fuel to that fire. Opposing your support of the war is the only thing that the republicans have to hit you with in key states. Polls show that if you run, you'll be lucky to clear 200 electoral votes."

"I see. But we stand a chance if I drop out of the race."

"Indeed, we do. If Hubert runs in your place, or if McCarthy or Kennedy win the nomination, then there's a decent chance that we could still win California, Illinois & maybe even Ohio."

"Would that be enough to win?"

"It would probably get us up into the 280s, not a great win, but a win."

"What if we don't get one of those states?"

"If we don't get Ohio or if we don't get Illinois, then our only hope would be if the American Independent party took a bunch of states in the south so that even with less than half the votes, we'd still have the most."

"So, you're saying that I should step down from the race."

"I'm sorry sir, but you can't win. The sooner that the other candidates can start distancing themselves from your Vietnam stance, the better for us."

President Johnson sighed as he took in the bad news.

March 30th, 1968

Church of the Lord's Son, Fort Worth, Texas

"They are giving up on the sanctity of the American spirit!"

Reverend Thomas Edwards shouted before his swollen congregation. In the last few months, as word of his fervent sermons spread across Texas, people had started coming from further & further away to hear him preach. From Amarillo to Houston, they were packing into his church to hear him preach the truth of the Lord's wrath.

The only place in his church where the congregants weren't being crushed like sardines was in the front pews where the large number of pregnant women were sitting with some breathing room. Each of the two pews for the pregnant women had an altar boy devoted to it to bring them towels or water as they needed it.

Looking out at the faces of his flock, he held up a copy of a local newspaper. The front page had a picture of President Johnson under a headline announcing that he was redrawing from reelection.

"President Johnson, a native to the great state of Texas, & one of the few liberals that was worthy of respect for his efforts to crush the communist menace in all parts of the world, is giving up on his God given duties as President. He intends to delegate the duty of protecting this country from communism to some soft hearted, godless liberal, who probably wants to bring communism to this country!"

The crowd shouted in anger.

"But this is merely a symptom of the democrat's refusal to stand up for God's way of life, for the American way of life. You've all seen it in the news. State after state, governor after governor, democrat after democrat, promising more funding for the study of the birth ratios, but also funding studies to look into alternative social structures for Americans. Do their scientists have no faith in their own work? The same scientists who built the bomb & are now sending Americans to the moon before the damned commies can get there? No, it's the Democrats who have lost faith!"

Applause broke out from the crowd.

"New York! New Jersey! Illinois! California! They have all begun research into new ways to organize society around the deficit of sons. This is their polite, clinical way of saying that they are studying how to integrate lesbianism into our society. Harems, matriarchy, the subservience of men to be nothing more than pumps for the few women that will want to have babies. They see this curse from

God, this deficit of sons to lead the next generation, & they are taking advantage of it!"

Shouts of devils & heathens erupted as the reverend stood at his pulpit, his coppery red hair seeming to blaze with his righteous fury.

"We must find a way to convince the good people of Texas that their favorite son, Lyndon Baines Johnson, stepping down from the presidency, is a sign that we must not let Texas remain in the hands of these liberal heathens! We must bring an end to this madness! They speak of needing to be ready in case a solution isn't found before the deficit of sons becomes too great, I say that we have the solution, the solution is to put our faith back into the Lord!"

Thunderous applause nearly deafened the reverend.

"Professors & analysts & sociologists are all talking about how even if we find a solution, things will have to change. That women will have to leave the home & work in the factories. That women will have to do the work of men. There are even some that are saying that women will have to be enlisted into the military to do the fighting. We cannot trust these men who relegate all of the God given duties of men to the weaker sex! They say that we need to have a solution, I say again, we have a solution!"

He reached his hand out to a woman in the second row. She stood up, holding her newborn son in her arms. The sudden movement disturbed his sleep, caused him to cry. As she tried to sooth him, Reverend Thomas slammed his fist on his pulpit.

"Let him cry Olivia! Let him cry out to the world that your faith has been rewarded with a son! A Son to lead us forward! A Son to stand against liberalism, against communism, against feminism & lesbianism!"

Most of the crowd cheered & applauded as the weeks old boy cried & wailed in his mother's arms. Reverend Thomas then signaled the altar boys who began passing the collection plates around.

"Our faith! Our vigilance! Our righteousness has caused this church to swell as our women swell with sons, the fruit of our faith! Our church must now swell as well, we must grow this humble chapel into a hall that is worthy of the parents of the new sons that will lead this nation back to God!"

Whether dollars or dimes, most of the congregation gave what they could spare so that the church could be renovated & expanded. Only when the collection plates reached the back rows did the donations dry up as the women who had given birth to daughters sat in the back, wondering if they were going to be cast out as Elisa had been.

May 6th, 1968
Capitol Building, Washington DC

Doctor Edward Swanson sat in front of the congressional overview committee. The seven congressmen sat at the long table opposite him, preparing to ask him questions that he didn't want to answer. He ran his hand through his brown hair, now streaked with grey, that hadn't been there three years ago. Once he had sworn to tell the truth, the congressman at the center of the table began the inquiry.

"Doctor Swanson. You're here to today to answer some of the questions that the American taxpayers have about the commission to study the birth ratio anomaly. This is not a criminal investigation. The main reason for all of us being here is to determine if your research should have a greater level of oversight & to find out why results have been so few."

"I understand congressman. I'm happy to answer any questions that you may have."

"Good. Now, for the record, when were you put in charge of the commission?"

"That was on day one of the whole thing, which if memory serves, was the ninth of April 1965."

"So, you can give us a complete accounting of the commission & it's history then."

"Yes, I can congressman."

"When you first started, what kind of oversight did you have over your budget?"

"None whatsoever congressman. I was told that an issue of this magnitude & consequence had full bipartisan support & that because this was completely unprecedented, I basically had a blank cheque. My budget was whatever I needed it to be."

"No oversight at all? Nobody asked questions about what the money was being used for?"

"No sir. Like I mentioned a moment ago, the phenomenon that we're studying is unprecedented & obviously has catastrophic consequences that will start to affect us within the next decade. We were told to get results & not to worry about the cost."

"I see. So, it was a similar situation to the Apollo program. Here's a cheque, do the job & fill in the amount you needed to do it."

"Basically sir. There was also the fact that we had no idea which of the dozens of different causes it might be that was causing this effect. It could have been viral, biological, chemical, environmental, genetic, etc. The list goes on too what might be causing it & some of these fields are brand new fields of study that we know nothing about."

"So, there was the issue of national importance, & the issue of having no idea how much it would cost. That's why you were given as much of a budget as you needed."

"Yes sir."

"I see. So, after you were given the key to the treasury department, you got to work assembling a massive team to start studying every reasonable possibility for the cause of this phenomenon."

"That we did sir. With so many possible causes & so many scientific areas that we've only just begun to probe, we had a lot of work ahead of us on this issue."

"Doctor Swanson, was there any real oversight in the early days?"

"No sir. As long as we were producing results, we were given free rein to do whatever we needed to do."

"Let's talk about those results. Very early on, you discovered a number of things that are not causing this phenomenon."

"We discovered a whole hell of a lot of things that it isn't."

The people behind him & a few members of the committee laughed.

"Yes Doctor Swanson. However, you don't seem to have found anything that could be the cause."

"Not as of yet. We've checked every possible chemical that could be causing this, we've checked for new viruses or bacteria, we've analyzed more semen than anyone should ever have to deal with. It all checks out as normal. As far as we can see, it's almost as if the sperm carrying the genes for boys are unwilling to fertilize a woman's eggs while women's eggs are at the same time, becoming very picky."

"Results that were published back in 65. The question now is, why has there not been any additional progress?"

"I... I don't know."

"You don't know."

"I don't know congressman. I don't know why we can't find an answer, I don't know why this is happening & that's the best thing that I, or the director of any other commission or study or research project into this can tell you. I don't know."

Edward could hear mumbling throughout the room as he took a sip of water before continuing.

"The best that I or any of my counterparts in other countries can figure is that either we lack the technology required to understand what's happening, or the cause is so esoteric that it's beyond our ability to understand."

"I... see... Is this the reason why some of your commissions' projects are so...?"

"Out there, fringe, new aged psychedelic nonsense & just plain weird. Yes. With a lack of results from any reasonable cause, we've also started looking into some things that many would consider to be unreasonable."

"I see. Have these... new aged psychedelic... theories... produced any tangible results?"

"Aside from I & my staff being more physically flexible & a few members of one team acquiring an appreciation for the smell of sage, no sir, there have been no tangible results."

"Doctor Swanson, if this council recommended that your commission should be subject to congressional oversight, what would your response be?"

"Honestly, I wouldn't mind. It might be nice if someone else's hair could start going grey."

"Doctor Swanson, does your commission need oversight?"

"We need results sir. If you think that oversight will help with that, then by all means. We've tried just about everything else."

June 6th, 1968
Sacramento, California

Patricia Torres looked at the symbol on her banner. A pink crown sitting above a Venus symbol. As she contemplated it, she wondered if this had been the right symbol to choose. As a young couple walked by the small booth that they had set up in the park, the woman next to her perked up & held out a pamphlet.

"Would you like to hear about the Matriarch Party? We're a new political party & we need your signatures so that we can appear on the ballot for the California legislature in November!"

The couple kept walking by.

"I think that we need to ditch the crown."

The young woman who had tried to hand out the pamphlet looked at Patricia curiously.

"It's the Matriarch party. What else should we have used?"

"It's just... I don't think that we're going to get a lot of Americans to sign on to a party that looks like it wants to put the Queen of England in charge. This country was started by throwing off the monarchy, now here we are with crowns saying that we should subjugate men."

The woman grew concerned.

"You're not having doubts about our new party, are you? It's your party, this is all your idea."

"I don't have any doubts about the party Sarah. We're moving towards a world where women will be running things, so women should be in charge. I just think that we're shooting ourselves in the foot with the crown & the name. I know that I came up with the name, but now I'm wondering how we'll ever get anywhere."

"We'll get there. It's like you said Patricia, we probably won't win this election, probably not the next one either."

"Right, we're making a name for ourselves so that when the XX generation grows up, they'll know who we are."

Putting the pamphlets down, Sarah turned around in her chair.

"What's wrong Patricia? You look like you've got the weight of the world on your shoulders."

"It's… Do you remember back in February, when we were just a bunch of middle-aged housewives who had had enough chardonnay & gin to think that we could change the world."

"The birth of a great idea."

"It seemed so simple then. Now, when we're actually out here, sober & trying to convince people that we might be worth voting for one day, it seems…"

"Insurmountable."

"Exactly Sarah."

"Does this have anything to do with that guy this morning that called us man cutters?"

"God. Don't even get me started on that. You know, I bet that guy had never even heard of Andy Warhol before he was killed. One crazy woman kills an artist while saying that men need to be destroyed & all of a sudden, any woman that says anything other than yes sir is a man killer waiting for her chance."

Sarah wrapped her arms around Patricia in a great big hug.

"Don't worry fearless leader. We don't have to overthrow the whole world today. Today we just need to get a few dozen signatures to get us closer to being on a ballot somewhere. At the rate we're going, we'll have enough by the middle of September."

"True. Did I tell you that Hank took a signature sheet to work for the secretaries? See if any of them might support us."

Sarah laughed.

"Yeah, you mentioned it yesterday. God, that must be a sight, that loveable meathead husband of yours trying to convince the gals to sign up for the matriarchy."

Both women burst into a fit of laughter as a pair of young women in very bright miniskirts decided to check out the booth & see what the matriarchy party was.

June 26th, 1968
McGill University, Montreal

Janet woke up to sunlight streaming in through her dorm window, her radio in the bed next to her, & a complete lack of any sensation whatsoever in her left leg. Slowly working the tangled sheet off of her body, she quickly noticed two things.

The first thing she noticed was that she was naked, something that she quickly picked up on as the sheet moved across her body as she tried to untangle herself. The second thing that she noticed was that Rebecca was next to her, just as naked.

Somehow, Janet's jostling of the sheet did nothing to wake her lover. When she could lift the sheet up high enough to see their bare bodies, she saw that their legs were entwined, which was leading to some of the issues with the sheet. It also explained why she couldn't feel anything in her leg.

Reaching into the tangled mess of their bodies, she heard Rebecca groan as she reached between their legs & spread Rebecca's far enough apart to pry hers loose.

Once her leg was liberated from the vice-like grip of her lover's thighs, blood flow returned to normal & everything from the tips of her toes to the middle of her thigh awoke with an excruciating pins & needles sensation. Every twitch of her bare leg was like lightning coursing through her waking limb. Each shock brought back memories of the night before.

Rebecca had convinced her to take a night off of studying so that they could listen to the election on the radio. They had stayed up late, listening to changing results as votes were counted & predictions were made. As the Atlantic provinces went to the conservatives & Quebec slowly started giving seats to the liberals, the two women began imagining what their lives might be like if the liberals won.

As the radio news hosts asserted that the majority of seats in Quebec had been won by the liberals, Janet could see her future brightening. The man leading the liberals to this apparent victory, Pierre Trudeau, was the same man who just months ago had moved heaven & Earth to make it legal for her & Rebecca to be together.

As predictions about Ontario started coming in, they found themselves sitting closer together on Janet's bed. As they talked about what it might be like to go to the movies together, or to go out to dinner together, or to be able to kiss each other in public, they were wrapping their arms around each other. As it became apparent that Trudeau had won the lion's share of Ontario, one of their hands had found a way underneath a shirt.

For the next few hours, neither of them heard more than a few words from the radio as it disappeared. Clothes had quickly been removed & thrown far from them. Lips, once locked together, were exploring each other's familiar bodies with hunger. Fingers soon found their ways to intimate places & by the time the Northwest Territories were being talked about on the radio, Janet was passed the point of caring that her neighbors might hear the sound of two women bringing each other to passionate climaxes over & over again.

Eventually, they collapsed from sheer exhaustion in each other's arms. The last thing that Janet could remember was Rebecca pulling the sheet over their pale, naked bodies.

Not even sure where her clothes were, Janet sat up & swung her legs over the side of the bed. Grabbing the radio, she tried turning it on to find out what the results of the election were. Realizing that the radio's batteries must have died during their passions, Janet put it aside & got up.

Realizing that her knees were in business for themselves, Janet struggled to get across the room for new batteries. As she reached the drawer that she was looking for, she heard clapping coming from Rebecca.

"For a second there, I didn't think that you were going to make it."

"I can't help it, after last night's marathon & then waking up with one leg pinned under you, this is how I walk now. Like a woman who was just split in half."

Rebecca grinned as she sat up. Janet marveled at her body in the early morning light.

"How many guys do you think there are in this school that wish they could be the ones to say they made you walk like that?"

"Probably not too many."

"I wouldn't say that. I'd be willing to bet that most of the guys here would do just about anything to see you walking around the room naked & limping from a marathon love making session."

"Too bad for them this sight is for your eyes only."

Rebecca laughed as she rolled onto her back & stretched while Janet made her way back to bed. As Janet took the radio so she could change the batteries, Rebecca laid her arm out on the bed & with her other hand, she patted the bed next to her, indicating that Janet should get back into her embrace.

With the batteries changed, Janet climbed into bed where Rebecca quickly wrapped her arms around her & held them close. As the boundary between their bodies got a bit hard to distinguish in some places, Janet turned the radio on.

"There wasn't much question among most voters about which party would win yesterday's election, but with only a handful of districts left to count, it's safe to say the results won't change. With 158 seats in parliament, not only did Trudeau's liberals win, but they also have a majority government."

Janet turned off the radio. Not only did the man that had made their love legal win the election, but his party had a majority, which meant there was next to nothing that could stop them. Possibilities that had once seemed like sweet dreams to be whispered between lovers suddenly felt real.

September 17th, 1968
Queens, New York

Mary Robinson was sitting on a bench in the park. It was just a bit chilly outside. Cool enough to wear some warm clothes, but still just warm enough for children to be playing outside. The bench was in front of a small sandbox where little Elizabeth, now three years old & curious about everything, was playing in the sand with another girl her age. As Mary looked out over the park, it struck her as odd that nearly three quarters of the children running around & laughing & playing were girls. What struck her as even more strange was the realization that when Elizabeth was her age, this sight would seem weird because of how many boys there were, not how many girls there were.

"Thanks for keeping an eye on Sarah."

The other little girl's mother sat down on the bench next to Mary.

"No problem. Sarah & Elizabeth were having so much fun that we could have run off to join the circus & they wouldn't have noticed."

"Don't tell that to Ben for a little while. He's still freaking out after seeing that new movie in the theater."

"Is that the World of Woman movie that I've been hearing about? Is it any good?"

"Yeah, it's an imagining of what the world will look like in about fifty years or so if we don't start giving birth to more boys soon."

"I heard on the news that a lot of people are freaking out over it."

"That's an understatement Mary. When we went to see it, people were protesting it outside the theater saying that it was indecent pornography. They weren't entirely wrong. There were a number of rather explicit & … up close lesbian sex scenes."

"Oh. I didn't know that."

"Nobody did. Everyone thought that it was going to be a drama or maybe a bit of a documentary. Next thing that I know, I was watching a married suburban couple, both women, go to bed & go down on each other."

"Oh my. Was it at least… tasteful?"

"No Mary. It was right up-close & it was gratuitous & that was the reason why just five minutes in, people were already walking out."

Mary actually blushed a bit.

"Was the whole movie like that?"

"Nope. That was the opening. It got worse, if you're going to see it, I won't spoil anymore for you."

"David is taking me to see it on the weekend, but perhaps I should know a bit more about it."

"Well alright. Without going into too much detail, the story is about a group of men living in the woods. One of the last groups of free men in the world. Then they get captured by this… military… government group called Seed. All the soldiers were women, & they chase most of the men down & arrest them."

"What did the men do?"

"Nothing, it was just illegal for them to not be in the seed facility."

"Dare I ask what the seed facility is?"

"Well, Martha, since you asked. It's one of the facilities in the city where the men are kept so that they can be milked."

"Milked?"

"For their sperm."

"What?"

"Yeah. They strap the men into these milking chairs every day for half an hour, put this pump tube thing on them & milk them like cows for their sperm so that they can impregnate women."

"Why would they do that?"

"Because it was the only way to keep the birth rate up, because in the movie, the boys born after 1965 are almost all queer & don't want to marry nine women, so the government, now entirely run by women, had them rounded up so they can be milked."

"Jesus. So is the movie just lesbian sex & men being sucked off by machines?"

"No, that's just the setup. In the movie, a small group of straight men are trying to fight for their freedom, arguing that since they aren't queer, they should be allowed to rejoin society because they would like to have a bunch of wives. The problem is that almost everyone thinks that's a bad idea because society has moved beyond men."

"I can see why so many people would be so upset."

"You have no idea, Mary. At the beginning & the end of the movie, there's a message on the screen reminding the audience that if nothing changes, then in fifty years, there won't be enough young men to keep the birth rate up & that there's been no real progress in finding a solution in almost two years."

"It sounds like they're trying to scare the audience into thinking that all of that could actually happen."

"That's exactly what they're doing & the scary bit is that it could happen."

"I guess that would have Ben all out of shape."

"Out of shape is one way to put it. Nearly all of the men in the neighborhood who have seen the movie are going to that town hall tonight, the one where the republican candidate is trying to drum up some votes for November. They have questions for him."

"What kind of questions?"

"They want to know why his party isn't mentioning funding for the commission, or what their plan is in case this birth ratio thing doesn't go away. That movie has them spooked that all of their daughters are going to become lesbians & that all of their sons are going to end up in a facility where a machine is sucking them off every day."

"You don't think that that could actually happen, do you?"

"The men in cages being daily pumped, I doubt it. But the rampant lesbianism, I would be surprised if that doesn't happen."

"Really?"

"Yeah, I mean, can you imagine Ben or David taking care of nine wives & a few dozen kids?"

Mary tried to imagine it & she couldn't see it working."

"I'm telling you Mary; things are going to change when they grow up. That's why I'm voting for Humphry. I never voted democrat before, & I don't really want to in November, but at least they're trying. They're pouring money into research & they're trying to figure out how everything will work when Sarah grows up if the research doesn't pan out. What are the republicans doing? Sticking their head in the sand & hoping that if they pray hard enough, it'll go away."

"Wow. Did you tell Ben about that?"

"Told him this morning. That's one of the reasons he's heading to the town hall. He says that if he doesn't get some good answers, he's voting Humphrey as well, for Sarah's sake. Better the liberals trying to find an answer for our kid then the conservative who won't acknowledge the problem."

"Mommy, play in!"

Looking over to the sandbox, Mary saw Elizabeth calling her over to play in the sand.

"In a few minutes Elizabeth, mommy is talking right now."

"Okay!"

As Elizabeth went back to playing with Sarah, Mary looked at her & thought out loud.

"When she was born, David & I agreed that I would be the one to talk to her about the birds & the bees & he would warn her about what boys are like. Now I'm wondering if we're also going to have to talk to her about girls."

"I know the feeling. The only reason that I haven't shared that insight with Ben yet is because in his current mood, he'd probably have a coronary. I'm telling you now, he does not get to check out until after we've had the talk with her because I am not doing that alone."

They agreed that the most awkward part of being a parent was now going to be much more awkward than either of them had signed up for as they both wondered about the future of their daughters.

November 6th, 1968
Hubert Humphrey's Home

Hubert had gone to bed the night before with a lump in his throat. He had been surprised when he had gotten the democratic nomination for president over Robert Kennedy & Eugene McCarthy. Nobody had been expecting the polls to swing in his favor near the end. What followed was months of campaigning to convince the people that they should choose him over Nixon.

Polls & surveys hadn't given him too much reason to feel comfortable. Every indication was that he was in a dead heat with Nixon.

The day before, as Americans across the country started going to the polls, Humphrey found himself glued to the television & the radio as he waited for the results to come in. As vote totals came in, some states seemed to be flipping back & forth, as if they couldn't make up their minds & it was driving him crazy.

Finally, his wife Muriel convinced him to get some rest & take a nap. Telling him that it wouldn't do anyone any good if he had a stroke, & that the final count would only be decided the next day, he had gone to bed for a quick nap at two in the morning. As he had been walking away from the news coverage of the election, the scales had been tipping towards Nixon in a number of important states.

A few hours later, when Humphrey woke up, he walked into the living room where some of his children were still visiting to watch the election with him.

"Why didn't one of you wake me up? I just wanted to take a quick cat nap."

His daughter Nancy looked away from the television for a moment.

"Sorry dad, we decided to let you get some more rest. But come here quick, you're winning."

"What? I was trailing Nixon when I went for my nap."

"Well, he's trailing you now. You've won New Jersey, New York, Ohio, Pennsylvania, Michigan, Illinois & it looks like Texas is just about a lock for you."

"What? Half those states were leaning to the republicans in the polling, how did I win all of those?"

"I told you dad; it was that movie that came out a few months ago. It made people wake up & realize what's been going on since 65."

"Nancy, do you really think a movie convinced half the country to vote for me?"

"It was one heck of a movie. You're up to 233 electoral votes. All you need at this point is one or two more states & you'll win."

"What do the western states look like?"

"Mostly red, wait, hang on."

She turned the tv volume up a bit as a news reporter that normally worked the evening news came on live.

"Walter, we're getting reports out of a number of red leaning districts in California apparently leaning to the left. Now, there's still about a million votes left to count in California, but Hubert Humphrey has once again pulled a few points ahead of Nixon. Now as I just said, with such a small lead, California is still too close to call, but what we've seen over the last few hours has been that Humphrey keeps taking the lead over & over again & every time that he does, it takes longer & longer for Nixon to pull the lead back."

Nancy turned the volume back down.

"You see dad, it looks like you might just win in the end."

Sitting down to watch with his family, they watched as his lead in California kept growing & growing. Eventually both Washington & Miami were found to have voted for the democrats. After a few more hours, news outlets across the country started calling

California for Humphrey as it became clear that he had won the state & the country with over 300 electoral votes.

1969

January 20th, 1969
10 Downing Street

"My fellow Americans, we stand in an age of unparalleled changes & crisis. As we strive to create a greater union, to bring freedom, liberty & justice to all within our borders & to inspire it elsewhere in the world, we are faced with hardships & challenges the like of which our nation & our world have never seen before. From the new frontiers of the space age to the rise of violent communism, to the realization that there are those in this country that are not truly free, to the challenges facing our children as one of the fundamental aspects upon which our society was built has been irreparably changed. Many challenges face us in the coming years & I am humbled & honored to be chosen by the people to face these challenges."

Harold Wilson turned down the volume of the television as the Secretary of State for Defense walked into the Prime Minister's home.

"Come on in Denis. I was just watching Humphrey's inauguration speech on the tele. Sizing up my counterpart on the other side of the pond."

"Yes, nobody was expecting him to win by such a large margin, but then his party has been pouring resources into the birth crisis & how they may adapt to it in the future."

"Yes. Speaking of which Denis, I don't suppose that you have that report that I asked you for."

"Yes sir & I'm afraid that it is not going to be very popular."

"I was aware of that Denis, but it is becoming more apparent every day that it will most likely be a necessity."

"Sir, if it gets out that you were considering implementing policies such as these, even if just for research purposes, it may just sink you in the election. It does not matter that it will most likely be something that we have to do, nobody wants to see women serving in the armed forces, particularly in combat roles."

"I'm not too fond of it either Denis, but it has to be done."

"Can it not wait until after the election sir?"

"Sadly, no. If the conservatives win, could we entrust them to have the army ready to have women in fighting positions by the end of the next decade? If they win, we won't have another chance to prepare our military until we win the next election. Besides, if we implement these policies after the election, they will most likely call for a confidence vote & have us thrown out."

"But sir, even if you could convince parliament of the necessity of having women fill combat positions, do you really believe that the Queen would give royal ascent to the removal of such restrictions?"

"I don't see why not. Don't forget Denis, she was the first female member of the royal family to actively serve in the armed forces."

"Yes Harold, as a driver & a mechanic. It will be an entirely different venture to allow women into combat positions."

Wilson stood up & walked over to the window. He stood in thought for a moment, smoking his pipe.

"Denis, does your report contain the estimated size of the population of the United Kingdom in 2000?"

"Best estimates put it at about fifty-five million people, assuming that Scotland, Northern Ireland & Wales don't break away."

"I see, & do you have an estimate for how large our military will have to be at the time?"

"Approximately two hundred thousand to two hundred & forty thousand people. I see where you're going with his Harold. If we don't allow women into combat positions, & if the birth crisis isn't resolved, then somewhere around three percent of the entire male population of the country will have to be serving in the armed forces."

"Exactly Denis, can you imagine it being acceptable for three percent of all men to be serving in the armed forces when they only represent a tenth of the population?"

"I can't, the problem is that the conservatives can imagine that as being perfectly acceptable. Hell, as far as they're concerned, nothing about our current way of living needs to change, even with this massive shift in demographics."

Harold took another pull from his pipe. He knew that Denis was right. The hardest part about preparing the country to function when women outnumbered men nine to one wasn't going to be figuring out how to do it. The hard part was going to be convincing the old guard, the people that prided themselves on tradition & the way things have always been done, to change in some of the most radical ways ever conceived of.

"We have to try now Denis. We can't be sure that we'll win the election & we might not have time to get it right if we lose."

February 14th, 1969
Chicago, Church of the Wives of Christ

"Tonight is a most unholy night sisters!"
Virginia Green stood at her pulpit in front of her congregation of women. Much like she had that day she met Hope in the park, she wore her white robes as she preached to her audience. The difference was that this time, there was more than just Hope taking her seriously.
"On this night of all nights, we must fight hardest to keep ourselves safe from the perversion that is man! Most other nights of the year, a man will at least think that he has to put in some effort to access your sacred womb. But on this cursed night, this unholy night, all the beasts of the land think that they can just show up with some cheap flowers & desecrate your divinity with their unworthy seed!"
While Virginia preached, she was upset to see that after a few years, they could only bring in about twenty women on this night. As she prepared to deliver her unique brand of man hating Christianity, she remembered what Hope had told her before she started, that three of the women in the front row were regulars that were showing up every Sunday. It was no longer just her & Hope. They had followers.
"We must remain vigilante tonight sisters! Let no man touch you tonight! Let no man speak to you! Let these lust & hate filled beasts know that they are no longer welcome within you! Let them know that there is only one man that is worthy of our bodies, the man that hangs on the cross!"

She pointed up to the large crucifix behind her as she made her proclamation.

"The end of days is coming sisters! God is allowing just enough men to be born to lure away those women not worthy to bear Christ's children into the world. Be strong! Keep your bodies clean for the coming of the King of Kings! Let no man inside of you!"

From behind Virginia, Hope watched as one of the regular partitioners turned to the woman next to her & pulled her into a kiss. The woman was clearly surprised & panicked at first, most likely having never been able to kiss another woman in public before. Hope watched as Virginia pointed them out & praised them. She listened as Virginia declared that until the Lord came back to lay with them, the only pure form of love was the love between women. Virginia then called Hope forward to her side.

Not sure what was happening, Hope, dressed in her own white robes, stepped forward & stood next to Virginia as she spoke to her crowd for the night.

"For those of you in the audience who have been brainwashed by the patriarchy of filth into thinking that happiness can only be found at the end of a penis, open your eyes & see the truth!"

Virginia then turned to face Hope as she pulled Hope forward into a deep & passionate kiss. Hope had been caught completely unaware. In the moment that it took her mind to realize what was happening, their embrace was awkward & clumsy. But once her mind caught up to what was happening, she gave herself over to the kiss & reveled in the boldness & intensity of it.

When their lips parted, Hope stood there blissfully stunned as Virginia turned back to an equally stunned crowd.

"All you need do is kiss another woman's sweet lips & you will see for yourself that the preachers of men have lied to you! See for yourselves, here & now, kiss the women next to you, learn that there's more than just the worm between men's legs that can make you happy!"

Hope was stunned to see that while one woman was getting up to leave the sermon, most of the others were turning to one of the women next to them & kissing each other.

As Hope found herself wondering how many of these women were kissing another woman for the first time in their lives, she saw

Virginia give the signal to prepare the collection bowl. Not wanting to seem overly greedy like the churches of men that put a plate on a long stick & shove in your face like a penis that you have to pay for, they simply put a bowl or two near the exit as the sermon was reaching its conclusion that people could donate to if they wanted.

As Hope went to check on the collection bowls, she wondered if this would be the night that a sermon broke ten dollars. Between the regular women that kept coming back & the growing donations that they received, Hope felt a new confidence that their church just might succeed.

March 9th, 1969
John F. Kennedy Space Center

Gene Kranz stood in mission control where he had spent most of his time over the last week. Acknowledging what the security guard had just told him, he flipped the small switch on his headset, calling up to the crew of Apollo 9, who had been orbiting the Earth for a week, testing the features of the Lunar lander & the command module.

"James. How are the pictures looking?"

James McDevitt, the commander of Apollo 9 flipped the switch on his headset as he stared through the camera setup.

"They're looking pretty good there, Gene. We're getting some lovely images of the Colorado river right now. Seeing things like this, I don't think that this could ever get old."

"That's good to hear James. Listen, this is going to sound like a weird question, but you're not pissing off any extraterrestrials up there, are you?"

There was silence for a few seconds.

"No Gene. Nothing but us & these incredible views in front of us."

"Just making sure."

"Is everything alright down there, Gene?"

"Do you remember that group that was protesting outside during Apollo 8, the ones that said we were pissing off the aliens with our space program?"

"The ones in the silver robes that said the moon aliens are responsible for the birth ratios because we're invading their sovereign domain. They're back?"

"That they are, robes & all. They're a little rowdier this time, apparently security is getting a little tighter."

"Are you guys in trouble down there?"

"Not at all, just as long as you three remember not to piss off the moon queen. Apparently, she doesn't like that our first ambassadors to her queendom are going to be men."

As most of the people in mission control chuckled, they could hear James, David & Rusty laughing on Apollo 9. As everyone shared a good chuckle, some of the people in mission control noticed a popping sound. A second later, two security guards came running in, hands at their holsters as they watched the entrances. Gene walked up to them as they listened on their earpieces.

"What's going on out there?"

"Shot fired sir. Apparently one of the protestors was armed with a revolver. Be ready to evacuate, just in case."

"We can't evacuate, we've got three guys a hundred miles up there."

"Sir, if this turns ugly, those three men may have to go on their own for a few hours. We..."

The guards both heard something on their earpieces. Listening carefully for a second, they both relaxed.

"Situation clear Mr. Kranz. It was an accidental misfire. The idiot had the revolver in the waist of his pants with the hammer cocked. Accidentally shot himself in the leg when he tried climbing onto a car they brought."

"Jesus. Were any of them armed last time?"

"We don't think so sir. Either way, we might want to consider a few of the changes to security we recommended a few weeks ago before we actually start sending these missions out to the moon. If they're coming armed to the tests in Earth orbit..."

"I'll talk to the guys upstairs about it. For now, just try to keep them back if you can."

"We're already working on it, sir."

As the security guard left, Gene realized that his mic was still hot when James called back down.

"Gene, everything alright down there?"

"It's all good down here. One of the Moon Queen's servants just shot himself in the leg. Security got a little jumpy."

"Gene, if you need to evacuate, we can handle ourselves for a few hours if we have to. We have plenty of extra provisions just in case. Don't be heroes down there."

"Thanks for the permission to save our own asses James, but we're in control down here. Everything is fine."

"If you say so Gene, it just sounded a little chaotic."

"Nothing to worry about, you just focus on the tasks at hand. We need to know that everything works up there."

"Alright Gene. If you say it's good, it's good."

May 22nd, 1969
Austria

Dr. Barbara Collins sat in the Austrian bar. When the director of the commission had insisted that she take a vacation, she had decided to call up one of her few friends to see if she could spend some time with her. A quick trip to a travel agency & a few days later, she had landed in Austria where she was met by Dr. Ester Beck, the only other woman working in the commissions & research programs devoted to the birth ratios in the western hemisphere.

During the day, Barbara would visit places that Esther told her about & at night, they would meet up in a restaurant or a bar. While Barbara continued to dress in her usual conservative manner, she found herself happy to let her hair down for the first time in a long time. She had been waiting for Ester in the agreed upon bar for about twenty minutes when Ester showed up at the little table & joined her.

"I hope that I haven't kept you waiting for too long Barbara."

"Barely any time at all."

"Perfect. How was your day today?"

"Wonderful. Austria is just beautiful."

"I'm glad that you're enjoying yourself. Even if your boss had to force you to do it."

"He didn't force me to enjoy myself, he just forced me to take two weeks off. My enjoying myself has everything to do with getting to spend some time with my friend."

"Well, I'll drink too that."

Esther then ordered two pints for them. A moment later, they had their drinks in hand. After a quick sip, Esther eyed Barbara curiously.

"So. Barbara. Are you ever going to tell me what's going on with Yale?"

"What do you mean?"

"Every single night, after a few drinks, you mention it as if it's an in-law that has overstayed their welcome. You curse them out & you still haven't told me why."

"Oh. That."

"I can't help but wonder what they've done that has you so upset."

Barbara sighed deeply before downing some more of her drink & telling the story.

"They want me to give the keynote address at their graduation ceremony in a few weeks for their graduating class."

Esther looked at her confused.

"You're mad because one of the best universities in the world wants you to inspire their graduates? I think that I am missing a few details to this story."

"The only reason that they want me to do it is because I'm a famous lady scientist who's working on the biggest problem of the century & they want me to be the one to announce that starting next semester, they'll be admitting women, just like me, to their hallowed halls of education."

"This still sounds like a great honor. I'm still not seeing the problem."

"The problem is that they refused to admit me back in 56, despite the fact that I had the highest scores in my district."

Esther suddenly understood the situation a little more as Barbara took a long pull from her pint.

"The highest scores in my district. My math teacher in my last year of high school demanded that I retake the exam because nobody had ever aced one of his tests before, let alone a girl."

"Arrogant bastard."

"Esther, you have no idea. I had to retake his exam with one of the school's secretaries present because they didn't like the idea that he was singling out a promising female student to spend two hours alone in his company."

"That's never a good sign."

"Aced his test again. He finally had to admit that I was just that good. He even wrote me a letter of recommendation to Yale, which he said would carry some weight because a dozen members of his family had gone to Yale, & they were well respected."

"Let me guess. They rejected you on the spot."

"As soon as they read my file & realized that I wasn't just a boy with a woman's name."

"So, they rejected you, & now they want you to announce to the world that they'll no longer reject women."

"Exactly. I mean, what would I even say? Hello men of the class of 1969, I wasn't allowed to come here because I have tits & the requirement was a penis. But if I fail to find a solution to the world's biggest issue within the next few years, your daughters will be allowed to come here."

Esther bent over laughing.

"I don't see that going over very well."

"Me either. So, I turned them down, but as you can imagine, they aren't interested in taking no for an answer."

"That doesn't surprise me."

"Did you have this kind of trouble getting into university?"

"Not exactly. Austria opened it universities to women in the 18... 90s... It was still challenging to get in, but my sex wasn't the issue at hand, at least not by policy."

"So much for the land of the free. Seventy something years later & not only have we still not caught up to Austria, but the only actual reason that we're making progress is because soon women will be nine tenths of the population."

"So, are you going to give the speech?"

"Would you Esther?"

"No. They didn't want me then; they don't get me know."

"I'll drink to that."

June 23rd, 1969
Oval Office

Edmund Muskie walked into the oval office. As Vice President, he was constantly bringing things to President Humphrey's attention. This news was not the kind of thing that he had been expecting to bring to the President's attention so early on.

"Edmund. You look like a man on a mission."

"I suppose that I am today, Hubert."

"Did you hear about Marcus Gibson?"

"Your appointee to the supreme court. Isn't he taking his seat on the bench today?"

"He just did an hour ago."

"Congratulation on your first supreme court appointment Mr. President."

"Thank you, Edmund. Now that it's done, I've got to start the process all over again because there's still another empty seat left for me to fill. No rest in this job. Sorry, Edmund, what was it that you wanted to talk to me about?"

"Well, coincidentally enough sir, I came here to talk to you about the supreme court."

"Oh. What's up?"

"Well, I don't think that it's going to be a problem, because from what I've heard, he doesn't have any actual support. But apparently, the senators from Kansas intend to publicly accuse you of stacking the supreme court."

"Seriously. Stacking the supreme court. On what possible grounds can they accuse me of that?"

"On the grounds that all eight of the court's members are democrats. They're claiming that you're creating a court that isn't representative of the people & that your next pick should be a Republican justice."

Hubert sat back in his chair for a moment in total disbelief at what he was hearing.

"Are they serious?"

"Quite serious Hubert. Their going around to all of the republican senators & congressmen to try & drum up support."

"I see. Are they succeeding?"

"Not from what I've heard. So far it seems that nobody is standing with them. Everyone else seems to understand that you won the election & you get to fill the vacancies."

"Stacking the court. Are we supposed to believe that if they had eight republicans on the bench, that they would be considerate enough to appoint a democrat?"

"I don't know Hubert; it looks like they're probably just trying to rile up their base. I'm willing to bet that we can expect more of this when you fill the ninth seat."

"What would stacking the court even look like?"

"Hard to say. It would probably look like one party trying to block a president's nominee because the election is imminent & they're hoping that they can win so they can give the pick to their candidate."

"Do you think that something like that could ever actually happen?"

"I don't see how. It would be an obvious ploy to steal a supreme court seat. Something like that could never work. It would be obscene."

July 20th, 1969
Robinson Home

Normally, Elizabeth would have been in bed hours ago. Either she would have gone happily, or her parents would have had to bribe her with stories & promises that she would forget by morning. That would be a normal night. But a man wasn't about to set foot on the moon on a normal night.

On a night that was like no other in the history of the world, children all over the country & all over the world were staying up late to watch a man get ready to set foot on the moon. All over the country, countless millions of Americans had offered up their prayers to those brave men.

Around quarter past three in the afternoon, the Robinsons watched the news with Elizabeth between them as Walter Cronkite described the trouble that Neil & Buzz were having as they tried to land in the Sea of Tranquility. Elizabeth, only four years old, looked up at her parents curiously as they cheered. She had no idea what it meant when she heard the crackly sound of a man saying Houston, Tranquility Base here, the Eagle has landed.

Over the next several hours, countless phone calls were made & received while neighbors came & went to talk about what was happening. Elizabeth didn't really know what was going on, all that she knew was that her normal bedtime had come & gone & her parents weren't making her go to bed.

At eight o'clock, instead of heading upstairs, they went next door to their neighbor's house where half the block had gathered to watch the moon landing on the best tv on the block. As everyone crowded around the television, they were dismayed to discover that the astronauts weren't ready yet.

They watched as Cronkite explained that while normally, it took the astronauts an hour & a half to get ready for their moonwalk in training, it was taking significantly longer than they had expected that it would take.

Elizabeth, Sarah, & a few of the other kids from the neighborhood started playing as the grown-ups waited breathlessly for what seemed like hours until eventually, at about nine thirty, it started.

The children were all gathered back up at the television as the scene switched to a dark imagine that was hard for Elizabeth to make out. When one of the older kids asked what was happening, one of the grownups explained that the man named Neil was at the bottom of the ladder, getting ready to step onto the moon. As they watched, he climbed back up a step for a moment before returning to standing on the landing pad.

"I'm at the foot of the ladder. The LEM footpads are only depressed in the surface about one or two inches. Although the surface appears to be very, very fine grained as you get close to it, it's almost like a powder."

Everybody watched closely as Neil took a step off of the footpad & onto the grey surface. The words Armstrong on the moon covered the screen as everyone remained silent for a moment.

"That's one small step for a man... One giant leap for humanity."

Elizabeth & the younger children were shocked when the grownups all burst into cheers & applause. When someone told her that a man was walking on the moon, she thought it was kind of cool. She didn't realize that once again, the world had just changed forever.

September 10ᵗʰ, 1969
Outside Birmingham Alabama

"I'm telling ya John; they got a cure."

Ronald Addams, known to his friends as Ronnie, had known that his old friend John would be hanging out at this bar. He usually did, & John seemed like the perfect kind of guy.

"What cure?"

"The cure for the baby thing."

"Seriously, Ronnie, you been drinking old man henry's bathtub brews again. You know that shit will fuck with ya. Just look at Henry, he wasn't born that crazy."

Ronald waved off the comparison to the town fool.

"Listen John. Think about it. They've had all the best minds in the world working on finding a cure for four years now & they say that they can't even figure out what's wrong. Don't that sound strange to you?"

John thought about it for a moment. A long moment.

"Yeah, it is a bit strange. Heck, it's probably just something very complicated."

"Maybe, or maybe it's a conspiracy."

"A conspiracy for what Ronnie?"

Ronnie cautiously leaned in close to not be overheard, so close that his stubble almost tickled John's ear."

"To take over the world."

John burst out into laughter.

"Ronnie, if you was a girl, I'd call you a blonde bimbo. Take over the world, explain that one to me John."

"Okay, remember what your sister likes to say about the government."

"That it's a patriarchy. That's where the men are in charge & women don't get a say. I mean, she ain't exactly wrong."

"Exactly. Now think about everything that's happened over the last ten years."

John thought about it for a moment.

"Well, men have been dying in war, women have been protesting, & then there's the whole baby thing, & we gone to the moon."

"Exactly. Let's start with the first thing, the war. All the wars since WW2 have been about drawing the lines between us & the commies. They're dividing up the world. Determining who gets to rule what."

"Okay, so?"

"So, now that they've almost finished divvying up the world, all of a sudden, there only just enough men being born to keep populating the world. Once the borders between God fearing & commie are set, there won't be any more armies because only the men do the fighting & now, they'll have to do the baby making."

"Sounds good to me, world peace."

Ronnie took a deep breath & ran his hand through his shaggy blonde hair.

"Listen John, do you really think that it's a coincidence that just as we start figuring out how to put things & people in space, that all of a sudden, there's a global baby making problem. How else could they do that?"

"Ronnie, how would they maintain the patriarchy if they not having any boys themselves?"

Ronnie leaned in close after John's next beer came.

"Because they have a cure."

"Do they now?"

"Yes. Look it here, the Nazis wanted to take over the world, but they couldn't even fight the commies, so how were they going to do it?"

"I think that you're about to tell me."

"Well, they were the ones that developed the first rockets. They then made the whatever it is that makes it so that we only have girls. They were going to use it on the rest of the world so that nobody else would be able to fight. They were going to put it in space, castrate everyone else's armies, then right around now, their armies would start marching on a world that couldn't defend itself."

"I'm way too sober for this Ronnie."

John then took a drink from his beer as Ronnie continued.

"They were going to launch into space, but their first rockets carrying the satellites that make girls flew off course & crashed into Poland. That set off World War 2, which they couldn't win because they had poured so many resources into space war."

"This was all back in the thirties right, during the depression?"

"Yes. Now we went over there & we saved Europe from the Nazi assholes & that was when their space plan was discovered."

"Okay."

"When Roosevelt, Churchill & Stalin all met to carve up Germany, they found the plans for world domination & they decided to set things into motion."

"What things?"

"They spent the next twenty-five years fighting proxy wars so that they could carve up the map while at the same time, they developed space technology so that they could put the Nazi baby satellites into orbit. Now they're going to watch as the armies of the world collapse, resulting in world peace that they control, because they also have the Nazi's cure that allows them at the top to have baby boys to replace them while we all have daughters."

"So, we found their plans for a new world order from the thirties, decided to do it themselves so they could rule the world, & now they're using it with rockets that work."

"That's it, John."

"Ronnie, seriously, have you been kicked in the head by a horse recently?"

"John, just look at what the democrats have been doing the last few years. They start a big, expensive commission that can't even find a cause. All the best scientists & doctors we got, & supposedly they found nothing. Then they start all of those so-called studies to see just how an all-woman society could function, even though we already know because it'll be like that movie that came out a few months before the election."

"Never saw it."

"Dammit John, just listen."

"Kay."

"Then Johnson steps down, when was the last time that a president stepped down from public office. Then his deputy throws his hat in & he just magically wins at the last moment. What happened to Kennedy or the other guy?"

"That win did just seem to come out of nowhere."

"Right! Now they are appointing even more negros to the supreme court & they're hell bent on taking over the moon before the Soviets do. Why? What's up there? Nothing. They're going up there because in 1961, the Soviets accidentally revealed that they had sent a satellite technician into space. A few months later, Kennedy announced that we were all going to the moon."

"So, you're saying, you're saying that NASA & the whole Apollo program…"

"Was because the sheep noticed all the work going on in space, so they created the moon programs as a cover. Think about it, do you really think that it cost four percent of the federal budget & that it takes nearly half a million people to build a rocket so that they can pick up a few rocks? What are they even going to do with a few moon rocks? It's all a diversion to distract us from what they're really doing in space, which is making sure that we don't make any sons to challenge their patriarchy."

Ronnie stopped & sipped his own beer for a moment so that John could think about the three daughters his wife had given birth to over the last four years.

"Ronnie. Even if this is true, & I sure ain't saying that it is, what can we do about it?"

"I'm glad that you asked that. Meet me out by the reservoir tomorrow night. I want to introduce you to a few friends of mine that have some plans."

"Friends of yours?"

"They like to call themselves the Sons of Adam."

November 23rd, 1969

Trenton, New Jersey

"1983! 1983! 1983!"

The crowd of people continued to grow as more & more protestors joined the movement against President Humphrey. All over the country, similar protests were erupting, but here, in the capital of New Jersey, it was growing faster than anywhere else, surrounding the entire capital.

"1983! 1983 for December 17th!"

As the crowd continued to swell, the chief of the Trenton police looked at the lines of officers that were surrounding the crowds.

"How the hell is this crowd still getting bigger, we've got them surrounded?"

The officers & staff around him remained silent.

"Well? Somebody explain to me how the crowd is still growing so quickly! Because I can only imagine that they're coming up through the sewers & I don't want to have to start dispatching units into the sewers."

One of the younger officers, so green that everyone was calling him cabbage, walked up to the police chief.

"Sir. I might know how they're getting through."

"I'm all ears son."

"It might be Hanson sir."

"Hanson? Why the fuck would he be letting people through?"

"Because his son was born on December 17th."

"Fuck."

The chief missed the day when he was a part of a police force small enough to know every detail about every officer's life. The whole point of the protest was that every man aged 18-25 that was born on December 17th was being drafted to fight in Vietnam.

"Let me guess, he refuses to protect the people that he sees as sending his son off to the jungle."

"It doesn't help that him & his entire unit vote republican. They see it as a party that they didn't vote for is sending his son off to war."

"Fuck. Head down to Lafayette Street, tell Hanson to report here immediately."

"Yes chief."

Cabbage ran off for Lafayette Street while the chief turned to another of his advisors.

"You, swap out the men in Hanson's unit with people from other units. Don't send them home, just put them in places where they won't be allowed to let people through."

"Yes sir."

As officers & assistants went on their radios to start barking orders, the chief looked at the baying crowd of protestors in front of him & thought out loud.

"Why the hell did he have to use the draft. Can't we just let Vietnam go? He was doing so goddam well. The moon landing, picking good justices for the supreme court. Now he probably just lost half the country in one bone headed move."

"What was that sir?"

One of the other officers was looking at him confused.

"Nothing. Just thinking out loud."

1970

January 19th, 1970
Sacramento, California

"We don't have a chance in hell of winning."

Patricia looked up at her neighbor. Gail was one of the newer recruits to the Matriarch party. Since the election in 1968, their numbers had swelled a bit, although they were still a tiny grass roots movement. One of the other founding members of the party put down her glass of chardonnay.

"We know we're not going to win Gail. You're pointing out the obvious."

"But we're not even going to get close to winning. In the last election, we got zero-point three percent of the vote. Now we're running for a congressional seat in the US Congress. What's the point of running if we won't even get enough votes to amount to a rounding error?"

Patricia was getting a little tired of having this conversation.

"It's for the name recognition Gail. The point isn't to win California's sixth congressional seat. The point is to get our message out to as many people as possible so that in the next election, we might actually be able to win something."

Gail looked at Patricia.

"So, we're going to lose massively on the national scene just so that people will remember us two years later at the local level."

"I wouldn't phrase it like that, but yes. We need to make some noise, rock some boats & be heard so that people will know what we stand for."

"Do you really think that we'll win anything in 72?"

Patricia sat forward & thought for a moment to choose her words carefully.

"I don't know. Four years is a short time to go from point three percent to a majority. If we don't make any progress in 72, I wouldn't blame any of you for abandoning the party. But I intend to keep going. If it takes two years or twenty years, I intend to keep going because I honestly do believe that this country is soon going to need leaders that will actually represent the majority of this country. Women, lesbians, bisexuals, feminists. The children of a female majority nation are growing up fast. We need to have people in charge that can move this country in the direction that it needs to move in for them. So, I'm going to keep trying, no matter how long it takes."

The women in the room all nodded their heads. Every time that Patricia spoke to them like that, it reminded them that the world was about to change fast & that they all had children that would be growing up in a very different world that the current crop of politicians couldn't predict.

At the mention of children, Gail was struck with a sudden idea for what they could do.

"Kindergarten."

"What was that?"

Patricia looked at her curiously, sensing that she wanted to say something that might just be profound.

"Kindergarten. You mentioned that the children of the new generation are growing up. You're right. They'll be starting kindergarten in August. Who better to pitch our ideas to then the very parents that'll be taking their children to school & seeing with their own eyes that the classes are almost entirely little girls?"

"That's... brilliant. It'll be one of the biggest moments of the century. Entire classes that'll have only two or three boys. At least a hundred parents at each school that'll be in for a shock."

"Exactly. They'll be sending their little girls off to school for the first time, only to see that there are basically no boys. Then we'll be there, talking about how we need to prepare the world for when those little girls grow up because the way everything is now, it won't work."

The women in the meeting grinned with excitement.

"Gail, since you came up with this, I'm putting you in charge of it. You've got about, what is it, six... no, seven months until the school year starts, but we'll only get one shot at this before the midterms."

"Got it."

The women attending the meeting gathered around Gail as they started coming up with preliminary plans for how they could

take advantage of the once in a lifetime shock that they believed
was going to occur when those girls went to their first day of school.
A shock that would stun the world & a shock that, very hopefully,
would catapult them up in the next election.

February 14th, 1970
London, England

Sarah Wilkins looked around at the performance stunt going on
around her.

"I can't believe I agreed to do this."

"Neither can I, I never thought that I'd see you take part in
performance art, let alone queer performance art."

"God, everyone out there is taking pictures."

"Of course they are Sarah, it's a show."

Outside the restaurant, hundreds of people were looking in to
see the performance piece that was being put on for them. A
performance artist that was trying to make a name for himself had
set up the strange event. He had rented out a restaurant for the
evening & put the word out that he needed a large number of
young women for the piece that he was calling Future Valentine's
Day.

Somehow, Sarah's friend had gotten an invitation to it. She had
then invited Sarah out of pure politeness & been pleasantly
surprised when she said yes. Having wanted to get out of her
comfort zone & try something crazy for once, Sarah had agreed &
spent the next week wondering what had possessed her. Looking
down at the silvery skirt that she was wearing, Sarah smoothed out
a wrinkle in the fabric.

"What are we wearing?"

"The clothes of the future Sarah. Apparently sometime
between now & the year 2000, everyone is going to start wearing...
whatever this is supposed to be. Chrome... I think."

"Well, I suppose that it's not any worse than what some people
have been wearing for the last ten years. Seriously, I almost backed
out of this when they showed us our costumes."

Sarah's friend laughed as their meals were brought to the
table. Sarah's jaw almost dropped when she saw that the waitress

was only wearing some very revealing black lingerie. Once she was gone, Sarah turned to her friend, blushing a bit.

"Isn't that a bit inappropriate."

"Well supposedly, according to the artist, the women of the future will be so liberated from the lack of men that many of us won't even bother with clothing."

"The lack of men or the lack of fashion sense? Maybe they just don't want to be caught in chrome clothing."

Her friend started laughing as Sarah started eating. As Sarah ate her spaghetti, she looked around the crowded restaurant & noticed that literally the only man in the room was a senior citizen that was pretending to be on a date with his wife."

"I think that the artist went a little overboard. There are going to be men in thirty years, not just one lone old guy."

"I don't think that it's an oversight. I think it's for dramatic effect. Easier to wake people up to the female future if you're not distracted by the men."

Sarah thought about it for a moment.

"It's ridiculous. What he should have done is have men here, but in non-traditional arrangements."

"Like what?"

"I don't know, you could have one man on a date with four women. You could have one man disappearing into the bathroom with random women while his wife looks the other way, that wat they can help keep the birth rate up. Stuff like that."

"Are you sure that you're not a performance artist Sarah? Those sound-like great ideas."

"I'm sure. It's a bit ridiculous to think that just because men are only one tenth of the population, that three quarters of women will become lesbians."

A particularly bright flash blinded them as a handful of photographers for the papers, women only in order to preserve the theme of the evening, were allowed in to get pictures.

"Of course, of course someone is going to take a picture of me on this fake date. Now my parents will half read the story, then they'll freak out & call me up to ask me why I'm going on dates with women when I came here to study engineering."

"How bad can it be?"

"Bad. They don't even like the idea that I'm getting a higher education. They figured that I look good enough to get a man, I should just put some effort in."

"I imagine that they're not fans of art either?"

Sarah shook her head.

"Nope. They'll like that I'm in a piece of queer street art less than they'll like the idea of me getting a degree as an engineer. They want me to stay home. They have no idea how far I'll go."

More flashes from the cameras blinded them as they tried to eat their mock romantic meal. As Sarah imagined her future as a mechanical engineer, journalists were picturing the morning headlines as news of this display in the heart of London reached everyone from the common working man to the Queen herself.

April 14th, 1970

National Institute of Health, Bethesda, Maryland

Doctor Fekete was taking a break from his mountain of paperwork to listen to the news on the radio. Like a lot of Americans, he had spent the last two days paying close attention to news coming out of NASA. As the latest report concerning Apollo 13 was wrapping up, Dr. Swanson walked into his office.

"Hey there Todor, any news on 13?"

"Nothing much. Everyone is still speculating on if the electrical issue is a manufacturing error or a design issue. Apparently, they're scouring the plans & the Apollo 14 rocket to look into it."

"Ah. You know I heard that if that glitch had happened on the way to the moon, it could have resulted in aborting the mission all together. Just slingshot around the moon & come home without setting down."

"That's nothing Edward. From some of the news articles I've heard, the electrical line leads right to an oxygen tank. If it had gone wrong when someone tried to stir the tanks, the entire command module might have blown up."

Dr. Swanson looked at him incredulously.

"Todor, they've got some of the smartest people on the planet designing & building it, not to mention they spent years going over the designs & testing it. I'm pretty sure that the damn thing can't just explode."

"Tell that to the original crew of Apollo 1."

"Okay, you've got a point there."

"Thank you, Edward, but as much as I love hearing that I'm right, I assume that you're not just here to talk about Apollo 13."

Doctor Edward Swanson sat down opposite Dr. Fekete.

"Five years Todor. It's been five years since we got this commission off the ground."

Dr. Fekete nodded his head in understanding.

"The annual report. I imagine that it's causing problems for you."

"That's an understatement. I've got to stand before a congressional budget hearing tomorrow to justify why we should keep getting so much funding despite the fact that by our own admission, we've made exactly... zero progress."

"We haven't made zero progress. We've safely eliminated a number of things that it could have been."

"That's not going to help us Todor. Congressmen don't think in the kind of long term where eliminating possibilities is progress. From their point of view, they asked us what two plus two is & five years later, we're saying it's probably not seventeen."

"They can't scrap the commission, that would mean admitting that we can't solve the problem of the lack of boys."

"They aren't going to scrap the commission, but we've been hemorrhaging funds for years & have next to nothing that they would consider progress. My few friends on capitol hill tell me that it looks like we're going to be dealing with budget cuts. Possibly major budget cuts, like at least a tenth of our budget."

"A tenth!"

Doctor Fekete was in shock.

"How can they do that to us?"

"We're not producing results. Plus, according to a friend of a friend, there's a rumor that the money might be going into military research."

"What military research?"

"This stays between us."

"Sure Edward."

The two doctors leaned in close as Edward passed along some gossip from the depths of congress.

"Well, apparently, it looks… sort of like the Soviets aren't even trying to get to the moon anymore, which means that a bunch of military hawks are seeing it as the ultimate high ground. Rumor has it that they want to research the feasibility of different kinds of lunar military bases."

"Lunar military bases. For what?"

"You name it. Spying, stealth attacks, using lunar resources to create weapons of mass destruction, the ultimate doomsday bunker to evacuate the upper government to in the event of nuclear war."

"Jesus. They're going to strip our funding just so they can see how many stupid ways they can militarize the moon."

"That's the rumor. More likely, Apollo is expensive, so they want to look like they're trimming the fat."

"I'm not the fat, am I Edward?"

Doctor Swanson looked up with a curious look of bewilderment.

"How can you possibly be the fat? You lead the genetics department. Your results are some of the closest things that we have to progress. They're not going to cut you."

"Thank goodness for that."

"That being said, your study on clownfish is probably not long for this world."

"What!"

Doctor Fekete stood up in a rage.

"Clownfish can switch genders, almost at will. If we can find out how they do it, it could open up all kinds of new research options for us to figure out what might be affecting our gender selection at conception!"

"I know Todor! I know. But try explaining a study of clownfish to figure out our own physiology to congress."

"Dammit. Maybe I can talk to some friends of mine, see if they can carry out the work from their universities. They probably won't be able too. Universities care more about the genetics of humans, crops & livestock."

"I'm sorry Todor."

"It's not your fault. There isn't much that science can do against politics. We'll just have to suffer through the cuts & carry on."

May 17th, 1970
Times Square, New York City

Lena Lewis was surprised that she had made it past the police line. Taking advantage of a brief moment when a gap was formed as a result of the police being distracted, she slipped through them & started hustling to get to the crowd of protestors.

Wishing that she was in better shape, she was out of breath as she reached the protestors. Cursing her love handles, she got her notepad out, hit record on the tape recorder slung over her shoulder & got to work. She regretted not writing the word press on the back of her shirt like she had wanted to. It wouldn't have helped much if she had. It's hard to convince the police that you're press when you don't actually work for a publication yet.

Dreaming of the day when she could launch her own newspaper in the not-too-distant future, she walked up to one of the women screaming for equality.

"Excuse me, I'm with the... Boston times... can you tell me why you're protesting here today?"

The tall woman put her sign down as she turned to talk to the strange woman with a tape recorder & a notepad ready to go.

"I'm here because I'm tired of being treated like a second-class citizen in my own country. Isn't this supposed to be the freest country in the world?"

"Any specific example of how you personally are being mistreated?"

"Yeah, I work at a record store over on 8th avenue. I found out last week that even though I've got more seniority than anyone other than the owner, I'm the only one making minimum wage. The new guy that they hired off the street is make two dollars an hour, I've been there for six years & I only got up to a dollar sixty an hour when the minimum wage was bumped up!"

"I guess that you're also the only woman there."

"Yeah. I asked my boss about it, he said he couldn't afford to give me more. But apparently, he can afford to pay some random dick off the street more than a woman with over half a decade of experience working for him."

"That's horrible. Thank you for taking my questions, I'll let you get back to the fight."

The woman raised her sign again & started shouting for equal rights & equal pay as Lena went over her notes. Wading a little further into the crowd, she found a shorter woman who seemed to be screaming out louder than half the crowd.

"Excuse me, I'm with the… Chicago Citizen… can you tell me why you're protesting here today?"

She didn't put her sign down, but she did decide to answer some questions.

"Why am I protesting? Because it's high time that our rights be something more than a gentleman's agreement between our husbands & fathers. I hate that if I get pregnant, my boss will fire me. I'm lucky that my husband is kind, because if he ever decides that I don't get to say no when he's in the mood, I'm shit out of luck that night."

"Is there anything in specific that made you want to protest today despite the police closing in?"

"Yeah, yesterday, Iraq granted its women equal rights in their constitution. If some fucking third world country in the middle east can do it, why can't we?"

"Can't argue with you on that one."

"Sorry lady, I've got to get back to it, looks like the police are reorganizing."

"No problem."

Lena made a special note about looking into Iraq & women's equality. That would be a news story. A country in the middle east getting more rights for its people than the US. Moving around, she found another woman who was protesting topless while holding up two signs, one that read Equality & one that read 1983.

"Excuse me, I'm with the… New Jersey Chronicle… can you tell me why you're protesting here today?"

The woman moved both signs to one hand so that she could rotate them & flash the two messages as she spoke. Lena was momentarily distracted by the woman's small breasts.

"The New Jersey chronicle, alright, I'm here because I don't want to have to wait until the government realizes that we're the new majority & that we should have at least as much freedom as a man. We're going to be 90% of the population, we're going to get our rights, I don't see why we should have to wait."

"A good reason. Can I ask, why are you…"

Lena pointed with her pen to the woman's chest.

"Screaming with my tits out."

"Yeah."

"Men are allowed to walk around without a shirt on. Why shouldn't I be allowed to? Why should I have to cover up my lovely little tits? Why shouldn't I have that freedom?"

"You make some very good points."

Lena tried to focus on her notepad as she talked to the topless woman.

"Is there something in specific that brought you out here today?"

"Nope."

"No."

"Nope. I just heard that women were fighting for our freedoms & decided to lend my voice to the cause."

"Your voice among other things."

"Yeah, I wanted to shock some people into hearing me, but I don't really have the kind of tits that can really grab people's attention. Hell, one time I got my hair cut short & everyone mistook me for a boy."

"That's unfortunate."

"Yeah. I've been trying to convince some of the women with real eye grabbers to strip down. Sadly, the best way for a woman to be heard is if she waves her jugs around. Unfortunately, I've got no takers. Oh shit, we've got to move."

Lena noticed that the whole crowd seemed to be bucking as the police tried to make a move. Not wanting to be caught, she moved against the crowd in the hopes that she now had enough sensational news for the first issue of a newspaper of her own.

As she made her way free of the crowd & through an alley that the cops weren't paying attention to, she began thinking of names for her newspaper. Unfortunately, the only thing that she could imagine was getting her hands on the woman's chest.

June 1st, 1970
CBC Newsroom

Walter Cronkite sat at the evening news desk, watching a monitor next to the camera man that showed the clip being aired on the news for the world to see. After watching two men remove the insignia from a woman's shoulders & replace them with the stars of a brigadier general, the two men shook her hand, gave her a quick kiss next to the lips as a new protocol for promoting lady generals, & stepped aside so that she could make her speech.

Jumping forward a few seconds into her speech, Cronkite watched as she spoke before chiefs of staff, her family & the world.

"First of all, I would like to thank general Westmoreland and general Jennings for honoring the army nurse corps by pinning these stars on my shoulders, & I am grateful to each of you for joining us this morning & sharing this memorable occasion for the army nurse corps. I shall wear these stars proudly, but with deep humility, for I know full well they represent no special merit of mine, but rather the dedicated, selfless & often heroic efforts of army nurses throughout the world since 1901 in time of peace & in time of war."

Almost missing the director's signal, Cronkite quickly straightened up as the camera focused on him & the broadcast switched back to his live reading of the news.

"For those of you watching tonight, that was an excerpt from the acceptance speech of newly appointed brigadier general Anna Mae Hays. Nominated by President Humphrey in early May, miss Hays is the first woman in the history of the United States military to be promoted to the rank of General."

"Like most women in the armed forces, miss Hays has had to endure a number of hardships throughout her career that few men have been faced with. While most are praising her historic achievement, a number of fringe & conservative groups are accusing President Humphrey of pandering to the far left & are claiming that he is forcing America to give up in the fight against the birth ratio deficits. However, with a lack of any significant progress around the world on solving the birth ratio crisis in years, most are viewing this moment as not only historic, but necessary in the need to prepare the military to function with a lack of men to serve. As brigadier general Hays continued in her acceptance speech, she pledged to help the military overcome the issues of sexism in the military in order to pave the way for more women to serve in the armed forces. While we congratulate brigadier general Hays, many of us can't help but wonder what the military & war itself will look like as the world approaches the twenty-first century."

August 26th, 1970
Queens, New York

A child's first day of school is supposed to be magical. It's supposed to be one of those moments a parent will always remember. The day that their little toddler lets go of their hand & walks into their first day of school. One of the great milestones on the journey that children & their parents take together in the story of growing up. It's often an emotionally overwhelming moment.

Mary had spent the morning preparing Elizabeth, making sure her clothes were perfect, that her hair was flawless, that she knew to be on her best behavior & that she would know to ask the grownups in her classroom for help if she was sad, scared, or confused.

David had been thrilled when his boss had given him permission to come into the office late today so that he could take his daughter to school for her first day of kindergarten. From the crack of dawn, when he opened his eyes, he could almost feel the day quickly building to one of the proudest moments of his life. His daughter's first day of school.

Upon arriving at the school, their moment of parental pride was dashed by the frenzied circus going on outside the school.

Camera crews, freelance photographers, protestors, low level politicians & full-blown whack jobs either trying to shout louder than the rest of the crowd or trying to shove a microphone or a camera into people's faces. Police had shown up to help manage the crowd, but their forces were being spread a bit thinly as this chaos was most likely going on all over the city. All over the country.

The police were struggling to make a corridor where the teachers could escort the children & their parents to the door. Every time that a boy who looked like he could be in kindergarten was escorted through, the police had to hold the crowd back that much more forcefully. As they approached the crowd, Mary turned to David.

"I know that you had to get permission to show up late to work today & that it might be a bit last minute, but do you think that you can get off of work early too?"

"I was just thinking that. I'm going to ask. Hopefully, news of this chaos is already on the radio. You should bring the car when you pick her up."

"We probably should have brought the car this morning."

"Too late for that Mary. Nothing to do but fly into the storm."

The two of them took Elizabeth's hands & pushed their way through the crowds of people that were swelling with onlookers who just wanted to see what the hell was going on. Making it to the beginning of the corridor, one of the schoolteachers led them & another family through the narrow passage. As they approached the front door, they heard chaos behind them as one of the few kindergarten boys was spotted & the journalist & photographers pushed forward.

Eventually they made it to the front door where a pair of stressed administrators were sorting through the chaos. One of them, a woman in her sixties that looked like she had just landed in Vietnam with nothing more than a clipboard looked up at them.

"Name?"

Elizabeth remembered what her mother had told her about roll call & shouted out.

"Robinson, Elizabeth!"

"Robinson… Robinson… Kindergarten, hang on a moment right over here please."

They moved inside to join a group of three more families. A moment later, the boy that had caused the crowd to buck behind them joined them as another administrator appeared.

"Alright, kindergarten students have to come with me. Parents, say goodbye. Sorry, this can't happen outside like normal."

Mary & David both pulled Elizabeth in for a tight hug & wished their daughter well. They then watched as the man from administration escorted the six children to their first class.

Mary & David smiled as they watched their Elizabeth walk away, beginning the long road of growing up & going through school. When the parents had had their moment & more students were starting to crowd in, one of administrators helped them head back to the madness outside.

///

Sacramento, California

Patricia Torres stood by the small booth that her team had set up in front of the elementary school. For the last hour, as the situation had become more & more chaotic, she & some of her fellow matriarch party members had been handing out their brochures & literature to concerned families that were now seeing that the world was changing a lot more than they had thought that it had.

Even with months to prepare for this event, they were still surprised by how many people were interested in hearing what they had to say on the matter of politics. Patricia had already had to send one of the women helping her to get more pamphlets as they were running low.

Looking at the entrance to the school, a bunch of camera flashes almost blinded everyone nearby as one of the few kindergarten boys was carried towards the school entrance in his father's arms. While she wondered if he would visit the Matriarch Party's booth like so many parents that had just dropped off their children, she was surprised when a camera went off in front of her.

"Sorry about that, ladies. Doing a story for the Sacramento Observer. Strange place for a fledgling political party to be trying to recruit voters."

Patricia smiled as she talked to the man who was already writing things down in his notepad while his tape recorder committed the conversation to tape.

"We're just here to point out that the current administrations running this state & this country have had years to prepare for this moment & that it's pandemonium out here."

"That's for sure. If you had been in power since the last election, what would you have done differently to avoid this scenario?"

"Well, the first thing that I would have done is to at least call in a few off-duty police just in case there was chaos. This has been going on for over an hour now & we only have four officers here because nobody thought that the first day of kindergarten for the first ninety percent female class might not go according to plan."

"That certainly does seem like a bit of an oversight considering the demonstrations & accusations that have been flying around in recent years."

"More police aren't the only change that I would have made."

"Oh? What else would you have done differently?"

"I would have staggered the first day of school, have it so that kindergarten & maybe first grade students would start tomorrow so that there would be fewer things for the schools to sort out."

"You think that would have worked?"

"Definitely, I mean right now they're trying to sort out the students for grades K through five into their new classes while all this is happening. Classes were supposed to start half an hour ago, but half the students haven't been able to get in yet."

"So, if the kindergarten students had started tomorrow, at least the other grades would already know where to go & they would be settled."

"Exactly."

"Any other ideas for how to avoid all of this?"

"Yes, they should have secured a side door for the other grades to go through so that they could get the students in faster & the crowd would be divided between two doors instead of concentrated around the main entrance."

"That's some clever thinking miss…"

"Torres. Patricia Torres, founder of the Matriarch Party."

"Torres. A lot of people haven't heard much about your party, can you tell me a bit about it?"

"With pleasure. Right now, there are two major points that our party is trying to make. The first is that it looks like there's going to be a sizeable percentage of the electorate in a few years that will be ninety percent women. In fact, it looks like entire age ranges will be ninety percent women, so we're going to have to elect more women to positions of authority to represent the changing nature of the population that our democracy represents."

"That makes sense. If everyone that is say… 18-35 is female, then the candidates from that age range should be ninety percent female as well."

"Exactly. The country is being feminized, & yet the government is doing essentially nothing to get more women into office. This has to change."

"Let me just get this down… A government that is representative of the changing population. Alright, you're second point?"

Patricia held her arms out.

"Look around. Democrats & Republicans are so concerned with what the military & marriage will look like in 83 & 85 & 2000. They aren't thinking about what society looks like now. I don't know how it was for you in school, but when I was girl, we were thought that it was the men who worked & the women who took care of the home. Have the schools changed that lesson plan yet? Are they going to start teaching girls that most of them will have to work? Because when these kids hit eighteen, they need to be ready for a very different way of life than what we're used to. Some of these girls will one day have to start businesses & buy their own houses. Will the banks allow them to take out loans without a husband to cosign for them? Will they be allowed to apply for a mortgage if they don't have a husband? Some banks don't allow women to take out loans & mortgages without a man, preferably a husband or father supporting her."

Before the man from the newspaper could respond, several of the women around them cheered her on.

"You make a lot of very good points miss Torres."

"All of them undeniably true. It's not just future battlefields & marriage licenses that will matter. We have thirteen years left to basically reorder every level of our society & there's so much that the men in charge aren't even thinking about because they don't know about the parts of society that don't affect them."

The growing crowd around them cheered loudly enough that some of the photographers started to turn away from the school entrance to notice the political movement in progress.

"The government is worried about the draft in thirteen years, what about next year when school sports teams run out of boys? The boys entering kindergarten in this school don't amount to enough to fill out a single team in a single sport. What's going to happen next year when the first grade only has two or three boys to add to a sports team? Will the boys be required to play on a team as part of their education? Will several schools have to band together to get complete teams? Will some sports just be dropped? Will they encourage girls to play sports? What is anybody doing about the issues that will be affecting families today, tomorrow, & next week? Everybody is worried about the next decade, what about next year? That's why the Matriarch party is running in the midterms for a number of positions in Sacramento, so that we can start dealing with today's issues, today."

The crowd around them erupted in thunderous applause as countless people took her words to heart.

///

Robinson Home, Queens, New York

David's boss had not been happy when, after being allowed to come in late, he also needed to leave early. But when David described the scene, his boss had relented & allowed him to go early.

When classes let out, there were more police than in the morning. The city had finally gotten the message at some point & was dishing out a good deal of overtime to get most of the police force on duty all at once. With more police, the reporters &

photographers were easier to deal with as news crews recorded the mess for the evening news.

Once they were home, they got about thirty seconds of conversation out of Elizabeth before she plumped herself down on the couch, exhausted. Shocked at the sight of a tired Elizabeth, David helped Mary make supper. Later, after Elizabeth had been put to bed, they sat down on the couch & turned on the evening news to see Walter Cronkite.

"Today, chaos erupted all over the country as the first day of school began for what some are calling the XX generation. All over the nation, what should have been a moment that every parent remembers for the rest of their lives will be remembered as the day they had to fight through mobs to get their children to school for the first time. Among the many people swarming the new kindergarten students were all sorts of tabloid photographers, protestors, & religious fanatics."

Cronkite shuffled his papers before returning his view to the camera.

"In Alabama, protestors picketing the opening day proclaiming that the lack of boys was God's punishment for desegregating the schools. In California, groups of hippies tried to block students from going to school, proclaiming that these purple children needed to be taught by mother nature who was lifting humanity into a new way of being. We have reports from multiple states of protestors demanding to know where the government was hiding all of the millions of boys that should have been born over the last five years while multiple groups called for radical changes to how we educate our children."

David ran his hand through his hair as they showed pictures of the day's chaos.

"Christ, I hope this isn't as bad tomorrow."

"A congregation from Texas was seen protesting at several schools, demanding that all the boys be placed in male only schools in order to ensure that they are not infected with feminism. Reports from interviews in the field have shown that in some places, he may have gotten his wish. A number of schools have segregated their kindergarten classes by gender, keeping the boys in one class & the girls in other classes. Parents sending their daughters to these schools are complaining that the boys' classes are getting disproportionately more resources as each school has only about half a dozen boys as opposed to fifty or sixty girls. Other schools put all of the boys into one class with girls so that they were closer to one fifth of the class while leaving other classes as being only girls. One school in Montana is experimenting with having all of the boys in one class but alternating which class they are collectively in so that they are not completely overwhelmed by the girls, but at the same time, the girls can spend time with boys in their class."

Mary was dumbfounded.

"How in the hell do they actually expect any of that to actually work? They're just trying everything they can think of & seeing what sticks."

Cronkite again shuffled his papers.

"One thing is clear. With five years to prepare for this day, school boards, police & legislatures were not ready for it. While we are all certain that this mess of how to educate our new generation of children will be sorted out, we can only wonder, if they were this unprepared for the first day of elementary school, what's going to happen when these kids reach middle school? High school? College & working life? Will we be ready?"

September 14th, 1970
New York City

Lena Lewis stared at the three front pages that she could choose from. The first one showed pictures of the demonstration from May where she had interviewed women in the field to ask why they were marching. The second front page showed an image from the first day of classes of an entire kindergarten class assembled in a schoolyard before heading inside. The picture was powerful in her mind because it clearly showed only two boys among the twenty-seven girls that were wearing skirts as part of their uniform. The third front page was just an introduction to the first issue of her newspaper, explaining what it would be reporting & who it was for.

Standing up from her desk, she walked around her small office. It wasn't as big as she had hoped for. It was basically just a small office in the front & a small press room in the back. A nice little out of the way corner for a fledgling presswoman & her idea for a newspaper.

Hanging over her filing cabinet was an empty frame, waiting for a copy of her first newspaper to show off. She imagined a huge office bustling with reporters passing by that frame every day, a monument to her humble beginning.

Walking into her backroom, she found herself crammed in among the printing supplies. Inks, toners, plates, mountains of paper, a window to air out the fumes & her press. It wasn't a massive press. Barely five feet tall & three feet long, it wouldn't be churning hundreds of thousands of copies of the Sunday times. It was her little workhorse, for her new little paper. It was also the same model as the one that her uncle had worked on for years. She had bought it cheap from a company that had just gone under & her uncle had even come over a few times to show her how to use it.

He had even painted the small flywheel lavender. He had said that it was a tribute to all of the people who had been afraid for their lives under the lavender scare.

For a moment, Lena was worried that she was in over her head. Starting & running a newspaper was going to be no easy business, especially when a lot of people were not going to be happy about it.

"Have I actually lost my mind? Can I actually do this?"

Resting her hand on the Lavender flywheel, she felt herself slowly calming down.

"I can do this. I've got six days to get this issue out, I can do it."

Walking back into her office, she sat down at her desk & she picked out the front page that she was going to use. It made sense. She wasn't going to hide anything about her paper. She was going to open with the truth. She selected the third front page, the introduction, as the first page of her newspaper.

The first story was going to be the story of the paper itself. The Lavender Press, a weekly newspaper for lesbians, by lesbians.

Taking her selected front page, Lena got up & held it in front of the empty display case, imagining it hanging there not just as a first edition, but as a mission statement.

"Hold on tight world. You might not be ready for this, but it's coming your way."

November 9th, 1970
Montreal, Canada

"Rebecca! Have you seen my blouse!?"

Janet was running around the small apartment that they shared together in her underwear. The blouse that Janet had picked out for her first day of work had apparently gone missing & it was getting dangerously close to when she would have to get a move on if she wanted to be on time.

"It's in here Janet!"

Janet followed the sound of Rebecca's voice to their bedroom where their master's degrees were hanging side by side on the wall over their bed. Rebecca was lying in bed, only wearing Janet's blouse.

"What's this Rebecca?"

"It looks like your blouse."

"Yeah, I need it if I'm going to go to work."

"What do you say then?"

Janet nodded her head.

"Could you please take my blouse off?"

"Sure."

Rebecca then sat up on the bed on her knees & began to slowly unbutton the blouse.

"Could you hurry up, I'm getting very close to running late."

Rebecca slowed down, taking her sweet time with each button while opening the shirt more & more to reveal more of her body beneath.

"Oh, for fuck's sake."

Janet rushed towards the bed & started undoing Rebecca's buttons as Rebecca laughed. With the last button popped, Janet slid the blouse off of Rebecca's naked body. Momentarily distracted, she quickly got her blouse on & went after her pants.

"It's going to be lonely without you here all-day Janet. What am I going to do?"

"You're going to pick out an outfit in case you get the call that a substitute teacher is needed."

"Maybe I'll go out & buy a yardstick so that when you get home, we can play teacher's pet."

Janet stopped in her tracks & felt a shiver run up her spine. Her lover was now an actual schoolteacher, with a degree in education. She couldn't even count how many times she had wanted her English teacher when she was in high school.

"You can't do that to me right before work Rebecca, how am I supposed to get through my first day with that in my head."

Rebecca smiled wickedly.

"You'd better hurry up & get ready Janet; you're almost running late. Do you want to be tardy? Do you want me to give you detention."

Janet worried that she would need a change of underwear if Rebecca kept talking like that.

"That's not fair. I've got to go."

Janet walked over to Rebecca & kissed her goodbye before heading out. Double checking that she had everything she needed, she left the apartment & made her way to the bus stop.

Thankful that the bus was on time, she climbed on & sat opposite a man who was reading a newspaper. Noticing that the front page was a story about Janis Joplin recovering from her near fatal overdose a month earlier, she remembered the night when she heard on the news that Joplin had nearly died.

Shaking the thoughts of Janis Joplin & her schoolteacher lover from her mind, Janet focused on being ready for her first day. One of her professors had called up one of his friends to get her an interview for this job. Not only was her boss a big shot in the agricultural community with connections to politicians, the military & even NASA, but she was the first woman that had been hired to work in this department as something other than a secretary.

Taking a deep breath to calm herself, she reminded herself that she had earned her master's in plant science & that her professor wouldn't have suggested her for the job & his friend wouldn't have hired her if they didn't think that she could do it. They knew, just like she did, that she was the right person for the job & that her work was going to lead to hardier crops, bigger harvests & all kinds of medical discoveries.

December 19th, 1970
Nashville, Tennessee

Ronnie Adams stood at the head of the crowd with pride. His crowd of a hundred men had taken over the mall & their voice was going to be heard. Nobody had expected them. They simply walked in while people were buying Christmas presents for their families & fired a few rounds into the air from their M1s.

Very few people had managed to get out. They were now holding hundreds of Christmas shoppers as hostages while police from all over Nashville rushed to the scene. In less than ten minutes, there were hundreds of police surrounding the mall as television news crews showed up to record what was happening.

With hastily constructed barricades made out of whatever was available, every main entrance seemed to be secured. Returning to the mall's security office, Ronnie picked up the phone that was ringing & switched it to the intercom so that all of his men could hear it.

"I'm guessing that you're the police."

"You guessed right. I'm Lieutenant Richardson, with the Nashville Police Department. We have the building surrounded."

"I imagine that you do lieutenant, but I have about four hundred hostages, many of them women & children, & my men are armed with military grade rifles."

There was silence on the line for a moment before the lieutenant came back on.

"You're in charge then?"

"I am."

"Who are you?"

"You can call me Ronnie. I am the leaders of the Militia of the Sons of Adam."

"I see. So, what exactly do the Sons of Adam want?"

"We want the federal government to admit that the baby boy shortage is being created by them with the use of stolen Nazi space technology to set up a new world order."

More silence on the line.

"Lieutenant, are you still there?"

"Yes."

"Did you hear me?"

"Yes Ronnie. Let me see if I've got this straight. You want the federal government, Washington, to admit that they are using stolen Nazi space technology, to engineer the birth ratio phenomenon, so that they, who already control the country & influence much of the world, can take over the world. That's what you said."

"Yes Lieutenant."

"I… see… Are there any other demands?"

"No sir. If they admit to what they're doing to us, we will release the hostages & surrender the mall back to the city of Nashville. You have twenty-four hours. Any attempt to stop us & we will kill hostages."

"Okay… I'm going to need a minute to talk to some people about your request, it is a big one."

"That's why we're giving you twenty-four hours starting now."

"We appreciate that. We'll call you back shortly with an update on our end."

"That would be appreciated."

Ronnie hung up the phone as he imagined televised news broadcasts confirming what his people believed. Outside, the police lieutenant & the people that had heard the call were dumbstruck. Richardson called for some shrinks since this militia was clearly insane. Inside, civilians cowered in fear, shielding their children as best as they could while a handful of the militiamen went over the conversation in their heads as if it was just dawning on them in that moment that this was insane.

Half an hour later, on the advice of the shrinks, Richardson called Ronnie in the security office.

"Lieutenant, has the government admitted to what they're doing?"

"Not yet. From what I understand, some high-level meetings are being called to discuss your request."

"Well, it's good to know that they're taking this seriously. Very seriously."

"Listen, Ronnie, you said before that there are children in there. From what I've heard, there was a bit of chaos when you took control. I need to know, is anybody hurt, & if so, would you be willing to let the injured go?"

"It's nice to see someone in authority that actually cares about the little people. There are no major injuries here. If that changes, I'll consider releasing the injured."

"That's good to hear. Do the hostages need any water or food or medications to get them through the day?"

"Not a problem Lieutenant, we have more than enough of everything to last the duration. We'll let you know if we need more."

"Also good to hear. While I've got you on the line, can I ask, why this mall in specific? There are plenty of malls between here & Alabama, why come all the way here?"

"We have our reasons to cross state lines."

Before the lieutenant could ask another question, one of Ronnie's men walked into the security office.

"Sir, we have a problem, we can't raise Matthew on the radios."

"Then send someone to find him, I'm busy over here."

"We did send someone sir, we sent John, it's been a few minutes & we can't reach him either."

Ronnie thought about the situation for a moment.

"Where was Matthew stationed?"

"By the food court."

"The food court... The food court. The loading dock for the food court, you bastards. Get everyone to the food court, their storming us!"

Ronnie hung up the phone as several of his men gathered their M1s & made their way to the food court. As Ronnie was kicking himself for not putting more security on that loading dock, the sound of gunfire could be heard coming their way. As the first cops appeared, taking careful aim to avoid hitting the civilians, Ronnie cursed.

"Fucking feds!"

He then took out his WW2 surplus radio & called out to his men.

"All sons, to the main staging area, we're under direct assault!"

Taking cover with several of his men, he waited for reinforcements to arrive. Instead, more cops showed up. Thinking that his men must have been defeated, he ordered the men that were with him to fall back to the hatch.

The hatch was their codeword for their escape plan, an old side door that had been painted over & had the exterior handle removed. The theory had been that nobody would think that it was a viable exit, so it would be left unguarded. Finding a group of his men that had survived one of the police assaults, he told them the situation had deteriorated & that they were bugging out.

He didn't mention that he had left another twenty men behind, fighting to cover their exit.

A minute later, they reached the side door & his men burst through it. The three that went through first were gunned down as the door did indeed have some guards on it.

"Fuck, there's no other way men, for our sons, we have to get out!"

Several of his men then screamed in a frenzy as they rushed the door, firing wildly as they ran for the small patch of forest next to the mall that was slated to be cut down in a few months.

As several police rushed to the side door to reinforce their fellow officers, Ronnie & about twenty of his men escaped into the woods. All but one of them made it to the parking lot where they had a bunch of their trucks waiting for them.

"Looks like the feds aren't willing to admit what they've done. They're going to shut us up by any means they can. We gotta get back to the camp before they find us here. Everyone take a truck & haul ass. We'll meet at the camp in four days."

One of his men then walked up to him with a look of concern.

"Ronnie, if we take that many trucks, they'll only be two left for the others. How will they get out?"

"I think it's safe to say that they didn't make it. Let's get the fuck out of here."

Downtrodden, his men each took a truck & peeled out of there before the police could reach the parking lot.

1971

January 31st, 1971
Fort Worth, Texas

Rosa was sitting on her couch, watching as three astronauts prepared to launch on Apollo 14. Normally, she would only be getting home from church at this time on a Sunday, but instead, she had spent her morning at home, alone, with her five daughters.

As she watched some scientists talking about the mission to the Littrow Crater, the front door opened up & her husband of six years walked in. The relative silence was immediately broken as their two oldest daughters ran to him screaming daddy at the top of their lungs. Behind him, her sister, Lily followed him into the small house.

"Hi Rosa, we missed you at church today."

Rosa's husband could be heard muttering for Christ's sake as he led his older daughters to the backyard.

"You missed me at church?"

"Yeah, it was a real shame you couldn't come today."

"Today? Lily! It's not like I was sick. I was fucking banished! Remember, it was just last week! You were sitting next to me when Father Edwards singled me out, called me a witch for having five daughters back-to-back, then kicked me out of the congregation!"

"Oh Rosa, I'm sure it's not a permanent thing. He'll probably lift the banishment in a few weeks."

"Really Lily. Like he lifted it for Elisa? Oh wait, that's right, she's still banished three years later. I spent five years almost perpetually pregnant because he told me to keep trying until a boy came out! Five years! Do you think that I wanted to have five kids? You think that I wanted to have five kids that are under five?!"

"He's just trying to keep the faithful vigilant. I'm sure that if the two of you have a son, he'll let you back in."

"Are you fucking stupid Lily? Five daughters in a row doesn't mean a boy is due. Even if a boy is due, I'm not having a sixth kid just so that I can get back into the flock that threw me out when I didn't even want to have the first five."

"Calm down Rosa, I'm just trying to be positive in these trying times. I'm trying to help you find a way back."

"I don't want a way back!"

Rosa's husband walked into the living room.

"The girls are outside chasing each other around, or playing a game that involves running, or maybe chasing a squirrel, I don't know, they're outside. Now what the hell is going on in here?"

"I'm just trying to help the two of you in this trying time & your wife is being unreasonable."

He stood silent as Rosa stood up, a look of fiery, apocalyptic rage in her eyes as she stared at her sister.

"Get... out... of my... house."

"Rosa, I..."

"Get out!"

"Fine. You want to burn in hell, you burn in hell."

Lily walked out the door. Before she left, she turned around & looked past Rosa.

"Remember what Father Edwards told you today, it's sounds like good advice to me."

Lily then left as Rosa turned to her husband, practically frothing at the mouth.

"What... did he... say to you?"

"Love of my life, I'll tell you in a second, let's just make sure the kids can't hear all of this."

As he went to the window to check on his older daughters, Rosa sat down & released her death grip on the remote.

"Okay, they don't seem to be hearing us, or they don't care."

He sat down next to his disgraced wife.

"Okay, so you know how I said that I would talk to Father Edwards about what happened last week & see if he would listen to reason?"

"Yes. Did you get a chance to talk to him?"

"I did, I did."

"What did he have to say?"

"Can I get you anything, water, some ice cream maybe?"

"What... did Father Edwards say?"

"He... he said that he spoke with the word of God & that God's commands could not be reversed because one man was..."

"Was what?"

"Was... ... showing... undeserved kindness... to his witch wife... that had cursed him to have no sons to carry on his name."

Rosa sat there in disbelief for a moment.

"Are you going to try to talk to him again next week?"

"I'm not going back next week."

Rosa looked at him, shocked.

"You're not? Why?"

"I was going to try to keep bringing up the topic of letting you back in, but I've changed my mind because of what he said next."

"What did he say?"

Her husband sighed.

"He said that he wanted to annul our marriage."

"WHAT!"

"Yes, he told me that I should not have to be tied down to a wayward sheep & that I should get remarried to a proper Christian woman."

"Jesus Christ. It's not enough that he wants me out, he wants me raising five young children alone as well."

"Not exactly."

Rosa looked at him confused for a moment.

"There's more, isn't there."

"He suggested... that I marry... Lily, that way I can take full custody of the girls from you & they can have a mother that they're related to who won't corrupt them. He also said that once I had custody, I should baptize them again so that he can wash away any curse you may have placed on them."

Rosa was speechless. She just sat there, dumbstruck.

"I told him that he was a snake & that he can go & fuck himself."

Rosa wrapped her arms around him & spoke through tears.

"What are we going to do now?"

He thought about it for a moment.

"Now..., now we are going to watch some very white men fly to the moon, then we're going to find a new church, one that understands that sons aren't in the cards for some of us."

"Let's make sure it's a church that thinks five kids is enough. I'm done being pregnant."

"Thank God, the ones we have already outnumber us more than two to one."

Rosa smiled. She then laughed as she imagined the look on Lily's face when Father Edwards told the congregation next week that her husband had left the flock to be with his witch.

February 7th, 1971
New York City

All over Switzerland, women were celebrating the fact that they now had the right to vote. Just a few short days ago, the news had broken around the world. For Lena Lewis, the story couldn't have happened at a better time.

After just a few months of barely managing to break even on the costs of printing her newspaper, a company had decided to put out an ad in the Lavender Press.

It was some fledgling clothing company that thought that they could capitalize on the idea of putting pockets in women's clothing. Pockets that could hold more than a tube of lipstick by sheer chance, one of the company's owners happened to be a big fan of the Lavender Press & had thought that a newspaper that was specifically targeting gay women would be the perfect place to advertise.

Hours after they had handed her a check to run their ad, that was when the news of Switzerland had broken to the world. The last western republic to give women the right to vote. While most American news outlets had made a minor note of it, if that, Lena was making the story the headline of this week's issue.

She had gone all out, researching studies that were being conducted on the effects that women had on politics, consulting with experts on the increasing presence of women in the political landscape, inquiring & speculating on the effect that the gender phenomenon was having on women in politics.

Not realizing how thick she had made the issue with her story about the emancipation of women in Switzerland, she had to work late into the night printing up the issue on Saturday so that it could be ready to go on Sunday morning. The wheels & rollers of her press spun wildly into the night, generating copy after copy of her new issue.

Early the next morning, with just two hours of sleep to sustain her, she loaded her bundles of papers up & drove around the city to the various newsstands that were willing to sell a lesbian newspaper. The man at the first stand that she delivered to noticed that the forty copies he bought from her every week were heavier than usual. She didn't mention that her paper was meant for lesbians when he told her that he took a copy home to his wife every week because she loved it.

All through the early hours, so early that most people would consider it to still be yesterday, she dropped off bundle after bundle at newsstands all over the city.

When she got to the last stand that she sold at, she found herself in for a surprise. The man there was very conservative, but he would sell anything. Normally he bought ten copies of the queer rag just in case some liberal woman got lost & wanted to know that she could buy stuff from him.

When he saw the new issue, with the front page devoted to a picture of women holding up ballots under the banner proclaiming that Switzerland had given women the right to vote, he asked her something that she had never expected to hear from him.

"You got any more copies this week that I can sell?"

"You want to sell more copies of a lesbian newspaper?"

"Hell no, I want to sell more copies of a newspaper that celebrates democracy. Giving people the right to vote in a free election is what separates us from the commies. All these other papers barely mention that Swizz women can vote now."

"I think that I've got about another dozen copies in my car."

"Perfect. It's going right upfront here so people can appreciate that the world is a freer place this week than it was last week."

Going back into her trunk to fish out her spare copies, Lena pinched herself to make sure this week wasn't a dream. Ad revenue, a great story, & even the hard right vendor wanted more copies of her paper. Certain that she was awake, she gathered up the last copies she had & handed them over while the vendor wrote her another check to cover the cost of the extra papers.

March 26th, 1971
White House Family Theater

"Three little boys. They have a very close bond between them. Some might say that it's the kind of friendship that will last a lifetime, while others say that it's simply a result of them being the only three boys out of a class of thirty. One thing is certain, these boys & the many girls sitting around them are the vanguard of a future that we cannot predict. Over the course of this documentary, we've seen these boys form tightknit bonds as teachers place them next to each other. We've also seen them form strong bonds of friendship with girls when spread out through the classes. We've seen boys ask the big question, why are there so few of them in the kindergarten classes when there are so many in all of the other grades? Perhaps most disturbing for some is the sight of boys playing with dolls & playing games that were very recently considered girl's games. Is this a temporary thing? The result of this handful of boys suddenly being surrounded by girls & not yet seeing that some toys are not supposed to be for them. Or could this be the new trend for our sons? Not just living in a feminine world, but they themselves becoming feminine. Are we destined to live in a world where the handful of men that exist don't know how to be a man? These are just some of the questions we've asked in the series & like the other questions, we do not know what the answer will be as government struggles to make any gains on finding a solution to this imbalance."

As President Humphrey & his wife, his chief of staff & a few of his aids watched the new documentary finish with an image of three boys in a corner of the classroom fading out, the Vice President stood up.

"This is the reason that protests have been raging across the country for the last three days Hubert."

"This one movie. This documentary is what has the people raging?"

"It premiered a week ago & it has shined a great big spotlight on something that most Americans weren't paying too much attention to."

"Not paying attention to? Edmund, the birth ratios are one of the reasons why I was elected. Every annual report from the commission hits me in the approval ratings. They've been paying attention."

"Yes, Hubert, but until now, the threat was... theoretical. They knew that it was happening, but they weren't seeing it. They just saw that for six years, people around them have been working, marrying, raising families & going about their lives like everyone always has. Now it's been shoved in their face that a complete reordering of everything we hold dear is coming up on us & we've made zero progress in dealing with it."

The President pinched the bridge of his nose.

"Of course, this also happens a month before the annual report from the commission. How much do you want to bet that republicans will have this in theaters in red states right up until election day."

"They can't do that, can they?"

Hubert turned to his wife.

"There's no law against it, Muriel. Can't prosecute a theater for continuing to play a popular movie."

"But it's basically a political hit job. It might as well have said produced by the GOP in the credits. There's got to be something that we can do. Edmund, can't we sue them for slander or something?"

"Sorry Muriel. Like Hubert said, they haven't broken any laws. As for slander, they don't actually specifically say that we're the ones failing. It also isn't liable if it's truth & the truth is that we've made basically zero progress."

"None?"

Hubert clasped his wife's hands.

"Not unless they've stumbled onto something since the last report to me a few weeks ago. Edmund, how are we going to calm them down?"

"Well, I say that we make a big deal at the next commission annual report. Really pull out all of the stops, make it look like we're on the side of a betrayed people & hope to high heaven that they've found some sort of a breakthrough that we can hold up as progress to show that we're getting closer to a solution."

April 27th, 1971
National Institute of Health, Bethesda, Maryland

Edward Swanson walked through the NIH in a beeline to his office. Ignoring his secretary & the paperwork that had piled up for him, he sat at his desk, pulled open a bottom drawer, & pulled out a half-finished bottle of rum. Pouring himself a generous amount of the Caribbean nectar, he started slowly nursing it as Todor Fekete walked in. For the first time in a while, Edward noticed the few greys showing up in Todor's hair. After six years of this, he wondered how grey he had gone without noticing.

"You look like you were just bent over Edward. How bad was it?"

"Bad."

"Care to elaborate?"

"Nope. I'm just going to sit here & nurse this rum until one of you finds a cure."

Todor grabbed one of the two chairs opposite Edward & brought it around to the side of the desk.

"I know that these annual congressional reviews can be overwhelming, but I've never seen you this beaten. Tell me about it."

"Todor. They wanted blood. The nation is enraged with us for not snapping our fingers & pulling a cure out of our asses, so now the mob wants its pound of flesh."

"That bad?"

"You have no idea. Half the republicans are trying to crucify me as an incompetent leftist that needs to be replaced. Apparently, they want to make a name for themselves before they make a bid for the senate next year."

"Jesus. What about the democrats?"

"Them, they're trying to find some poor scapegoat to blame their lack of success on. After that documentary came out a few weeks ago about the kids in kindergarten, the country is freaking the fuck out. Apparently, half the country has only just now started taking this stuff seriously. They want a solution that we don't have, so a scapegoat is needed to appease the sudden anger of the crowd. I may as well have been bleating up there most of the day."

"That doesn't sound good. I imagine that a series of budget & personnel cuts are in our future."

"No, we're actually getting a desperately needed boost."

Todor looked at him confused. In his thick Hungarian accent, he tried to get some clarification.

"How strong is that rum, one of us has missed a chapter here."

"Apparently, they were desperate for a way to increase our funding to appease the masses, make it look like they're working the problem. But with the republicans bringing the hammers & the nails, they didn't have much to go on. Then I mentioned that new technique that your team developed to read individual genes. Saved my fucking career Todor."

"They like it."

"They like it alright. An efficient way to compare the genes of people born before & after 1965 to see if something in our genetics has been changed. A major scientific advancement that nobody else was even close to & will open up all kinds of new revenues of research. They jumped on the chance to fund us to use this new technology."

"That's great, but somebody would have eventually figured this out."

"Yeah, in a few more years. Todor, because we can actually compare genes, actually look at a very likely candidate for what caused this with new advanced technology, we've got the kind of funding we had before congressional oversight was forced on us."

"That's incredible."

"It is. Starting tomorrow morning, I want you to start drawing up proposals for research using this new process."

"Not a problem, but the thing is, it isn't an efficient process. We can only transcribe one gene at a time, not to mention that each gene takes some time to process. It's not exactly fast."

"Yeah, well, don't tell anyone until the cheque clears."

"Deal."

They sat there for a moment while Edward took a slow sip from his rum. Sitting up a bit, he held the glass in his hand.

"What worries me is what's going to happen next year, or the year after that. Now that people can more easily see the problem as it's growing up, the need for answers is just going to get worse & worse."

"Well... hopefully we can find an answer soon."

"Hopefully."

June 2nd, 1971

Chicago, Church of the Wives of Christ

Hope stood at the pulpit. Normally, she would have stood by the side as Virginia gave the Sunday sermon, but Virginia was currently upstairs battling a cold like no other, so she had given the task of leading their fledgling flock to Hope.

When she had first walked into the small chapel, she had been stunned to see how many women were there. The two-hundred seats that they had space for had filled up fast & more women were standing where they could find space. When Hope had stood at the pulpit to announce that Virginia was sick & that she would be leading them today, she found herself looking out on a diverse group of women from just about every demographic the city had to offer.

She saw young women, old women, rich women, poor women, white women, Asian women, Hispanic women, Black women, hopeful women, desperate women. Every single one of them seeking salvation for their souls & salvation from the world of men & husbands & fathers.

Stealing her courage, she led the congregation in prayer. She preached about the vile inadequacies of man, about how God almighty had lost faith in them & determined that those that wield a penis will never be worthy or righteous. About how man had fallen short in God's eyes. World Wars, racism, bigotry, rape, pollution, God could see that almost all men were completely irredeemable & decided to recreate the world in woman's image.

She ignored the part about the end of days as she felt that from time to time, it was better to have the flock focus on the here & now. She spoke about how even with new males in short supply, men still waged bloody wars. She spoke about how women were still expected to stay home & tend to the household despite the fact that such a philosophy was soon going to be completely untenable.

They hung on to her every word. While many of them weren't entirely happy about the idea of giving up sex with men, they could all see that a lot of what she spoke was true. The world had changed & was changing still, yet the powers that be couldn't seem to get their acts together.

When her sermon was finished, the congregation watched as she brought out a large bowl to place on the altar. She then filled it with water & blessed it before turning to her flock.

"Those among you who seek to unbind yourselves, please step forward."

As Hope moved to the side of the altar so that everyone could see what was going to happen, a middle-aged woman stepped forward from the front pew. Hope had seen the woman at a few sermons over the last few weeks. She had always seemed to be exhausted, as if she was always carrying the weight of the world on her shoulders. She stood at the altar opposite Hope.

"Racheal. Are you ready to unbind yourself? To free yourself from the bondage of man & to live free as God now intends us too."

The woman lifted her hand & looked at her ring finger for a moment. She then pulled her wedding ring off in one fluid motion & held it over the bowl of water.

"I'm ready to be free."

"Then let go of your chain & say goodbye to all it represents."

Racheal stood there for a moment.

"Goodbye Dan. Goodbye to the endless days of keeping your house clean for your ungrateful ass. Goodbye to slaving away over a stove to make dinner just the way you like it only for you to get home at ten & tell me that you ate with the guys. Goodbye to pretending that I don't see the lipstick stains on your shirt collar. Goodbye to never being able to see my friends because you think they're a bad influence. Goodbye to pretending that I was satisfied when you climbed on top of me & grunted for twenty seconds. Goodbye to your disappointment that I couldn't give you a son you ungrateful bastard. Goodbye to you & everyone like you."

Racheal then dropped her wedding ring into the bowl of holy water & returned to her seat where her fourteen-year-old daughter welcomed her with open arms as the congregation cheered her on. Hope then stood before the pulpit & waited for the applause to die down a bit.

"You see sisters. Even those who were bound to men can free themselves. Here we have a mother & daughter who are now free of an ungrateful prick that saw them as nothing more than his property. We will show the men of this world that their time as our masters, is over. We are free & we are righteous."

The congregation cheered her on as she kept preaching about women's ultimate emancipation from the shackles of men. As her sermon came to an end, she gently reminded her congregation to donate if they could on the way out so that they may acquire a larger house for their growing flock to worship the lord in.

July 26th, 1971
Endeavor Command Service Module, 22,000 kms above Earth

David Scott was nearly finished with his checklist. So far, everything had gone off without a hitch. The launch, docking with the Lunar Module, the trans lunar injection burn, everything had gone off perfectly & as commander of Apollo 15, he intended to make sure that it kept going off without a hitch. Naturally, it was at this moment, when he was nearly done with the checklist that he got a call from Houston.

"Endeavor, this is Houston, do you read us?"

"Houston, this is Endeavor, we hear you."

"Are Alfred & James there as well?"

Alfred Worden checked to make sure that James Irwin was hearing everything before he answered.

"We hear you Alan, what's up."

Alan Shepard lit a cigarette & took a long pull on it before continuing with the news that he had been told to relay to them.

"Alright guys, I know that you've had one hell of a day so far, by this point you're probably looking to finish up your checklists, grab a bite & then check out for the night."

"You're not wrong Alan."

David signaled to James to be quiet.

"Right, well, I won't keep you for long, we've just received some news from the President himself concerning Apollo 20 & we're telling you before it hits the evening news tonight."

The three astronauts braced for the news that everyone had been hearing rumors about. Apollo was expensive, & with no sign that the Soviets were ever going to make it to the Moon, it was getting harder & harder to justify the cost. They were certain that this was news of twenty being cancelled.

"There's been a crew change for Apollo twenty."

The three of them perked up at the news. David was the one to answer.

"Twenty isn't cancelled?"

"We were surprised as well. Twenty is still a go, but they've decided to make some changes."

"What kind of changes?"

"The President has ordered us to reserve one of the two Lunar Module seats of Apollo 20 for America's first female astronaut, whoever she'll be."

The crew were silent for a moment.

"Sorry Alan, say again?"

"Twenty is going to have a woman on board David."

"What brought this on?"

"I have no idea; we were just informed that we now have to train a female astronaut for Apollo twenty. Originally, the President wanted her to be on eighteen, but the director told him that we were going to need more time to properly train a new astronaut candidate for a lunar mission."

"Where the hell are you going to get lady astronauts from?"

"Well, we're thinking about looking up the women from the Mercury 13. At least they started the training, so we wouldn't be at square one with them."

"That's smart."

"This won't affect your mission or the next few, we just wanted to let you know about it before the country finds out."

"Thanks Alan."

"Alright, I'll let you get back to your checklists."

A moment later, the call came to an end & the three astronauts were simply floating there on the way to the Moon. While James went back to his Lunar Module checklist, Alfred hung around with David.

"They couldn't have waited until after we got back from the Moon to tell the country that twenty will have a woman?"

"I guess not Al."

"Why do you think that the President wants us to do this?"

"Who knows. It could just be a stunt to keep the public invested so he doesn't have to cancel the missions."

"You think this is going to delay twenty?"

"Maybe. Can't train astronauts overnight & they'll probably want to take their time if they're really going to send a woman up."

Alfred hung around for a moment, just floating there.

"What's up James?"

"You think that all astronauts will be women in twenty or thirty years?"

"What?"

"The birth thing. What if in twenty years, they're only sending up women?"

"Well then that'll be an interesting time. But I don't think that they're going to completely cut men out of space."

"Right, just a silly thought. I've got to get back to my own checklist."

While Alfred got back to his own checklist, David wondered if any of the women from the Mercury 13 would come back after all these years.

August 15th, 1971
NASA Headquarters, Washington DC

The sun was streaming into the room as the Administrator of NASA, & a number of high-level NASA officials reviewed the data that was being presented to them by the CIA. The administrator leaned back in his chair & took a long pull on his cigarette.

"You know, it was just over a year ago, that you told us, in this very room, that the Soviets had given up on their manned moon program & that they were slowly gearing down production."

The CIA analyst sighed for a moment.

"That's right Mark. I remember the day quite well."

"That's good. Because this looks distinctly like an N1 rocket on the launch pad with a picture of a rather large crater nearby."

"That's right Mark."

"This would also seem to indicate that they aren't giving up if they're still testing N1s."

The CIA analyst took a drag off of his own cigarette for a moment.

"I don't know what to tell you Mark. All indications were that they were ramping down the program. We humiliated them when we got to the Moon while they couldn't get their first stages to work. Combine that with the fact that they were shifting materials, money & personnel away from the program & it became clear that they were closing it down."

"These pictures paint a different story."

"I don't know what to tell you. A month ago, we got a report saying that they were suddenly moving things back to the program & then a week ago, a new N1 rolls out to the launch pad."

Taking a close look at the image of the crater, the administrator carefully analyzed the grainy image.

"Well, the good news is that it looks like they still don't have a working super heavy lift rocket. I don't suppose that you've managed to acquire any information on how it preformed?"

"Not much I'm afraid. Our mole in the Soviet Space Program was only able to get a minor report out. The kind of thing that's usually dumbed down for us non-science types. There should be a translated copy in each of your folders."

Mark flipped through the report until he found the document in question. As he read it, he grew concerned.

"Well, this isn't as good as I had hoped for."

"We can ask him to get a better report if you'd like."

"No, not that. I mean, if he can, go for it, but don't risk him if it's too dangerous, this tells us plenty."

"It does? What does it tell us Mark?"

"It tells us that this launch faired a lot better than previous launches. Nothing exploded until it hit the ground, nothing ripped apart mid-flight. It looks like a bunch of the engines just shut down & the onboard computer failed to compensate."

"It still crashed."

"Yes, but if the engines shut down because of some sort of safety feature engaging & the computer failed to compensate for it, then that means that they are a lot closer to having a working rocket than we thought that they were. The others either ripped themselves apart or blew up mid-flight. This looks like a minor guidance issue."

"Shit. A software bug would probably be a lot easier to fix than a hardware issue. Do you think that this means that they're on the verge of being able to reach the Moon?"

"I don't know if they're close, but it looks like they are closer."

"Shit. Last thing we need on top of everything else is a second space race when we just finished the first one."

October 10th, 1971
Montreal, Canada

Janet's heart was pounding in her chest like a drumbeat. It beat like that every time that she brought Rebecca home & passed her off as her close friend who didn't have anywhere to be for the holidays. For the last two years, the plan had been that she was going to come out to her parents with Rebecca by her side. Of course, back in high school, the plan had been that she would come out to them with Charisma by her side. She had learned several times that planning to do something brave & actually finding the courage to go through with it were two very different things. Rebecca squeezed her hand as they sat in the car.

"Should we wait until supper, or should we just walk up to the door hand in hand & grope each other in front of them."

Janet laughed nervously, which told Rebecca all that she needed to know about her girlfriend's plans.

"It's alright Janet. You don't have to say anything tonight. I can keep playing the role of good friend until Christmas."

"No, Rebecca, it's not fair. You shouldn't have to hide just because I can't tell them."

"It's fine. At least this way they won't be upset about me sleeping in the same room as you."

Janet smiled.

"You're so good to me like that. Charisma used to give me all kinds of crap for not coming out, not that she ever would."

"I'm ready when you are Janet."

"I still say that you shouldn't have to put up with this. I just hope that I can do it tonight at supper."

Rebecca smiled evilly.

"How about this Janet. If you don't come out to your family before we go to bed, I get to punish you tonight."

"Punish me how?"

"You'll have to go down on me tonight, in your bed."

"Okay, it's not like we haven't fooled around in there before."

"True, but this time will be different. This time, we'll keep the light on & the door unlocked."

Janet paled.

"Rebecca, you can't be serious. Last Thanksgiving, we would have been caught if the door wasn't locked."

"I remember. Think of it as motivation to tell your parents the truth."

"What if I still can't?"

Rebecca got out of the car & took the pumpkin pie that the two of them had lovingly bought at the store together. Janet quickly got out of the car as well, locked it, & followed Rebecca up the walkway to the front door. Once Janet rang the doorbell, Rebecca leaned in close & whispered in her ear.

"Be ready to have the riskiest sex of your life if you can't tell them."

Janet blushed just as the door opened & her father stood there smiling to see his daughter home.

"Hi Daddy."

"There's my little girl, come inside. Rebecca, good to see you again."

"Good to see you too John. We brought pumpkin pie."

"Well then get in here already."

The three of them hugged each other as they made their way into the house.

"By the way, Janet, I know that Jane usually helps your mother with serving & the dishes, but she's out of commission this year, swollen ankles from the pregnancy. would you be willing to help?"

"Fine Dad, although I don't know how swollen her ankles can be, she's barely showing."

"Oh, she's showing Janet. I don't know what happened in the last month, but she's already bigger than your mother ever got & she's still got three months to go. Apparently, the doctor is concerned about this."

"Is that my other daughter out there?"

Jillian Hill walked out of the kitchen wearing a pink & brown striped apron. She then wrapped Janet up in a bear hug.

"Thank God you're here. With Jane in her condition, I'm shorthanded in the kitchen. Harold tried to help, but he's almost as useless with a mixing bowl as your father. Would you be willing to help me out?"

John laughed as Janet agreed & went to say hello to her sister before joining her mother in the kitchen. John indicated the way to the living room for Rebecca.

"Thank you, John. Have I ever mentioned that I think it's adorable that your whole family has names that start with J."

"I tried to get Harold to change his name Jerold when he got married, but he was named after his grandfather."

Rebecca laughed as she followed him into the living room to say hello to Janet's sister.

Over the next few hours, Janet regularly helped her mother with all sorts of tasks to get things ready while Rebecca mostly kept Janet's sister company while the boys watched sports & talked about their jobs. Eventually, the meal was ready, the table was set & Rebecca helped Harold lift his wife to her feet so that she could waddle to the table while complaining about the mutant giant that he had put into her to gestate.

After Janet & her mother had spent endless hours cooking the meal, John took over at the last step & with his carving knife, & he cut into the succulent turkey.

"Dear Lord honey, perfection once again. A feast fit for a king."

"Thank you, John. I wouldn't have been able to do it without my helpers, which was all of you a bit this year."

John smiled.

"How are you doing over there, Jane?"

"Hungry, I'm eating for a mutant here."

John laughed as he stacked up the first plate nice & tall & handed it to Jane covered in turkey, stuffing, potatoes, mashed yams & gravy.

"There you go Jane, don't wait up for us to start, you dig in."

"Thanks Dad."

John went back to carving.

"So, while I'm serving & before we say grace, anyone have any big announcements? Like maybe the name of my granddaughter?"

"It'll either be… Jill, June…, or Susan."

Everyone laughed as Jane answered through mouthfuls of supper.

"Anyone else? Any big announcements?"

Rebecca looked at Janet. Janet took her plate.

A belly breaking meal & a few hours later, Janet & Rebecca were lying next to each other on Janet's bed from high school. As Janet stared up at her ceiling, Rebecca turned onto her side.

"God, your family makes one hell of a thanksgiving meal."

"Yeah. It would have been nice if I could have told them what I'm really thankful for."

"What would that be?"

"For having the most patient girlfriend in the world, a woman who's willing to sit at family event after event next to me & pretend to just be a friend with no other plans."

"Your right, that is something to be thankful for."

"I am thankful Rebecca."

"I know, & in the spirit of that gratitude, maybe you could do something for me."

"What?"

"Unlock the door."

Janet paled.

"Seriously?"

"I told you, if you don't come out, we're having risky, family could walk in at any moment, high school bedroom sex."

"Is there any way I can get out of that?"

"You can go & tell your family that you're a carpet muncher."

"What, just wake them up in their rooms & come out while their half asleep, I don't think so."

"Then go unlock the door, then get over here & start munching."

Janet stood up. She knew that there wasn't really a risk. Nobody had barged into her room unannounced since she was fourteen. Her parents were probably in bed, asleep & her sister was probably too tired to care about any strange noises that she heard in the night. She was also fairly sure that Harold wouldn't barge in unless they really got vocal. Still, the idea that it was hypothetically possible was doing something for Janet.

She wouldn't tell Rebecca, but a part of her was suddenly hoping that she would get caught, just so that she wouldn't have to say it out loud, everyone could just know. So, she got up, walked over to the door, & felt a tingle of excitement as she unlocked the door. With her heart beating faster, she turned around just as a pair of pajamas came flying at her.

"What the?"

Looking at the bed, she saw Rebecca sitting on the side of it, naked, smiling, & with her legs spread to reveal her trimmed golden bush.

"Come on Janet, time to get on your knees."

Janet walked over to Rebecca, slipping off her own pajamas as she went. If somebody walked in, if her parents heard noises & John Hill came to see what was happening under his roof, oh the sight that he would see.

December 8th, 1971
Oval Office

President Humphrey looked over the shocking numbers in the report that his generals had just presented to him. The report spoke of ultra-low morale among soldiers, outright dereliction of duty, drug use & falsified battle reports.

"How in the hell did it get this bad?"

One of the three generals in the room found the courage to do what so few military men ever wanted to do. He told his superior officer things he didn't want to hear.

"Simply put sir, they don't want to be there."

"Excuse me? They don't want to be there?"

"That's as simple as it is sir. Most of the soldiers that we have in Vietnam were drafted. They didn't want to serve to begin with. On top of that, a large percentage of our soldiers are questioning why we're even there, they don't see the point in us fighting the North Vietnamese. It's also kind of hard to convince soldiers that were effectively press ganged into service that they're defending freedom. It also doesn't help that Australia & New Zealand have pulled out of the war."

"So, what you're saying is that one of the most powerful armies in the world doesn't want to fight. How do we fix this?"

The generals all looked at each other.

"None of you have any ideas?"

Once again, one lone general worked up the courage to say what had to be said.

"Mr. President, I think that the time has come to consider the idea that Vietnam is unwinnable. We've been throwing bodies & resources at the problem for almost ten years & we've gotten nowhere. The soldiers don't want to fight, the people want the soldiers to come home & quite frankly, even if we could win by some miracle, the public doesn't really see the value of such a victory."

"So, what, I should just give up on the war? We can't just back down."

"Sir, we don't have much left to fight with. Our forces are in such a poor state that many of them aren't even trying to resist the enemy. Unless you want to go nuclear, which I do not recommend, every indication is that we we're not going to win."

"So, what, you want me to just go on TV & tell the people that we're quitting the biggest war since World War 2? How do you think that'll go over?"

"Actually sir, it would probably play in your favor."

The President looked to his chief of staff who was searching through some reports of his own.

"They want us to lose?"

"It's not so much that they want us to lose, it's more that they want the fighting to stop & for the soldiers to come home. Polls show that without the war, the people think that you're doing a great job. Appointing Gerald Forestman & Sandra Fletcher to the supreme court, increasing funding to the commission, your support of the equal rights amendment, the promise to send a woman to the moon. It's putting you forward in all of the polls, but the war has become such an albatross that it's threatening to seriously undermine us in the midterms."

The President leaned back in his chair, contemplating the situation that his chief of staff had just described. As he considered it, his general spoke up once more.

"Sir, Vietnam is a quagmire, & if we don't pull out, we'll be stuck there forever. I recommend that we start slowly pulling our forces back & bringing them home. Instead of your plan to send thirty thousand more men to Vietnam, I recommend that you withdraw thirty thousand."

"What would we do after we brought some of our men home?"

"From time to time, we bring even more men home, after a while, we stop sending more men to fight. We push for a peace treaty & hope that we can bring an end to the war in the next two or three years."

President Humphrey didn't like it. He didn't like the idea of losing a big war. Korea had been bad enough. But looking at the report that his generals had presented concerning the state of the military & the unwillingness of the people to be involved in the war, he had to concede that the war was most likely not going to go his way.

"Thirty thousand home then. But I want some sort of a plan on my desk about how we'll get the enemy to the negotiating table before I commit to not sending anyone else to fight."

The generals breathed a sigh of relief. For the first time, many of them could see a potential end to the war that had been going on since some of them were majors.

1972

January 16th, 1972
New York City

The headline on the front page of the paper read the rise of the queens. Sarah hoisted the last of the bundles into the back of her station wagon. Hoisting the hundreds of copies into the wagon was causing it to ride a little lower than it usually did. Yawning from the work & from how early it was, she stifled her yawn just in time for her new boss to walk out of the building's back door.

"Got everything loaded up Sarah?"

"Yes Ms. Lewis."

"Ms. Lewis, that's going to take some getting used to. You've got your route?"

"Completely mapped out."

"Good. You've got quarters for payphones?"

"Yes mam."

"Good. I'll be back here in about two hours. If you have any problems before then, leave me a message & just use your best judgement. Don't piss anyone off, I'd rather you make it back with an unsold bundle or two then get into a fight. Some of these guys aren't too happy about selling a lesbian newspaper."

"My father isn't too happy that I'm working for one either, I'm used to older men that disapprove."

"Then this should be a walk in the park for you. Remember, be careful, drive safe & avoid arguments."

"Yes Ms. Lewis."

Lena shook her head as she made her way to her car so that she could deliver her bundles of the Lavender Press to newsstands in the city. She watched in her rearview mirror as her first employee drove out to deliver her newspaper to stands & shops that were much further afield.

Lena wasn't sure what was causing it, but in the last few months, business had been booming. Almost every vendor that she sold too had started asking for more & she had been able to convince a few more to start selling her Sunday paper. One stand had even called her up & requested a few copies of her newspaper. With business surging all over the city, the weekly early morning crawl had been brutal.

Looking into how much money she was making, she decided that the best thing to do was to hire someone to help her out part time. When she had put the help wanted ads out, she had been surprised by how many women showed up looking for work.

Sarah had won out because she brought an enthusiasm to the early morning rush & because she had a car that could carry a ton of papers. A few days earlier, she had taken Sarah around to the stops that she would be making to familiarize herself with their customers. Now she watched as her first employee went to work.

Sarah felt like she had been at it for days by the time she got to her last stop. Driving all over half the city of New York in the early hours with the people who were only vertical because of the semi-lethal amounts of coffee they had consumed.

Along the way, the people buying the bundles from her had been impatient, rude, condescending & more than one had tried to shortchange her. Now, as the morning rush of commuters began with the people making their way to their jobs, Sarah, thoroughly exhausted, made her way back to the office with the money & cheques for her boss.

"How did it go?"

"I should have brought a crowbar for some of their wallets, but it all worked out in the end."

"Good to hear it. Can I assume that means that you won't be quitting after your first run?"

"It's going to take more than that to scare me off."

"That's what I like to hear."

Lena then picked up two rolled copies of the paper that they had just distributed.

"Here, these two are for you. One copy to read, one copy to keep as a reminder of your first day."

"Thanks Ms. Lewis."

"Still not used to that."

With their Sunday work finished, they both headed home. When Sarah walked in, her father had just gotten home from Sunday mass.

"How was your first Sunday working?"

"It was good, I'm exhausted, but it was good. Here, I got you a copy of the paper in case you wanted something to read."

"Thank you, Sarah. I suppose it would be a good idea to see what kind of news you're distributing."

Taking the rolled paper that she handed him, he opened it up & took a look at the front page.

"The rise of the queens? This isn't going to be one of those manifestos that says I'm evil because I have a... beard."

Sarah had been ready to cringe if he hadn't said beard instead of certain other answers he could have given.

"No, the King of Denmark died a few days ago, so now his daughter... Margrethe... I think, is the now the Queen of Denmark."

"It says queens, as in more than one."

"Yeah, she has two daughters, Frederica & Josefine if I remember right. The article talks about how if not for the birth ratio anomaly, at least one of them might have been born a prince & how monarchies all over the world are being affected by the fact that nine out of ten new royals born since sixty-five have been princesses."

"Interesting. I imagine that will change a few things. Makes one wonder who these princesses will marry when they get older."

"That point comes up in the article. I won't spoil it, but unless a solution is reached, a lot of royal lines might come to an end in sixty or seventy years."

Sarah saw her father look at the paper & hoped that the paper won over his approval before he got to the article on how to best apologize when you accidentally hit on a straight girl.

February 14th, 1972
Church of the Wives of Christ, Chicago

"Welcome sisters! Welcome to our new church. Come in, we have plenty of space for our congregation!"

Hope welcomed women into the new church that they had gotten. A part of her still couldn't believe that they had a proper church instead of a space that they had rented from a strip mall. Sure, the building needed a good bit of work done, & they were going to need a lot more people to donate to the church if they didn't want rent to be an issue, but it was theirs. A church all their own where they could preach the word of Christ's Wives.

As a grand opening of their new church, they had decided to open it with their annual denouncement of Valentine's Day. Every year, this special sermon drew in more & more women, not to mention, more donations. It was their biggest day of the year, a day when women were most fed up with the inadequacies of men.

As the sun set, the last stragglers came in. Hope turned to the two women helping her welcome people to the church & signaled to them that it was time to go inside. Hope had known that with so much more capacity, most of the church would be empty. They didn't even have enough pews to fill out the main room yet. But when she walked in, she was stunned by how full the church was. It looked as if they had packed over four hundred people in.

As Hope walked up the center aisle, she saw a lot of women who were clearly couples. It warmed her heart to see that there were women who felt safe enough here that they didn't have to hide. She also saw a number of women who seemed rather nervous, most likely their first time here or worrying that someone might recognize them. Eventually Hope reached the altar where she made sure that everything was in order. She then kissed the copy of the book of revelations that Virginia kept on the altar at all times & stood to the side.

A moment later, Virginia walked out onto the dais. The entire crowd gasped, causing Hope to turn to see what was going on. She pretty much had to pick her jaw up off of the ground. Virginia had walked out onto the dais wearing nothing but a pair of black panties & a black lace bra.

Her curly blonde hair had been swept back behind her shoulders to prevent it from obscuring anyone's view of her pale body, sharply contrasting against the black lace. Some of the women in the pews cheered. Some of them got very nervous, wondering what kind of sapphic orgy was about to begin around them. Hope felt her heart beating faster as she wondered what the hell the priestess was up to. Virginia stood at the waist high table & took a deep breath before beginning her sermon. The entire congregation watched her chest rise & fall.

"Sisters! We all know what a wretched day of the year it is. It's the day that husbands expect to come home to their wives dressed like this because they remembered to get a card & some flowers. The night when we're just supposed to let them in because they came home for supper & remembered that it's the fourteenth of February. This is what men expect us to be on this day, a mindless toy in sexy underwear who gives it up for a box of chocolates."

A lot of the women attending the sermon nodded their heads. Some of them had husbands that they had cooked a delicious meal for, that they had prettied themselves up for, just because it was the day that men were supposed to put their wives first. Yet here they were while their husbands worked or claimed to work. Some of them, like Virginia, were even wearing sexy underwear underneath their clothes because that had been what they were preparing for.

"How many of us have spent entire evenings forcing ourselves to wear underwear that was not designed for comfort just so that some man can see it on you for a minute & get hard? How many of us have squeezed into these sheer bras that hoist our tits up as if they were torpedoes ready to be fired, all so that some idiot man can delude himself into thinking that his wife is three cup sizes bigger than she actually is?"

Countless women throughout the church remembered the struggle of forcing themselves into bras that were too small, or made out irritating fabric, or bras that tried to lift, squeeze, push, mold or hoist their breasts into uncomfortable positions just so that the guy they were seeing could drool over them.

"Why do we constrain ourselves in these contraptions just to make men horny? God has declared that men aren't worthy of existence, why should we be trying to please them? I say enough! If you want to wear a bra, fine, but forget about what men think will make your tits look better. They look great as they are!"

Several women in the crowd cheered her on.

"Our world is changing! The age when man gets to dictate how we live our lives is coming to an end. Yet we are still expected by society to never leave the house without a bra on & we are expected to wear crap like this on certain nights of the year just because sometimes, a man can remember why that day is supposed to be important. I say enough! Let us be free to be comfortable! Let us be free to take these off!"

As several women cheered, Virginia shocked the congregation by reaching behind her back & unclasping her bra. In the blink of an eye, she threw the sheer black garment away, inadvertently hurling it towards Hope.

Standing in front of the group of women topless, she let them take in the sight of her pale, slightly sagging breasts & her stiffening nipples. Just now realizing how chilly it was in the room, she spoke a little faster so she could get to the part of her sermon where she put clothes back on.

"That sheer piece of underwear that was designed to put men in the mood is the very last bra that I'll ever force my tits into. I refuse to make myself look proper or sexy according to the tastes of the inferior sex. In this new age of women, we will be free of men & their contraptions."

As the crowd applauded, Virginia picked up the white robe that she had left on the altar earlier. Wrapping herself up in the soft robe, she reveled in the sensation of wearing it with nothing beneath but a pair of panties.

With Hope in shock & the congregation questioning why women can only be considered proper if they're wearing society approved underwear, Virginia held up her copy of revelations as she preached to her growing flock about how men were bringing about the end of days, & about how they had to deny men who were not worthy of their bodies in the eyes of the lord on high.

Later that night, when the sermon ended, Hope & a volunteer stood at the front of the church, next to the donation bowls, to thank people for coming & to silently encourage them to donate to the church. About three quarters of the women gave something, leaving Virginia & Hope quite certain that they would be able to pay the bills.

March 22nd, 1972
Sacramento, California

The small office space had once housed a number of small companies. Some of them were legitimate companies that lasted for years, others were fly by night companies that popped up, made some money, got in some trouble & shut down. Now the office was the headquarters of the Matriarch party as they prepared for the 1972 presidential election.

With six candidates running for various seats in the city of Sacramento & a desire to start winning races, this was no longer something that they could do by just meeting in Patricia Torres' living room once a week. While a door knocking campaign was being organized near her, Patricia was looking over polling data that had recently been published so that she could get an idea of where her party stood in certain races. That was when one of the volunteers working for them rushed in to talk to Patricia.

"Patricia! They passed it!"

Patricia looked up at the young woman who had just burst into the room & was now distracting her from the important information that she was looking at.

"Who are they & what did they pass?"

"The senate, they voted on the ERA & the vote passed with the two-thirds majority that they needed."

Patricia put down the papers that she was looking at. The equal rights amendment had been the dream of women's movements since the twenties. An amendment that would prevent any kind of discrimination based on gender. It would force countless laws & policies to be rewritten in order to ensure that men & women were truly treated as equals.

"When did it pass the senate?"

"About half an hour ago."

"They got sixty-seven senators to vote in favor of it?"

"They got eighty-nine votes in the senate."

"Eighty-nine!"

When Patricia screamed out, everyone in the office stopped what they were doing & looked to her to see what was going on.

"You're telling me that the ERA passed the senate with eighty-nine votes."

"It sure did."

"Now it just has to be ratified by the states."

"Well, apparently half a dozen state legislatures are already calling for emergency sessions to vote on it over the next few days."

The whole room went silent. The handful of men in the room were stunned by the look of joyous shock on the women's faces. Dreams of true equality were playing out in their minds. Patricia took a breath to center herself before turning back to the volunteer.

"Has California called for a vote on the issue?"

"Not as far as I know, like I said, the news only just broke half an hour ago."

"There are still a lot of hardline conservatives in the legislature, so the democrats might not want to call for a vote until after the election so that they can campaign on it."

The people around her could almost see the gears turning in her mind as she tried to predict how the California legislature would react to the news of the ERA.

"Alright everyone, change of plan! The Matriarch Party's position on the ERA is that if we're elected to the state legislature, we will vote to ratify the ERA. I want it included in our literature, I want it mentioned when we knock on doors, I want everyone who will be voting in November to know that our candidates for the legislature will vote to ratify the ERA."

By the time that she finished her last sentence, most of the groups in the room were already hard at work coming up with plans, strategies & redesigning pamphlets. For a party that wanted to go from a rounding error in the vote counts to an actual contender, this was a once in a lifetime opportunity.

April 16th, 1972
Fort Worth, Texas

The first three rows of pews in the chapel were filled with pregnant women who were being tended to by the altar boys & the church's first altar girl, affectionately referred to as the handmaiden. The back of the church was occupied by women & their infant daughters while the few women who had born a son sat just behind the pregnant women. As the crowd was just starting to get a bit restless, Reverend Thomas Edwards emerged from the back room behind the altar.

Despite the grey that was slowly weaving its way through his copper hair, his eyes still burned with a righteous fire as he walked up to the altar to address his flock. He was slightly concerned that the number of women with a hoard of daughters at the back was much larger than the pregnant women at the front. Unfolding a piece of paper, he placed it on the podium next to his microphone & went over it before addressing the crowd.

"My children. We are losing the war against the Godless & the depraved."

A silence fell over the congregation as they all looked up to their Shepard as he proclaimed the terrible news of the world.

"Hawaii. Massachusetts. Rhode Island, New York, Ohio, Michigan, Illinois, Wisconsin, Minnesota... South Dakota, Alabama, Florida, California, Oregon... Washington & even our own beloved Texas. In less than a month, these sixteen states have foolishly ratified the ERA."

The members of his flock were stunned.

"Less than a month my children. The corruption of radical feminism has spread so far into the fabric of our great nation, that in less than a month, sixteen of God's United States have fallen to the ways of the Godless. Upon seeing that God was depriving the non-believers of sons to carry on their names, did the federal government cleave to the Lord. No. Did they stand up to ratify that this is a Christian nation under the one true God. No. Instead, they delude themselves into believing that women are equal to men, in complete violation of the word of the Lord!"

As he held up his old, leather-bound bible, the crowd erupted into moans & tears as they realized that equality was spreading faster than they had feared it would.

"My children, if nothing is done to stem the tide of false equality, we will live in a world ruled by women! A world where the handful of boys are encouraged to play with dolls & where skirts!"

Thomas knew that everyone in the congregation had seen the documentary about the elementary schools & the confused kindergarten boys. He had arranged a screening of it for his congregation to whip the fear of feminism into them.

"The news from the trenches, I fear, is worse than even this my children. Across this great land, even houses of the Lord are being corrupted!"

The people looked around at each other as if they were searching for the corruption.

"You will not find this filth in our house. But all over the country, houses of God are making concessions. Churches in New York are considering allowing lesbianism! Churches in California that are considering allowing women into the priesthood! Churches that are losing sight of the sacred!"

He calmed down for a moment as his flock took in the news that he was preaching to them.

"In many ways, the corruption is spreading without even trying to conceal itself. In constitutional amendments & government studies on alternative reproduction strategies. Yet in other ways, this filth is spreading in more subtle ways. I know that many of you are eager to get home so that you may watch the launch of Apollo 16. I can't blame you. I want to watch it. Three brave men launching into the heavens to bring America & God to the moon, for God made the universe for us as he made the Earth for us."

Several space fans in the crowd cheered & clapped.

"Yet, our liberal president, who allowed this wretched amendment, has declared that Apollo 20 will carry a woman to the moon!"

The crowd gasped.

"Even the moon, all but untouched by man since the dawn of creation, will now be touched by a woman who thinks that her place is that of a leader instead of that of a housewife as God decreed!"

Thomas stopped preaching for a moment as the people mumbled to each other about what kind of a woman could think that it was her place to explore the universe with men of action & courage.

"Yes. NASA, at the behest of our inglorious President, is carrying the flame of feminism to the Moon! However, we need not fly out a quarter of a million miles to find subtle corruption. Tomorrow, in Boston, the annual marathon will be run. A tradition of men showing off their physical prowess in the streets of Boston.

But this year, they are allowing women, three of them, to compete in the marathon!"

Most of the crowd gasped in shock, except for a few young girls who had from time to time imagined themselves in sports.

"My children, it would be one thing if they created a separate marathon for women. I could tolerate that. Let these young women compete so that they may demonstrate their health & inherit strength to men looking for women that can bear them sons. But to allow women to compete against men directly, it is insanity! Women cannot compete against men! They are weaker, slower, they will accomplish nothing but to demonstrate that they are inferior as God made them! Yet still, they will be allowed to run next to, or more likely, far behind men in a competition of physical ability."

Most of the crowd booed.

"My children, we must double our vigilance! We must make sure that no more states ratify this feminist agenda! We must make sure that those that have, especially our beloved home state, reverse these ratifications! We must protest & fight the encroachment of women into the domains of men! Only when the world has been restored, with men in charge & women subservient, only then, will God restore the sons that he has taken from us!"

The crowd applauded thunderously. When they began to calm, Thomas continued with the most important part of his sermon.

"My children, we must remain vigilant, even against our brother congregations!"

The parishioners looked at him confused.

"I fear that the archdiocese has requested of me that I tone down my rhetoric about resisting feminism. He claims that it's scaring away & pushing away those who would seek God. I told him that if someone is seeking God, they will not find it in a bible that was written by a lesbian!"

The crowd cheered.

"Still, he persists. In June, I am supposed to attend a meeting on how we can make our churches more friendly to a changing world. But I will not attend. We must not bow to corruption; we must force the world to change back. If that means breaking away from a diocese that may be about to lose their way, then that might be what we have to do!"

Shocked murmurs ran through the crowd.

"So, I ask of you my children, over the coming weeks & months, to look into your hearts & measure your souls. I do hope that our brothers in Christ see the way to righteousness, but if they do not, we will have to take drastic actions. We will have to move to a new church that is not owned by them."

His flock fell silent.

"If you agree with the priests & the bishops that are saying that God wants to go down the corrupt path of feminism, lesbianism & emasculation, then perhaps you will need to find a new place to worship. I'll even give you a list of the churches in & around Fort Worth for you. But if you want to stay true to the word of God, true to the truth that men were made to rule over women, then I ask that you donate & tithe all you can so that we can be ready to build a new place of worship, one fit for the God of men."

As the altar boys started passing around collection plates for their first go around, many worshippers started digging into their wallets for more to donate so that they could help the fiery preacher in his quest to save their souls from a world ruled by women.

May 16th, 1972
Maryland State Department of Education

Doctor Barbara Collins found herself sitting in a poorly decorated conference room. The décor seemed to embody the word institutional. Around her at the conference table were about twenty men. Principals, school board members, the superintendent of schools, many of the men that were in charge of the state's duties to educate its children.

Jeremy Young was a heavyset man with thin, greying hair. He was one of the dozen members of the board of education & he had walked into the meeting a few minutes late & took a seat next to Barbara.

"Thank you for coming in Ms. Collins. Sorry I'm late."

"Dr. Collins."

"Hm, yes, my apologies, that's actually why we're here, we need to stop making such shameful mistakes."

"I'm glad to hear that. For a moment I was worried that this was some sort of subterfuge to confront me about that homework assignment that I never handed in in the ninth grade."

The men around her chuckled. It put her at ease to see the room full of men in a good mood.

"Right, well, as you know, the oldest children that are nine tenths female are coming to the end of the first grade. In a few months, Kindergarten through the second grade will be almost entirely female & it appears that there is no end in sight to this gender imbalance."

"Yes, as a member of the commission into the birth ratio anomaly, I am very aware of this."

"Of course. As such, we need to... adjust some of our educational policies to be more encouraging for women to enter the workforce in nine years. We're quite proud of the work that we've done so far, but we thought that it might be best to consult with women who have succeeded in completing the higher levels of education to see if there are any more improvements that we can make."

Barbara held her tongue. She didn't think that it would be a good idea to berate them for waiting until now to think to ask women who had overcome an educational system that didn't like the idea of women being educated for ideas. Truth be told, she was surprised that they had gotten to the idea this quickly. She had been entirely expecting the first mostly female class to be in high school before it dawned on them to ask women how to make the system more friendly to women.

"I think that's a wonderful idea Mr. Young. Lord knows that I had to get past a few obstacles on my way to a doctorate."

"Exactly. We were hoping that you & other successful women could provide us with a few insights that perhaps we haven't had yet."

"Well, right off the top of my head, you could make sure that your teachers aren't telling young girls to avoid higher education."

Many of them looked at her confused.

"From the very moment that I developed an interest in chemistry back in middle school, right through to getting my doctorate, I was constantly being told by teachers that science was men's work & that I should give it up for something more… womanly."

Barbara was surprised by how many of the men opened her notebooks & wrote down her suggestion to make sure that teachers weren't actively discouraging women. Seven years into the birth ratio anomaly & they were only just now realizing that they should check for this.

"Obviously, such behavior is no longer something that can be tolerated. While it may make some uncomfortable, we're going to need to reverse that trend & actively encourage girls into industry, science & all employment levels of society."

"If you're serious about that endeavor, I have another suggestion for you."

"We're all ears Dr. Collins."

As the men in the room looked to her for her advice, Barbara felt a strange feeling. She felt valued. For the first time in her life, all of the men in the room were not just respecting her opinion, they were asking for it.

"Well, you may want to see if you can hire on a few female teachers in some of these fields, that way the students can see that women can succeed in these areas. When I was pursuing my degrees in chemistry, literally every teacher that I had was a man. It sent a strong message to the handful of women in the class. This course of study was not for us."

Again, the men took careful notes. One of the younger men, a principal at some Maryland school or another looked up from his notes.

"Perhaps, it might also be beneficial to have some successful women come to some schools to give presentations on what they do & to encourage young girls to pursue higher education."

"That would be a very good idea."

Once more, they all noted it down in their books. Barbara watched as her opinion as a woman & a scientist was respected & honestly didn't know what to do with herself.

July 4th, 1972
Berkley, California

In a small class that had been set aside for club activities, a group of students calling themselves the UC1983 had gathered to hear the president's Independence Day announcement. The University of California 1983 Movement had almost a thousand members consisting of current students, former students, teachers, a few local politicians & a growing number of people in society. Yet it was here, in this small classroom, that a dozen individuals, representing the unofficial leadership of the leaderless group, had gathered to strategize. As one might suspect, the room smelt of a certain herb that was technically illegal.

This emergency meeting on Independence Day had been called in order to see if there were any last-minute changes that they needed to make to their protest plans. Independence Day, or 1983 day as they liked to call it, was a day that they devoted to protesting the draft & wars that the US had no business being in. At least as far as they were concerned.

With the Independence Day parades set to begin all over the state of California in two hours, they were going over everything quickly when a student burst into the room with a large radio in hand. He swept some of his elbow length hair out of his face before explaining his bursting in.

"The President is making an emergency announcement about the war in Vietnam, I thought that you would all want to hear it."

They all instantly agreed & put the radio on the teacher's desk where a number of their plans lay haphazardly sprawled out. Plugging the cumbersome radio in, they turned up the volume & listened as the broadcaster mentioned that the announcement was coming live from the Oval Office.

"Again, we do not know what the purpose of this announcement is. Some speculate that President Humphrey will be announcing a new round of drafts to fortify our forces in Vietnam. A small number of analysts believe that this may be an announcement of peace talks. We will soon find out as the President is about to start. Ladies & gentleman, the President of the United States."

Everyone in UC1983 paid close attention as the President started talking.

"My fellow Americans. For many years now, we have been fighting a long, arduous battle in Vietnam to hinder the spread of communism & authoritarianism to a people who crave freedom & democracy. The cost of the war has been catastrophic in both dollars, damages, & lives lost. Well over two million Americans have served to combat the red spread, & sadly, many of them have not come home. The sacrifices this nation has made have been costly, which is why I am delighted to announce that going forward, the United States of America will no longer need to play as important a role in the conflict as we have up until now."

The unofficial leaders of UC1983 stood around the radio, feeling hope that the war might be coming to an end.

"While the conflict rages on & is in fact likely to continue for a number of months, possibly even years, America will no longer need to devote such vast resources & personnel to the conflict. Because of this, it brings me great pleasure to announce that as of today, no more Americans will be drafted to serve in the war."

The members of the 1983 movement erupted into cheers. Ending the draft for Vietnam had been one of their main goals for years. It seemed that the President's speech writer had known that many people would be cheering, & so the President had paused his speech for a moment, giving people all over the country a chance to say quiet down. As the students & teachers in the room calmed themselves, the Presidents continued.

"While those drafted up to & including the 3rd of July will be expected to serve their time in Vietnam until either the end of the war or until they rotate out, there will be no more Americans drafted into the war. I ask all Americans today to pray for a swift end to the conflict, & to hope that we never again need to implement a draft. God bless you all, & happy Independence Day."

As the broadcast ended, the group started cheering once more, until it dawned on them that a number of the protests that they had organized were in opposition to the draft that had just ended. With time until the parades & protests began quickly flowing away, they all quickly agreed to move people protesting the draft to groups protesting the war. They then made a mad dash to the payphones to get the message out so that protests all over California could rearranged at the very last minute.

August 22nd, 1972
CBS Newsroom

As the commercials wore on for the viewers at home, Walter Cronkite looked over his notes as his guest was prepared. Confident that he had everything in order, he sat up as the producer counted down until they were back on the air.

"Welcome back to our special edition of the evening news. Over a month ago, the country was shocked when Richard Nixon won the republican primaries to become the presidential nominee for the republicans to challenge incumbent Hubert Humphrey. Tonight, to discuss the issues of Nixon's campaign, we have a special guest, a member of the California senator's campaign team, Larry Tolls. It's a pleasure to have you on the show Larry."

The lights came on to reveal Larry, a relatively young man with a severe buzzcut, a million-dollar smile, & a red tie with his grey suit.

"It's a pleasure to be here Walter."

"Now, Larry, A lot of people on the left, & the right, & in every other facet of American life are wondering, why is Nixon running again? In 1968, he was thoroughly defeated by more than a hundred electoral votes. Even if the votes awarded to Wallace were added to Nixon's, Nixon would still have loss by almost ninety votes."

Larry chuckled.

"Yes, 1968 was not a good year for us Walter. But 1968 was a unique situation. The democrats were succeeding in beating the Soviets to the Moon, people weren't as sick of the Vietnam war as they are now, & the birth ratio anomaly was still fairly new & the country had hope that it could be resolved quickly. Clearly, the situation has changed, therefore, we feel that Richard Nixon will be significantly more successful this time around."

"Indeed, the situation has changed & it continues to change. Ever since Nixon announced his candidacy, he's been talking about ending America's involvement in the Vietnam war."

"That's right Walter. We've been involved in Vietnam for almost a decade now & quite frankly, nobody can really explain why we're still there or what we can possibly hope to gain. With everything that the democrats have poured into Asia, first in Korea, & now in Vietnam, what exactly are we getting for it? That's why Nixon has vowed to bring our boys back home."

"While that's something that most people in America support, it was less than two months ago that President Humphrey announced an end to the draft for Vietnam. Since then, we've seen more & more soldiers coming home as they rotate out of the war. It seems that Humphrey is winding down America's involvement in the conflict, what is this doing to Nixon's chances at winning in November?"

Larry nodded his head for a moment.

"Well, that certainly wasn't something that we saw coming. While we are glad the democrats are finally seeing reason & are winding down our efforts on the other side of the Pacific, the war continues. The men that were drafted just before July will still have to go through training & then earn enough rotation points to come home. This typically takes two years. So even with Humphrey winding down the war, it'll take until 1974 for these last draftees to come home. We need to pull out now."

"A lot of people on both sides of the aisle are saying that just pulling out all of our forces at once could destabilize conditions, giving the communist forces just the opening they need to make large gains."

"That is a minor risk. Obviously, we would coordinate with other countries that are still in the war to ensure that there's as little chaos as possible."

"It's good to hear that you plan on being careful in your goal of withdrawing."

Walter took a second to flip his note cards.

"It's long been known that there's more than one way to defeat the Soviets. One of those ways was by winning the space race. Nixon has stated that not only does he not want to continue the Apollo program after twenty flies, but he wants to scrap the Apollo program outright. If he got his way, Apollos twenty, nineteen

& possibly even eighteen would never fly. Do you really think that it's such a good idea to give up our lead in space?"

"Well, it's not like we're giving it up to anyone. Like you said, we went to the Moon to beat the reds there. Mission accomplished. We've been there a few times now & they can't even get off the ground. The fact of the matter is that the Apollo program is expensive, & other than collecting a few rocks to do some esoteric science on, what value are we getting from pouring two or three percent of the federal budget into it?"

"Well, the Soviets haven't exactly given up. Reports have shown that they are continuing to develop their super heavy lift rocket & some analysists are saying that it appears that they've made progress. What happens if we give up on the Moon & then a year later, they start going there & building military installations?"

"Going to the Moon is even more expensive for them than it is for us since they have a smaller budget & a bigger population. Even if they can get there, odds are that they'll just gather a few rocks of their own & pat themselves on the back. We have more important issues here at home, such as our impending population crisis."

Cronkite quickly switched out his notes again.

"I'm glad that you brought that up. One of the core components of Nixon's platform is his promise to come up with a solution to the birth ratio crisis."

"That a massive priority to us Walter. The US is already missing seventeen million boys & around the world, well over four hundred million boys have been born as girls. We need solutions now."

"I don't think that anyone is arguing against that, but your campaign has yet to address what it would do differently than the current administration. What changes does Nixon plan on making?"

"An excellent question. Obviously, we would make sure that the best scientists & doctors in the country are working for the commission. The rate of progress that the current team has made has been devastatingly slow. Clearly, there's room for improvement."

"To be fair, most of the researchers in the commission are considered the best in the business that America has to offer. I would also point out that all over the world, the best scientists have been working on it for seven years & they've made even less progress than we have. Simply saying that you're going to find better people is a bit simplistic."

"Obviously overhauling & expanding the commission's staff is not our only solution. We're working on a number of ideas for how we can improve the situation, I wouldn't want to offer up details before we've had a chance to finish analyzing all of the data & reports to make sure that our plan is perfectly tailored to address the crisis."

Cronkite took a moment to let that response settle in with the audience at home.

"Staying on the topic of the birth ratios for a moment longer, a number of people on the left have criticized your platform for ignoring the effects that the birth ratio crisis will have on our society. As you yourself said, the new generation has seventeen million more girls than boys & that's just in the states. Even if a solution were found today, the shortage of men will have an effect on society in the 1980s. Yet, your platform makes no mention of how we might prepare America for a society in which an entire age range is only ten percent male. Is the republican party looking into solutions for how the economy will work or how marriage or getting pregnant will work?"

"Another great question Walter. We're fairly confident that as long as a solution is found soon, then society should be able to compensate by simply adjusting hiring policies for a few years. Once the balance is restored, this will be nothing more than a blip."

"While I can see how that might work for the economy if a solution is found soon, what happens if we don't find a solution until 1990, or 2010?"

"We're confident that it won't take that long once we've made our adjustments to the commission. If we win the election in November, I predict a solution will be discovered by the end of seventy-four & fully implemented by the end of seventy-five."

"Even if your prediction holds true, I don't see how just changing a few hiring policies will make up for a ten-year age range that is ninety percent female. Who will these women marry or have children with? Even if we only implement temporary societal changes for this generation, we will have to make changes, or starting in the eighties, we'll see a population crash."

"One problem at a time Walter. Once we figure out how to fix the birth ratio anomaly, then we'll figure out how to clean up the mess. I do believe that a good part of why we're seeing so little progress in the commission is because so many resources are being devoted to deciding if we should allow men to have harems or if we should let women marry each other. We need to stop thinking about ridiculous notions like those & work the problem."

While Walter tried his best to remain neutral in these discussions, as he looked to the camera, he couldn't completely conceal his concern for what he was hearing.

"We all agree that the problem needs to be worked on. However, it looks like you're not taking into account the possibility that you might not find a solution. Sure, you're very confident, but it takes more than confidence to fix a problem. What if you don't find a solution, or what if the solution is so expensive that we can't afford it? What is the republican plan if it takes another twenty years to find a solution?"

September 18th, 1972
Robinson Home, Queens, New York

David Robinson looked over the letter that his daughter had brought home from school. For about the hundredth time, David wished that his daughter had been born a year or two later. Having been born just three months after the anomaly began, she was always among the first children to be subject to teachers who had no experience with almost all female classes. First her kindergarten class where nobody could figure out if the boys should be allowed to play with girl's toys & vice versa. Then there was the first grade where the teachers didn't know how to respond when some of the girls started teasing & making fun of the few boys in the class.

Now Elizabeth was starting the second grade & her teachers were proving just as ill equipped to teach female classes as the previous teachers. The latest issue was from the gym teacher, who also served as the coach of the football team for children aged six & seven. Now that the entire first & second grades combined contained only ten boys, & only three of them wanted to play football, there weren't enough boys for the youngest football team.

David wondered why they were waiting until the school year had started before having this meeting since they had known last year that this was going to happen. The letter proposed a number of potential solutions that the school wanted to discuss since they didn't want to disband the team.

The first idea was to change the age ranges of the teams so that the youngest team would have third-grade students on it. Then there was the idea of seeing if they could somehow merge their team with a few neighboring schools. If they combined their team with three or four others, they could have enough players for a full team. Another idea, the one that seemed the craziest, was to make the team co-ed, which would make locker room discussions very difficult. The last idea was to make the team a girls' team & hope that they could convince eleven girls in the first & second grades to play.

When they got the letter, Mary was concerned about the issue until David asked Elizabeth if she was interested in playing football. Elizabeth looked at him as if he was an idiot & said no. With that matter solved, David declared that the problem didn't affect them & they didn't have to worry about what the school did. Even if they let girls play, they couldn't force them to & they most certainly couldn't force Elizabeth to play.

Still, it shook him to realize that most of the options that they could come up with to save football were pipedreams at best. Watching football with his friends, or the Super Bowl with his family was something that he had been doing since he was a boy. If the schools couldn't even drum up enough players to make teams, what would happen to the NFL? Would colleges still have football teams in fifteen years? Would there no longer be enough interest in football to justify the costs of the Super Bowl?

He put the letter down & walked by Elizabeth's room for a moment. He wondered if she would one day cheer on NFL teams made of women. Would it still be the same sport if there weren't enough men left that were interested in playing the game?

Putting such thoughts aside, he headed downstairs to sit next to his wife. There was some new show that she had heard about & she wanted to watch the series premier with him.

"Is Elizabeth asleep up there?"

"Yes Mary. She's gone out like a light."

"Good, from what I hear, this show is a bit too racy for children."

"What's it called again?"

"Nine girls & a guy. It's about the lives of a bunch of twenty-year-old people set in 1992."

As he sat down, the commercials came to an end & the series began. It opened with a clip from a speech given by some government official in sixty-five, telling the country about the anomaly. It then cut to a scene of a house with a caption that read September 20th, 1992. The camera moved through an empty house until it moved through an open door into the bedroom where it then showed two half naked women, covered only by the sheets that they were tangled in, waking up next to each other. David & Mary were stunned as the two women kissed each other good morning.

"Good morning, Alice."

"Morning Margaret."

"Today's the day."

"That's right, tomorrow will be waking up in a hotel in Miami, celebrating our honeymoon."

As they started to kiss, the camera zoomed out & panned away to show a pair of white suits. As the opening title sequence started to play, David looked to Mary.

"If this show doesn't get cancelled by dawn, then we really are in a whole new world."

"Definitely."

"A sitcom that starts with two women in bed on their wedding day, & they're going to wear suits. If this is how they open, I can't wait to see how this show plays out."

October 25th, 1972
NASA Headquarters, Washington DC

The office room where the administrator of NASA met with individuals from intelligence organizations was coming to be known as the black box, or the black room, or the black hole. Several employees constantly wondered what was going on in there & what was being said during these top-secret meetings.

"I've had to stop eating supper when we're watching that show. Last week when the soldier came home from war & her girlfriend cried & kissed her at the front door, I damn near chocked on my potato."

Smith, the man from the NSA, laughed & nodded his head at what the administrator of NASA had just said.

"I know. I mean, when I got home from Korea, that's exactly how my girlfriend greeted me, with tears & a kiss, but it's just so weird seeing it on TV between two women."

"You know, I hear that eight different state legislatures are trying to sue to get the show taken off the air."

"I hadn't heard that, but I have heard that the FBI is hiring female agents for the first time since hoover took over."

It was at that moment that the door swung open & a sharply dressed man named Gerald Hives walked in with a set of CSI dossiers under his arm. He quickly closed the door behind him & handed out the dossiers to the other two men in the room. Mark took the dossier from the agent.

"Hello Agent Hives, it's good to see you too."

Hives looked up at Mark & agent Smith before it clicked in his head that he had forgotten to say hello.

"Sorry, it's been a long few days for me. Hello Mark, it's good to see you again. It's also good to see you again, Smith. Still don't believe that your name is actually John Smith."

"Well, that's what my mother called me. What's today's cloak & dagger about? I assume that it's something to do with the Soviet space program."

"You assumed correctly. The dossiers that you see contain reports on the latest Soviet test of the N1 rocket for their manned moon program."

Mark opened the dossier to see a lot of Russian documents & their translations as well as a number of satellite photos with labels & scales.

"This looks suspiciously like they've made progress. Just the scale of the photos & the labels tells me this rocket got a hell of lot further than the previous ones."

Agent Smith looked over the photos & came to the same conclusion.

"You're both right. Our new specialists have explained to us that the rocket's first stage succeeded with only a minor bug. The test only went wrong when the stage failed to separate from the rest of the rocket."

Mark looked at the reports submitted by the Soviet rocket scientists & agreed. The first stage of the flight had been rocky, but it had worked until it came time to separate.

"Damn. If they've got a working first stage, then they could be just a matter of months away from a working moonshot rocket."

Agent Smith looked up in a rare moment of worry.

"I assume then that they're increasing resources to the program & getting ready for another test."

"No."

Agent Hives stood there as Agent Smith & the administrator of NASA looked at him confused.

"They are pulling resources away from their lunar space program. They're pouring more resources into robotic exploration of the solar system."

Mark put his dossier down on the desk.

"Does this mean that they're actually giving up this time?"

"Unlikely, they aren't moving too many specialists away from the program. Our best understanding is that they don't believe America will keep going to the Moon after Apollo twenty, so they're taking their time & telling their engineers to take their time & get it right. N1 rockets are expensive, they're tired of them exploding. So, they're going to work all of the kinks out, wait for America to call it quits, & take the Moon once we have given up on going there."

Agent Smith pinched the bridge of his nose.

"They want to say that America is giving up because it's too hard for us while they send up a fleet of their cosmonauts."

"We think so."

"When is Apollo twenty supposed to go up?"

Both agents turned to Mark.

"July of seventy-four."

"Can they have the N1 working by then?"

"Hard to say, we were able to get the Saturn V up & running in a few years, if they're just ironing out glitches, then it's definitely possible. Although, even if it does work in seventy-four, they'll probably test it a few more times & then there's the issue of their lunar lander. They'll want their hero cosmonaut coming home so they can parade him around."

"So probably in seventy-six or seventy-seven, but we can't rule anything out for seventy-five."

"Basically."

The three of them sat in the black hole, realizing that the space race might not be as over as everyone thought that it was.

November 9th, 1972
Oval Office

President Humphrey looked out the window at the snow gently falling on the ground. The last two days had been gut-wrenching as votes had been counted with numbers so close that by the end of the second day, newscasters were refusing to venture even a guess at who would win the election. With the third day of counting nearly over, the race was neck in neck.

With several states having been won by no more than a few thousand votes, if that, he knew that no matter the results, at least twenty states would be spending the next week conducting recounts & audits. Never in all of his years had he seen a race so close. He knew that he had no hope of winning Alaska, the numbers that were already being reported were proof of that. It was now down to California.

Assuming that the recounts didn't change anything, California would be the determining factor & it was split down the middle. With the lead dancing between him & Nixon, he wished that he had listened to advisors earlier in the war. Sure, not cancelling Apollo & drawing more anticipation on twenty with a lady astronaut had allowed him to hold onto Florida, Alabama & Texas, & sure, his support for the ERA had women all over the country cheering for him, especially now that twenty-six states had already ratified it, but then there was Vietnam.

He should have learned from Johnson's lesson. That was why he was even President to begin with. That quagmire of a war was an albatross, an anchor around the neck of any president. Sure, he had scraped back some votes by finally ending the draft & starting to dial down America's efforts. But he had clearly waited too long. Countless states that had voted for him four years ago were turning to Nixon.

It was as he was deep in contemplation that one of his aides entered the Oval Office with a sheet of paper in his hands.

"Excuse me, Mr. President."

"Is that an update for California in your hand?"

"Yes sir, their final numbers are in."

"Well don't keep me waiting. What is it?"

"Oh, sorry sir, you won California by about four thousand votes, which brings you up to two hundred & seventy-one electoral votes."

"Two hundred & seventy-one electoral votes. Jesus."

"It was a close one sir."

"Was? It still is, do you have any idea how many states I only just managed to win? If one recount goes wrong, it'll be Nixon sitting here come January."

"Still sir, congratulations."

"For what, even if the recounts maintain the result, this isn't a win."

"Sir?"

The aide looked confused as the President continued to stare out the window.

"Back in sixty-eight, I got three hundred & one electoral votes. My stubbornness in Vietnam has sent millions of Americans fleeing to the republicans. They took congress, they took governorships, we barely held onto the senate. A number of state legislatures just turned red which means that progress on ratifying the ERA is going to slow right down to a crawl. Instead of months, it'll take years, assuming it passes at all. I'll still be sitting in this chair next year, assuming recounts & all, but this was a loss."

"I understand sir."

"I hope so. We have two years to convince America to come back to the left. If the republicans win in the midterms, we'll be completely crippled. Then it'll be far too easy for them to win the white house in seventy-six."

December 7th, 1972
Rural Alabama

The crate made a loud thud as it slammed down on Ronnie's desk. He looked at the massive crate & the bulky equipment inside of it for a moment.

"John, I know that you said that some of this equipment isn't close to being state of the art, but some of this looks like ya got it out of WW2."

"Well, some of it is. WW2, Korea, even one from the early days of Vietnam. Military surplus, God's gift to America. They all work."

Ronnie picked up one of the smaller signal jammers. It was about the size of a New York phonebook & it looked like it was built by NASA.

"I don't suppose that these come with manuals?"

"Sorry Ronnie. What you see is what you get."

"Well, we'll just have to figure it out."

Ronnie wondered if these surprisingly heavy devices would make a lot of noise as his militia intended to install them in their bedrooms.

"Ronnie. Can I ask ya something?"

"What's up John?"

"You really think this will block them government baby satellites?"

"Of course they will. Satellites give off radio signals, these things jam radio signals. We install these in our bedrooms, get them working & in a night or two, our women will start making sons again. Nice & easy."

"I hope you're right."

"Don't worry John. Say, the guy who runs the store, did he give you any grief over all of this?"

"What'd ya mean?"

"Did he ask any questions, like say, why are you buying a whole bunch of signal jammers?"

"Nope."

"Really. Old Tom didn't ask you any questions."

"Nah, he was listening to the news on the radio, he was real interested in it."

"What was so interesting that old Tom didn't care about what he was selling?"

"NASA. Apparently, Apollo seventeen launched this morning. They are saying that they put a rock scientist on this mission. A geologist."

"Nice story. They ain't putting no geologist on a mission to service the baby satellites."

"I figured that Ronnie, but I didn't say nothing."

"Good job. The last thing that we need is attention on us. We'll set these up, have some kids, then we'll be able to show the world that we were right & the feds & the commies are doing this to us."

"Sounds good to me Ronnie. I'll try & get some more jammers. From other surplus stores, in other states."

"That's why I put you in charge of logistics for this mission John. In the meantime, get the others here tonight so we can start figuring these things out."

John actually saluted Ronnie before leaving to make sure that the rest of the guys knew to be in Ronnie's barn. Ever since that mall takeover that went sideways, Ronnie Adams had been living in a country house that technically belonged to his aunt under her maiden name. The numbers in his militia had dropped off after the mall incident, but he was slowly rebuilding. He routinely held militia meetings on his property, far from prying neighbors & authorities.

Looking down at the jammers, he wondered for a moment how long they would have to be in the jammed areas that these things created before they could make boys again. He hoped that it was like a light switch, turn it on, maybe give it a minute & presto, you can father sons again. If it took days or longer, that could be a problem. John had told him that some of these jammers had a range of less than twenty feet. It would be hard to convince a woman to stay within twenty feet of one of these things for days just so that you can make baby boys.

Hell, it would be hard to convince some of the men to do that & some of them ain't exactly picky.

December 24th, 1972
Montreal, Canada

Rebecca's threat still lingered in her mind. Janet had sworn that this was going to be the day that she came out to her family. She had been telling herself that it would work out because her parents liked watching Nine Girls & a Guy. That was the closest thing that she had ever had to proof that they might accept her. With that in mind, she had sworn to Rebecca that this holiday was the one where she would finally admit the truth to her family & get to kiss her girlfriend in front of other people.

Rebecca went along with it, not believing a word of it. As much as she wanted to believe that there would be a place where they didn't have to feel like they had to hide, Rebecca kind of enjoyed punishing Janet for breaking her promise to herself.

Last Christmas, she brought a pair of fuzzy handcuffs so that if someone heard them & opened their bedroom door, Janet wouldn't have been able to cover herself up. On Canada Day, she had done the same, but with the covers thrown off of them & the lights on in case anyone walked through the unlocked door. When Thanksgiving rolled around, Rebecca upped her punishment by making Janet handcuff her to the bed & making Janet go down on her while she lay there moaning in the unlocked room.

The whole ride to her parents' house, Janet had been wondering what kind of punishment Rebecca had in store for her if she broke her promise & didn't come out again. The only thing that broke Janet's nervousness was the news stories on the radio about the success of Apollo seventeen, the last of Australia's servicemen coming home from Vietnam & an unfaithful elector in Virginia bringing Humphrey's win up to two hundred & seventy-two electoral votes. It was only when they pulled up to the house, parked the car & were about to get out that Rebecca grabbed Janet's arm & told her the price of breaking her promise again.

"I've got Richard in my luggage."

Janet paled. Richard was the name of their favorite man shaped bedroom toy.

"Why in the hell did you bring him?"

"Because if you don't come out to your family today, like you promised that you would, you're going to cuff me to your bed tonight, & you're going to fuck me with him."

What little color had still been in Janet's face drained away. Every single time that Janet had used Richard on her, she screamed like a porn star. The whole house would come running to see what was going on.

"You wouldn't Rebecca."

Janet's heart was racing in both fear & arousal. She knew that she could just not cuff her girlfriend to the bed tonight & not ravage her with their favorite toy. Rebecca couldn't actually make her do it. Still, a part of her liked the way that Rebecca's punishments kept getting more severe every time that she broke this promise. She could almost see herself pumping Richard into Rebecca with one hand while trying to keep Rebecca quiet with the other & knowing that one cry of pleasure could finally reveal the truth.

Rebecca had just grinned wickedly, knowing that Janet would do it as an apology for only acknowledging her as a friend once again. She didn't like the idea that she might humiliate the woman that she loved, but she knew that Janet wanted to come out & that she needed a little help in the courage department, even if it was only a bluff.

Janet had managed to regain her composure in time to be greeted by her father John. Her mother Jillian & her sister Jane were both in the kitchen working on the feast. Jane's husband still hadn't changed his name from Harold to Jerold & all of the business of their J names brough a fit of laughter to Rebecca as it did every time they got together.

Endless hours passed, John, Harold & Rebecca watched sports & kept an eye on baby June. Janet almost ended up slicing into her fingers with the carrot peeler a few times as she wondered how she was going to tell her family. Janet could feel a mountain of anxiety building in her chest as the day wore on.

Eventually, supper was served. The family gathered in the dining room & admired the feast fit for a king. The food was passed around & as he often did, John stood up & asked anyone if they had any announcements.

Jane stood up & told them all that she & Harold had decided that they were going to try for another baby, in a year or two, when June wasn't running them ragged. Everyone applauded them for their growing family & their wisdom in waiting until they had a bit more energy to start the job all over again.

When John turned his attention to Janet, Rebecca expected Janet to answer with a polite no to the question of any announcements. She was surprised when Janet stood up.

"Actually… I do… have something to say…"

Janet's heart was pounding like a jackhammer in her chest. She had spent the last fifteen years making this announcement in her mind, or her bathroom mirror, but now that the time had come, she couldn't remember a single word of all of the ways that she had come up with to say it. So, she just said whatever came out of her mouth.

"I've actually been meaning to tell you all this for a very, very long time. Since high school actually. I'm… I'm…"

The whole family looked at her as she struggled to get the words out. She looked to Rebecca for a moment before turning back to her family.

"I'm… gay."

Her parents were dumbstruck. Harold sat there with his mouth actually hanging open. Jane sipped her wine & smiled & June sat there looking at her food.

After another moment of stunned silence, where Janet felt like an animal in the zoo that had just said hello to the crowd in perfect English, Jane refilled her wine glass & turned to her mother.

"I told you that it was a bit weird that she was always bringing a… what did she call it, a good friend to family events."

Jillian turned to Jane with an angry look.

"Jane, don't go bringing Rebecca into this."

"No Mom, Jane is right."

"What?"

Jillian just stared at Janet confused.

"Rebecca isn't just my friend; she's been my girlfriend for six years now."

Jillian sat there shocked while Jane continued.

"See Mom, & before Rebecca, it was what's her name, her good friend form high school."

Again, there was silence as John, Jillian & Harold desperately tried to catch up to what Janet had announced. Janet just stood there for a very awkward moment until the silence was deafening.

"Well… say something. Dad…?"

John leaned forward & opened his mouth for a second before speaking.

"Gay… gay like… gay… like Linda & Pam."

Jane laughed hysterically as her father referenced the only lesbians he had ever heard of; the characters from the sitcom they watched. Janet just stood there, dumbstruck that that was the comparison he was making. Rebecca finally spoke up.

"I'd say we're more like Ashley & Clara, just without that Martha business. Three's a crowd."

Janet sat down as her parents went over every scene that had Ashley & Clara, but not Martha in it. Jane closed Harold's mouth & picked up her fork.

"Congrats Sis, I think Mom & Dad need a minute, or a month to work through that one. I suspected something was up when I heard you laugh at Rebecca's jokes for the first time. You laughed the same way I laughed at Harold's jokes."

Janet laughed as Harold started coming back to reality. Jane took a bite out of her mashed potatoes.

"We should probably start on supper before it gets cold."

They all started eating supper very awkwardly. Throughout supper & afterwards, the conversation was rather subdued. Eventually, John & Jillian went off to bed, still in shock. Shortly afterwards, Jane & Harold decided to turn in for the night.

"Janet, we're heading up to bed."

"Alright Sis, we're probably going to head up in a minute or two."

"Glad to hear that you're going to be here in the morning."

"I'm glad that everyone isn't upset."

"I see this as a good thing Janet."

"You do?"

"Yeah, when June starts dating, it's going to be slim pickings in the boy department. I plan on dropping her off with you when she has questions about other girls."

Janet laughed & agreed to be June's fairy godmother if the need arose. Shortly afterwards, Janet & Rebecca were turning in for the night, with the door locked for the first time in over a year.

"I'm proud of you Janet. That takes guts."

"I couldn't have done it without you Rebecca, especially without you threatening to wail like a banshee. You don't still intend to use Richard do you, my folks are still shaken, I don't need them to hear it."

"No, I actually didn't bring Richard. That was a bluff."

"a bluff! You were bluffing!"

"Come on Janet, you know that I wouldn't humiliate you like that."

"I mean, yeah, but still, that was cruel of you to bluff like that."

"I know."

"Thank you, Rebecca."

Janet kissed Rebecca before they cuddled together.

The next morning, Janet's mother had an uncountable number of questions for her daughter. Many of them were questions that Janet didn't want to answer & many more were questions that Jillian clearly wasn't ready to hear the answer to. As everyone was getting ready to head home in the afternoon, John had only one question, for Rebecca, as they were leaving.

"Say, before you go, I was wondering?"

"What's up John?"

"Would you be willing to change your name to Jennifer?"

After a few seconds of silence, everyone burst out laughing hysterically.

1973

January 23rd, 1973
Sacramento, California

Across the country, liberals, progressives & even a small number of conservatives were cheering as the new year got off to an incredible start. As Patricia Torres sat down with some of the other leading members of the Matriarch Party to dissect their recent election loss, she was still thrilled about some of the things that were going on in the country at large. As the meeting hadn't started yet, a number of the women present were still talking about the roe case from Texas that the Supreme Court had just used a few days ago to legalize abortion nationwide. Patricia sat down & as the group quieted down, she opened the meeting with some news.

"Before we begin, I just got off of the phone with my contact at the Sacramento Bee. Despite the massive republican wins a few months ago, progress marches on. The West Virginia & Pennsylvania legislatures voted today & they both ratified the ERA."

The women before her cheered as twenty-eight states had now ratified the ERA. With only ten more ratifications needed, they were all confident that the Equal Rights Amendment would pass within the next three or four years.

"Alright everyone, I'm thrilled too. We're inching closer to equality. Now we need to figure out why we only got six percent of the vote & how we can change that next year."

One of the women, Kathleen Howard, a relatively new face in the movement, sat up straight & spoke up.

"Part of the problem is that every time the conservatives say that they'll come up with a solution for the gender imbalance, everyone forgets that it's been going on for seven & a half years already. We need to remind people that even if a solution is found & implemented by the end of the year, there will still be major issues that need to be addressed & the republicans, as well as a number of democrats are just not proposing solutions or even acknowledging the long-term issues."

Everyone in the meeting could recall a number of interviews & debates where the question of how society will handle the lack of sons in ten or fifteen years was either answered with platitudes or just waved off as something that'll be easily handled.

"We need to focus on what's going to be happening after 1983 when these kids grow up."

"Exactly. If the elementary schools have shown us anything over the last two years, it's that even the ones that did try to prepare were not ready for grades that were almost entirely female. What's going to happen when these children grow up & walk into a world built by men, for men."

"Alright Kathleen, what do we do about it, & how can we convince more people than just hardcore liberals to go along with it?"

"We do it by doing the same thing that the military is doing."

All of the other women in the party meeting looked around at each other. Imitating the military wasn't exactly something they were known to do.

"You're going to need to explain that one a bit Kathleen."

"The military knows that in 1983, their recruitment numbers are going to plumet. Even if they can triple the percentage of men volunteering for service, they would still be losing more than half of their annual recruits. On top of that, implementing a draft will probably be an administration ending mistake. So, they've accepted the fact that they will have to open up recruitment to women."

"How does that help us here & now?"

"Because they aren't going to wait until 1983 to open up the doors for women. They've been running studies over the last few years. Studies on everything like how to convince women to enlist, how to train them, how to build units & platoons out of them. On top of that, they're going to open up recruitment for women long before 1983, possibly before 1980, that way when the transition happens, they'll already be used to working with large numbers of women."

"They're making the necessary changes before the problem arrives."

"Exactly. We can't just say that when 1983 rolls around, we'll have a solution ready to go. We need to implement these changes before the new generation shows up & disrupts everything. New hiring policies, new job recruitment campaigns, college acceptance policies, lesbian marriage, polygamy. Whatever we are going to be doing in 1983, we need to start doing them now. We need to show the voters that we'll have solutions by putting them in place now."

The women surrounding her agreed with her as Patricia sat there dumbfounded by the idea that their solution would come from the military of all places.

February 14th, 1973
National Institute of Health, Bethesda, Maryland

Doctor Barbara Collins marched through the building from her department on a mission. Along the way to the boss's office, she walked into Doctor Fekete who seemed to be coming from where she was going to. He lit up when he saw her.

"Barbara. How's it going?"

"It could be better Todor. My department head is sending me to deliver some final results to the boss."

"Hope it's good news, he needs all the good he can get right now."

"Does that mean that he's in a mood?"

"It sure does Barbara."

Barbara took a deep breath.

"Isn't everyone thrilled by the new breakthrough in genetics?"

"They are, but he's in a funk about something else."

"Just my luck."

The two of them chatted for a moment before heading back to their jobs. Barbara made her way to the boss's office where after a quick knock, she was welcomed in. Entering his office, she saw Edward Swanson holding a glass of bourbon in one hand & holding a magazine in the other hand.

"Doctor Swanson, is everything alright?"

"No Barbara. Everything hasn't been alright for nearly eight years & today, everyone feels like pointing it out."

Edward threw the magazine onto his desk & took a sip of the bourbon. Wondering whether or not to report him for drinking on the job, she looked at the magazine & saw the reason for the bourbon. It was an issue of Nature magazine & the front cover was made to look like a missing poster announcing that there were now half a billion missing boys as that was how many more girls had been born than boys. Barbara decided not to report him.

"Rough day?"

"That's putting it mildly. You would think that everyone would be talking about how we sequenced a whole bacteria genome, meaning that we can now read dozens of genes at once instead of doing them one at a time. A quarter of our studies can now go exponentially faster. But no. Some asshole decided to crunch some numbers, so now, a week where we should be celebrating the fact that we can accelerate our progress in several studies, everyone is instead raging that we're estimated to be half a billion boys short."

He took another sip of his bourbon.

"I don't suppose that you're bringing me good news there Barbara. I could really use a pick me up."

"Sorry Edward. The final results on the study of corn syrup. It turns out that corn syrup is not causing the gender imbalance."

"Remind me again why we were testing corn syrup?"

"Because we found out that commercial production began in 1964, right around the time that ninety percent of newly conceived fetuses were suddenly female. It seemed to fit, although we wouldn't have been able to explain how that affected everyone on Earth."

"I see. & how long did it take us to figure out that it wasn't corn syrup that's causing all of this?"

"About two years."

"Well, I suppose the corn farmers of America will be happy about that. It'll be nice to know that we made someone happy."

Barbara sat down opposite Edward.

"Are you going to be okay Doctor Swanson?"

"Yeah. I'm just having one of those days where I'm wondering why in the hell I went into reproductive medicine. It seemed like such a good idea at the time. Something about money & prestige."

"You have plenty of prestige. You're in charge of the largest medical investigation in American history."

"Yep. Everyone knows my name. Too bad we haven't made any real progress in half a decade."

"Don't worry Edward. We'll find something. We still have a lot of rocks to overturn."

"Yeah, & some of those rocks are getting a bit out there. I've got one proposed study that says we should build a base on the Moon & see what the birth ratios are outside of Earth's environment."

"Wow. Okay. That's out there."

"That's nothing. It follows up by saying that if the Moon is still too heavily influenced by the Earth, we should repeat the experiment on Mars."

"Well… you might have to coordinate with NASA on that one."

"Yeah… Half a Billion boys. It's kind of hard to believe that the population has grown by over half a billion people in just eight years. But I did the math, it checks out. Just over half a billion people in less than a decade. Maybe that's the problem. Maybe there's just too damn many of us."

"So, what… Somebody just… flipped a switch… or turned a dial?"

"If only it were that simple. Then we'd just have to find the switch. No. I was just wondering how crowded the world would be in a few generations if we had kept growing at such an extreme rate."

Barbara nodded her head.

"There have been a lot of people concerned about how many people the world can sustain. I heard a few months ago that in a few years, there'll be four billion people alive on Earth."

"I don't know Barbara, maybe this anomaly will turn out to be a blessing in disguise."

"I'm pretty sure that we can't think that way Edward."

"True. Pretend that I didn't say that. What's next for the Chemistry department after corn syrup?"

"Antibiotics. It's probably pointless. Plenty of people have never had any & there's no one antibiotic group that a majority of the population has been given, but we're turning over every stone."

"To every stone being overturned."

Edward had a final sip of his bourbon before attacking the stack of papers in his inbox.

March 21ˢᵗ, 1973
Grand Forks, North Dakota

"What the hell do you mean it's cancelled?!"

The crowd of angry parents burst into a fit of yelling about how it was unacceptable & how they couldn't do this in the middle of the school year. The principal of South Fork Elementary let the parents rage for a minute. They had come a long way & they were entitled to be a bit upset about what they were being told. This was the school where children from a dozen small towns & hamlets in North Dakota came to go to school. Children from neighboring towns made up the bulk of the student body. Eventually, when the parents calmed down the principal gave the coach a nod to indicate that he should continue.

"I'm sorry. I really am. Believe me, I wish that I had different news for you. Unfortunately, due to the lack of interest & the logistical issues involved, we can no longer continue to offer football or soccer to the younger grades."

Another wave of anger ran through the crowd for a second until one man near the front stood up to demand answers.

"What happened to the interschool teams!? We've been working our asses off around our schedules for months so that the boys could make teams with the boys from other schools! Now all of a sudden, that doesn't work anymore. What's going on!"

A number of the parents nodded their heads in agreement. The coach took a breath & tried to explain.

"The problem is that too many boys from these two sports have quit the teams. Don't forget, it hasn't been easy on anyone. Combining teams from four different schools has led to logistical nightmares. It's hard to coordinate a team when they are spread out across four different schools. Even here, this news is being broken to the parents in multiple meetings because we couldn't coordinate a parent teacher meeting for the parents of four schools."

His attempt to explain the situation wasn't going well. It didn't help when a large woman with slightly greyed brunette hair stood up to speak.

"So, because a few boys in the other schools couldn't be bothered to keep playing on the team that they agreed to play on, my boy has to give up football? Why don't you get off your ass & find some more boys from these four schools to fill out the team!"

The crowd cheered as the coach took his cap off & spoke to them.

"We tried. We held a new round of tryouts. We made it very clear that we would accept any boy that showed up onto the team. The simple fact is that even offering team spots to any boy that showed up, we couldn't get enough boys in these grades in these four schools to make a full team."

Many in the crowd didn't believe him. Many more weren't happy about what he said. As some of them cried out about whether there was anything that he could do, he continued despite knowing they were about to get a whole lot angrier.

"There's nothing that we can do I'm afraid. We can't force the boys to play. We can't include boys from the third grade, they're too large to play against the younger children. The only way that we can get enough players to make a team is if we make the teams coed, & that…"

Many parents in the crowd were not having that. As they seethed with rage at the suggestion that the boys play sports with girls on the team, the coach struggled to talk over them.

"Making the team coed is not an option, at least not this late in the year! As I was trying to say, we can't make the team coed because no other team would be allowed to compete against us & it's too late in the year to work out the locker room situation. We would need to sort that out with the other teams & schools over the summer & that was assuming that a majority of you were alright with it."

As the crowd calmed down, the coach continued.

"I know it's upsetting. Hell, I started playing football at this age right here, in this very school. I used to love competing against the teams from the schools that we're now working with. I played through middle school, high school, & college. There is nothing that I would love more than to find a way to finish the year. But the simple fact is that we don't have enough players for a team. We can't reorganize the teams with the other schools this late in the season, & we can't go coed. I'm sorry. I truly am. But for our four schools, there will be no way for the grasshopper team to continue. We'll try again next year, but for this year, I'm afraid it's done."

As the news sank in, the parents became resigned to the fact that they would be telling their sons that there would be no more football or soccer for them this year.

April 18th, 1973
Oval Office

President Humphrey walked into the oval office to find the director of the CIA seated on one of the couches. He stood up to shake the President's hand immediately.

"I assume that you're here about the situation with the N1."

"You would be correct Mr. President."

Hubert sat down on the opposite couch. In just a few hours, he was going to be briefed on the situation concerning the peace talks in Vietnam. The last thing that he needed was a second space race starting up when they hadn't even finished with the original Apollo missions.

"Give it to me straight. Are the Soviets still trying for the Moon?"

"It would seem so sir. While resources to the N1 rocket still appear to be minimal, vital resources, like engineers & scientists are still working on the project. We can't be certain of the timeline, but it looks like they're aiming for another test launch sometime next year."

Hubert sat back on the couch. The reds weren't giving up.

"They seem to be very stubborn about coming in second place several years later."

"That they are sir. We were confounded by that stubbornness. It didn't seem to make sense, especially after they moved multiple sets of resources to other projects. Normally, after such a defeat, they would try to make everyone forget about the program, pretend it didn't happen. Yet now they're continuing forward, we're not entirely sure why, but we do have a few ideas for their motivation."

"What're the ideas?"

"One idea is that they are trying to distract their people from the birth ratio crisis. Either they're trying to distract their people from the major issue because they're going to struggle to transition to a majority woman population, or they're trying to show the people that they're still strong & doing incredible things."

"They're trying to pass it off as we're still glorious, still strong, a few extra girls are nothing to worry about."

"Exactly Mr. President."

"Are there any other possible reasons for why they would still be reaching for the Moon."

"Another possible theory is that they have determined that coming in second place in a two man race a few years later is not as bad or embarrassing as giving up & never getting there at all."

"So, the race isn't over then."

"No Mr. President. It certainly isn't."

Hubert sat there silently for a moment as he contemplated what this all meant. If the Soviets landed a mission or two on the Moon, that would be alright. They would brag for a little while that they were equal to America & that would be that. But if they kept going, if they were able to regularly launch, America might have to up the ante & the Moon program was already expensive.

"Alright, if the Soviets can get to the Moon like we do with Apollo, what might we be looking at?"

"If they can get to the Moon reliably, they may decide to build a base, to show that they can have a permanent presence where we can only visit."

"Meaning that we would have to build a base up there. How much would that cost?"

"It's hard to be certain sir, but it would most likely cost somewhere on the order of five to ten billion dollars a year."

Hubert paled.

"That's about five percent of the federal budget!"

"Yes sir. We've asked NASA to perform their own analysis, including ways to make it more cost effective. But they estimate that even if they can lower the costs, it'll still cost on the order of billions of dollars a year."

"Here's hoping that the Soviets are just going for a quick look."

"One more thing sir."

"More, what now?"

"Well, it's possible that the Soviets might include female astronauts on their missions, possibly to show that communist women are just as capable as men & that even when women are in the majority, they'll still be a glorious nation."

"How does that affect us? We're putting a woman on Apollo twenty."

"Yes sir. A woman. We may want to create room for female astronauts on other missions as well, that way the Soviets won't be able to show us up. We might also want to include women in some other leadership roles in mission control."

"We probably should. Hell, we're probably going to have to in a few years anyway."

"Exactly sir."

"Make sure that I get a copy of the report from NASA. I want to know how much our options are going to cost us."

"Understood sir."

"Is there any chance that the Soviets will give up on the Moon?"

"Unless their next N1 tests go horribly wrong, I don't see them backing down sir. They've got something to prove."

"Just great."

May 10th, 1973
CBS Newsroom

Walter Cronkite read through his notes carefully. This was the biggest story in years & he was about to announce it live on the air. He couldn't afford to get it wrong. As his producer gave him the signal & counted down, he took a deep breath & readied himself as the lights came on.

"Good evening, I'm Walter Cronkite, & this is the evening news for May tenth, 1973. Our breaking story, the news that so many have been waiting to hear for several years, the Vietnam war is over."

All over the country, men & women who were only half paying attention to the news as it played in the background suddenly forgot what they were doing & watched intently, they had known about the peace talks, but they hadn't known that any real progress was being made on them.

"Reports emerged early this morning that a peace treaty has been reached & that all fighting has ceased. While many of the exact details of this treaty are not yet known, what is known is that over the coming weeks, all prisoners of war will be exchanged as American & allied forces pull back from North Vietnam."

Tens of thousands of hopeful parents watched closely, completely oblivious to their surroundings, hoping for news of when their children would be coming home.

"Unconfirmed reports tell us that American soldiers & servicemen will begin returning home in the coming days & weeks. It will take some time to fully evacuate all of our military forces from Vietnam, current estimates indicate that all of our forces should be home before August first."

Unbeknownst to Cronkite, countless people around the country started cheering as they realized that their children would be coming home soon. As they cheered, a number of people across the country wondered if perhaps their children might have come home sooner, might not have died, or come home with too few limbs if Nixon had been in charge the last five years.

July 15th, 1973
Schroter's Valley, The Moon

As over a hundred million people watched from Earth, the spidery, cramped little lunar module slowly descended to the grey surface below. Gently burning the retro rockets to come down to a safe landing, Doctor Andrew Gomez carefully navigated the lunar module away from a small impact crater that they were descending towards. As a geologist, he never imagined that he would one day be piloting a lunar module into Schroter's Valley. Yet here he was, a quarter of a million miles from home, slowly landing in the sinuous valley while the commander, Richard F. Gordon Jr. called out the time remaining on their descent fuel & the altitude.

As they reached an altitude of just ten feet above the dusty surface, the exhaust from the rockets began scattering the dust around as they slowly & carefully descended the final feet to their goal. When a red indicator light went on to show that the probes descending from the module's feet were contacting the surface, Gomez cut the engine & they slowly dropped the final three or four feet before landing on the lunar surface.

For a moment, the two men stood there in stunned silence as they took in the fact that they had landed on the Moon with plentiful fuel to spare & that their lander had almost zero degrees of tilt as they sat on the smooth surface beneath them. Richard patted Gomez on the back as Gomez called Houston on the com.

"Houston, Endurance has landed."

As the people in mission control celebrated the historic landing, David Robinson watched with his daughter Elizabeth in their home in Queens. David always loved watching the Moon landings. While many Americans were growing bored with watching men land on the Moon, David was still thrilled every time they landed & every time that they set foot in the lunar soil.

He was particularly thrilled because now that Elizabeth was eight, she wasn't just watching because she got to stay up a bit late. She was old enough to fully understand that those two men were on the Moon. The same Moon up in the sky.

"They're on the Moon Daddy!"

"That they are Elizabeth. Do you know where on the Moon?"

Elizabeth thought about it for a moment.

"Schroter's Valley!"

"That's right. They're the first people to ever go there."

"Cool!"

David was ready to tell his curious daughter all kinds of interesting things about the valley, but that was when Mary, with her pregnancy starting to show, walked in & informed them that Elizabeth's special Apollo bedtime was five minutes ago. Reluctantly, Elizabeth followed her mother to bed while David, promising to join his wife before the late hours turned early, stayed in the living room to keep watching the news.

As much as David would love to stay up nearly all night, watching the early hours of the mission unfold, he knew that he had work in the morning. He watched for another hour. An hour later, as Gomez & Gordon were doing checks & gearing up for their first moon walk, David decided to pack it in as he would need to be at work in the morning. That was when the announcement came on.

"As our Moon explorers prepare for their first steps onto the grey landscape of the Moon, NASA has just released the official crew for Apollo twenty. Joining Pete Conrad on the lunar surface next year will be Myrtle Cagle, with Jerrie Cobb as her backup. Cagle & Cobb are both veterans of the space program of a sort as they were original members of the Mercury 13, a group of women who in 1961, passed all of the same medical & psychological evaluations that male astronauts have to get through. Along with Marilynn Adams, a rookie to the space program who applied last year as part of the initiative to send women to the Moon, these three women stand as America's lady astronauts since they qualified four months ago. At the age of forty-eight, she will be the oldest person to go to the Moon, beating Alan Shepard's record by almost two full years, allowing her to push the boundaries of space travel as both the first woman & the oldest person to set foot on the Moon when she launches next year on Apollo twenty."

David turned off his television & made a mental note as he went to bed to call in sick the day that Apollo twenty landed. He intended to watch as much of that mission as he could.

August 19th, 1973
Church of the Lord's Son, Fort Worth, Texas

The morning light shone in through the large window, illuminating the pulpit as if a shaft of God's divinity was lighting up the altar. The air conditioning worked tirelessly to bring relief from the summer heat to the pregnant women in the front pew & moderate relief to the families with a son. The all-daughter families in the back had to make do with what little relief reached them. Normally, the service would have begun half an hour ago. The service was being slightly postponed this one week as it was being held in a new church, a good distance from the old church & a number of people had gotten turned around despite the directions that had been handed out & explained to them the week before.

Reverend Thomas Edwards, instead of emerging from behind the altar, walked around the large building so that he could walk in through the main entrance. The crowd watched in admiration as he approached the illuminated altar as if he were being chosen by God to lead the flock of the faithful. With the morning light shining in his hair like a fiery halo, he climbed up into the pulpit, he took his old, leather-bound bible in hand, held it up high & proclaimed to his people like a prophet.

"This! This is the word of the Lord's son!"

He then raised his hands above him.

"This! This is the church of the Lord's son!"

The congregation erupted into shouts & cheers. Thomas allowed his followers to adore him for a minute before indicating that they needed to calm down. After all, he needed to appear humble.

"Today, we separate ourselves from the archdiocese that sought to kneel before the sins of rampant feminism & we start along our new path. The true path to salvation!"

The crowd roared in support before he could continue.

"However, while I am honored to lead the Lord's flock to salvation, it is thanks to all of you that this is possible. Your vigilance against corruption, your dedication to the true way, your charity & generosity are what have made this possible. I thank you, my children, for making this possible. I only ask that you not harden your hearts to those who chose to stay with the old church. This new world that the devil & his feminist whores have unleashed onto us is a trying world. We can only hope that our wayward sheep will find their way back to the flock."

Most of the congregation cheered & applauded Thomas's words of compassion. Only a handful of women in the back, tending to five or six young daughters were not overjoyed by his speech.

"Our vigilance has been great, but it must be greater still!"

Reverend Thomas than picked up a thick book that had been sitting on the altar next to his old bible.

"This is a federal study that the commission completed & presented to the government a few days ago. I would like to thank Albert here in the second row for using his connections at the university to acquire a copy of this study for us."

Albert raised his hand modestly as a few people congratulated him.

"In this study, the commission looked at what would happen to the birth rate & the population of humanity as a result of the birth curse placed on us all by the good Lord. With this study, they sought to show how the population will change once these cursed children reach adulthood & take on the responsibility of becoming parents themselves. The news is not good."

The crowd murmured. They weren't used to the use of science in their sermons.

"The scientists say that if this curse had never happened, if we could continue to grow as we had before this all began, then by the time these cursed children retire, the population on God's Earth would have tripled to over twelve & a half billion people!"

The congregation was stunned by the numbers. It seemed impossible that there could be so many people in the world.

"Now, even I'll say that that's a bit much. They seemed to agree with me, which is why they showed what the world would be like if each woman had only two or three children. Even then, the population would still reach over eight billion. A large number, but a healthy number that we could figure out how to feed. But at last, the Lord's curse is upon us, & this must be accounted for."

The flock could almost sense that something shocking was about to be said. Many of them gripped the pews they sat on.

"In their worst-case scenario, where the curse doesn't go away & we continue to live as we are now, with a man & his wife having a global average of five children, the population would stop growing in 1995, & would begin to decline sharply. By the time that these children reached retirement age, the population would only be a quarter of what it now is, leaving the world empty as humanity slowly dies off, with each generation being smaller than the last until there were none left to carry us forward in just a few hundred years."

The crowd gasped as they imagined their grandchildren in empty cities with no sons to carry on their lines. They all looked to the preacher for guidance.

"In the study, they proclaim that if we intend to stick to traditional marriages of one man & one woman, then each & every married woman will have to have eighteen children just to maintain the size of the population. They proclaim that to be unreasonable,

& I admit, it sounds like a bit much. However, they then propose that the solution is to change our views on marriage. They say that these boys, born after 1965, should either be allowed to step out of their marriages in order to impregnate unmarried women, or that they should be allowed to take multiple wives. They proclaim that if each man could take four or five wives, then each wife would only need to have four or five children & the population could keep growing & that this would allow the other half of women to work in the economy where the missing men once worked!"

The people in his flock were shocked by what the commission had proposed. They envisioned their daughters as parts of harems or working a nine to five while once a month, some cheating husband stopped by to impregnate her. They were all shocked to attention at the sound of the thick study slamming to the ground. The good reverend had thrown it to the ground & had once again picked up his bible.

"My children, despite their own math showing them that this rampant feminism will lead us to a literal extinction, these scientists refuse to see the path to salvation! We must show God that we are worthy of his mercy!"

The congregation cheered.

"We must be vigilant! We must be faithful! Only when we are worthy will he return our sons to us! We must be loyal to the word of his son, so that we may have our own. Those of us who are righteous will bear sons into the world!"

The few families that had young sons & the families with children on the way all cheered in celebration.

"But to be righteous, we must be pure. We cannot allow even a hint of the corruption out there to infect us! Therefore, as God separates the faithful from the sinners at the gates of judgement, & as the farmer pulls weeds from his fields, we must cleanse ourselves of the unworthy. Those who's wombs have been poisoned by corruption & a lack of faith, must be cast out!"

The women with sons cheered as the women at the back with only daughters suddenly became nervous.

"From here on, any woman who births four children, & does not produce a son, must be forced to leave the church, to avoid corrupting the righteous. She & her ill seed must be cast out! Her husband will be allowed to choose if he will walk the wicked path with his wicked wife, or if he will take a new wife from within our congregation."

A number of women in the back with four or more daughters started staring either at the reverend or their own husbands who might leave them high & dry with a new way out.

"To those women who have birthed so many daughters already, fear not. The Lord is kind & forgiving, I will not cast you out just because the rules changed without notice. You will each be given one more chance to get right with the Lord & to bear your husbands a son."

The rest of the congregation applauded & complimented the reverend's generosity & mercy, comparing him to Jesus. The women who were already pregnant for the fourth, fifth, sixth or seventh time with no sons grew nervous.

September 30th, 1973
Church of the Wives of Christ, Chicago

Virginia Green stood at her pulpit with a million-dollar smile as she delivered wonderous news to her followers. In the last month, they had almost doubled the number of women who regularly attend church services, leaving their church at three quarters capacity. She partially attributed it to the good work that they had been doing in the last few months helping to support the wives of disabled veterans. She stood before her flock & offered her personal thanks to Hope & the rest of the women in charge of the charity.

She also took a moment to sing the praises of the New Mexico state legislature for ratifying the Equal Rights Amendment. As she read the list of twenty-nine states that had ratified it, the over sixteen hundred women in attendance felt the hope of a better future swelling in their hearts.

As Virginia began speaking about how the age of women's oppression was coming to an end & how that meant that they should liberate themselves from their bras, Hope looked out into the crowd. A part of her missed the days when she knew all of the regulars. While she could still pick out some of the regulars that had been attending weekly service since the early years, she had little to no idea about who many of these women were. While she missed that connection, it brought her joy to see so many women finding salvation in the church.

It was as she was looking out into the crowd that she happened to spot a familiar face that she had not seen in years. She had to look away & find her again to make sure her eyes weren't playing tricks on her. She had lost some of her youthful glow over the years, but there was no doubt that it was her older sister, Grace, sitting in the third row of pews.

She hadn't seen her sister since just after she joined the church. She hadn't seen any of her family since then. As Virginia continued her weekly sermon, Hope kept looking back to see her sister, as if to make sure that she wasn't an illusion. When the service came to an end, Hope had one of the assistants take over for her at the donation bowls up front while she made her way to her sister.

Hope wasn't sure about what to expect as she walked up to her sister for the first time in over four years. As Grace got out of the pew & separated from the crowd of people, she smiled as her white robed sister approached her.

"So do you burn your bras, or just throw them away?"

Hope couldn't help but laugh as Grace grinned playfully.

"Neither. I but rocks in them & throw them at republicans."

They both started laughing, just like they used to when they were kids, making up all kinds of stupid things.

"I didn't expect to see you here Grace. Don't tell me that you've left Roger?"

"No, no. Still happily married to him, penis & all. You won't find me dropping my wedding ring into a bowl of holy water anytime soon."

"To each there own I suppose."

"Are those three women really divorced from doing that? Like is that legal?"

"Sadly, no. They've either already gotten divorced or they're in the middle of the legal battle. The unbinding ceremony is symbolic."

"Are they lesbians now?"

"No, just single, you can't become a lesbian. I'm pretty sure that you didn't come here to talk about the church."

"Right, sorry, I was expecting something smaller, less organized religion & more…"

"Lesbians dancing naked in the woods?"

Grace chuckled.

"Not that small, but definitely not this. There's like, almost two thousand people here."

"Yeah, this place has been filling up fast. A month ago, we had half the number of people coming in for weekly service."

"I heard. Listen, Hope, are you free to get a cup of coffee, I'd like a chance to catch up a bit."

"Sure, just give me a minute to get changed."

"Okay."

Hope headed to the offices in the back & changed out of her robes & into normal city clothes. In Jeans & a simple long sleeve shirt, she rejoined her sister & they headed down the road to a coffee shop. Sitting down together with their coffees, they sat there awkwardly for a moment.

"So, Grace, how are the kids?"

"They're doing great, the oldest is in fourth grade & we just had our third about a year ago."

"Congratulations."

"Thanks, I just hope that she's the last one. Three is enough."

"I'll pray for you."

Grace smiled.

"You know, when you told us six years ago that you were going to devote your life to this street preacher, we all thought that you were losing it. But it seems to be working out."

"I know. Truth be told, I had a few doubts along the way in the early days, but hard work, determination & a message that resonates with people & here we are. About to outgrow the church that we just moved into."

"I'm glad that it's working out."

"How's the family doing?"

Grace sipped her coffee before continuing.

"Mostly alright. Mom's eyesight got so bad that she failed her driving test. Finally had to get glasses so she could get her license back."

"Wow. Does she actually wear them?"

"Sometimes, when she's driving."

"Wow, never thought that I'd see the day."

"Same. Dad's alright now, although we had a bit of a scare a few weeks ago."

"What happened?"

"The mole on his shoulder changed color."

"Jesus."

"Yeah, we dragged him to the hospital, they said that the mole was turning cancerous, but it was still early. They removed it & he's fine."

Hope breathed a sigh of relief.

"Wow. So that bulbous mole is gone now."

"That it is. That was actually the reason why I came to see you today."

"It is?"

Grace nodded.

"Yeah. We got a little too close to losing Dad for my comfort. That was when I realized that I had basically lost you. I mean, we haven't seen each other in years. I miss my sister."

Hope smiled.

"I've missed you too sis."

"Maybe we can get together sometimes."

"I'd love that, Grace."

"Maybe you can come to Thanksgiving this year? Mom & Dad would be thrilled to see you."

"I'd love too."

"Great. Out of curiosity, would you be bringing Virginia? I mean, are you two... a thing?"

"No. We're not a couple. Virginia isn't a one-woman kind of girl."

"Ah, okay. But you're... into... women?"

"I'm not into anyone. Not like that at least. I prefer to spend time with women, but I just, I don't feel the need for that kind of company. You know what I mean?"

"Nope. I don't know anything one way or the other about being with women in any way. But if you're happy coming to Thanksgiving without a partner, that'll make it easier to deal with Mom & Dad at least."

"I bet."

The two of them sipped their coffees before Grace opened up with about a hundred questions about the church.

Oct 7th, 1973
New York City

Lena looked at the new truck with awe. For three years, she had been transporting newspapers to stands in whatever cars her & her employees had. Now they had a pair of trucks. A pair of trucks that had the words Lavender Press in large, stylized, lavender font for the world to read. With the first truck having just left with her newest employee to deliver to the outskirts of New York City, she helped Sarah pack the second truck.

"You know Sarah, I always dreamed of seeing a fleet of newspaper trucks carrying my news out into the world. I just never thought that I would get here this fast."

"It's impressive. It certainly looks more legitimate when we're dropping papers off. We're no longer some crazy ladies with a press. We're a proper organization now."

"Yeah. Makes these early morning runs a little more bearable."

"Says the boss who doesn't have to go out anymore."

Lena grinned as Sarah hopped into the truck & got a start on her Sunday morning route. She then walked back into her office where she proceeded to hang up a copy of the week's paper on her wall. She usually kept a few of her recent issues on the wall, but this one was going to be one of the few that stayed up permanently, right next to her first edition.

Stepping back, she admired the image on the front page of a stack of psychiatric textbooks. She almost jumped as a woman behind her read the headline.

"American Psychiatric Association removes female homosexuality from DSM-II."

Visibly surprised, Lena turned around to see who had wandered into her office. Standing there was a woman in her early twenties with untamed hair, wearing a bright orange t-shirt with a large pin that said ERA YES!

"Sorry Ms. Lewis. I didn't mean to scare you."

"That's alright. Who are you?"

"Oh, sorry, I'm Alison Higgs. I'm a student at Cornell University, I'm also the president of the Lesbian Rights Club."

"Hi there Alison. How can I help you?"

"Well, we'd like to sell your newspaper in the Cornell newspaper stand, if that's alright with you, & if we can get permission from the administration."

"Well, I'm always in the market for new customers, but would Cornell University actually be willing to sell a lesbian newspaper on campus?"

Alison tried her best to act like she was sure of herself.

"Not normally. We've been advocating since last year that we need to see more female oriented newspapers & magazines for the student body to read. The thing is, most of the things that we've been able to find are either deemed by the administration to be obscene, or they devolve into long winded manifestos, or they quickly fall out of business."

Lena nodded her head.

"I'm familiar with some of those. I even interviewed one of the women that try to sell those... papers."

"Right, then last week, one of our new members mentioned a queer newspaper that she regularly read back in New York City. At first, we didn't believe her, but then she produced a copy from a few weeks ago that she had. It was the issue where you did a biography on Myrtle Cagle, the woman going up on Apollo twenty."

"The woman about to make one small step. I remember it."

"Exactly. Your paper isn't just a feminist rant, it's exactly what we need. A proper newspaper, covering actual news in the world, with a focus on women's & queer issues."

"I'm glad that you see that, but don't you still need permission from the administration to sell my paper on campus?"

"Yes, that's why I'm here today. I was wondering if you had a few old copies of your newspaper that I could take back to Cornell

& show them. I figure that if they can see that it's a proper newspaper with their own eyes, they might be more likely to say yes to selling it on campus. I'd pay for the copies, of course."

Lena looked at her curiously.

"You mean to tell me, that you drove all the way from Ithaca, I think it's about four hours each way, just to buy a few back copies of my newspaper."

"Yes. I know that Ithaca is a long way away for two or three bundles of newspapers, but we wouldn't need them on Sunday morning. I'm sure that we could work out the logistics & costs."

"The logistics would be an issue. I'd have to pay a driver to spend about eight or nine hours driving, it would probably take... at least a hundred & fifty issues to be sold just to break even each week, unless I charged you a little more for the long distance. Do you really think there's a market for that kind of an order in Cornell?"

Alison was speechless for a moment as she thought on her feet.

"If there isn't, we could do a monthly thing where you bring say, thirty or forty copies of each week's paper from the last month, or we might be able to send a volunteer down to pick the issues up. Like I said, we can work on the issues & cost of getting the paper to Cornell. I just need to convince them to let us sell the newspaper there. Besides, think about how good this could be for your business, we have students from all over the country, including all over New York City & the areas that are closer to it. This might allow you to drive up much more local demand."

Lena thought about it. She did like the idea that her newspaper would be sold all over the state instead of just the city. Not to mention she could be bringing a whole new perspective to young minds at an ivy league university.

"Alright."

"Really!"

"Yes. If you can convince them to sell it, we can try to find a way to make this work. I've got a bunch of old copies that you can take back with you."

"YES! Thank you!"

Alison wrapped Lena up in a great big hug. Lena wondered how hard it would be to convince Sarah to spend nine hours driving to & from Ithaca once a week.

November 30th, 1973
Montreal, Canada

Janet walked into her boss's office. It wasn't often that he asked her into his office & it was even less often that he asked her to close the door. Janet knew that he wouldn't try anything, although a part of her was still nervous now that it was just her & her boss alone in a room.

"Thanks for coming in Janet, I know that everyone is eager to finish up for the week & start the weekend."

"That's alright, I figure it's important if you're calling me in here just before the weekend."

"You're right. It's important."

Janet tensed up a bit. A part of her was worried that she was about to be fired. More than one of her colleagues wasn't too happy about working with a woman.

"I'd like your permission to run a background check on you."

"What?"

Janet looked at him confused.

"As you know, we do some work on government projects. We've got a new project that we'll be starting in a few weeks with NASA."

"Wait, is that the project that Hank was talking about, trying to grow things in simulated lunar regolith?"

"That it is. We've been tapped by NASA to do the first major study on growing plants, particularly food crops, in simulated lunar soil. We're even going to get a sample of lunar material so that we can analyze it for things like drainage & salt content."

"That's incredible, but why do I need to get a background check?"

"NASA is a government agency in the US, anyone working for them needs to pass a background check, especially someone from a foreign country."

"I know that, but why am I getting a background check, I thought that Hank was leading that project & he certainly wouldn't pick me to work next to him on the biggest study of his career."

"There was an… issue… with his background check."

"What kind of an issue?"

"Nothing serious. I can't go into details for legal reasons, but suffice to say, there's something there that the FBI doesn't like. So, we need someone else to lead the study. The board met & discussed it at length. We want you to lead the project."

Janet was speechless. She was being given an opportunity to lead a massive study for NASA. One of the greatest botanical studies in history would be written by her. With that kind of notoriety, she'd be famous in the botanical community. It was a dream come true.

"Janet?"

"Sorry sir. I was just… taking in what you said."

"It is a major opportunity. So, can I run the background check?"

"Sure."

"Great, just sign this so we can start."

He handed her a document from the government of Canada, authorizing him to perform a background check & another form that would grant the American government access to it. She paused for just a moment.

"Uhm, sir, just how personal do these things get?"

"It basically just checks if you have a criminal record. Why, is there something I should know about?"

"Well… back in sixty-four, I may have been arrested for taking part in a gay rights protest that got a little out of hand."

"I see. Were there any charges brought against you?"

"No, no charges, just a night in jail. Nobody in my life even knew about it, the college I was attending didn't know, my family didn't know. Until recently, the only person that knew was… my partner."

Janet wasn't sure if calling Rebecca her partner was enough of a clue for her boss to figure out that she was with a woman. A part of her wondered if she should come out to her boss. A more panicked voice told her not to as it could cost her this once in a lifetime opportunity, not to mention her job.

"I don't think that should be a problem. We were all young once, a lot of people had to spend a night in jail for being a little too rowdy. Boys will be boys; I suppose girls will be girls."

"That's good to here."

"You were marching for… gay… rights?"

"I was young, it was… college."

"Right. I remember those days. Don't tell anyone, but back when I was in my college years, I might have tried a cigarette or two that weren't cigarettes."

Janet grinned, trying to picture the old man back in the fifties getting high on refer or grass or whatever they called it back then.

"Wild child. I won't tell yours if you don't tell mine."

"Deal."

As Janet signed the papers, a part of her wondered if she had just made one of those closed doors, backroom handshake deals that allow some people to ascend in society. She doubted it. She handed back the signed papers.

"Excellent. Assuming that one night doesn't give anyone cause for concern, which I doubt that it will, I think that it's safe to say that you'll be starting work on this project just after the holidays."

"It's a pleasure. Please thank the board for their faith in me."

"I'll pass that along. Just don't go announcing that you're on the project until after the background check comes back."

"Understood."

Janet left his office thrilled. She could barely understand how a Canadian company had gotten the job, let alone how she had gotten to work on it, but this was going to be big for her.

December 12th, 1973
Hyginus Rille, The Moon

Fred Haise took in the sight around him with awe. When an electrical issue had caused a caution & warning in Apollo thirteen, he had been worried that they would have to abort the mission & that he would miss his chance to go to the Moon. Now here he was, three years later, the first man to reach the Moon twice.

Looking up & seeing the Moon overhead, he wondered how he could possibly be so lucky as to get to do this twice in a lifetime. He figured that it had something to do with the rumor that the Soviets weren't giving up on the Moon. His being there was a chance to one up them again before they got there. By the time they got a man to the Moon once, the Americans had sent a man there twice.

Whatever the reason for his selection, he didn't care. Standing on the blasted grey landscape, staring up at the Earth was just as magical the second time around. He wanted to take in every detail that he could because in a few hours, he would be heading home.

"Hey Fred, I've got the last samples, should we head back?"

"In a minute Gerald. Trust me, you're going to want to take in the view. Just in case this is the last time you can see it."

"It is something."

In mission control, exhausted technicians & directors listened as the two men on the Moon took in the scenery. A moment later, as the two astronauts were setting out on their way home, every person in mission control felt their adrenaline pumping as they heard a scream over the radio.

Flight director Gene Kranz hoped this was a prank. His hopes were dashed when the flight surgeon reported that Haise's heartrate & vitals were going wild.

"Gemini, what happened? Gerald, is Haise alright?"

On the lunar surface, Fred Haise was on his back after Gerald had helped to roll him off of his side. Struggling to kneel on the dusty surface in his stiff suit, Gerald Carr got on the radio.

"Mission control, this is Gemini, Haise is hurt."

"What happened?"

"We were hoping along back to the rover when Fred landed funny, I think that he landed on a rock that slipped. He fell hard & landed on his arm funny."

"How bad is it?"

"It's hard to tell through the suit. But judging by the pain he seems to be in, I'd say that it might be broken."

"Can he stand, can you get back to the lander?"

"I think so, we're just going to need a minute here to get him on his feet. It's not easy in these suits."

"Understood, get Haise back to the rover, secure him in carefully, & get back to the lander."

"Working on it."

With no small amount of effort, the two men were able to get back to their feet. They then walked very carefully & very slowly to the rover. Walking normally was hard in the low gravity of the Moon, but they didn't want to go hoping around like astronauts often did on the Moon. Twenty minutes later, they were in the rover. An hour later, they were in the lander, where getting Haise out of his suit was no easy task. Once he was free from the top of his suit, which involved a significant amount of screaming & cursing, Gerald was able to see the problem.

"Houston, I can see the problem now. His arm isn't broken, but his shoulder is most definitely dislocated. I can pop it back in, but I'd like a recommendation on pain killers, aspirin ain't going help much on this."

"Stand by Gerald."

They waited for a minute as Gene consulted with the flight surgeon.

"That's a go on the pain killer. Start with one dose, wait until he calms down before relocating his shoulder. Be advised we're pushing back your launch time by six hours."

"Understood."

Gerald cracked open the first aid kit & opened a package containing a pain pill. Fred took it & waited for it to kick in. A few minutes later, he felt the pain in his shoulder begin to fade away. A quick pop & a scream later, & Fred's shoulder was back in place.

A few hours later, they were both sitting in the lunar lander, waiting to see if Houston was going to clear them for launch. To pass the time, they were listening to Jim Lovell, the commander of Apollo thirteen, reading them news articles over the radio to help pass the time.

"Apparently, the military is concerned because recruitment numbers are incredibly low & all of the drafted soldiers are rotating out. They're saying that if it keeps up at this rate, we might fall below critical levels if war breaks out."

"Here's hoping the world has had enough war for a while."

"You said it, Haise. Let's see, what else, oh, apparently, Kentucky has ratified the ERA."

"How many states is that now Jim?"

"Uh, it says thirty. Eight more & it'll pass."

"That'll be something. Any idea on when it'll pass?"

"It doesn't... hang on guys, Gene wants to have a word with you."

They both straightened up a bit as Gene came on.

"Alright boys, the flight surgeon has reluctantly given a go for you to launch. Hopefully zero G & reentry won't be too rough on your injuries. But we need to know, Fred, will you be able to help, or is Gerald going to have to control this solo?"

"I can still help with my good arm Gene."

"Alright then, we're going to review the procedures for lunar launch with an injured man. We'll also be pushing your launch back another three hours so that you have the best chance of splashdown near American waters. I know you're getting a bit bored up there, but we want you landing as close to us as possible."

"Understood Gene."

"In the meantime, I'll let you get back to your news, feel free to ask Jim how the Cleveland Browns did a few days ago."

Fred & Gerald laughed as they heard Jim moan over the radio.

1974

January 24th, 1974
Cedar Rapids, Iowa

The ads started showing up everywhere a few days after New Year's. The response from several parts of society was outrage. Protests popped up all over the country, especially in more conservative areas. There were calls from the public, from religious leaders & from conservative politicians for military leaders & President Humphrey to resign over the ads.

Next to images of Uncle Sam pointing to the reader & saying I want you for US Army, there were now posters of a tall woman, wearing a long flowing dress made to look like the American flag with a golden shield to match, with the caption at the bottom reading: Ladies; Columbia is calling you for the army.

It was the first poster of its kind that Debra Foster had seen when she went into town with some of her friends. They had been drawn to it when they heard a group of old men raving about it. Her friends had passed it off, but something about the image resonated with her.

Over the coming days & weeks, she saw more ads like it. Some of them, like a Navy recruitment ad calling for seawomen to enlist, were on the news as people debated them & the direction that the country was going in.

As experts & quacks debated if this meant the commission was giving up, or the government was giving up, or the military was realizing it would be hit with a decade of reduced enlistment at least, Debra saw more ads. She began to imagine. She recalled her grandfather's stories of his time in the service & her mind began to drift to all of the possibilities.

Then the army started posting stories in the newspapers & magazines about women who had served in combat. Women who had become marines, snipers, heavily decorated war heroes that heard their country's call & stood up to defend freedom, democracy & America herself.

Her friends would think that she was nuts. Her parents would try to stop her from being able to go. Her grandfather would probably laugh & say that she had more balls than her father before being the first to salute her.

She asked her friend who had a car of her own for a ride into town. When she found out where Debra wanted to go, she was stunned. Little Debra Foster, Darling Debra to her friends, wanted to enlist in the military. Her friend tried to talk her out of it, saying that she probably wouldn't make it through training. Debra thanked her for the ride & the concern before walking up to the only military recruitment office in Cedar Rapids.

Just outside the office, she saw a larger poster of the image of Columbia & her golden shield pointing to her, calling her to serve. Taking a deep breath, she walked into the office where Tom, a geeky guy that she had known in high school, was sitting behind the desk, waiting for recruits.

"Debra? What are you doing in here?"

Debra took another deep breath.

"I'm here to enlist."

"Seriously? You? Did Bobby put you up to this?"

"I haven't seen Bobby in years. I'm here to enlist."

Tom took on a serious look.

"Seriously. You want to sign up for one of those all-girl units?"

"Yes."

"Fuck, the whole town is going to flip."

"Yeah, probably."

"Holy shit Debra. Okay. Let me get the papers, they gave us some special forms for women."

Tom looked through his drawers for the papers for women to enlist. When he had first gotten them three weeks ago, he didn't expect that any woman within spitting distance of Cedar Rapids would enlist, let alone short little Debra.

"Got them."

He pulled out a small set of papers.

"Are those it?"

"Yep. Enlistment papers & contract. First you answer this questionnaire, then I review it, then assuming that it's all in order, you read the contract carefully & sign it. Then you're in the army."

"Perfect."

"Just so you know, once you sign the contract, there's no turning back, you're in the army. If you don't show up for basic training, it's desertion, which is frowned upon by the army."

"I understand."

"Jesus Debra. You're really going to do this."

"I'm really doing it."

"Alright. Here's the questionnaire, here's a pen, let me know if you have any questions or if you change your mind."

"Thanks Tom."

"No problem. Just one thing."

"What's up?"

"When you tell your family that you enlisted..."

"You were never here Tom."

"Thanks Debra."

February 12th, 1974
National Institute of Health, Bethesda, Maryland

Barbara walked into the office that had been vacant for weeks. It used to belong to Doctor Barber, a happy go lucky old man who was one of the premier virologists on the East coast when it came to viruses that could damage the reproductive tract. His credentials were the various papers that he had written about how some viruses had left lasting or even permanent damage to some women's uterus's.

Barbara wasn't too keen on socializing with another doctor. She was certain that this Doctor Lopez would be just like all the men in the office. Smart, somewhat respectful, but not someone that she would have a lot in common with. Still, it paid to be friendly with your colleagues. In the years that she had been working here, she had had to work with several people that she had never predicted that she would have to work with.

Walking into the office, she saw a tall woman with golden-brown skin setting up medical textbooks on a shelf & no sign of the doctor.

"Excuse me miss, I'm looking for the new virologist, Doctor Lopez."

The young woman turned around, her long dark hair flowing as she turned to face the woman that had walked into the office & spoke with a thick Colombian accent.

"You've found her. I'm Doctor Ruby Lopez, the new virologist."

Barbara's eyes went wide.

"I'm sorry, I thought that you were…"

"The young assistant, that's alright, I'm used to it."

"I'm so sorry. I know the feeling; I've been working here since sixty-five & most new researchers mistake me for an assistant. I'm Doctor Barbara Collins by the way."

"Doctor Collins, yes, you're in the chemistry department."

"Yeah. God, I can't believe that I assumed you were an assistant."

"It's alright. I know what it's like. I would probably have done the same. I've seen so few women in these positions that I make assumptions as well."

"Still, I'm so sorry. Is there any way that I can make it up to you?"

Ruby grinned wickedly.

"You could introduce me to our colleagues & we can see how many of them are assuming that I'm your new assistant."

Barbara imagined half the doctors in the commission stuttering & stammering apologies with looks of shock on their faces.

"I'd love that."

"Great. Just give me a minute to finish unpacking my books."

"No problem."

As Ruby put her medical texts on the shelves, Barbara took a look around at the credentials that she had hung up.

"National University of Columbia. I take it that's not the one in New York, I'm pretty sure that they still don't permit women to attend."

"No, I received my degree in Columbia. The national university has allowed women to attend since the thirties."

"Maybe I should have gone there. I was the only woman in my class, which was one more than a lot of people wanted."

"Yes. No offence Doctor Collins, but your country isn't exactly living up to its reputation as the home of the free. Don't get me wrong. I have many freedoms here that I didn't have back home, but there are a few things, like education, where you are falling behind."

"No offense taken. Probably the only good thing about this anomaly is that when we make up sixty, seventy, eighty, ninety percent of the voters, we'll finally get some real freedoms."

"Yes, but in the meantime, let's go make some men apologize for making assumptions."

Barbara grinned as she rarely did. She had never had a female colleague that she permanently worked with. She sensed that she was going to like it.

March 18th, 1974
Baikonur Cosmodrome, Kazakhstan, Soviet Union

Tikhon Smirnov looked over the final checklists one last time. The moment was finally here. Within the next twenty minutes, he & his team would either be heroes of the people, or they would be the cause of the final embarrassment of the Soviet program to put cosmonauts on the Moon.

It had been a few years since an N1 had been launched. By some miracle, the party had given them the one thing that they actually needed to build a working rocket. Time. His team had been given years of time to work out all of the problems & to properly test all of the systems out. Now, it was time to see if it had all been worth it.

A number of political figures were sitting in the observation booth, putting all kinds of pressure on Tikhon & his team, not that they needed reminding of how desperately they needed to get this launch right. Protests across the union were quickly put down, but they were growing in number & size. The people wanted to know what was happening to their children & the party wasn't even willing to admit how severe the problem was. The party wasn't even willing to discuss what had happened to the researchers who had failed to produce a result after so many years & had been *reassigned*.

The Kremlin desperately needed a win, preferably a big one. They needed a grand achievement that they could parade around to show that they were still great & glorious & capable of incredible things so that the people would believe them when they said that the boy crisis would be solved. They also needed to show up the West.

With the countdown nearing the final seconds, Tikhon gathered the final confirmations from the various people, confirming that all appeared ideal. With that, the last few seconds counted down & as they reached zero, the launch began.

The rocket fired with such awesome force that even a few kilometers away, the launch complex shook with the force. The N1 lifted into the sky & rolled slightly onto its side as it needed to in order to climb into the heavens.

After a few minutes, the rocket reached the moment of terror for the crew. Once the first stage cut out, the onboard computer automatically separated the first stage, causing it to fall back down to Earth as the second stage engaged. The men & women in the room were ecstatic. The first stage hadn't ripped apart or failed to separate. They were now further into the launch than any N1 had ever gotten before.

When an alarm light came on, Tikhon almost felt his heart stop. Fortunately, it was just a single engine failure & the onboard computer shut down the opposite engine. The second stage had been designed to be able to function with just six of its eight engines firing. Once the rocket climbed into space, everyone was elated when the second stage separated cleanly.

All that was left for this test was for the third stage to put the rocket in orbit. As the engines fired, the entire team was certain that they would be receiving medals for their success.

Over the next few hours, military men & intelligence organizations all over the world called their superior officers to inform them that a large rocket from the USSR was now in orbit around the earth. Soon enough, Presidents & Prime Ministers would be informed about the new chapter in the space race.

President Humphrey cursed when he was informed. Putting down his notes about an upcoming state visit to England to meet with Harold Wilson who had just been reelected with a slight majority in the English Parliament. Humphrey set up a meeting with NASA officials to discuss what their next steps might be.

April 7th, 1974
Church of the Lord's Son, Fort Worth, Texas

The three women & their children cried & wailed at the Reverend. They cried to the congregation; they begged God for forgiveness & some begged their husbands for mercy. None of these women had suspected that Reverend Thomas Edwards would actually make a huge spectacle of throwing them out of the church like this. He had started off his sermon by talking about how the population had now reached four billion people on Earth & there were over half a billion girls that should have been born as boys.

The four women had watched from the back with the other girl bearers as he proclaimed that the church must be kept pure of the feminist taint. That was when he had called the three of them up to the front by name. The four women were helped out along the way as they had each recently given birth & had not fully recovered.

Reverend Edwards then pointed to the four women standing before the congregation & he cursed them.

"Satanic, Feminist, Whores! You've strayed from the light of the Lord! You've ignored the words of his Son! Your wickedness has birthed nothing but vile girls who will one day lay with each other rather than with a man! Those who refuse the mercy of the Lord have no place in His House! I cast you whores out!"

Three of the four women fell to their knees, their newborn daughters in their arms & their young girls around them. They begged him for mercy. They pleaded with him as he turned to their husbands & commanded them to either divorce their families on the spot by renouncing them or to leave the church with them. Molly begged him with her mousey voice & her slight Irish accent.

"Please Father! It's not fair! I was already pregnant when you gave us another chance, there was nothing that I could do about it! Please! Give me one more chance!"

The Reverend spit at her. Her husband lifted her up to her feet. He then flipped off the Reverend before escorting his wife & their young daughters out the door. He had no intention of ever returning.

Autumn, a woman who had followed her boyfriend into a free love cult & couldn't remember anything that happened between

1962 & 1964, begged for another chance until it became clear that she wouldn't get one. She then stood up & looked the Reverend in his blue eyes.

"Some mercy. Some redemption. I found more love & compassion in the men that spent two years meditating between my legs. Come along John."

When she turned to her husband, he looked at her as if he was thinking. He then took a step back from her.

"Be gone Whore! Our marriage is over!"

Autumn wasn't surprised that he wanted out. They had only gotten married because she had gotten pregnant their first time together. She took her daughters, all five of them, & walked out of the church, ready to go back to the cult if need be.

Alaina cried & begged for mercy. She had been baptized by the Reverend. She had attended every single sermon he had given since she was a baby. She had been married by him to her husband. She had gone to him for advice on countless things all throughout her life. She had listened to everything that he had ever said. She had asked him to bless all four of her pregnancies. She had even forgiven him that one time he had accidentally groped her butt.

Now he was casting her out of the flock that she had called her family all of her life. As her husband helped her up & led her out, ignoring the encouragement from the reverend to divorce his wife, she turned on Father Edwards.

"You snake! I did everything that you ever told me to do! I asked for forgiveness every single week since I was old enough to confess! You blessed each & every one of my pregnancies! You said that God would look over me & give me sons! You lying, treasonous snake!"

As Alaina left, Dory continued to stand in front of the shocked congregation. She didn't cry, beg, or plead. She wasn't even upset when her husband renounced her & their seven daughters before the Reverend even had to encourage him to. She simply looked at Father Edwards & pointed at her husband of ten years.

"Just so that you know, he only ever fucked me from behind, like a dog, he never let me get naked, he always had to be drunk, the lights always had to be off & he always called Antoni's name as he came."

She then turned around on her heels & marched out the door with her children, fully intent to walk to the pay phone in front of the church & call her cousin Aldric, the divorce lawyer. If her husband thought that he wasn't going to be coughing up a fortune in child support, he was going to be as surprised as Antoni was when she walked past him.

With all four women gone, the two husbands who had renounced their marriages took seats among the pews reserved for single men. The Reverend then continued with his sermon.

"You see how quickly they turn on the Lord, these witch women. One proclaiming more love from a satanic cult, one trying to besmirch my good name & another throwing wild accusations at the husband that labored to give her seven children. See how the wickedness flows from them as they are rooted out & cast out of the house of the Lord!"

As the preacher spoke, most of the flock cheered & praised him whenever he paused, certain that he was cleansing the flock & protecting the righteous from the wicked. In the front rows, some of the women who were nearing their due dates were suddenly getting nervous.

May 4th, 1974
Montreal, Canada

Janet Hill sat at the café table, sipping a cup of coffee & reading about an all-female team of Japanese mountain climbers that reached the summit of Manaslu in Nepal as she waited for an appointment. Over the last few months, she had gotten to know a few people from NASA as part of the study that she had been conducting. About a week after the initial study had been completed, one of the people from NASA had approached her asking if she would be free for a quick meeting on the weekend.

At first, she had thought that he was coming on to her. As she was trying to find a good way to refuse his offer, he eventually got around to mentioning a job that they wanted to give her. They set an appointment & she now found herself waiting for a man that was almost ten minutes late.

"Janet, sorry, I only know where three things in this city are. I got completely turned around."

"That's alright. Do you want to order anything?"

Janet put down the magazine that she had been reading.

"I would, but I've already had three… no four… I've had way too much coffee today. I hope that you don't mind getting straight to business."

"Not at all Albert."

"Great. Along with continuing our current study into plant growth in lunar regolith, we're going to be starting a few more studies in the field of astrobotany at the Kennedy Space Center in Florida."

"Astrobotany. You mean growing things in space. Like not just in lunar soil, but actually in zero gravity?"

"Exactly. We intend to begin looking into what it would take to grow important plants like crops in space & on the Moon. Discover what challenges they'll face, what they may need, what the costs & benefits would be. That sort of thing."

Janet was stunned. That would be decades of work where nobody has ever done any research. Where nobody had ever even thought to do research. She tried to keep her composure at being presented with this opportunity of a lifetime.

"Is this research that will actually go somewhere, or is this for some hypothetical mission in the distant future?"

"I honestly don't know. Officially, we don't have any plans to go beyond Earth orbit after Apollo twenty. Even if that stays the case, there are rumors of space stations in earth orbit, although that's all just preliminary talk. It'll probably be a few years before we start any work on that."

"Are we actually going to stop going to the Moon?"

"Like I said, officially, yes."

"What about unofficially?"

"Unofficially, rumor has it that the recent Soviet N1 launch has the government spooked. Supposedly, Humphrey is going to order a few more Apollos."

"Just a few?"

He leaned in closer.

"You didn't here this from me, alright?"

"Alright."

"We've been told to conduct studies on how to send more people & equipment up there, as well as how much it would cost. Rumor has it that if the reds reach the Moon, we might be ordered to build a base up there, so that we can stay ahead of them."

"What if they build a base up there?"

He grinned.

"Well, that's when shit would get really interesting. Point of the matter is that we need quality people doing cutting edge research, & you do quality work."

Janet tried to contain her excitement so that she could ask some important questions.

"Not to shoot myself in the foot here, but couldn't you find a botanist in the states? I know that I'm good, but Montreal seems like a long way for NASA to go for a plant girl."

"Well, it helps that your work has already impressed us. But yeah, you're right, it is a bit far to go. The thing is, Apollo is expensive, & potential base building is going to be even more expensive if it happens. So, we're looking to include some international help in these potential endeavors."

"You're hoping that if you hire enough NATO allies, some of those NATO countries will start picking up some of the tab."

"Yes. Full disclosure, we're also looking to increase the number of women that we employ in important roles. That's not why I'm offering the job to you. Most of the names on my list after you are men. It's just something that I thought that you should be aware of."

Janet thought about it.

"It's tempting, but there's a personal issue of concern for me that's rather worrying."

"Your... *partner.*"

Janet suddenly became cautious.

"I don't..."

"I'm just guessing by the fact that you always refer to your partner as your partner & not your boyfriend."

"Right..."

"Assuming that my assumption about what you were implying is accurate, I'm not going to lie. Certain... acts... that are legal up here are still technically illegal in most of the states. That being said, a number of locations have started easing up on women doing those things."

"Is Florida one of those places?"

"No. Not in any significant way. Although Florida authorities have been willing to overlook a few minor incidents for NASA, especially if we're working to fight the reds in space, especially in counties near the space center. I can't guarantee that you & your... partner... wouldn't face issues."

"Hmmm."

"Look, think it over, talk it over with your partner, let me know by the end of Friday. You've got my number."

"I have it. We'll think about it. Montreal to the Space Coast is a big move."

"That it is. I've got to get going, promise me you'll consider it. The team at KSC wants you."

"I'll consider it."

He then packed up his equipment & headed out, leaving Janet with a major decision that could impact her & her relationship with Rebecca in all kinds of ways.

May 16th, 1974
Havana, Cuba

Estefania was outraged. Absolutely furious. It had been bad enough when all of those liberals & queers & counterrevolutionaries had started using the birth anomalies as an excuse to demand things from the government. That was to be expected. They were always up to something that would corrupt the country & let the capitalists back in. She, like most of her people, had believed that these individuals were just a handful of misguided people that had been confused by American propaganda.

When President Torrado had made the announcement with Prime Minister Castro next to him, it rocked the country to its core. Like many Catholics, Estefania was marching down the streets in protest of the government's lapse in judgement.

While it was true that she, like everyone else, couldn't ignore the plethora of little girls & the near absence of little boys, she could not abide by the government's decision to legalize lesbianism. Many of her university's classes had been cancelled as the protests started ramping up. Walking out onto the campus, anger coursing through her veins, she chanced upon a small group of protestors being led down the street by a priest.

The man was handsome & passionate. He spoke with fire & conviction. He would not stand for his country to fall from righteousness. Estefania followed the crowd as it slowly grew. She quickly found out from the other protestors that the man was known as Father Domingo Tome, & that before the President had even finished announcing the change to the country's laws, Father Domingo was already knocking on the doors of his congregation to demand that they march.

Within the hour, they had hundreds in their group & they were just one of many marching through the streets, causing chaos & upheaval. Unlike other groups that had been broken up by police or even military forces, they only came across a small number of cops who backed away from them. As they reached the heart of the city, Domingo stopped them & pointed out the enemy to them.

Arsenio was disgusted by the announcement. Sure, it would allow women to be together, but what about him? He & Bernardo had a right to be together. They weren't hurting anyone. They weren't destroying the moral fabric of society. They were just in love. Was that really so wrong?

After a long chat, the two of them decided that if women would be allowed to be together, so too should they be allowed. They went to the homes of their friends & in what seemed like no time, they organized a small protest to the new freedom that they would be denied because they were men.

They found a place for themselves that the police seemed to be ignoring. The last thing that they needed as queer men was to have the police come down on them on the day when the whole country was losing its mind. As they shouted at anyone that passed by, they saw a small group of women marching towards them under a banner that read what about us?

Judging by the symbols & slogans on their signs, it was clear that these women were not interested in the desires of men. This left the group confused. Why would a group of lesbians be protesting the legalization of lesbianism? Since it was Arsenio who had basically started the group, he was chosen to talk to the approaching lesbians. He steadied himself & approached them.

"My name is Arsenio; we are demanding that the government extend these new rights to men as well. Can we ask why a group of lesbians is protesting this new law?"

The group of women seemed to part as one of the women from the center was selected to confront this man.

"I'm Lupita. We're protesting because the new law doesn't apply to us. Its only women born after 1965 that will be allowed to be together. For those of us over the age of nine, it is still a crime for us to love each other!"

The women behind her cried out in anger. Arsenio thought about the absurdity of the law for a moment & the group's passion.

"It would seem that we share a common cause."

"A freedom dangled before us but denied to us for trivial reasons."

"Yes. We should join forces, & march on the government united."

"Yes. We need to make them see that we should all be free to love!"

The two groups cheered & joined together, intermingling & reorganizing themselves. With over a hundred men & women among them, they sought out to begin their march.

Just as they were about to set out, they saw a group of hundreds being led by a priest who was pointing at them. It quickly became clear that this new group were not friends. As the two groups charged at each other, a police officer appeared & called for backup.

Some hours later, Arsenio woke up in a hospital bed, tied to the bed with a bruised cop standing over him & the priest named Domingo in the next bed. Domingo was also just coming around & was tied to his bed. The police had apparently run out of handcuffs.

A mile away, Estefania & Lupita found themselves in the same jail cell. Despite their mutual hatred for each other, they agreed to be civil as a brawl in a jail cell where everyone was packed in like sardines was a bad idea.

Outside, shots could be heard as the police & infantry tried to establish order in a country that had lost its mind.

July 14th, 1974
Tycho Crater, The Moon

"Be a dear & zip me up."

Pete Conrad chuckled as he checked the seals on Myrtle Cagle's equipment. By far, one of the most tedious parts of going to the Moon was for the two astronauts, crammed in like a pair of sardines, to put on the bulky equipment that they needed to set foot outside the lander. In the over two hours that it took them to suit up, Myrtle thought about all of the times that she & Pete had spent training & practicing putting these suits on.

"You know Pete, aside from Walt, I don't think that anyone has ever seen me put my clothes on as many times as you have."

Pete laughed.

"I know the feeling. For Apollo twelve, I spent so much time training to put these suits on with Alan Bean that I could barely remember what Jane looked like. I think that she's more upset about it this time around."

"Well, as usual, I'll try to need as little help as possible undressing later."

"Jane & I both thank you for that Myrtle, but don't be overly heroic. I don't want to have to explain to your husband that you slipped & got a concussion while you were changing next to me."

Myrtle laughed.

"Don't worry about Walt. He trusts you & he understands that these would be extreme circumstances. How am I looking back there?"

"All zipped up & ready for a night on the town. Thought about what you're going to say out there?"

"I'm still choosing between Death to all men, & I am woman, hear me roar."

Pete laughed again. With their pressure seals & life support connections checked out, they signaled Houston that they were ready to step out. A minute later, they got the signal from NASA that they were good for an EVA.

Back on Earth, the better part of a billion people were huddling around the glow of their television screens in preparation for a historic moment. Even more people had watched as the lander had descended, listening to the broadcasts as they watched an animation play on TV. When the Valkyrie landed in Tycho crater, women all over the world cheered.

Now, they watched as for the first time in history, a woman climbed out of the lunar lander & began to descend towards the surface. As she descended down the few steps, she worried about what she was going to say. She had spent months thinking about it. The first words from the first woman on the Moon. These words would echo into eternity. As she stood on the last rung, hardly a foot from the grey regolith, she took a deep breath, calmed her nerves as best as she could with the world watching & countless millions of women looking for inspiration, & hoped that her next words would be appropriate for the occasion.

"One small step for a woman, one giant leap into humanity's future."

Myrtle Cagle then stepped off of the lander & took her first step onto the Moon. The moment that she had dreamed of when she had applied to the women in space program fourteen years earlier. The dream that the Mercury 13 represented. A woman standing on the Moon.

Pete Conrad followed close behind her. By the next morning, nobody would remember what he said as he set foot on the Moon for the second time in his life.

Over the next three days, countless people watched & listened as Myrtle & Pete explored Tycho crater. Myrtle was constantly amazed every time that NASA reported how many people were tuning in as she drove a golf cart around & collected some rock samples.

The work was long & grueling. Even in the lower gravity of the Moon, the suit was heavy & stiff. It didn't help that the lunar dust clung to everything & got in everywhere. Whenever she drove the rover, it was like when she was working, she was focused entirely on the task at hand. But when Pete was driving, she found herself staring out at the vast grey landscape, taking in its pristine, unspoiled, unearthly beauty. Here she was, having gone from the youngest pilot in North Carolina, to the oldest person to set foot on the Moon. From that little girl whose brothers taught her to fly, to the first woman on the Moon.

After their three days were up, they climbed into the ascent module & flew up to meet the command module. As they broke lunar orbit to begin the three-day trek home, Myrtle recalled her days on the Moon & couldn't believe that they were over.

It was on the way home, as she was wondering if some miracle would ever bring her back out this way that Gene Kranz called up to them from Mission Control.

"Hey there folks. Listen, before we let you get some sleep, we've just gotten an announcement from President Humphrey. On top of congratulating all of you on your successes, he's going to be making an announcement to the country in the morning. Apparently, with backing from congress already secured, he's ordered four more Apollo missions. They're going to start launching in 1976. He's also going to announce that he intends for there to be a woman on each mission."

After letting the news sink in for a moment, Myrtle got on the mic.

"Gene, I'll give you a hundred dollars if you send Adams before you send Cobb up."

Pete & Don burst into fits of laughter about three quarters of a second before the folks at mission control did. All throughout the training, she had been competing with Cobb to see which of the Mercury 13 would be the first to go. They had both constantly joked that the new girl would go before the other one went.

"I'll see what I can do for you Cagle. In the meantime, goodnight to all of you up there. You're all heroes."

Pete came onto the mic this time.

"Gene, Myrtle is the hero this time around, we're basically her chauffeurs."

Myrtle smiled & turned to Don.

"Driver, Pacific Ocean please, I have a parade to get to."

The three of them laughed before signing off for the night.

October 11th, 1974
Billings, Montana

The chill in the evening air had the promise of snow in the not-too-distant future. It didn't bother the crowd as they sat in the stands, bundled up against the chilly air. They were there to see something that many of them had never thought that they would get to see, their children playing in a soccer match.

Many of the men in the stands had given up on the idea of ever getting to watch their kids play sports after their wives had given birth to two, three or even four daughters in a row. They had assumed it wouldn't happen, yet here they were, watching their daughters run out onto the field.

Some of the men were thrilled to get to watch their children compete. Some were going along with it to make their girls or their wives happy. A few were complaining to each other that it just wasn't right. Among the fathers were mothers worried about their girls & also excited. More than one had wanted to play sports like this as a kid but had not been able to. Now they were getting to watch their daughters storm the field.

Judith was one of those mothers. Having grown up with four brothers who all played soccer in school, she had wanted to join the team as well. She had almost burst into tears when her parents told her she wasn't allowed. She had gotten furious when the coach told her there were no girls' teams for her to play on. She remembered telling him that she would be alright playing with the boys, but he just laughed her off, saying that it wasn't allowed.

Now here was her daughter, eight years old & wearing the red & silver uniform of the Kickabouts. As the girls were warming up for the game against the Hens, Judith's oldest brother showed up & sat next to her.

"Did I miss anything?"

"No, they're getting ready. Thanks for coming, Derrick couldn't make it tonight."

Her brother gave her a look that told her he wasn't buying it.

"Okay, he didn't want to come. He's not too happy that our oldest is playing sports."

"His loss. She's on the Kickabouts, right?"

"Yeah. She's right there next to the goalie."

"I see her. She looks like she's ready to kick some butt, just like you were."

Janet smiled.

"I'm just glad that there's another school with a U9 girls' team. She's been having so much fun in practice, she was thrilled when she found out that they were going to get to play an actual game."

"Glad to hear that soccer isn't going to die in our family."

"How was Billy's practice yesterday?"

"It wasn't."

"What happened?"

"The coach from his school was out sick & they couldn't agree on which coach from the other schools should replace him. Do you have any idea how hard it is to run a team that's led by a committee from three different schools? Honestly, a third of his practices aren't happening because these three coaches can't coordinate."

"That's horrible."

"Yeah. It certainly doesn't help that he isn't really becoming friends with his teammates. It's a lot harder for kids his age to become friends with teammates from other schools."

"That's rough."

"It can be. I think their starting the game."

Judith turned back to the game & watched as they started playing. Everything else seemed to fall away as her daughter chased the ball & the other team back & forth across the field. More than once, Judith stood up & cheered her daughter on with some of the other moms in the stands.

One of the men, a reporter for the local newspaper, busted out his camera & took a few pictures of the crowd cheering. He thought that his editor might like it, the surreal sight of mothers, cheering their daughters to victory on the soccer field.

Judith felt the adrenaline pumping all throughout the game. She wished that she could have played like this when she was young. Partway through the second half of the game, she watched as her daughter got the ball, charged across the field, & made a goal scoring kick about half a second before one of the other girls tripped her.

She went down hard, clutching her leg. Judith didn't panic. In her head, the procedure was simple. Get to her daughter, make sure she was alright, kiss her hurting leg, then find the little bitch that tripped her baby & end her.

Just as the voice of reason was kicking in to tell her that she couldn't actually kill an eight-year-old girl, Judith realized that she was on the field next to the coach with her brother failing to keep up.

"Is she alright? Is she alright?!"

"I'm fine Mom. Can I get up now?"

Hearing her daughter's attitude in full force calmed her down. Hearing the coach's words helped as well.

"In a minute. It looks like a bit of a scrape there, so the nurse has to sign off on you getting up & playing."

"Come on."

Two school nurses, one from each team, showed up to examine the scrape on her leg. They quickly determined that nothing was broken & that she was going to have one hell of a bruise. When she asked if she could keep playing, they told her that she shouldn't. She wasn't happy about that. Judith felt the weight of the world fall off her shoulders.

"Come on baby girl, we can watch the rest of the game together."

"Fine. But did you see that goal?"

"Yes!"

Judith lied. The ball could have transformed into a dinosaur & she wouldn't have noticed. She just wanted to keep her daughter from going back out onto the field for the rest of this game. She loved watching her girl play, but an injury was an injury.

Taking her little soccer fiend into the stands so she could watch the rest of the game, some of the other parents congratulated her on such an incredible goal & on being so tough. She smiled with pride as Judith got her an apple juice to drink while they watched the rest of the game.

Once one of the two girls on the reserve team got to take over the empty spot, the game continued. While the Kickabouts didn't score anymore goals, they did end up winning the game. With her leg feeling better, Judith relented & let her daughter go & celebrate for a bit with the girls. Judith's brother leaned over while clapping.

"I guess soccer isn't dead in our family."

"I guess not."

Judith smiled as her daughter celebrated her first win.

November 6th, 1974

Sacramento, California

Patricia Torres had spent the entire night watching midterm results come in from all over the country. Her own Matriarch Party had failed again, though not by as much as in seventy-two. In one congressional district, they had managed to get almost a third of the vote, making them a contender to be taken seriously in the next election.

Still, even with their defeat, Patricia was thrilled as the results from across the nation came in. The Democrats had made sweeping victories despite the anger from the right about letting women into the military. By four in the morning, news stations all over the country were announcing that they had retaken Congress from the republicans. Patricia, along with her party members who were still up, cheered.

As experts analyzed & tried to understand this hard swing to the left, each station played a number of clips from the night before of voters being interviewed about why they voted for the democrats. A number of them had said that it was because of the renewed investment in the Apollo program. Some said that it was to get the ERA passed. Most said that it was about the birth anomaly. One clip showed a man from Texas, with a belt buckle bigger than his fist & a snow white Stetson.

"Look, I voted for the republicans in seventy-two because I felt that the dems weren't getting the job done. They were lingering in Vietnam & we were still running short on boys. I thought some new management was just what the doctor ordered. Then it turned out that their solution for a decade of next to no boys being born was to bury their heads in the sand & hope that the free market magically just sorted everything out. I have two girls at home, four

& five, who they gonna date when they're older? Who are they gonna marry? Who they gonna have kids with? Our congressman's answer was to go on about how marriage was a sacred institution. That don't help my little girls!"

While there were still a number of districts that would need a while to count, the simple fact of the matter was that the democrats had made serious gains. Almost a decade into the anomaly & more & more people were aware that the liberals were right, sacred institutions & traditions were going to need to be updated. The world was changing & they were long past the point where it could be ignored or easily compensated for.

Patricia almost jumped when the door to their headquarters opened, letting the light of dawn in. Seeing Kathleen walk in, she smiled.

"Is it morning already?"

"Well, the sun thinks so. I disagree. The not so gracious winner had me on the phone last night for an hour complaining that I took away so many of his votes that the congressional seat we were fighting for almost went to the republicans."

"He sounds fun."

"So, what's the verdict boss? Am I trying for that seat again in seventy-six, or do I have to find myself a real job?"

"Oh, you're trying again. You got a third of the votes for a congressional seat. That's the best we've ever managed at that level by a lot. You've got some magic working for you & I want it again."

"You've got it Patricia. So did we win anything in the end?"

"Not much. We won a spot on a school board & a seat on a city zoning council."

"Hey, that's better than nothing. Yesterday we had nothing, now we get to be part of local government."

"A small part, but you're right Kathleen, it's more than we had. I think that seventy-six will be our election."

Kathleen hugged Patricia before they both sat down to start going over the results of the election, district by district.

1975

January 27th, 1975
CBS News Desk

Walter Cronkite sat at his desk as the commercials ran. He had wanted the second news story that he was going to present to be the headline news of the night. Instead, the senate had voted 91-3 to have Frank Church, a senator from Idaho, lead a new committee to investigate the CIA. Having gotten that breaking story out of the way, it was time for what Walter felt would be a much larger set of stories. As the lights came on, he heard the countdown & turned to face the camera.

"Welcome back. It was in March of 1972 that the government of the United States of America submitted the ERA to the states for ratification. The new constitutional amendment would seek to remove any distinction between men & women from American law. This would help to usher in true equality for women & to remove any & all discrimination based on gender if it becomes law. While republicans have referred to the effort as the far-left pandering to a people panicked by an unprecedented anomaly, it has indeed seen significant support, including from a number of traditionally conservative states. Within just a few short months, sixteen states had already ratified the amendment. Despite major Republican wins in the last presidential election, progress towards ratification continued, albeit at a much slower pace. But despite thirty states ratifying the amendment by the end of 1973, progress came to a grinding halt. 1974 saw no states ratify the ERA & multiple republican controlled legislatures attempt to repeal their ratification for it. While this effort ultimately failed, it did create a sense that the effort was doomed to fail. But just a few weeks into the new year with several states having returned control of their legislatures to the democrats in the recent midterms, it seems that the effort to ratify the ERA is back on. This morning, Alabama became the third state this year, along with Oregon & New Jersey, to ratify the ERA."

Cronkite waited a moment before continuing to let the news sink in for the viewers.

"This brings the total number of states to have ratified the amendment to thirty-three. While it is not likely that we will receive any more of the five ratifications that are needed by the end of the year, it is clear that the battle is not over in the fight for equality among the genders. As we move closer to a world where ninety percent of the people entering the workforce & beginning to vote will be women, it seems ever more likely that the ERA will succeed & help to reshape the future."

Turning to another camera to indicate that a new story was beginning, Cronkite quickly read the teleprompter to make sure that he had his information right.

"Speaking of a future being reshaped by the birth ratio anomaly, it was about one year ago that military recruitment ads targeting women for full combat roles in the us army began appearing around the nation. While many groups around the country protested this move by the military & several experts claimed that no more than a handful of women would join, the military was stunned to find so many women enlisting that many had to be placed on a waiting list. By March, these new female units began basic training & the results have been beyond the wildest expectations of even the most optimistic military analysts. They've performed so well in fact that the military is already moving some of them into potential combat zones."

At home, thousands of American families watched the news as they realized that some of their girls might actually be getting deployed.

"Two all-female platoons, both led by female first lieutenants who have been serving in non-combat roles for a few years are being deployed to American bases overseas. One unit is being deployed to West Germany, less than sixty miles from the iron curtain that separates us from the USSR. The second platoon will be stationed in South Korea, just outside of Seoul, where they will operate near the demilitarized zone with the North."

All over the country, concerned parents started calling military bases to reach their daughters & find out if it was their girls being deployed around the world to stare down the communists.

February 13th, 1975
Ferris Barracks, Bavaria, West Germany

Debra Foster slumped into the empty chair in the common room. Leaning her head back, she tried to relax a bit as another long day came to an end. As glad as she was to be finished with training, there were still parts of life as an infantryman that could be downright exhausting. It certainly didn't help that the women in her platoon were being forced to jump through a ridiculous number of inspections. When someone sat down in the chair next to her, she hoped that it wasn't another guy that was thrilled to be serving with women.

"How's your day going Debra?"

Opening her eyes, she saw another woman from her squad cracking open a newspaper from back home that was only a few days old.

"Ich brauche ein Bier."

"I see the German lessons are coming along."

"I just found out that in German writing, they capitalize all of the nouns & now my brain is a little broken, which is why, like I said, I could use a beer."

She laughed.

"Why are you learning German?"

Debra looked over to her.

"I figured that we're in Germany & we have a lot of free time on our hands, so why not."

"I guess you've got a point."

The two of them paused their conversation to flip off another private that whistled as he walked past them.

"So, Debra, any plans for the weekend?"

"Figured I'd write home at some point."

"How about for Valentine's Day?"

"Nope. I'm trying to stay out of trouble."

"What trouble, a few of us girls are just gonna head into Nuremberg, find a nice restaurant for some lonely gals."

"A restaurant or a bar?"

"Restaurant first, then see what we're in the mood for. We could use someone that speaks German."

"I'm not that fluent."

"You're more fluent than the rest of us."

Debra thought about it for a moment.

"Sounds like fun."

"Sweet."

Sitting up a bit, Debra nodded to the newspaper.

"What's that you got there?"

"Newspaper from Monday. Figure that I'd catch up on what's happening back home."

"Anything interesting?"

"Oh, you could say that."

She handed Debra the paper, showing her the headline.

"President Humphrey calls on states to relax sodomy laws."

"Yep. Them Nine to One girls are gonna be old enough to start dating in a few years."

"And there aren't going to be enough men to go around."

"Exactly what he says in his speech. We're gonna have to do it eventually, let two thirds of the country be dykes while the rest of them fight for a handful of very lucky boys."

Debra cracked open the paper to take a glance at it.

"Makes sense that we should start softening the laws. If we don't, there'll be a revolution one day. Even if we can avoid that, eventually most of the people voting will be girls that'll vote for one of their own who'll repeal the laws."

"Yep. That's our future. Keeping the commies East of the iron curtain so that in twenty or thirty years, half the girls can be rug munchers while the other half share the handful of men so they can push out as many kids as they can. Can you imagine what that'll be like for them?"

"Which them? The lesbians or the man chasers?"

"Hell, either of them. Can you imagine sharing a man with three or four or five other girls just so you can get knocked up? Either that or going at it with a woman?"

She physically cringed as she finished her question. Debra thought about sharing a man.

"Sharing doesn't feel right. Marriage should be built on love, not on whether your monthlies line up with his other wives or not. That would be more like renting a piece of equipment."

"Damn straight Debra, ain't right. But if you were one of those girls, would you rent a man, or would you go cave diving?"

"I… I don't think that I could go… you know…"

"Rug munching, clam licking, kitty kissing."

"I get it. I don't think that I could do that."

"So, what would you do?"

"I would… I would get a girlfriend for all the love bits, you know, sharing a home, having someone to talk to & care for, someone to spend time with. But we would both be sharing the same man, so that he would spend twice as much time with us & he wouldn't be like a disposable toy."

Her squad mate thought about it for a moment.

"That's brilliant. Get to have a great romance with someone that's considerate & understands you, then you got a man around for when you're in the mood."

"It would still be weird with another woman."

"Maybe, but you know what, I think that's the way I'd go. Sharing a man ain't ideal & dating a woman take some getting used to, but it sounds like the best alternative to me. Better than climbing into the sack with another woman, although, I suppose if there were no men, after enough years, I might be inclined to get drunk enough to try it."

Debra looked up from the paper.

"Really, how many years?"

"A good number of them. I ain't remotely interested in girls, but I ain't a nun. Sooner or later, I need somebody else in there."

"Prison rules."

"Prison rules. Ya make do with what ya have."

As her friend started contemplating other scenarios, Debra tried to imagine what it would be like if her only options really were being part of a harem or another woman. Grateful that she was born a decade before anyone who would have to make that choice, she felt sorry for the young girls who would be faced with that choice in a few years.

April 9th, 1975
800 kilometers above the Pacific

The new lunar craft, designed by soviet engineers to carry two people to the moon & back, sat in orbit above the Earth, unmanned, & ready to begin its voyage. The N1 rocket had successfully delivered the lander to orbit two days ago where Soviet engineers had been testing its systems to make triple sure that everything was working correctly. They couldn't afford to screw this up.

The test was scheduled to begin in just a few minutes. High ranking party members were taking positions to watch the test of the Blok G. If it worked, it would carry the unmanned lander on a slingshot orbit around the moon. If it didn't, either the moon program would be scrapped, or the new team would wonder what happened to their colleagues. It didn't help that one member of the team was already missing. Tikhon got off the phone. He went into the control room with a grim countenance. The news he had to deliver was not good.

"I have just gotten off the phone with Moscow. Petya will not be arriving today due to a personal emergency. He is on his way to Novopolotsk to attend the funeral of his brother. I have asked Moscow to pass along our well wishes to him in this dark hour. His substitute will be here momentarily, please review your procedures."

As he turned to his desk, the man next to him leaned in close & kept his hand over the microphone.

"Why were we informed by Moscow? Shouldn't the program director have told us?"

"There are complicating factors."

"What kind of complicating factors?"

Tikhon looked around & double checked to make sure the microphones were off.

"The kind that can get his security clearance revoked."

"Petya? Never. He is one of the most loyal people I know, he received a medal from comrade Brezhnev himself. What could he have done to warrant suspicion?"

"Not Him, his brother, the one with seven daughters."

"Is his brother really dead?"

"If not, he'll soon wish that he was. He was in one of the daughter protests."

"Fucking hell. Which protest?"

"Does it matter? There are so many of them. At this rate, we're going to run out of fathers long before we run out of sons."

"So Petya's brother was caught protesting, now he's being removed from his secure position right before a major test. He's not coming back, is he?"

"No. Toma Tarasova just got promoted. I'm going to make the announcement next week when we'll be informed that Petya has decided to take work closer to home to support his brother's family for an indefinite period of time."

"Damnit. Well, we are still here. I've never had a woman work for me, is Tarasova any good?"

"She's the best. Top of her class, brilliant & fiercely loyal when the political officers are around. Make sure that you tell her about the computer error when she gets here."

"God help us. I'd almost forgotten about that."

Toma Tarasova arrived just three minutes before the test was to take place. The test was then delayed three hours so that she could do the work that her predecessor was supposed to do. Once everything was confirmed to be ready, the test began.

Above the Pacific, the navigational computer confirmed that it was properly aligned & located. Then, at the newly appointed time, the Blok G rocket fired & the entire contraption began to accelerate. As the engine burned, an alarm sounded. Panic hit Tikhon until Toma confirmed it was just a sensor malfunction. A few moments later, the burn came to an end & the engine shut down properly.

"Trajectory!"

The man tracking the flight of the lander took a minute to examine his readings.

"It would appear that we are within acceptable tolerances. Blok G was successful."

The room erupted into cheers. The political officers & officials congratulated the men & woman involved. Above the Earth, the spent Blok G stage separated from the lander as the experimental craft began its journey towards the Moon.

That night, the success of being able to break orbit was played on Soviet news & propaganda channels all over the union. While many believed that it was just something to keep the masses fooled into thinking that the party had everything under control, a handful of people felt safer in knowing that their nation was still doing great things as they sent their daughters off to bed that night.

Before the craft could perform its first course correction, President Humphrey, the Pentagon & the people in charge of NASA were being briefed on the Soviet advance in space.

By the time that it was halfway to the Moon, the story broke & news agencies all over the world were talking about how the USSR was making a push for the Moon.

Since the lander was on a simple free return trajectory, it didn't need to perform any maneuvers to slingshot around the Moon. While it was there, it got a few decent photos of the Moon's far side before coming home. By the time that it landed in the North Pacific, President Humphrey was already ordering NASA to develop the Saturn V's replacement & to come up with plans for how they would continue to be one step ahead of the Soviets as the reds slowly caught up to the milestone of being able to land on the Moon.

May 2nd, 1975
National Institute of Health, Bethesda, Maryland

Edward Swanson groggily woke up when Barbara nudged his shoulder to gently wake him up.

"Bar... Barbara... what time is it?"

"It's nine in the morning, everyone is coming in, except for you it seems. Did you sleep here?"

"I guess. I was looking over some reports from two years ago... then I guess I passed out."

"Right, well I hope that you had copies of that report, because this one is soaked through."

Edward held up the drool covered report.

"Yeah, that was a copy."

"Are you alright Edward? You look like you haven't seen daylight in weeks."

"What's daylight?"

Barbara put the amended budget request for a new project in her department in Edward's inbox & then sat down opposite him, looking over the piles of paper on his desk.

"What's going on Edward? What is all of this?"

"This is my worst nightmare. The decade report on the commission's investigation into the birth ratio anomaly."

"Right. I take it that it's a little bit more than a quick recap of the last ten annual reports."

"To say the least. It's a complete inventory, report & dissection of everything that we've done, discovered, invented & attempted in the last decade. Starting with when I was tapped to lead this shit show because the other guy was a little too close to retirement, & I had heard a lecture on... on... what the fuck was it... it was Madeleine... Charnier, talking about the effects of testosterone on females of... some fucking lizard or another, I don't remember."

"That's why you were put in charge! Because the other guy was a fossil & you went to a lecture on lizards."

"Yes mam. Now I have five months to sift through everything we've done in a decade, including all of the joint work with commissions & projects around the world, & to assemble it into a single report the size of a phonebook that describes how in ten years, all we've really done is invent new ways to get negative results at a faster rate."

"Jesus."

"You know what the most horrible thing about this is?"

"I'm afraid to ask you Edward."

"The most horrible thing is that in ten years, when it comes time to do the 1975-to-1985-decade review, I'll be sixty-five, which means that the second decade report will probably be the last thing that I do before I retire. A second monument to a second decade of failure."

Barbara wasn't exactly sure of what to say.

"Maybe we'll find a solution by then."

Edward looked at her in disbelief.

"No Barbara. We won't. Let's face facts, we're running very low on plausible causes. Hell, we're running low on improbable causes. Last week I looked through the fringe theories for whatever hippie aluminum hat whack a doodle ideas were being suggested, & it was a list of stuff that we've gone through & studied. Even the crazies are running out of ideas & just throwing stuff out there."

"It can't be that bad."

"One woman from Georgia suggested that some new horse dewormer can fix the problem. What in the actual fuck am I supposed to do with that? Put a hundred mothers to be on a dewormer made for horses & see if more than ten of them give birth to boys? Oh, and apparently, the drug can cause miscarriages in horses, which means we shouldn't be giving it to pregnant woman."

"Wow. Admittedly, that is a bit out there. But there has to be something reasonable that we can try."

"I wouldn't count on it. We've been scrapping the bottom of the barrel for years. The only studies that we have that are panning out are the ones that look into how we might adapt to the new way of the world."

"I see. How are those coming along?"

"Great. Wonderfully great. We're going to have to tell America that their children will be embracing lesbianism & polygamy while their daughters run the economy & fight the wars. How do you think a country that's majority Christian is going to handle that?"

"You need a vacation."

"What I need is to go back to 1965 & refuse this job."

June 24th, 1975
Montgomery Alabama

Two trucks & a van were parked just outside the Alabama State House. Ronnie Addams sat in the driver's seat of the lead truck ahead of the van. For the last two hours, he had been carefully trying to keep his team calm. For two & a half years, they had tried to use signal jammers to block the satellite signals that were stopping them from having sons. It hadn't worked. Among their group, they had had about forty children & only four of them were boys, just like the national average.

Their plan wasn't working, & most of the Sons of Adam didn't have the patience to try another technical solution. They wanted to have sons to carry on their legacy. They didn't want the feminists & the queers to take over & remake the world in their image. They wanted answers. This left Ronnie & the senior leadership with only one option. They were going to have to do something big. They were going to have to get someone to talk.

They had spent weeks looking over targets that could tell them how to set things right. Obviously, President Humphrey had been the first on their list of people who would know. He was the President & they were mostly convinced that he hadn't actually won either election. But Ronnie was smart enough to realize that they would never get close to him, so they decided to look a little more locally.

For two months, they had watched the comings & goings of the members of Alabama's government. From its us senators to its aldermen. They wanted to go after someone with relatively little security, but at the same time, they wanted someone high up enough that they would know what was happening. Eventually, they settled on the Lieutenant Governor of Alabama.

They spent weeks subtly observing his movements. Watching him come & go, figuring out his security which seemed fairly lackluster. Most of them believed that the highest-ranking member of the state senate must know the truth, or that he could at least get them closer to the answers. In order to convince the members of the Sons of Adam that were hesitant or were subtly hinting at a leadership change that this was a good idea, Ronnie joined the mission personally. With the voices of descent calmed down, it was time to make their move.

At about eleven thirty, Ronnie heard one of the lookouts call out on the walkie talkie that he had on his dashboard. He had been expecting the call at this time. The Lieutenant Governor always went for lunch at that time on Tuesdays.

"Tango is on the move. Normal route. Plus, one. Slightly more crowded than normal."

Ronnie felt a chill run down his back. It wasn't uncommon for the Lieutenant Governor to go to lunch with someone. Politics was all about connections & backroom deals. But something just felt... off. Unable to put his finger on it, he called out to his men.

"Alright everyone, Bravo strategy, we don't want any random bystander getting hurt. Don't pull your weapons until you're up close."

The van opened up & four guys got out as well as a few more guys from the trucks. The original plan, if the sidewalk hadn't been too crowded would have been to jump out, guns out, charge him, grab him, get him into the van & haul ass. But with so many people, that would have been a challenge, so they stuck to handguns & kept them concealed.

"Tango approaching corner one. You'll have eyes any second now."

Once he was around the corner, he would walk close to them & then it would only take a few seconds to get him in the van. As the Lieutenant Governor came around the corner, Ronnie got a look at him & the guy he was with. The guy looked familiar. Ronnie felt that same nervous chill. As his men started approaching the Lieutenant Governor with the intent of surrounding him, Ronnie noticed that some of the people on the street seemed to be a little to suit & tie.

As his men parted to let the Lieutenant Governor walked through them, at which point, they would spring the trap, that was when Ronnie realized who was walking next to the Lieutenant Governor. It was the US Senator from North Carolina, the one in the papers because he was relentlessly hounding the North Carolina Legislature to block a vote on the ERA. He had received threats when he announced that he was coming to Montgomery to try & grease the wheels to get Alabama to withdraw their ratification of the ERA. The extra suits must have been the added security detail for him. The detail that was expecting men with guns to take a shot at the Senator. Ronnie grabbed his walkie talkie.

"Abort! Abort! Retreat immediately!"

It was too late. The six men pulled their guns. The one in front of the Lieutenant Governor moved forward.

"Jeremy Foreman, you're coming with..."

A loud bang cracked through the air as the lead gunman went down. One of the suits, an armed bodyguard, had drawn on an unsuspecting gunmen & had taken him down with one shot. At this point, the rest of Ronnie's men realized that they were surrounded by state security. Ronnie could see one of them calling for backup. Some of them pulled guns on Ronnie's men while others grabbed the Lieutenant Governor & the Senator from North Carolina.

Shots were soon fired. One of the bodyguards & two of Ronnie's men went down. Sirens were blaring in the distance, & people were running for their lives. Ronnie's men tried to retreat, but they were surrounded. As some of them gave up, Ronnie did the only thing that he could think to do that wouldn't make things worse.

"Scatter!"

The two trucks & the van pulled forward & hit the gas. With the van door still open, one of Ronnie's men tried to jump back in, but he was tackled by state security. The three vehicles then went off in different directions, two of them away from the sirens.

A few hours later, Ronnie was driving through Tuscaloosa when he finally got a decent news station on his radio.

"Breaking news, the four men who were arrested by the police & the three that were killed were all part of a radical group that call themselves the Sons of Adam. This is the same group that tried to take over a mall in Nashville five years ago, demanding that the federal government admit that they were using stolen Nazi space technology to create the birth ratio anomaly. The group's leader, Ronald Addams, also known as Ronnie, was not apprehended, or killed at the scene. He is at the top of the FBI's most wanted list. If you have any useful information about his location, or the location of his group, the Sons of Adam, please contact the FBI or your local law enforcement."

He cursed in his truck as he drove out of Tuscaloosa. He should have realized that with such a controversial senator in town, there might be increased security. Not knowing if either of the other two vehicles made it out, he now had to head back to base camp, empty-handed & knowing that a number of the people in his movement were going to be calling for him to step down.

August 11th, 1975
New York City

Lena was swimming in stories. As the Lavender Press was growing in popularity & slowly spreading across the state, Lena was also getting more & more access to more & more stories, including friends in places where they could tell her about things that hadn't quite reached the mainstream yet. Such was the nature of the call that she had just gotten.

With her regular Sunday issue having just gone out the day before, Lena had already been swimming in new stories to cover & look through when she got the call. It was a nurse friend of hers that worked at New York Methodist Hospital.

Normally, when she called, it was to update Lena on things like hospital policies & things that were happening in the medical world. Lena had been certain that the call was going to be about the hospital's decision concerning its treatment of queer patients. Some of the doctors were unwilling to follow the new DSM guidelines that said homosexuality was no longer considered a disease & Lena's contact was keeping her updated-on policy changes & what the hospital was doing about these doctors that refused to get with the times. Lena was expecting such an update, that was not what she got.

The nurse had been in a rush, calling from a payphone outside the hospital just to be extra careful that nobody overheard her. Lena was stunned when she heard that Janis Joplin had been wheeled into the hospital, suffering from a near fatal overdose.

Lena was dumbstruck. For a moment, it felt like 1970 all over again, hearing the news that one of the voices of a generation was fighting for her life. She had just barely survived & it had changed her. Sure, she had never actually given up the heroin & sure, she was still a bit of a wild child, but she had gotten more careful, not wanting to slip into the darkness just yet. She had even gotten the number twenty-seven tattooed on her wrist to remind her of when she nearly died.

It was hard to hear that she was in the hospital for this again. She was supposed to be in New York for a concert performance of

Needles, Love & Visions, her seventh album. Lena thanked her friend & sat in her office looking over the small pile of stories in front of her. A decade into the anomaly, there was no shortage of news. Stories about resistance to conservative resurgences in the middle east to reports of massive protests behind the iron curtain to the women preparing to go to the Moon.

She already had enough stories to fill her paper well into September & to make matters worse, with this bombshell dropping on a Monday, it would be old news by the time her next issue went out on Sunday. She didn't want to be the last to report it & she had no idea how she was going to fit this story in with everything else that she was going to publish on Sunday. Looking to the stories that she already had typed up & ready to print, the story about how many women were enlisting, the story about how New York middle schools were preparing for the first children of the XX generation. She realized that she had nearly enough prepared material to release a new issue already.

She would need a few hours to type up the story about Janis Joplin, & a day to print & call her distributors, but it could be done. Lena grabbed the old phone on her desk & called up Sarah, her senior delivery girl.

"Hello?"

"Sarah, it's Lena, do you have a minute?"

"Sure, is everything alright?"

"Yeah, I was wondering if you would be available to deliver another issue on Wednesday."

"Wednesday? When did we start sending out on Wednesday?"

"Since Janis Joplin is in the hospital & I have enough other material to go to print tomorrow."

"Who's in the hospital?"

"I'm going to pretend that you didn't just say that. Can you deliver on Wednesday?"

"Sure. I don't know if Susan will be available to drive the other truck, but she's more reliable than the girl before her, so we'll see."

"Great."

"Is this going to be a regular thing, are we twice a week now?"

"No, this is a special issue."

"Alright, I'll check with Susan & get back to you."

"Great."

Hanging up the phone, Lena looked around at all of the stories & leads that she had backing up & she started to wonder if she could make the Lavender Press a bi-weekly paper, sending out twice a week instead of every week. Shaking her head of the notion, she got to the typewriter & started going over her notes about what her nurse friend had told her before she started typing up a rough draft of the story of Janis Joplin ending up in the hospital again.

October 18th, 1975
Oval Office

The final report was so thick that it had to be split into multiple volumes. All in, they made the phone book for New York City look skinny. President Humphrey looked at the report sitting on his table & turned to the Secretary of Health, Education & Welfare who had just lugged the report into the oval office.

"I'm amazed that you didn't throw your back out lugging that in here."

"I'm fine, just don't pay too much attention to the trail of broken interns leading to this room."

Humphrey chuckled as he picked up the first book, over a hundred pages thick & he realized that it was just the index for the report.

"This Doctor Edward Swanson, seems to be a very thorough man."

"I won't argue with you on that sir. Based on my quick skimming of the report, it looks like he's covered everything that the commission has done, looked into, discovered & cost us over the last decade."

"Well, I suppose that is what we asked for. I don't suppose that you could sum it up for me. I intend to read it, but I've only got another year or so in office."

The secretary laughed.

"Well, sir, basically, it says that they found nothing."

"Nothing."

"Nothing sir. They spent ten years combing through every possibility. Everything from genetics to corn syrup, from viruses to astrology, from chemistry to latent radioactive fallout from nuclear testing. They have no idea what's causing it."

President Humphrey put the index down. He then stood up & walked over to the window to look outside.

"I don't suppose that he mentions his plans for the future?"

"He does sir. The commission is going to continue looking into what's happening. However, they request that we invest more in their programs for technological development. Apparently, they are starting a number of programs to develop better tools to aid in their research & open up new avenues of exploration into the nature of the anomaly."

"Well, at least they're still trying."

"Yes sir, but I believe that the consensus among most of the people working in the commission is that there is no hope."

"Why do you say that?"

"Because sir, their final recommendation is that we prepare for this anomaly to be the new official status quo. They'll keep trying, but they seem to be of the opinion that even if they can find a solution, it'll take so long that by that point, society & culture will have permanently changed & that large parts of the population won't want to go back."

Humphrey turned around to face the secretary.

"Tell me you're joking."

"Truth of the matter is sir, there are already small groups of people that are happy this is happening."

"Really?"

"Yes sir. The longer that this goes on, the more that people will get used to it & the more that people get used to it, the fewer who will want to go back."

"I see. And it's already been going on for a decade."

"Exactly sir. There's another issue as well sir."

"Great, it gets worse. What's the issue?"

"Even if they find a solution tomorrow, in about a decade, we'll begin experiencing a population crash as the XX generation reaches its main childbearing years."

"The XX generation, is that what we're calling them now?"

"It seems to be the term that's sticking. Now we can do everything that we can to encourage the girls in this generation to have big families. We can run ad campaigns to make having half a dozen children look fun, we can convince the ones that get married to share their husbands with their friends, to a degree, in some places. We have a decade to try & convince this generation to have lots of kids, but the simple fact is that unless we can find a way to make the common man in this generation father nineteen children on average, there will be a population crash."

"I don't like where you're going with this."

"I've consulted with the secretary of the treasury & he agrees. In about thirty years, either we're going to have to dramatically increase immigration to levels not seen since the eighteenth century, or we're going to have to find a way to make our growth-based economy function while it's shrinking with the population."

President Humphrey sat back down.

"Thank God I'm not up for reelection. How long until this report goes public?"

"Copies are already going out to government bodies & allied NATO governments. It'll be released to the public in a matter of days."

"This is going to unleash a firestorm."

November 20th, 1975
CBS Newsroom

"A renewal of the traditional American values that this country was built upon. We need to restore faith, faith in the American people, faith in American institutions, & faith in America itself to overcome adversity as we rise to the challenges facing this great nation of ours. Crime, drug use, radical liberal ideologies & the threat of communism. The challenge posed by these issues is the reason why I am announcing my candidacy to run for President of the United States, to restore the great American spirit of Freedom, Faith & Fortune."

In millions of homes across the country, the scene of the famous actor announcing his candidacy paused & was quickly replaced by the more familiar Walter Cronkite.

"That was footage recorded earlier today from famous actor & former single term Governor of California, Ronald Reagan. He's Also famous for his role as Robert L. Howser in the hit television show Western Horizon which ended its four-season run six months ago. After his back-to-back failures at getting reelected as the Governor of California, Reagan was assumed to be stepping out of politics with the amount of time that he has devoted to his acting career over the last several years."

"While some expected his scheduled announcement today to be another bid for his lost governorship, it seems that he has surprised everyone by announcing his intent to run for President. While some in the republican party see this push by Reagan for more traditional conservative values as great for the nation, many others see it as problematic."

An image of Reagan appeared on the screen with a number of bullet points for the audience to see.

"Several Republicans are not in favor of how he raised taxes on sales, banks, & corporate profits during his single term as Governor. Furthermore, a number of republicans, as well as many democrats & independents call his use of the term radical liberal ideologies as being shortsighted. They point to it being an indication that he & many other members of the republican party are completely out of touch with reality. In recent months, a number of more liberal republicans have pointed to issues such as lesbian marriage, polyamory, & matriarchal households as necessities that whether for the short term or for the long term, will be needed to contend with the growing gender imbalance."

The image on millions of screens returned to Cronkite talking into the camera.

"Perhaps the greatest criticism put to Reagan's candidacy is the fact that he completely neglected to even mention the birth ratio crisis. This is a tactic that has been seen in many members of the republican party, an almost ironic unwillingness to acknowledge the elephant in the room. Many do not give Mr. Reagan any significant odds of winning the party nomination, let alone the election itself."

1976

January 14th, 1976
Chicago, Illinois

Hope Baker sipped her tea. Despite the grey weather outside, she was in a cheery mood. Seeing her sister always brightened up her day. Just as Hope was starting to get worried that Grace was a bit late, her sister came in through the door, shoulders slumped, bags under her eyes & her brown hair barely kept together. She dropped into her seat & immediately started drinking the coffee that Hope had ordered for her.

"You look like you've had a rough morning."

"A rough week is more like it. Thanks for ordering my coffee for me. With three children, this sweet bean juice is the only thing keeping me going. Last night wasn't much help."

"Wasn't the middle school board meeting last night?"

Grace sipped more of her coffee. Hope could almost see it beginning to take effect.

"That it was. God, I wish that Charity had been born just one year earlier, or even one year later, just so that we wouldn't have to put up with all of this crap."

"How bad was the school board meeting?"

Grace laughed lethargically.

"Hope, if I tell you that it was a three-ring circus, know that I'm not exaggerating."

"God. What happened?"

"Exactly the same thing that happened six years ago when the elementary schools were figuring out how to deal with classes that are almost entirely girls."

"Haven't they had eleven years to prepare for this?"

"They have, but not only did they waste that time, but they haven't bothered to ask the elementary schools how they handled it & on top of that, the kids are now on the verge of puberty. So, there are those issues to."

"Jesus, is it like that everywhere or just for the schoolboard in charge of Charity's school?"

"From what I've heard, it's nearly everywhere. Some places are worse, some are better, but it's like nobody learned from the first go around."

Hope was about to say something when Grace continued.

"You know what it's like, it's like they expected the solution to have been found by now & didn't realize that half the girls of a generation wouldn't magically turn into the missing boys."

"It's run by men is it."

Grace looked at her sister & they both started laughing.

"Yes, yes it fucking is. I don't suppose that your church has opened a private school that I could send Charity too. Maybe a school run by women would know how to teach girls."

"Sadly, no. Although it is an idea."

"God, Hope, you can't believe what it was like last night. The school board was looking for opinions on putting all of the incoming boys this fall into one class just for them. There are going to be enough students in each middle school that they can each have an all-boys class. Well didn't one guy stand up & accuse them of trying to turn the boys queer."

Hope almost chocked on her tea.

"Seriously?"

"Seriously. He stood up & shouted that if we segregate all the boys, it'll make them all gay."

"Does he think that boarding schools make boys gay? Does he think that everyone coming out of college before they let girls in was gay?"

"No idea. But when they suggested that they divide the boys up evenly, some mother stood up & yelled that if it's two or three boys to a class, they'll turn into Nancy's. She said her son was already turning into a Nancy because he only had one other boy in his classes & he barely had a chance to play on sports teams."

"Right, because God forbid that boys play with dolls."

"Right, they have to play with action figures."

They both chuckled for a second before Grace continued.

"So, then someone suggested that they go back to random class placement. Well didn't the whole room erupt as parents became afraid that their boys would be the only boy in a class."

"So literally every option that they suggested, someone was worried that the boys would turn gay."

"Yeah, pretty much."

"Did anyone worry about the girls turning gay with so few boys as their hormones are about to start raging?"

"One woman brought it up when they were suggesting all the boys be lumped together into a single class. She was concerned that it was sending a message that boys are bad. But other than that, one little peep, nobody cared that the girls might go that way."

"Really? I would have thought that that would be a big one."

"I don't know, I think that a lot of parents have just had time to get used to the idea that their girls might end up with other girls. Like they've been worrying about it for so long that they've gotten used to it. Either that, or they're hoping their girls will find older boys."

"Well at least they didn't blow up about that."

"At least. I'm just glad that they're having this meeting nine months in advance. Six years ago, the meeting was held a few weeks in advance. We couldn't figure a few things out & it turned into a case of throw everything against the wall & see what worked."

"So, they have learned something."

"If they've learned anything, it's not how to organize girls' sports teams."

"Oh, this is going to be good. What was their grand idea?"

"Their grand idea, Hope, was to simply not have any. They figure that unlike the elementary schools, they have enough boys to form proper teams, so they don't need to make girls teams."

"I'm guessing that didn't go over well."

"You guessed right Hope. A lot of the parents, especially ones with younger children, aren't too happy with that idea."

"I bet."

"The parents with younger boys are talking about how a lot of their boys don't want to play sports because they don't like them, or they don't want to play them just because the grownups say that they should."

"Makes sense. Who wants to go to the trouble of playing on a sports team because someone else thinks it's a good idea."

"Yeah, well, gets better, the parents with younger girls who are playing sports were shouting that it's not fair to let their daughters play football & baseball & soccer & whatnot & then take it away because now they think that they'll have enough boys."

"Doesn't sound fair to me."

"Yeah, then the more conservative parents that have been resisting girls' sports talked up. I swear, it almost descended into a fistfight."

"Jesus, was anyone hurt?"

"Only egos. In the end, they decided to hold more meetings in a month or so after we'd all had a chance to contemplate all of the options presented & suggested. I think that they just wanted to get the hell out of there."

"I would in their shoes."

They both sipped their dinks.

"So, Hope, how's the church going."

"Pretty good. We've still got some room most Sundays, although with V-day a month away, I suspect that the next few Sundays will be standing room only."

"Is that for morning & afternoon services?"

"I imagine that it will be this year, especially with V-day being on a Saturday. We're planning on afternoon & evening services on Saturday, then morning & afternoon services on Sunday."

"I imagine that on Monday, you'll just be comatose."

"Probably."

"Is Virginia going to be doing something crazy in her sermons this year? Last year was quite the show that you told me about."

"Yeah, I've made her promise that if she talks about freeing ourselves from bras, she's not going to flash the congregation this year."

Grace burst out laughing. After a moment, Hope joined in. Eventually, they managed to calm down before continuing their conversation with the minutia of their daily lives.

When one of the baristas coming onto her shift recognized Hope from Sunday service & said hi, Grace realized how late it had gotten.

"I'm sorry Hope, I'd love to stay, but I've got a meeting with some of the other parents in Charity's class. We're going to talk about some of the things that we went over last night with some of the teachers who don't have a class at that hour."

"That's probably a good idea."

"I've got to tell you Hope, it's something else walking down those school halls, especially in-between classes."

"Really?"

"Yeah, it's a bit surreal, hundreds of children moving around to get to their next class & barely any boys. Did you know that some of the boys are growing their hair long & even wearing a bit of pink."

"I had no idea."

"Yeah, the whole elementary school is nine tenths girls & it looks like it's even more because you can't pick out some of the boys."

"That does sound surreal."

"I have to tell you, it's not what Roger & I imagined when we settled down & decided to have kids."

February 4th, 1976
400 kilometers above the Moon

The two cosmonauts sat next to each other in the tight confines of the lunar lander. They had no idea how the Americans could possibly fit three people into one of these. They must be very friendly. The two men had been both honored & terrified when they were chosen for this mission. The first Soviets to go beyond the Earth & to orbit the Moon. It was a huge honor that would put them up with the like of Yuri Gagarin. Of course, Yuri Gagarin had never had to ride an N1. He had simply had to jump out of his module & parachute to the ground.

After two & a half days, they were thrilled when they saw the Moon looming large in the window. They both imagined what it would be like for the first cosmonaut to set foot on the dusty surface & reclaim it from the Americans. As they approached the Moon, they were preforming their final system checks before the radio blackout. This would be one of the most important parts of the mission. If this engine burn failed, they would simply slingshot around the Moon & fly back home. They actually needed to park in orbit & then orbit the Moon for at least three days. As they were approaching the point of signal loss, they heard Kazakhstan over the radio.

"Comrade Konstantin Orlov. Comrade Gavriil Pushkin. You are approaching the point of signal loss where the Moon itself will block communications. You will be out of contact for approximately ten minutes. Good luck in performing your historic maneuver. Make your country proud."

Konstantin flipped a switch to respond.

"Thank you for the well wished comrade. We will bring glory to the people of the Soviet Union."

A few seconds later, the radios went dead as the Moon blocked out the signals to Earth. Gavriil turned to his commander.

"We will bring glory to the people. I didn't realize the propaganda department was paying us."

"Didn't you hear about how much of their budget went into this mission?"

"That's just a rumor, isn't it?"

"Nope. They paid part of the bill & in exchange, when we come back as heroes of the people, they'll get to parade us around in all of the places that are seeing protests."

"Great. Then after that, we get to go home to our daughters."

"Exactly."

"Konstantin, what is that sound?"

They both listened to the quiet hum reverberating through the ship.

"It's just the turbopumps, you know that they sound like that before the engine fires."

"Yes, but it's only supposed to be a few seconds before the engine fires. The maneuver is not for another four minutes."

They both suddenly went wide eyed as they realized that the turbo pumps were coming on too soon. Looking at the computer display, they saw that the engine fire sequence had started as soon as contact with Kazakhstan had been lost.

"Fuck, Gavriil, emergency shut down, don't let the engines fire."

Their hands flew over the keypads & switches as they tried to abort the launch. It wasn't enough. Almost four minutes ahead of schedule, the main engine fired, putting the ship on the wrong trajectory. About halfway through the burn, they managed to shut off the computer & manually shut off the engine, cursing the whole way.

Kazakhstan knew that something was off when they reacquired the signal three minutes too early. As the cosmonauts explained that the computer fired the engine as soon as contact was lost, reports came in about their new, highly elliptical orbit around the Moon. It did not look good. As American, European & Australian governments watched the scene unfold over radar images, the Soviet space program worked tirelessly to get their men home.

While the cosmonauts were conducting what tests they could, their scientists managed to find a way. As they came close to the Moon again, they very carefully used what was left of their fuel from the original maneuver & some more that was supposed to be for the next maneuver to correct their orbit.

A day later, after completing most of their tests, & running dangerously low on fuel, they performed another burn to come home. Just barely meeting the requirements for reentry, they managed by some miracle to survive the trip home. While the rest of the world congratulated them on getting their people home safe & sound, everyone west of the iron curtain wondered if the Soviets would try another test to get it right, or if their next move would be to try & land on the Moon.

March 1st, 1976
National Institute of Health, Bethesda, Maryland

Doctor Swanson walked into his office & sat down at his desk. For the first time in a long time, he was happy, almost hopeful. As he sat there smiling & staring out the window, Doctor Fekete walked in.

"Edward, the boys down in the computer lab... What... the hell is that?"

"What's what Todor?"

"That thing on your face, it almost looks like... no it couldn't be... no, it is, it's a smile."

Edward Swanson laughed as Todor continued.

"It's been a while since anyone has seen you crack one of those Edward."

"What can I say Todor, it's been a while since I've had a reason to be happy. Ever since that damn report."

"Yes, that was a rough one. But you sure seem happy today."

"Why wouldn't I be happy. For the first time in months, I don't have people yelling or questioning me about why we haven't produced any useful results. It's all about our new computer system & how it's going to speed up our research."

"Well, to be fair Edward, the Cray-1 is more than just a new computer. It's the most powerful computer ever built on Earth. It makes our old computers look like they're still using vacuum tubes. The amount of time that we're going to save & the amount of work we'll be able to do is phenomenal. According to some of the guys that operate the damn thing, it was supposed to go to the Los Alamos National Laboratory to do nuclear research."

"Damn, how did we get it?"

"Apparently, someone in the government thinks that we need it more. Plus, with the space race heating back up, nobody wants to look aggressive."

Edward suddenly understood.

"If they give the most powerful computer in the world to the people who design nuclear bombs & intercontinental missiles, it could be seen as aggressive."

"Exactly. Apollo 21 just took another woman to the Moon, the Soviets will land their first cosmonaut there at any time, tensions are getting a bit high."

"They don't want to throw fuel on the fire. Well, whatever gets us our new supercomputer."

As Edward sat there, he ran his hand through his greying hair while Todor ran his fingers through his incredibly thick mustache as the room went silent at the talk of nukes.

"So, Todor, do the boys downstairs like their new toy?"

"They're in love. I'm glad to see you smiling, this whole room seems brighter for it."

"Thanks, Todor. Hopefully, this lets us accomplish something more than failing at a faster rate."

April 7th, 1976
Rural Alabama

Ronnie had known that this day was coming. The failed mall occupation. The failure of the signal jammers. The failure to catch a man that shouldn't even have had a security detail. It was clear to the Sons of Adam that under Ronnie's role as Shepard, they were not only struggling to recruit, but they were now being actively hunted by multiple government agencies.

Now it was time to pay the piper. Over the years since he had founded the Sons of Adam, he had appointed twelve of the greatest believers to the level of Patriarch. These twelve men acted as community organizers, preachers of the real truth & in some cases, as judges who decided important issues like who in the group could marry or divorce & who could be promoted. In order to help convince the people that followed him that he wasn't a mad tyrant trying to take power, he had given the Patriarchs the power to strip him of his title as Shepard.

He had thought that the twelve men he picked would be loyal. He had been mostly right. But twelve days earlier, he had been presented with a notice that the Patriarchs had put a challenge to his authority. That meant that at least three of them wanted him out.

Appearing at the summons, he walked into the large barn to see the twelve men sitting around him in a half circle made of folding tables & chairs. These men looked just like all the other men in his followers of the truth. Strong, tough, conservative, wise & with thick beards, most of which had some amount of white or grey in them. The only thing separating them from any other man in the group was the small gold pin of the Mars symbol used to denote the male gender. One of the men, a man name Gregory stood up, his beer belly resisting his suspenders as he spoke.

"Ronald Adams. You stand before God almighty & the council of Patriarchs to determine if you truly are our shepherd, or if are you leading us astray. Mark, Albert & I do believe that you cannot lead us to the sons we ought to be having. You stand here to defend yourself."

Ronnie had been expecting Gregory to be one of the three. He was an asshole. A self-righteous firebrand that was only promoted because his passion & charisma had convinced over a third of the followers to join the Sons of Adam. Without him, Ronnie would lose the entire Huntsville contingent & he needed them to monitor & spy on NASA. But Mark & Albert, impossible. Albert was one of his oldest friends & Mark had been one of the first recruits.

"Defend myself. Against what? Being the only one to come up with good strategies to expose the truth?"

"Good strategies! Don't make us laugh! You botched a simple kidnapping. We should have had the Lieutenant Governor here, telling us where we can find the proof. Instead, some of our men are being held captive, including my nephew."

There it was. Gregory had played his hand. His nephew was rotting in a prison cell somewhere & he wanted to do something about it. Ronnie didn't know if that something was just punishing him or trying to break his nephew out, but whatever that something was, it was why he was here.

"So that's why you've convinced the Patriarchs to hold this meeting. You still blame me for your nephew."

"He'd still be a free man if you hadn't turned coward & ran."

"No Gregory, he'd be a free man if the lookouts that you had given me had been able to spot armed bodyguards or the most famous Governor in the South. Those lousy eyes let security get the drop on us & here we are."

Gregory slammed his fist down on the table causing it to bend a bit under his fist.

"It's not just the kidnapping! Every operation & strategy that you have tried has failed spectacularly. Every time that you try something, a large part of our organization can't go back home cause they're wanted men!"

"I'm well aware of that Gregory, my face is posted in every precinct & post office from here to North Carolina. I haven't been home since the mall went sideways."

"That just proves my point. We need a fresh leader that isn't on the FBI's ten most wanted list. We need someone who can actually pull off his clever plans."

"Like your clever plan to invade the prison where your nephew is being held, even though we don't actually know which prison that is?"

Gregory looked like he was about to boil over. Before he could say another word, Ronnie took a step closer to the Patriarchs & made his case in his defense.

"Look, I know that my plans have not yet borne fruit. I could stand here and rightly point out that it all has to do with a number of chance events & poor sightings of key details. Instead, I'm going to simply point out one key thing. The reason that you have all continued to follow my plans is because you knew that they were good & because you know now as you knew then that I am always open to suggestions & new ideas. If you or the people that trust you have a good idea for what we can do next, I'm all ears. Instead of ripping this mission apart from the inside, work with me to figure out our next steps."

"Is that your defense?"

"It is Gregory."

"Then please wait outside for our judgement."

Ronnie thanked the members of the Patriarch's council & walked outside to where dozens of people had gathered to hear how this was going to play out.

As the twelve men deliberated, Ronnie found himself getting irrationally nervous. If seven or more of them voted to boot him, he was out. He knew that three wanted him gone. Could Gregory convince another four to vote his way?

He thought about how his group had started. He thought about his idea to create the very council that was judging him. He thought about how he had gone to lengths to make sure that none of their plans would ever trace back to the council in case they needed to choose a new leader. He wondered for a moment why he created the council in the first place & then remembered that it was so that he could have a system of checks & balances, so that the people would trust him because they knew there was a way to keep him in check.

He thought about all of these things & more for the hour that it took the council to think it over. When he was invited back in, he stood before the council while the growing number of followers stayed outside.

"Ronnie, we've discussed the matter. Do you have any last statement to make before we vote?"

"Nope."

"Very well then. All those in favor of naming a new shepherd, raise your right hand."

Gregory, Albert, Mark & another man named Luthor raised their hands. A Patriarch named Samuel then spoke up.

"All in favor of continuing to follow Ronnie."

The remaining eight members of the council of Patriarchs raised their right hand, bringing the vote in Ronnie's favor. Samuel then stood up.

"It's decided. Ronnie shall remain our Shephard for the time being with the next vote to be held no later than the 7th of April 1980."

Ronnie, while grinning, turned on his heels & walked out the door to announce to his followers the good news, that he was to continue leading them for at least the next few years. With up to four years secured before the next vote, he decided that it would be time to try a new tactic & to begin implementing a longer-term plan. Something that could take several years to pull off but would get him what he wanted. Proof of the greatest conspiracy of all time.

May 9th, 1976
Boston, Massachusetts

Matthew was rather exasperated. This was the third time this week that he was going to have to have this conversation & he could only hope that it would go more smoothly than the last time. Walking into his wood paneled office, He saw Mr. Marks & his wife seated at his desk. As with most of his clients, their appearance screamed of inherited wealth & conservative values. While a lifelong conservative himself, he preferred having this conversation with more liberal individuals. They tended to understand that it was beyond his control.

"Sorry to keep you waiting for so long. I hope that you've been comfortable. Is there anything that I can get for the two of you? Water? Tea?"

Miss Marks looked up from her white gloves & waved off the hospitality.

"Thank you, but we don't need anything other than to know if we qualify for adopting a sweet little boy from your orphanage."

"Yes, my wife & I have been through interviews, financial reports, background checks. Tell us, are you finally ready to let us adopt or not?"

"Sweetheart, they're just being thorough, they need to make sure that we can take care of him."

"You're right darling, I'm just getting a little eager to take our little boy home, whoever he will be."

The two of them looked at Matthew who suddenly felt an unpleasant conversation coming on.

"As you said Miss Marks, we have to be thorough when determining fitness to adopt. The good news is that you have been deemed superbly fit to adopt."

"Wonderous."

As Miss Marks cheered, Mr. Marks imagined enjoying some cigars with his friends & associates at the country club.

"Yes, wonderous, your home has been deemed the perfect environment to raise a child in. There is however, one... minor issue... I'm afraid to say."

Mr. Marks' expression suddenly turned sour.

"What kind of an issue? I thought that you said we were ideal for adopting. What hoop have we not yet jumped through?"

"I'm sorry Mr. Marks, the problem is not with you or your wife or your home. The problem is that on your application, you specified that you were only interested in adopting a son."

"I don't see the problem in that. A son to carry on our name without forcing my wife to give birth up to ten times like some kind of... rural folks."

"Well, the problem is... & this should have been mentioned to you earlier, I admit, the problem is that we have no boys to give you."

They stared at Matthew in complete disbelief. It was Miss Marks who spoke first.

"What do you mean when you say you have no boys to give us?"

"I mean just what I said, our facility has no boys for anyone to adopt at the moment."

It took Mr. Marks only another moment to catch up to the conversation.

"How… can you not… have any boys? This is not supposed to be an all-girls orphanage."

"I assure you that it isn't. We do take in & care for boys when they arrive, it's just that at the moment, there are no boys for us to adopt out."

"But how is that even possible?"

"It's possible for the same reason that many of our clients want to adopt a boy in the first place. The anomaly. You see, a few years after the anomaly began, the number of boys being put up for adoption began to fall drastically. These days, there are hardly any arriving here at all. Furthermore, the number of couples only looking to adopt sons has surged in recent years as couples realize it will probably take four to nine births to have a son & they don't want such massive families."

Mr. Mark sat back in his chair. It wasn't often that he slouched, let alone in defeat. He understood the laws of supply & demand. His entire business was manipulating demand & understanding supply. He understood that there was simply a short supply of orphan boys & a massive demand for them. The demand was simple enough to understand, he wanted a son to carry on his legacy & he & the misses didn't want to have half a dozen or more children before a boy was born.

Miss Marks was not as understanding.

"Surely you have a boy somewhere here. He doesn't have to be perfect; we can afford tutors & nannies to contend with any character flaws or issues."

"I'm truly sorry Miss Marks. It's not a matter of quality, we simply have no boys."

"You can't possibly have no boys at all. You must have some poor miscreant that we can adopt, we're not going to be picky if you are so lacking."

"Honey, they have no boys, leave it alone."

"Nonsense, they have boys, they just don't think they're good enough for us. What's wrong with them? Are they traumatized? Daft? Deformed? Negro? We really don't care."

"Miss Marks! First off, we do not consider a child being negro to be an impediment or defect of any sort in this facility."

"Of course not, my mistake, we're not allowed to say such things anymore."

Matthew cringed a bit in his soul. He hated that his orphanage wasn't yet required to disqualify people with attitudes like Miss Marks.'

"Secondly, it's not that we have no suitable boys. The problem is that we do not have any boys at all. So, few come in & they are in such demand that as soon as a boy arrives, he is immediately adopted."

Before Miss Marks could reply, Mr. Marks sat up straight once more.

"Is there anything that you can do for us?"

"I'm sorry Mr. Marks, This is an industry wide issue & not just in this country, but all over the world. I'm afraid that if you're hellbent on adopting a boy, all I can do is put you on the waiting list."

"I see, & roughly how long would it take for us to get a son on the waiting list."

"It's hard to say, but at the rate that things are going, it could easily be three or four years."

"Years."

"Yes, if you'd like, I can put you on the list now & after the two of you have had a chance to think & talk it over, you can decide if you want to stay on the list, adopt a girl, or try the old-fashioned way."

"Thank you, I think that would be best for now."

The man shook Matthew's hand before the couple departed. It hadn't been as bad as he had feared. Still, he opened up their file & added in a note to remind him or anyone else who handled this file to ensure that no negro children go to this couple.

June 18th, 1976
Ferris Barracks, Bavaria, West Germany

The two men hid in the greenhouse. It was their last safe refuge. With the solid steel door locked from the inside, the women just behind them couldn't simply force the door open. As such, one of them, the brunette with the thick Russian accent, was using a special set of emergency tools to pick the locking mechanism. As she worked to unlock the door from the outside, the other half a dozen women, all in red jumpsuits, were waiting outside with pipes & wrenches n hand, ready to deal with the only two men on Mars.

At the other end of the long corridor, a perky blonde in a green jumpsuit & disheveled hair calls out the other women with length of pipe in her own hand. The leader of the women in red jumpsuits turns to her.

"Stay out of this Abigail, we can never be free until Mars is once again free of men, unlike Earth."

"Don't do this Natasha, we still need them."

"No, we don't. We'll find a way to live without them."

"Natasha!"

Before Abigail could charge into the corridor to face off against the other women, the door closed automatically & sealed the women in the corridor. Before they could breach their way into the greenhouse, a hissing sound came over the scene to indicate to the audience that the air was being pumped out of the corridor as the women in red jumpsuits gasped & fell to the ground. As Abigail watched the would be mankillers fall, a voice came over the intercom.

"Glad that I was able to close the door before you charged in there."

"Julia, is that you? I thought that I lost you!"

A few moments later, the scene showed Abigail running into the control room where her beloved was monitoring the rescue efforts for the men. Everyone in the theater watched as Abigail, played by Farrah Fawcett, wrapped Julia up in her arms & kissed her. The movie then ended with the man hating lesbians dead & the man tolerating lesbians getting their happily ever after as Mars City recovered from the mankiller attacks.

Private Debra Foster walked out of the theater with her friend. Men on Mars had been all the rage all over the states & after a few months, a copy of it had finally gotten to West Germany. It was unlike anything that Debra or Harriot had ever seen before. Harriot was going on about the last scene.

"Like, I get it that before the men showed up, it was a town of four hundred women alone on Mars, but I still say that Fawcett should have gotten one of the guys."

"I think that the men are going to be fine, don't forget, the whole reason they're there is help the women that want families get pregnant."

"Yeah, but they would do that with test tubes & turkey basters or whatever they use in those clinics. I hear they're working on doing that in real life."

"They never said that they were going to do that in the movie. I got the sense that they would be getting pregnant the old-fashioned way."

"Aren't all those women supposed to be lesbians?"

"Not all of them, besides, I think the message of that movie was that some queer girls are going to have to take a turn or two with the fellas for the good of the population."

Harriot laughed as they walked across the base on the sunny afternoon.

"So, Debra, only two more weeks until you go on leave, gonna be home for July 4th?"

"That's the plan."

"Family still upset about you enlisting."

"Oh yeah. Every time that I go home. Fortunately, I can hit them with the whole I'm not allowed to just quit the army thing. Not that I would if I could."

"Yeah, as long as the reds don't come over the line, this life is a lot better than I thought that it would be, with the obvious exceptions of course."

A trio of men whistled at them as they walked by. Debra & Harriot ignored them, which only egged them on.

"Hey ladies, come on over to our place & undo those buns!"

As the other two guys laughed, Harriot flipped them off while Debra ignored them.

"What's a matter, don't tell me army girls are already dykes!"

Debra & Harriot just kept on walking, not wanting to start a scene or risk getting into trouble. Too many people didn't want them there already, no need to give them a reason to be sent back home. Once the guys were out of earshot, Debra tried to change the conversation.

"Hear anything about Apollo 22?"

"Well, they landed yesterday, so I think that they're doing their first moonwalk right about now."

"Who's the woman on the mission this time?"

"Marilynn Adams. I bet that she doesn't have to put up with assholes like that."

"I hope not. Especially when she's off world."

August 8th, 1976

Church of the Lord's Son, Fort Worth, Texas

The heat was suffocating. It was all over the news, not that it needed to be. Damn, nearly every part of the world was experiencing a summer like no other that they could remember. In Europe, people were literally dropping dead. All over the states, churches had posted on their front signs that it'll be hotter in Hell & nobody believed it.

In one not so little church in Texas, fans were working overtime & alter girls known as handmaidens were bringing endless amounts of ice chilled drinks to keep the pregnant women in the front pew cool. In the second row, the church's few altar boys were tending to the families with young sons. In the back, the families that only had daughters felt like they were dying of heat stroke.

Reverend Thomas Edwards swept through the church like a force of nature, leaving a small breeze in his wake. As he took his position to preach to his congregation, he waited patiently for his two deacons to hand out copies of a small flyer to his congregants. Everyone was confused when they looked at the flyers & saw them advertising books & tapes that would allow someone to learn

Russian. Once most of the people in the church had a copy, he breathed deep & began his sermon.

"In case the temperature outside hasn't been enough of an indication, we're all going to Hell. Everywhere we look, it's getting harder & harder to find godliness. We have countries all over Europe that have legalized abortion in recent years. We have feminist movements all over the world in countries where women knew their place as little as a few months ago. The great & wonderful scientists of the commission who were supposed to find a way to solve the crisis have basically given up & are now focusing most of their efforts on adapting to the new world. Every month, every week, every day & every hour, these witches & whores drag us further from God & further from salvation."

Thomas paused for a moment to let the message sink in.

"This world is on the path to Hell. That's why the heat is unbearable, especially in Europe where the most egregious of sins is occurring. It wasn't bad enough that the government, that group of liberal sissies, brainwashed by the same feminists that damn us all, had decided to send a platoon of women to guard us against the commies in Europe & Asia. No, now their sending more!"

There was a murmur among the crowd.

"Two more of these pussy platoons are being sent to defend us from the Godless commies! How far will they take this? Are they going to have the entire iron curtain watched by women? Are they going to have the entire demilitarized zone checked by childless lesbians? If that peanut farmer from Georgia that the Democrats nominated wins, how long will it be before there are so few men on the line that the Soviets can just march across the border? Hell, even our so-called allies in NATO have started recruiting women!"

He held up a copy of the flyers that he had had distributed.

"You may as well start learning Russian now! That way you can be fluent when they take over, put you to work on a commune & force you to start calling everyone comrade. Here's your first lesson, Bog umer, pereday khleb! That's commie for God is dead, pass the bread!"

As shock & fear rippled throughout the congregation, Thomas raised his hands to call their attention back to him.

"All is not yet lost my children! We still have a chance to protect the American way of life."

He gave the crowd a moment to calm down.

"While the fools on the left have nominated their peanut farmer, we have nominated a true, red blooded American. Now I won't lie to you, I'm not overly fond of Reagan giving women the right to leave their husbands in California. I hope that he doesn't bring that to the nation. I'm also not to fond of his idea to create a pathway to citizenship for illegal immigrants. The man isn't perfect, then again, there was only ever the one that was & he died on the cross for us. We need to ensure that Reagan gets elected to the white house. Just looking at him, you can tell that he is a real man who knows how the world ought to work. He understands what a woman is supposed to do with her life. He understands that something needs to be done about these confused women that are falling to lesbianism. He knows that the Soviets won't be kept in check by soldiers that are too busy putting on their makeup & doing their hair!"

The crowd cheered in agreement.

"But we alone don't have the power to get him into the white house. There are too many Godless heretics that have the right to vote. We need to spread the message to the country. Those of you who are not pregnant or nursing, you need to be doing all you can to get the message out! Pound the pavement, ignore the heat, it's just the devil trying to stop you! Knock on doors, make people see reason! We must not allow the Democrats to drag us closer to the days of revelations!"

Picking up his trusty bible, Reverend Thomas opened it to the book of revelations.

"Speaking of the end of days, let's take a look at what we'll be in for if the liberals win again & continue to corrupt mankind."

August 30th, 1976

Queens, New York

The scene before Elizabeth Robinson was reminiscent of the scene six years ago when she went to her first day of kindergarten.

While it wasn't as chaotic as it had been back then, it was still a zoo as she prepared for her first day of middle school.

"At least they were smart enough to stagger it this time."

Elizabeth looked up to her father David who had taken the morning off of work to be here in case it was wild again.

"What do you mean?"

"The other classes are all starting an hour late so that they just have to get your grade through this insanity."

"They didn't do that before?"

"Nope. When you started Kindergarten, they just had everyone come in together. The result was a madhouse that took forever to get everyone through."

"Wow. Is that why it was so crazy?"

"That's one of the reasons."

Mary stood by the parked car with her family, nervous about her daughter's first day in middle school as Elizabeth stood there in her colorful skirt.

"At least this time they were smart enough to have the police ready & waiting. Last time, they waited until everything had already gotten out of hand, & so it took a while for the police to show up since they were getting calls from all over the city."

"Wow."

As another group of girls walked through the secured path, they heard a familiar voice behind them.

"Hi Elizabeth! Hi Mr. & Miss. Robinson."

The three of them turned around to see Elizabeth's friend Sarah standing there in pants & a tee shirt.

"Hi Sarah! Where are your parents?"

"They're talking to someone from the administration over there."

She pointed behind her & they saw her parents talking to one of the school administrators. Mary waived to them & got a waive back.

"They're probably asking about your walnut allergy again."

"Yeah. They keep asking if there's going to be walnuts in any of our lunches. It's getting embarrassing."

"It just means that they love you. But at this rate, they're going to miss watching you walk into the school."

"Speaking of which."

Davis pointed to the small group of students waiting in a safe spot to wait for their turn to go into the school.

"I think that there's room for you girls."

"Finally! Come on Sarah!"

Elizabeth held out her hand & Sarah immediately reached for it.

"Come on, let's go! Bye Mom, bye Dad!"

"Bye Mr. & Miss. Robinson!"

The two of them then ran off together hand in hand to where teachers were organizing the students before they ran the gauntlet of reporters & photographers. Sarah's parents had heard her shouting & looked up in time to see her run off. As they made their way to the Robinsons, David hugged his wife.

"Our little girl, growing up before our eyes. It's not going to be long before she starts talking about dances & dates."

"David don't even joke. She's my baby & that's not allowed to change."

David laughed as he imagined the day that his little girl brought a girl home to introduce to them before they went to the prom. That was the moment when David realized that he wasn't even considering the idea that Elizabeth would ever bring a boy home to meet them.

"She might be our baby, but she's changing alright."

Mary glared at him.

"As long as you both admit that she's still my baby girl."

"Alright."

As Sarah's parents caught up to them, the cameras flashed as Elizabeth & Sarah walked into the school, still hand in hand, in front of a boy that had gone to a different elementary school.

"There they go Mary. There they go."

October 24th, 1976

100,000 kilometers from Earth

"Apollo 23, Houston, the flight surgeon would like to know how John is feeling up there."

Myrtle Cagle looked to the LEM tunnel & what she saw was not good. John was clearly not well. Not only did he look green around the gills, but judging by the way he was holding a vomit bag in front of him even after taking anti-nausea medication, he was in a bad state.

"Any better John?"

John's response was to bring the bag to his face & start filling it. Marcus, the mission commander looked at the thermometer & shook his head.

"Sorry Myrtle, I know that you wanted to be the first woman to set foot on the Moon twice, but he's getting worse, we need to abort the mission."

"Damn. Take it easy John, we'll get this boat turned around."

Myrtle adjusted her headset & flipped on the mic.

"Houston, Apollo 23. John's getting worse. The meds barely seem to be taking the edge off. Marcus & I agree that he's going to get a lot worse before he gets any better… … Recommend abort."

There was silence from NASA for a minute as several people argued furiously. Eventually, the flight director came back on.

"Abort approved. Come on home."

A few minutes later, they were all strapped in as best as they could be as Marcus flipped the red switch that no Apollo astronaut had ever had to flip before. As the main engine kicked in, the entire ship stopped flying to the Moon & started falling back to Earth. Thirty-nine hours later, they splashed down in the North Atlantic, just South of Iceland where they became the first Apollo crew to ever be picked up by the Icelandic Coast Guard.

November 2nd, 1976
NASA Quarantine Facility, Houston, Texas

"What the Hell!"

John turned up the volume on the television so he could hear the news better. Myrtle put her book down to see what the fuss was about.

"What's up John?"

"They just called Virginia for Carter!"

"Good, the last thing that this country needs is Bonzo's costar as president."

"So, you'd rather stick with the party that put women in the army?"

"I'd rather stick with the party that realizes that we're going to need women in the army."

"It's not right."

"Regardless of whether or not it's right, it is what it is. We need a president that is willing to deal with the new reality. Reagan just wants to pretend it's still 1964."

John simply sat there in silence as he watched the election unfold. Marcus had already gone to bed having simply asked to be told who won in the morning & Myrtle went back to her book, occasionally looking up when new results started coming in.

A few hours later, as Myrtle was imagining what it would have been like to set foot in Copernicus Crater instead of reading the book in her hand, she was snapped back to reality by John shouting.

"Finally!"

"Everything alright John?"

"Not really. Sorry for interrupting your book, I'm just glad that another state has finally been called for Reagan. Good old Illinois."

"How much is Reagan losing by?"

"Doesn't matter, he'll take the big states & overtake Carter."

"That much."

Myrtle got up, put her bookmark in its new place & walked closer to the TV to sit next to John.

"A hundred & fifty-two to Twenty-eight. I admit it can still go either way, but damn John, it's Carter South of Illinois. Who's that? She looks familiar."

Myrtle pointed to the woman standing next to the reelected governor of Illinois.

"That's Phyllis Schlafly."

"Oh her. The albatross around Reagan's neck. Makes sense she would be in Illinois. One of the few places where she wasn't booed out of town."

"I wouldn't call her an albatross, sure her views are a bit extreme, but she's just giving a voice to a large part of the population that doesn't like the direction this country is going in."

"A bit extreme! She said that me, Cobb & Adams are mentally unfit & should be committed until we want to return to our husbands!"

"Okay, yeah, that was a bit much."

"Going around the country trying to convince people that women who enlisted of their own free will should be bounced out of the military. Saying that queers should get straightjackets instead of rights. It's like everywhere she talked, she was trying to shoot republicans in the foot."

"I guess she thought that America was pulling to the right after seventy-two."

"More like she desperately wants to pull America to the right. Half the stuff she says makes her sound like a battered housewife."

"Yeah, a lot of what she says hasn't been helping conservatives. She's right that putting women in the army was a step to far, but after that, she & Reagan really need to stop fighting against women's rights."

Myrtle laughed before returning to her book with the intent of actually reading it & not daydreaming about the crater she didn't get to visit.

A few hours later, as the late hours were starting to turn into the early hours, Myrtle finished her book & then walked over to John.

"Hey John, I'm going to head to bed. Are you going to head off soon or are you going to be here all night?"

John looked away from the television.

"I'm staying right here until someone wins."

"What's Carter at?"

"Two hundred & sixty-one."

"So, you're not going to be here much longer."

John glared at Myrtle.

"As soon as Reagan wins Ohio, it'll prove that he's still in the game. Wait, here it is."

John turned up the volume on the news so that they could hear it.

"... here at the democratic headquarters in Ohio where senate candidate Howard Metzenbaum is celebrating his election to the Ohio senate as Carter wins Ohio, bringing his total up to two hundred & eighty-six, making Carter the next president of the United States of America!"

John turned the TV off.

November 3rd, 1976
Sacramento, California

The pops of champagne corks echoed throughout the Matriarch Party headquarters along with the sounds of laughter, cheers & celebration. Patricia Torres, Kathleen Howard & other members of the party were ecstatic. They had spent the last year campaigning hard. Sending legions of mostly women out door to door, raising funds for commercials across the district & making their view of how the country should be run heard across Sacramento & a decent sized swath of California.

They had set up candidates & offices in San Francisco, Santa Rosa, Modesto & San Jose. Patricia's husband Hank was astounded by how far his wife's movement had gone. While all of the candidates in those other cities had failed, Patricia hadn't expected them to succeed. They were just starting out in those territories after all.

The celebration for the night was for Kathleen Howard, the star of the party who had just won California's sixth congressional district with nearly three fifths of the vote.

They had spent all night watching the local news on one tv & state news on another & the national news on another tv as the results for California slowly trickled in. As the night had started, they were neck in neck with the republicans as the Democrats pulled ahead. Fearing that their peak had come & gone in seventy-four, they were thrilled at about one in the morning when they started pulling ahead.

One of the few districts that had been a republican stronghold for the last decade went from red to purple in a landslide, leaving the rightwing representatives stunned & confused. On one channel, they played a clip that they had recorded earlier of interviews they were conducting with people lined up to vote. One older woman had leaned into the microphone & explained herself quite clearly.

"I don't believe I can ever vote for the Democrats, the way that they throw money around & the way they kept us in Vietnam, I can't do it. But God knows that I can't vote republican anymore, they clearly have no clue about how to fix what's going on. Thank God the Matriarch Party came along. They got good heads on their shoulders. They're going to work on the problem like the Dems, but they ain't going to waste money or start pointless wars on the other side of the planet."

That interview soon found itself being played across the state & even received mention on the national scene. At four in the morning, when news anchors started calling California's sixth district for Kathleen, they were jumping for joy. In just eight years, from their founding as a party that most people laughed at, they were now part of the federal government. By dawn, there was no doubt that they had won. With a lead of thirty thousand votes & only twenty-seven thousand votes left to count, it was official, they had won.

As champagne & wine turned to coffee, reporters were nearly knocking down their door, begging for a statement from the newly elected, soon to be sworn in as congresswoman of California's sixth. Both Kathleen & Patricia took strong swigs of their retched industrial strength coffee as they let the reporters in & they began setting up. As the first reporters got ready, Patricia put her hand on Kathleen's shoulder.

"Congratulations. We couldn't have done this without you."

"No Patricia, I couldn't have done this without you. You're the one that set all of this in motion."

The light from the camera was blinding as the reporter started talking into his microphone.

December 22nd, 1976
Montreal, Canada

"Is it possible to get jetlag going from Florida to Montreal?"

Rebecca tried to rub the sleep out of her eyes as Janet drove them towards her parents' house.

"No, they're in the same time zone."

"Then why am I so tired?"

"Probably because we just spent the last five hours flying two thousand miles & dealing with customs. That would leave anyone tired."

"Makes sense. Maybe we should have driven."

Janet had to stop herself from staring at Rebecca as she drove down the snow-covered & ice slick highway.

"It's a twenty-six-hour drive, & that's without waiting at the border."

"Right. Forgot about that. Still, maybe in the summer, we can make a road trip of it. Take a nice vacation, drive up the East coast, see the continent. Stay in motels & break the sodomy laws in at least three new states."

Janet almost lost control of the car. Thankful that she wasn't on a patch of ice, she blushed a bit as she grinned.

"That does kind of sound like fun."

Rebecca smiled & flirted with Janet until they finally pulled up to the house. With the sun setting despite how early it was, they grabbed their suitcases from the rental car & headed inside. Jane answered the door, seven months pregnant & with her belly sticking out like a house.

"Janet! Come in!"

"Jesus Jane, I thought that you were only having one."

Jane laughed as Janet & Rebecca walked into the house.

"I know, I'm as wide as a house! Look at this!"

As Janet was starting to worry that her sister was being a bit too happy, Harold came from the basement.

"Jane, you shouldn't be on your feet."

"What are you going to do? Put me on my back?"

Jane then wrapped her arms around Harold & pulled him in for a kiss. As Janet & Rebecca stood there dumbfounded, Jane eventually let Harold come up for air.

"You need to shave before Christmas, that stubble has to go."

Jane then turned around & got really close to Janet as if she was whispering something, even though she was talking normally.

"It's like kissing a porcupine, all those prickly little hairs tickling, you know. No wait, you wouldn't know, advantage of kissing girls I guess, no prickly stubble kisses."

"Yeah. Definite advantage. Uhm, Jane, how do I ask this, are you high on something?"

"Just life, love, & this bundle of growing love."

"Right. Harold?"

"Sorry Janet, the last few weeks, she's been getting these manic episodes. The doctor says that it's an uncommon side effect of pregnancy, possibly related to how large she's gotten. It usually only lasts for about half an hour, so she should come down in a few minutes."

Jane then reached forward & started trying to unbuckle Harold's belt.

"Woe there, Jane, we're in your parents' hallway, in front of your sister."

"Oops, sorry, got a little carried away."

Rebecca gave Harold a look.

"I didn't say it was all bad."

"Janet!"

Janet's mother, Jillian, came up from the basement.

"Sorry, I didn't hear you there. Come in, come in. How was your flight from NASA?"

"Hi Mom, we didn't fly from NASA, we flew from Florida."

"Not the way I'm going to tell it to my friends."

Rebecca & Jane both burst into laughter. Janet smiled as her mother hugged her tightly. The five of them eventually made their way into the living room where after a few minutes, Jane came down from her manic high & felt embarrassed for trying to reach down her husband's pants in front of her gay sister. After a few more minutes, Janet's father came upstairs & announced that the downstairs toilet would be in working order tomorrow, after he got a new part for it. Eventually, Jane & Harold went home to relieve their babysitter, leaving Janet & Rebecca with Janet's parents as they all had some tea.

"I'm so glad that you two could make it home for the holidays. I know that the two of you are very busy with your work."

Janet looked up from where she had been unconsciously entwining her fingers with Rebecca's.

"Of course we would come home. Unless they send me to the Moon, which I highly doubt will ever happen, I'm spending Christmas right here."

"Same for me Jillian."

"Well, aren't you two sweet. I assume that you're going to spend a bit of time with your family Rebecca."

"Definitely, I figure I'll stop by tomorrow & see how they're doing."

"That's good. How's it going at the school?"

"It's going well. One or two coworkers think it's a bit weird that I have a "roommate" at thirty-two, but they don't pry."

Jillian looked a bit concerned as she turned to her daughter.

"They're not prying to much at NASA I hope."

Janet thought about it for a moment.

"Not too much. There are two or three people there I trust, one of them is a higher up, he's helping to tamp down on anything that might come up."

"Are you sure that you're alright? Florida isn't Canada, you can still get in trouble if you get found out."

"I'm alright Mom. Nobody is really that concerned about a little old highly recommended & vetted Canadian botanist. Besides, with the big left swing in November, you never know, things might ease up."

"The big left swing?"

"The election. Carter won... what was it... four hundred fifty-three to eighty something. The liberals made sweeping wins all over the country including Florida. So maybe things will ease up over the next few years."

"I hope so."

"Don't worry Jillian, Janet knows what she's doing. She's a smart girl, that's why NASA hired her to figure out how best to grow crops on the Moon."

"Thanks Dad. It has been fun working with actual lunar regolith, despite how messy it is."

"Messy?"

"Yeah, the Moon's surface is so damn dry that the regolith is statically charged, it clings to everything. I have to wear an anti-static suit when handling it & it still gets everywhere."

"Wow. Speaking of lunar samples, any news about more missions?"

"Nothing concrete Dad. Everyone knows that Carter is going to add a few more numbers to Apollo, but nobody knows how many. I think he's waiting to see if the Soviets launch anything early in the year."

"Smart. See what the enemy is up to."

"Exactly."

Janet took a moment to sip some of the tea that her mother had brought out earlier.

"So how are things going here now that the separatists are in charge of the province?"

Jillian & John both sighed before sipping their tea. While John cursed under his breath, Jillian voiced their opinion.

"They're thrilled & excited because of their two-seat majority. Not exactly something worth bragging about."

"Are they going to try to separate from Canada?"

"Not if they're as smart as they think they are. They've stopped talking about it for now. I think that they've realized that with such a narrow majority, they probably don't have enough support to actually leave."

"That's good. Means that I won't have to take time off of work to come up here & help you guys pack for Ontario."

"You laugh, but your father called up his cousin in Thunder Bay, he said that if we have to get out fast, we can stay in his cottage while we look for a new place."

"Wow. Good to know that you're taking this shit seriously."

John cursed out the election results before changing the topic. Eventually they turned on the news & watched TV until it was time to head off to bed.

1977

February 8th, 1977
Seventy thousand kilometers above the Earth

Jerrie Cobb floated in zero gravity as she flew to the Moon on Apollo 24. With her daily tasks finished, she was happily listening to the radio when the host interrupted his own talk show. They had spent the last half hour talking about the effects of Jimmy Carter pardoning Vietnam draft dodgers as his first move as President. The conservative guest had just accused Carter of weakening the American draft system when the host had to silence the crowd.

"Sorry to interrupt you Victor, we'll get back to your point in just a second. We've just gotten word from our producer. The North Carolina legislature has just ratified the ERA, becoming the thirty-fifth state to do so."

As the audience cheered the fact that the ERA only needed three more ratifications, the host apologized for the interruption & promised that there would be more news on the matter in the evening show. As the talk show continued, Ronald Evans floated into the module. He was about to ask what was on when mission control came on over the radio.

"Apollo 24, Houston, do you read us?"

Evans was closest to the controls, so he flipped the switch so that they could all talk to mission control through their headsets.

"Houston, this is Apollo 24, we read you."

"Sorry to interrupt your evening, but we've got a bit of a situation happening."

"What's up down there?"

"More like what's up, up there. We just got word from the Pentagon that the Soviets launched a manned mission an hour ago. About ten minutes ago, they performed a trans lunar injection maneuver. The reds are on your tail & we think that they intend to land on the Moon this time."

The three of them floated there in silence for a moment before Cobb responded.

"Any idea on where they intend to land?"

"Not a clue. Some are guessing that the fact that they launched less than a day after you implies they want to set down somewhere nearby. With the issues that they had on their last flight; it could be that they want to set down next to you in case there's an emergency."

"Or it could be a coincidence & they're going to land on the other side of the Moon."

"Exactly. The state department has people who are trying to work the diplomatic channels to find out where the Soviets want to land, but there's a good chance that they'll land before we find out. For all we know, they want to drown out our news about the first woman to land on the Moon twice with the news of their first moonwalk."

Cobb, Evans & the command module pilot all wondered if they were going to be having neighbors soon.

February 11th, 1977
Ptolemaeus Crater, 16 kilometers South of Apollo 24

Maksim Grigorev struggled with the controls. The LK-1 was being temperamental as it descended towards the lunar surface. He was certain that one of the thruster assemblies had a bad regulator. Nothing that he wasn't trained for, but it was making his job a lot harder.

When the altimeter read that he was just three meters above the surface, he cut the main engine. A second later, the insectoid looking craft touched down on the Moon. Lana Koroleva, his copilot, checked several dials & flipped a few switches before confirming the landing was a success. Maksim grinned.

"Roscosmos, this in Lenin base. We have successfully landed on the Moon."

They could hear cheers & celebrations as the people in Kazakhstan celebrated their landing. A man that neither of them recognized came on the radio.

"Congratulations on your successful landing. The two of you are heroes of the people & have brought glory to the Soviet Union. Your names will forever stand in the history books next to Yuri Gagarin."

As the man kept going on, the two cosmonauts nodded at each other. A political officer, reminding them of their duty & that they couldn't afford to fuck this up now. Once the bureaucrat was finally finished, their mission control instructed them on the procedure that they had been training on for the last two years. Confirm that all the systems are good, that all engines are shut down & redress for an immediate moonwalk.

Suiting up for their first moonwalk was not easy. The capsule they were in was cramped. Personal space was a foreign concept to them, as was modesty. It hadn't been particularly easy for either of them to spend the last few days cramped together like this, but they did what they had to do. As they were suiting up, the radio came on. Another Soviet political officer ordered them to write down a message that would be their response. It quickly became apparent that the message was a phonetically spelled out English message. They were then ordered to tune their backup radio to a new frequency & to give that response after someone called them. About twenty minutes later, someone started speaking to them over the emergency radio. It with an unfamiliar woman talking in slow, broken Russian.

"Lenin Base, this is Jerrie Cobb of Apollo 24. On behalf of the American... people, we welcome you... & your country to the Moon & we look... forward to a peaceful coexistence."

Since Maksim had slightly more experience with English than Lana had, he was the one to respond. He reached over to the microphone, which required that he & Lana basically be pressed together in an awkward position that made him grateful that there were no internal cameras. As he tried to ignore what was pressing into his back, he picked up the paper that they had written on & replied in his shaky English.

"Claudius Base, this is Maksim Grigorev of Lenin Base, Thank you for the warm welcome. We are... proud... to join you on the Moon. We look... forward to peace &... coexistence between our great nations."

Both of the astronauts & the cosmonauts knew that that broken & shaky exchange, spoken by two people who had little idea what they were saying as they read out phonetically spelt messages, was going to be played all over the world. The Americans

& the Soviets were now on the Moon & the world would never be the same for it.

With that in mind, Maksim & Lana finished their awkward suit up & after an uncomfortable suit check, they depressurized their lander & carefully took their first steps onto the Moon. As the lander mounted camera transmitted the image to the world, they both hoped that neither of them would slip.

March 16th, 1977
New York City

Lena was exhausted. At thirty-seven years old, she finally had to admit that she couldn't go all night the way she had fifteen or twenty years ago.

With how long it had taken her to write the Wednesday edition of Lavender Press, she had burned through the midnight oil & the two am oil & the three am oil to get the papers printed for their early morning delivery. Now it was just after four in the morning & with the papers ready to go, she had decided to hit the diner down the street for some coffee & something to eat. She needed a way to stay up until Sarah could show up to pick the papers up & take them out.

The corner diner had large glass windows that wrapped around the curved corner of the building that looked out onto the intersection. Inside, the yellow walls & the red bar were illuminated by the blindingly bright ceiling lights that were fighting off the middle of the night. The only other customer in the place was a young man in a blue three-piece suit & a matching blue fedora. The bald server in his white outfit & little white hat served up her coffee.

"Waking up early or run out of yesterday's steam?"

"That depends, what day is it?"

"It's Wednesday now. Almost Wednesday morning."

"Then I'm running out of steam. God, I haven't pulled an all-nighter like this in years. I don't remember it being this hard."

"Happens to the best of us, reaching the point where we can't say we're twenty anymore."

"Shh, that's sensitive information there."

He grinned & mimed zippering his lips closed. He then left Lena to enjoy her coffee. A minute later, he handed her the sandwich that she ordered & left her to check on the other customer.

At a time of day so early that the sun hadn't even considered waking up to crest the horizon, Lena contemplated how far her little newspaper had come. From struggling to find her first customer, to having her own small fleet of trucks. Twice a week, people all over New York were reading her little paper. She was even at the point where she was considering hiring a part-time printer because she could afford it & not just because she never wanted to pull an all-nighter again. She even realized that it had been almost two years since she was legitimately worried about being late with the rent.

As she slowly nibbled her sandwich & sipped her tea, the front door opened & a woman in a red dress walked in. Running a quick hand through her red hair, the woman looked as tired as Lena felt. She scanned the room quickly & decided to take a seat next to Lena. Lena was too tired to worry about how she looked when a beautiful woman sat next to her & ordered with a slight Irish accent.

"My usual nightcap Harold."

The server behind the bar got to work preparing her coffee. Lena found herself getting curious.

"I guess you're here often if you're on a first name basis."

"Six nights a week, singing in a club down the street."

"Wow. Sounds exhausting."

"It can be, especially in the beginning when you're not used to it."

Harold handed her the nightcap. She thanked him before turning back to Lena.

"So, what brings you here so late, or early?"

"I was up all night running the presses for my newspaper."

The redhaired woman's eyes went wide in surprise.

"Not what I was expecting to hear. You work for a newspaper?"

"I own a newspaper, a small one, but I own it, & write for it, & do most of the printing."

"Damn. Do you also deliver it?"

"Not anymore, I used to back in the day, but I have people for that now. Which is good, because once they take the papers this morning, I'm going to crash on the nearest soft surface & sleep the day away."

The redhaired woman laughed.

"Well, I have to say, I've never met a newspaper owner here. Usually, the only women in here this late are waitresses, nurses, dancers & women of ill repute."

"Sounds like good company to me."

"Cheers."

They both sipped their coffee before the woman in red continued.

"I'm Cassie by the way, Cassie O'Dowd."

"It's nice to meet you Cassie, I'm Lena Lewis."

It took a moment for the name to sink in.

"Wait, Lena Lewis. The Lena Lewis? The one that writes the Lavender Press?"

"Yeah, you've heard of me?"

"I sure have, I've been reading your paper for a few years now."

"Really?"

"Yes, it's incredible. The issue that you just put out on Sunday, with the profile for Lana Koroleva, the first Soviet woman on the Moon. I was blown away. A woman born of lowly potato farmers like my mom's side of the family."

"I'm glad that you liked it."

"I always like it. Even the stories that aren't Earth shattering, they still feel different, like a different kind of person is writing them."

Lena almost jumped into the air when she felt Cassie's foot brush against her calf.

"Well… yes… that's kind of what I was going for. A newspaper for… certain women."

"Hmm, for certain women, maybe written by a certain kind of women."

"I don't call it the Lavender Press for nothing."

Cassie smiled.

"I imagine that today's issue will be another good one."

"It's definitely going to be a big one. I went all out on it."

"Sounds promising. Care to give a fan a preview of the headline?"

Lena grinned & slowly sipped her coffee, drawing out the time a bit.

"Gay marriage or polygamy, 83 is coming."

"Jesus! That's going to hit hard. Your paper might make the news."

"Thanks."

"Let me savor that headline. Hmm. It's going to be good. Are you going to tell us which choice is right?"

Lena sat there for a moment, enjoying being the center of attention for this beautifully freckled woman.

"Nope. I talked to a sociologist about how the country would work with harems, or women marrying women or both. Then I point out that the government is going to have to make a decision at some point & we're not really hearing much from them on the matter."

"God, I can't wait. Sounds like it'll be a hit."

"Would you like a preview of the other big stories?"

Cassie's eyes lit up.

"Yes. Yes please."

"Well, I mention how we're only one more state away from ratifying the ERA."

"Really, just one more?"

"Just one more, & Arkansas is set to have a vote on the subject in a few weeks. We could have constitutional equality by Mother's Day."

"If Arkansas votes to ratify. What are the odds of that?"

"Not a guarantee by any means, but when you read through it, you might just find the odds are a bit better than you think."

"Sweet Jesus."

Cassie leaned her head back & imagined it for a moment.

"Wait, you said that there were other big stories, plural. Is there another one?"

"There is, & it's going to be very different from anything that I've ever written before."

"You've got me hooked Lena Lewis."

Cassie's foot started caressing Lena's leg again.

"It'll be different because I didn't write this one."

"I thought that you write all the stories?"

"Not anymore. One of my delivery girls is finishing up her degree in journalism. So, I'm letting her write the occasional story. Today is her debut to the world as a journalist & I'm very proud of her."

"Well, I have to know what her story is about with an endorsement like that."

"She does an in-depth exposé about schools & doctors across the state & country that are still saying being gay is a disease despite the fact that it was delisted as a disease very publicly a few years ago."

"Coming out of the gate hard. That's a hell of a first story."

"It sure is."

"God I can't wait to read it."

"Well, you won't have long to wait. I'm going to have to go soon so I can give the girls their new routes."

"I'm looking forward to it."

As Lena finished up her sandwich, Cassie decided to roll the dice.

"Say, Lena, what are you doing Sunday night?"

"Not much, probably resting after I get my next issue out. Why?"

"Well, a friend of mine is having a little rooftop sunset get together at her place on 57th street. She says there's going to be a beautiful sunset that lights up the street & the buildings. If you're free, we could see if it lives up to the hype, then maybe we could go out on the town."

Lena found herself very interested in the idea of a romantic sunset with a beautiful woman.

"Sounds tempting."

Cassie smiled. She then borrowed a pen from Lena, because like any good journalist, Lena always has a few pens on her. Cassie then took a napkin & wrote down her name & phone number.

"Give me a call. We'll have a night, maybe a morning, maybe you can interview me for your life in the closet segment at some point."

"I'd like that."

Lena carefully folded the napkin & put it in her pocket before pulling herself away to get back to the office before Sarah showed up.

April 14th, 1977
Streets of Little Rock, Arkansas

The crowds of people, mostly women, had been gathering from all over the state of Arkansas ever since it had been discovered that the legislature was debating ratification of the ERA. For the last two days, the growing crowd had spent a great deal of time shouting the word ratify to anyone coming or going from the state capital building.

Most of the republicans in the house tried to discourage ratification. They proclaimed that it would open the door to women being drafted, homosexuality, & radical feminism. These arguments fell on deaf ears as many in Arkansas agreed that the country was heading that way anyway. After all, there would only be three more election cycles with women & men voting in equal numbers. After that, women would make up a greater majority of the population & the electorate with each cycle.

Democrats pointed out that women were already serving in the military rather happily. As for homosexuality & radical feminism, it was going to happen anyway. One republican lawmaker suggested making the votes of men born after 1965 count for nine votes in order to balance out the population imbalance. He was not supported.

Eventually, a vote was called for. The proposal for ratification of the ERA passed with almost two-thirds of the vote. News then quickly broke to the state & the nation that Arkansas had ratified the ERA, becoming the last state needed for the ERA to pass into law.

Celebration erupted in the streets. As conservatives lamented, impromptu parties began springing up all over the country. Within a matter of hours, as some parties were getting so wild that police intervention was being called for, the Equal Rights Amendment was published in the national register, completing the amendment process. Women's rights were now a fundamental right, forcing judges at every level to apply strict scrutiny to all cases in which women could be considered to be discriminated against & forcing the courts & legislators to ignore any difference between men & women in their dealings.

While some expected the country to change overnight, & in some ways, it would, many of the changes to come would play out over months & years as new kinds of lawsuits & petitions were brought to courts that now had to weigh evidence & make decisions in new ways. Nobody could be sure exactly how it would play out, but one thing was certain, things were going to change in ways that most people would consider to be for the better.

May 8th, 1977
Washington, DC

Congressman Joseph J. Davis was learning a hard lesson about politics as he stared out of the window at the crowd. What's popular in Utah is not always what's popular in America. The protestors in front of him were like an ocean of people screaming that he needed to be stopped. According to reports from the police, there were about half a million people in the crowd, far more than the police could actually contain if they got violent.

He stood there dumbfounded as to how his rather commonsense bill could generate so much animosity. He was wondering how so many people could be so blind when he heard someone behind him.

"Davis, meet Goliath."

"Very funny Kathleen. You know that David won in that contest."

"Yes, but he had a sling. You've got a piece of paper that's going to fail at getting passed Congress."

"You don't know that, Kathleen. Just because your beloved Sacramento is willing to abandon normalcy, doesn't mean America is."

"Oh Joseph. It's a miracle that you were able to get that bill out of committee. Trying to have homosexuality listed as a mental disorder. Your party is sinking & you hang this albatross around your collective neck."

"It's just hysteria about the future that's led to this permissive attitude. Once a cure is found for the imbalance, it'll all go back to normal, I'm just trying to speed up the process."

Kathleen Howard looked at him for a moment in stunned silence.

"It's never going back to normal Joseph. It's been twelve years already. Even if a cure were found tomorrow, there's an entire generation of girls that'll outnumber their available boys nine to one. In a few more years, they're going to be voting. Even if the imbalance is reversed, it'll be decades before their generation can be overpowered, & by that point, what they're fighting for will be tradition. They're the new normal, well, they're the parent s of the new normal."

Joseph slouched a bit as Kathleen made sense. Getting his bill passed was going to be an uphill battle & most people were pushing it back down the hill. Still, he couldn't give up. His bill idea was what got him elected to Congress.

"I don't see your bill to legalize gay marriage getting anywhere Kathleen."

"True, but that's just because everyone is nervous about working with the new party in town. Deep down, most of them know that this has to happen in the next few years or protests like that will get all too common."

Joseph nodded his head. It was quickly becoming apparent to him that the changes that were coming were not in his favor.

June 9th, 1977
Ferris Barracks, Bavaria, West Germany

There is nothing better in the world than a steaming hot shower after a long day of running yourself ragged. That was how Debra felt as she stood under the hot water that was working her sore shoulders. Debra found it amazing how quickly things changed. Three years ago, she was struggling with the idea of communal showers. Now she barely noticed the other women washing a day's worth of Bavarian dirt off of themselves.

At 0600 hours that morning, she had been in formation with the other volunteers. Her roommate had called her crazy when she volunteered for yet another training day. As far as her roommate was concerned, the mandatory ones were more than enough. Not Debra. She volunteered for one every week & the results were showing. Before joining the army, she had never seen a muscular woman. She wasn't even aware that it was a thing. Yet here she was. Sure, her muscles weren't bulging or rippling like Mr. Olympia, but she reckoned that she could easily go toe to toe with any of her brothers or cousins.

Still, even the strongest of soldiers gets tired after a day of hiking, running, pushups & obstacles designed to sort out the girls from the women.

With the days exertions washed off & the soreness in her muscles eased slightly, Debra was making her way to her quarters where she had a copy of a slightly out of date American newspaper waiting to be read. While she liked reading the German ones because it gave her practice & they weren't a week behind, she was curious about what was happening back home. All that she knew of this issue was the headline about Anita Bryant's crusade failing again to stop legislation to help queers.

Halfway to her dorm, she was stopped by a Private from her platoon.

"Hey Debra, I was just coming to look for you."

"What's up Helga? I'm just heading back to my dorm to crash after today."

"Tell me about it, I'm scheduled for a training day of running through the German woods at the end of the week & I am not looking forward to it. Anyway, the Colonel is looking for you."

"Shit. What does he want?"

"No idea, but I wouldn't keep the old man waiting. You know how he is, if you're not early, you're late."

"Thanks Helga."

Turning right around, Debra marched her way to the office of the base commander. As she approached the door to his office, Major Schultz, the head of the MPs, was walking out.

"Major. I don't suppose the Colonel is in a good mood."

With a slight hint of a German accent, the Major looked back to the office for a moment.

"I would say he's in a good mood. You're not in trouble, are you Private?"

"I hope not sir. I was just told to be here."

"Well, I wish good luck Private…"

"Private Foster, sir."

"Viel Gluck, Private Foster."

"Danke, Major."

Walking into the commander's office, Debra found herself standing before Colonel LeBeau as he was shuffling through some papers. Speaking with a French accent, he welcomed her into his office.

"Come in, Come in Private Foster. Have a seat."

"Thank you, sir. I'm afraid that I'm not sure why I'm here."

"You're here, because I've been reviewing your service record & I'm impressed by what I see."

"Thank you, sir."

"In the two & a half years that you've been here, it's clear that you've gone above & beyond the requirements of a Private. You've learned a valuable language to almost perfect fluency. You routinely sign up for special training courses. You volunteer for more training days than anyone else, going far beyond just the ones that are required. You get along well with your teammates; women & men & your superiors all speak highly of you. It's clear that you're not a *what can the army do for me* kind of lad… err… lady. Sorry, old habits. The point is, it's clear that you mean business & that you are one of the most disciplined & dedicated Privates that I've ever seen."

"Thank you, sir."

"With all of this in mind, your platoon Commander & I agree that your insignia doesn't have enough chevrons on it."

"Sir?"

Colonel LeBeau reached into his desk drawer & pulled out a small box which he handed to Debra.

"Congratulations Corporal Foster."

Debra opened the small box to see the two-bar chevron insignia of a Corporal intended for her shirt collar & the matching patch for a dress uniform.

"I… I… Thank you sir."

"Thank you for your dedication corporal. Make sure that you get your new patches sewn on before your next inspection or roll call."

"Yes sir."

A minute later, Debra was walking back to her dorm, staring at her new insignia as she walked. Before she knew it, she was in her room where her roommate was reading her paper.

"Hey Debra, since when do you take that long in the shower?"

"I was called down to the Commander's office."

"Shit, what kind of trouble did you get into?"

"I got promoted."

"What?"

Debra showed her roommate the new insignia that she would have to pin to her collar & sew to her uniform.

"I just got promoted to Corporal."

"Jesus Christ, Debra, congratulations!"

"Thanks."

"Hey, this makes you an NCO, doesn't it?"

"No, it... actually, yeah, this makes me a noncommissioned officer."

"Wow. Does that mean that you're going to get your own room, or a new roommate or are you still expected to rough it down here with us grunts?"

"I have no idea. Guess I'll find out soon if I get assigned a new room."

"Either way, congratulations Debra. I bet your grandfather will be proud."

"My grandfather, yes. My parents are probably going to freak out."

August 20th, 1977
NASA Headquarters, Washington DC

The various heads & leaders of NASA had been expecting this day for several months now. Every time that a new President was elected, NASA was given new marching orders & directives to accomplish. With President Humphrey, it hadn't been too bad, just continue the Apollo program. But Humphrey had been Johnson's vice president & Johnson had been Kennedy's vice president, so it had been a bit of a continuation of Kennedy's original marching orders. Carter on the other hand was not part of this chain of presidents & their vice presidents. He could have an entirely new direction for NASA to take & everyone in the conference room was wondering what that direction could be.

As the various directors & certain key people talked among themselves, the recently appointed administrator of NASA, Dr. David Gomez walked into the room where he handed everyone a small booklet before taking his coat jacket off & putting it on his chair.

"Alright gentlemen, the moment that you've all been waiting for. NASA's new directives from on high. Strap yourselves in, the news is mostly good & there's a lot of it."

They all sat down & opened the thick booklets containing the basic information about NASA's new direction as Gomez walked them through it.

"Alright, for those of you worried about budget cuts & the end of manned Moon missions, I have good news. The Soviet LK-1 mission that landed two cosmonauts on the Moon has riled everyone up. The people complaining about the cost of NASA have gone silent for the time being & congress, for now, see the value in what we're doing here. So, for now, we're seeing small increases in our budgets."

Everyone in the room cheered & clapped.

"Yeah, yeah, we're all happy. That being said, try, if you can, to avoid wasting money. Be cost effective, if possible, we all know how congress can swing in their opinions of NASA."

Everyone nodded their heads.

"Now, the big points which Carter is going to talk about on the news tonight. We'll start with Apollo."

This got the attention of everyone in the room as the Apollo program touched nearly every part of NASA.

"Apollo has been extended through Apollo 30, with even further missions a possibility to be discussed in his second term, assuming he wins."

The room exploded in rapturous applause.

"I'm glad that you're all happy, but there are one or two caveats for this. The first launch will be late next year, the remaining launched to be in seventy-nine & eighty. At some point in there, we need to start launching the Saturn V-a, it's more cost effective & it's increased capacity will allow for significantly longer missions of seven to ten days on the surface. We're to fly the V-a as soon as we can."

The engineers groaned.

"I know, I know. I've informed the administration that it won't be ready to go before seventy-nine, so Apollo 25 will be a Saturn V. This will also allow us to run the next requirement on a tested system. We need to have a female command module pilot. We'll do that on 25."

Gomez was almost surprised by the lack of reaction from having the command module pilot, who has to be alone in the command module for days, be a woman. He guessed that it was a combination of their three female astronauts having proved themselves & the changing times.

"Well, since there are no objections to that piece of news, the next big caveat is that Apollo 30 is going to be... an all-female crew."

That did not go over as well as Gomez had hoped it would. Shouts erupted from all over the conference room. Accusations of political theater & shouts of too much too quickly & one person demanding to know if men were being phased out of space flight & questions of what if they got their periods at the same time on the Moon. Amidst the anger was one voice which said something that somehow calmed the room.

"We only have three lady astronauts!"

As the noise died down, the chief of the astronaut office, John Young, stood up.

"We only have three lady astronauts. Crew selection rules currently say that an astronaut has to be Earthside for at least six months in-between missions. If we want all three of them on one mission, either we have to scrap that rule, which the flight surgeon will never allow, or they can't be part of any mission or backup crew for Apollo 28 or 29, which would interfere with our current policy of having a woman on each mission. Either we're going to have to change some of our policies, or we're going to need more lady astronauts."

The entire room looked to Gomez.

"Well, John, that actually brings up another part of our new plan. I was going to bring it up later, but now's as good a time as any. We're going to be recruiting more women in the next group of astronaut candidates. In fact, our new policy is that women should be selected to take part in each candidate training group from now on."

A lot of the old school guys from the days of Mercury & Gemini weren't thrilled about this.

"Look gentlemen, I know that this will be seen as a radical change by some of you, but our current ladies have clearly demonstrated that women can handle space flight & the Moon. We're not lowering standards or guaranteeing that people can get through just so we can meet a quota. They'll be held to the same standard as men. That's our new policy."

With only a bit more grumbling, he was able to continue.

"One more note about crew selection for Apollos 25 through 30. Somewhere in there, we need to send a non-American astronaut to the Moon."

The grumbling quickly returned.

"Look, I know, it's a lot, but after some talks, we've agreed that sending an astronaut from a NATO ally will both help to strengthen the relationships with our allies & show the world that there's advantages to being part of NATO. Not to mention it might encourage some of our allies to help pay for some of these missions. Europe has gotten its space agency running & is looking to get people in space in the next few years. We can also extend an invitation to Canada. They were the third nation to put a satellite in orbit & they've been helping us with Apollo since the early days. It'll be good to send a message to the Soviets that they aren't just against the good old US of A."

As the complaints & grumbling died down, Gomez turned to the next section of his booklet.

"Alright, now that we've gotten through the near-term events, we can talk about the long-term efforts. First off, we're to continue working to develop the Saturn VI. The hope is that it'll be up & running before 1985."

The engineers took down several notes despite it all being in the booklet already.

"Furthermore, work on the shuttle program is to continue as well. If we can get a vehicle that can get to medium Earth orbit, we might get the go ahead to start work on a space station. Finally, the big one. The one that we've all hoped for & dreaded since Neil & Buzz landed on the Moon. We're to get a proper moon base up & running by 1990."

The room was silent for a minute before it erupted into frenzied questions & comments. The cacophony of noise made it almost impossible for anyone to actually hear what anyone else was saying. Questions of where, how, why now, where, enough astronauts, cost, where, overblown reaction, where, congressional approval & seriously, where are we going to build it?

Eventually the room calmed down again & Gomez was able to speak once more.

"I know that we have a lot of questions concerning a base. Where will we put it? How will we sustain it? How much will it cost? These are all good questions. For the time being, we're going to use these new Apollo missions to also look for suitable base sites. Preferably places that may have some reserve of water we don't know about or access to mineral resources. We're also going to be running a number of studies & trials to develop the kind of equipment that we'll need to have a base on the Moon."

Gomez saw one of the flight directors raise his hand.

"Yes."

"Is this base going to be permanently manned?"

Everyone looked at Gomez.

"Probably not, at least not at first. If we manage to get a base going & if we can keep this space race going, maybe. Also, we're not to announce the plans for a Moon base until we have at least some of our questions answered."

Murmurs started up again as everyone began discussing the logistics of a potentially permanently manned lunar base. Gomez looked at the men in front of him & realized that the next few years of his life were going to be more hectic than he could have imagined.

November 14th, 1977
Buckingham Palace

Prince Philip was relaxing on the couch, reading a newspaper when Queen Elizabeth came into the room on her way to her bedroom. Curious as to whether her husband was ready to turn in for the night, she approached him & was about to ask when she saw what he was reading.

"The Washington Post?"

"Oh, I didn't see you there."

"Yes, I was wondering if you were going to be coming to bed soon?"

"How can I say no to that, cabbage?"

Elizabeth smiled at the use of his nickname for her.

"You've been reading quite a few American papers lately."

"Just keeping an eye on the prodigal sons."

"I see. Anything interesting?"

"Indeed. Some woman named Anita Bryant was booed off a stage in Iowa. She was there to support some republican congressman that's running for reelection."

"Aren't their midterms a year away?"

"You know the Americans, they finish one election & a few days later, they start the next."

"Yes. Why was this woman booed offstage?"

"Oh, apparently, she's falling far out of favor with the Americans. She been saying for a number of years now that men & women need to return to more traditional roles & she's been trying to rally Americans behind candidates that support traditional marriage."

"That's a bad thing?"

"For the next generation it will be."

"Ah yes, I suppose so."

"Yes, but enough about events in Iowa. You said something about going to bed?"

Elizabeth smiled. She turned to lead the way to her room when her private secretary, Philip Moore almost ran into her.

"Sorry for the intrusion mum, & for the near collision, I was hoping to catch you before you turned in so that I wouldn't have to interrupt you so late."

"What's the matter?"

"We just got word from Gatcombe Park. Her Royal Highness, Princess Anne has gone into labor."

Two days later, after Princess Anne had had a chance to recover a bit & arrangements had been made, Queen Elizabeth & Prince Philip arrived at St. Mary's Hospital to meet their first grandchild. They were very quickly escorted through the journalists & paparazzi, to the private room where Anne was resting & holding her newborn child.

"Hello sweetie."

"Hello Daddy, hello mum, come in."

Making their way in & handing their coats to their respective secretaries, they took seats by Anne's bedside.

"Mum, Dad, say hello to your granddaughter, Pietra Phillips."

The two of them each took a turn holding their granddaughter, the first of their grandchildren as it sunk in that they were now grandparents.

December 24th, 1977
Church of the Wives of Christ, Chicago

The Wives of Christ church was well beyond capacity. The pews were packed in like sardines as women filled the aisles. Hope was astounded by the sheer number of women who were here on Christmas Eve instead of with their families. She was also stunned by how many women brought the entirety of their female families here. Stepping up to the lectern at the altar, Hope raised her hands & quieted down the women before her.

"It warms my heart to see so many here on the eve of his birth. On this most holy of holy nights, it is important that we be together with friends, with family & with community. At this time of year, the time of the longest nights, it is important that we open our doors to loved ones & our hearts to love."

Hope could see among the endless faces that most were agreeing with her as she spoke of love & community. At her behest, everyone bowed their heads & followed her in prayer. When she finished, she introduced Virginia.

"Sisters, the time has now come for me to surrender you to our shepherd, our guiding light to lead us through bright days & dark nights. Mother Virginia Green."

The congregation cheered as Virginia walked onto the altar. As per usual, her white robes seemed to be flowing around her as she walked.

"Thank you all for that warm welcome & thank you to Mother Hope for leading us in prayer. It is always a wonder & a pleasure to see so many of you here to find your way to our great redeemer, the only man not in need of redemption. It is a far greater pleasure to see so many of you here tonight, at the celebration of his birth. On this night when we honor the holy son & the mother who labored to bring him into the world, let us give thanks to them & the almighty for our many blessings in our lives & the chance to be a part of this community."

Virginia then led the congregation in the light of the world prayer, slightly modified to omit the part about remembering brothers. This was followed by two more prayers of the season that had been slightly modified to remove mention of men other than God or Jesus.

"Daughters, we are fast approaching the year of his coming, 1983. We have just over five years before the great redeemer returns to Earth, returns to his faithful wives."

Hope could see that while there were a few people in attendance who had taken Virginia's message of revelations to heart, most were not exactly willing to bet money on this part of the faith.

"Only we who are worthy of him will be able to serve him. However, to be worthy of him, we must free ourselves from all corruption, & there is no greater corruption than the men of the Earth."

At this point, more of the congregation was agreeing as the message that men weren't worth it resonated with many.

"We have done well to deny them our bodies, but their corruption spreads from more than the serpent tween their legs. They have many subtle ways of bending women to their perversions & one of them is this contraption."

Virginia reached into the pockets of her robes & pulled out a bra.

"For those of you who remember, I vowed to stop wearing these accursed creations five years ago. For those five years, I have encouraged you to do the same, for these are not elements of fashion. These are constraints, designed to make your tits more flattering to men. Bras to hold your tits up, to press your tits together, to make them look perky when they sag, to make them look round when they're flat, to make them look nubile when they've been nursed from, all to arouse their serpents!"

A number of women in the congregation began nodding their heads as they thought about all the time that they spent wearing uncomfortable bras that dug into their shoulders or backs just to make some guys pay more attention to them.

"We cannot be free or truly worthy as long as we bind our tits in these devices of male perversion. I dream of a day when a woman will be free to walk down the street, her breasts hanging low & free without judgement. Such a dream will never come to be until we learn to set ourselves free."

As more women got into the sermon, Hope was a bit concerned that this was going to turn into a Christmas to remember because Virginia might strip down again.

"I cannot & will not tell you how to dress when you're at home, which is for you to decide, but I must insist that you all free yourselves in this place. Here, in the house of the holy, we must cleanse out bodies, our souls & our church of every trace of man's corruption. So, from now on, not one among you is to wear one of these vile things in this place. Let today be the last time that you wore these confines in this holy place. Go home & know that you'll never wear another one here again. In fact, if you so feel like it, take them off now & throw them out in the street side garbage on your way out tonight!"

Virginia paused. Hope had been expecting Virginia to make a spectacle of herself on Christmas, she had never expected what she was now seeing. Throughout the congregation, hundreds of women stood up & began working to get their bras off from under their clothing. A few women even undressed to make it easier figuring that it was fine since there were no men in the church.

Within two minutes, hundreds of women were holding their bras up, vowing to never wear them again. Chests that had once been high now hung lower & as the women who hadn't stripped their bras off watched those that had, they resolved to come to mass unencumbered from now on. This was how Virginia had chosen to preach on Christmas Eve & as weird & possibly inappropriate as it may have been, Hope could not help but laugh & was both glad & disappointed that her sister wasn't there to see this. She believed that Grace was going to lose it when she described this event & told her that from now on, all attendance would be braless.

1978

January 24th, 1978
Phoenix, Arizona

When a number of middle schools in Arizona had implemented their new boys & girls policy a number of years earlier, it had flown under the radar as it wouldn't have any sort of significant effect until the mostly female generation reached middle school. The administrations of these schools had hoped that the policy wouldn't cause too much controversy if they were introduced years before these children reached middle school. They were wrong.

The policies were different from school to school, but they were all variations on a singular theme. No romantic relationships allowed between the girls.

For some of the schools, it was a simple policy of girls could only go to a school dance with a boy, or in a group of three or more. No girl only couples allowed. For other schools, it was a set of subtler policies like girls can only give valentines & presents to boys, or that girls weren't allowed to go to the bathroom in pairs. Some of these policies were subtle enough to fly under the radar, or they would have been if not for the ones that stood out.

One school had a policy where two girls caught hugging could get detention. Another school adopted a policy where the only girls allowed at dances were girls with a male partner, leading to very small dances & over half the population being unable to attend. Some schools encouraged the girls to compete against each other for the attention of the limited boys. Several of the schools had posters & announcements that went a long way to encourage the girls into thinking that boys were the only option that would be allowed.

When the classes had been half & half split between boys & girls, it hadn't caused too many issues. But now that the sixth & seventh grades were nine tenths girls, problems were occurring. Lots of problems.

Girls being thrown into detention or forced to watch educational videos simply for hugging another girl or spending too much time with one specific girl. Girls getting into fist fights & humiliating each other in order to get the attention of the minuscule number of boys. Girls that had been friends since they were infants being forced into completely different classes to avoid them being too friendly with each other. Girls were always getting into trouble & parents were always raging at school officials as their daughters were being unjustly punished for innocent friendships, misunderstandings & a lack of traditional options. For a year & half, this manageable fury persisted among Arizona middle schools, until one winter formal dance in Phoenix.

The school in question had adopted a policy where their winter formal was open to all students, but girls could only go to dances if they went with a boy. One couple tried to cheat the system. One of the girls, a twelve-year-old named Joan, had figured that if everyone thought she was a boy, she could take her friend to the dance & they could go together for the first time.

She got herself a crew cut the night of the dance. She had spent the week before the dance wearing heavy makeup so that nobody would recognize her when she didn't wear any makeup at all to the dance. She dressed herself up in a boy's suit & practiced keeping her chin down to avoid accidental eye contact.

She managed to get her & her friend into the winter formal where they spent most of the night trying to avoid drawing attention. Some of the boys even unknowingly chatted with her as if she were one of them. She might have gotten away with it if she hadn't taken her friend to the dance floor. One of the teachers noticed her & started shouting loud enough to get the song stopped & every eye on her. The rouse was up & Joan was in trouble.

Crossdressing, entering a dance under false pretenses, dancing with another girl. She was expelled. The news then spread as the students told their friends in other schools. They told their parents & in less than a week, the parents of the new generation were no longer willing to let things stand. After all, their girls outnumbered their boys nine to one. Something had to give.

The superintendent had to negotiate a way through the crowd by promising dozens of angry parents that he would get to the bottom of this, that wrongs would be righted & that heads would roll. He made his way through halls teaming with students that were three quarters girls, a fraction that would shift heavily when the last normal class moved on to high school next year.

Entering the principal's office, he was greeted by a stressed man who was tired of getting angry phone calls.

"Sir. I wasn't expecting you so soon."

"I was going to come tomorrow or Thursday Ed, but then I heard about the crowds that have been growing since yesterday. It's not just middle school parents out there. Elementary school parents, activist groups, rights groups, progressive reformers. It's turning into a circus out there."

"Well, I don't know what more I can do sir. I've reversed Joan's expulsion, even though she violated half a dozen major rules concerning student conduct. I've apologized in the local papers. What more can I do?"

"What you can do, Ed, is scrap the policy that led to the expulsion in the first place."

Ed was not happy about that.

"Sir, we can't give into radical demands like that. These protests will die down in a few days."

"Sorry Ed. But it's time. The fact of the matter is that as much as some parents might not be happy about it, it's time to adjust to the reality of the situation. The Arizona state board of education is going to be releasing a statement later tonight announcing that it is striking down all of the girls & boys policies."

"They can't do that!"

"They can & they have. These protests aren't just at this school. Hell, they're not even just in Phoenix. They're happening all over Arizona. People are pissed. They're tired of us pitting girls against each other to compete for boys. They're tired of us not allowing girls to go to the dance unless they can lure away one of the handful of boys. They're tired of the entire anomaly & at this point, they just want for their daughters to be happy."

"Even if it means lesbianism?"

"What can I say Ed. There aren't many other options."

Ed slumped into his chair as the superintendent continued.

"All Principals are being given until the first of February to shut down these policies. After that, anyone who doesn't comply will face disciplinary actions."

"You want us to allow the girls to date each other starting two weeks before Valentine's Day?"

"The timing isn't ideal. But this is happening now. Take the posters down, any girls in detention for being over friendly are to be let out. Teachers & hall monitors are to stop harassing girls who seem to close & you're going to have to send out a memo by the end of the week informing everyone about our policy change. You're still allowed to enforce rules against public displays of affection, just remember that those apply to heterosexual couples as well."

"I... Jesus Christ... Fine. Goodbye, normalcy. Goodbye decency. Goodbye heterosexuality."

"Calm down Ed. Some study out of California was published to show that at least seventy percent of these girls are still only interested in boys. This isn't the fall of Rome, it's... an adjustment."

Ed sat there for a moment & thought it over.

"Well, at least the... I don't know... the teen pregnancy rate will drop like a rock. I mean that was going to happen anyway, but I guess that now it'll be even lower."

"That's the spirit Ed. Look at the bright side of our new reality."

"I'll try. Since my job is on the line."

"More than just your job if tonight's announcement doesn't appease them. Now, if you'll excuse me, you're not my only chat today."

"I bet."

The two men bid each other farewell as the superintendent rushed out to his next appointment.

March 23rd, 1978
Niavaran Palace, Iran

Mohammad Reza Pahlavi, the Shah of Iran, lay in his bed, his condition was deteriorating. His cancer was progressing aggressively & his ability to rule over Iran was slipping away from him. He had hoped to hold on to power until his oldest son was old enough to take over from him. Twenty would have been old enough, even eighteen would have been acceptable, but at seventeen, he was still practically a boy. Just ten more months he had asked for, nine more months, eight more months he had prayed for.

But now, in his failing health & with mounting protests against him, he knew that it was time. In one of his more lucid moments, he signed the paperwork to make it official. He would abdicate the thrown due to his failing health & his wife, Farah, would serve as Regent until his oldest child & only son's eighteenth birthday in October.

News quickly spread. Most, including the leaders of western nations, were shocked to realize that the Shah had been fighting cancer for the last two years. As news of his condition & medication regiment spread, some of his decisions & inaction over the last few months finally began to make sense. To address the concerns of the people & to calm the protests, the new Regent & the Crown Prince called the media to the palace so that they may speak to the nation.

Farah Pahlavi spoke to the people, confirming that her husband had fallen ill & that realizing that he no longer possessed the strength or the courage to rule over Iran, he had ceded power to her until the Crown Prince reached his eighteenth birthday. Once she was finished reassuring the people, she allowed her son to stand before the media & to speak to the people that he would soon be ruling over.

Reza Pahlavi II stepped into the metaphorical limelight & tried to speak with gravitas & authority.

"It is with a heavy heart that we can finally reveal my father's ailment to the world. He has been a titan in our family, in our nation, & in our world. He has reshaped the very core of Iran in ways that many thought to be impossible or too radical. He took a struggling country & through his white revolution, he changed us into a thriving, world class nation the envy of the entire developing world. The jewel in the middle east. He saw how the world was changing & he brough us forward, into the twentieth century."

Taking a deep breath, he looked at the cameras & reporters & decided to be as bold as his father had been.

"Today we live in a very different world. A world that is changing in ways that nobody saw coming. While there are many in our nation calling for a return to more traditional ways of life, for a restoration of an Islamic theocracy, we cannot allow this to happen.

Make no mistake, I respect a person's right to hold their beliefs in their heart. If you personally wish to live by the traditional laws of Islam, that is your faith & your choice. But as a nation, we must not only preserve the great success of the white revolution, but we must also push it further. My father's white revolution has turned this nation into a prosperous twentieth century economy that competes with the world's giants. But a new world is upon us. A world in which there will not be enough men to keep pushing this country further. As much as some men may not want to hear this simple truth, we will not be able to function in a world where every man must support nine wives."

Taking another deep breath, he steadied himself before continuing.

"I understand that some among us feel that we have already moved too far forward too quickly, but the state of the world refuses to wait for us to be ready to change. I do not know why God almighty has condemned us to be so without sons, but we have only a few years until this generation of daughters is grown & we need to be ready to live in a world where our daughters are the vast majority. Therefore, for the sake of Iran, I am calling for a second white revolution, a revolution to not only empower Iran, but to empower our daughters for the new world that they will have to live, work & be mothers in. Over the coming months, as I prepare to ascend my father's throne, I shall consult with scholars & leaders both here in Iran & around the world so that we may remake Iran into a nation that will be the jewel of the world in the twenty-first century to come."

Over the coming days & weeks, the reaction to the Crown Prince's call for a second white revolution was met with mixed reactions. Many progressive both in & out of Iran rallied behind him, proclaiming him to be a forward thinker with Iran's best interest at heart. Others proclaimed him to be worse than his father, a blasphemer who sought to take Iran even further from God, a Muslim in name only.

Hardline conservative dissidents made plans for propaganda & demonstrations to force a religious revolution while fearing that their few numbers & the growing progressive movements led by men without sons would derail their efforts to return Iran to sharia law & the will of God.

April 25th, 1978
St. Paul, Minnesota

Anita Bryant walked through the crowd of reporters that were eagerly throwing questions to her about her latest failed attempt & what it means for her going forward. She had tried to rally support for a new measure to repeal part of the city's human rights ordinance, the part that protected gay people from discrimination. She had been a bit worried when Minnesota had voted so heavily for the Democrats, giving them a clear landslide victory. She had redoubled her efforts & worked hard to promote traditional values. Still, she had been no match for a parents group lobbying to protect the ordinance & expand on it.

The protecting our daughters group had canvassed the city & fought hard to protect gay rights for the simple reason that nine tenths of the people under thirteen were girls & in a few years, they were going to need the protection of these laws. Anita had had no choice but to watch as a large number of conservatives gave into this hyped fear that just because there weren't enough boys to go around, that large swaths of these girls would turn queer.

With yet another defeat haunting her, she had left St. Paul to head back to Oklahoma with her head held high as she prepared to keep fighting. Shortly after she arrived home, an issue with her future work knocked on her door.

Dennis Higgins, a conservative MP from the Canadian parliament was standing at her door. He had been one of the people that had been working to help organize her upcoming tour of Canada.

"Dennis, come in."

"Thank you, Anita."

Once inside, she quickly offered him some coffee, which he graciously accepted before they sat down in her living room to talk.

"I have to say, I wasn't expecting you to show up unannounced."

"That's strange, I left a message with your husband, didn't he tell you that I was coming by?"

"No. To be fair, I just got home myself an hour ago, so I haven't yet had a chance to go through all of my messages."

"Ah, I see."

"I assume that you're here to talk about some of the logistics of my Canadian tour, although I wasn't expecting a member of Parliament to show up in person for the nitty gritty of travel arrangements."

"Yes, well, I'm actually here to discuss another matter of your tour, specifically the scale of it."

Anita smiled.

"I'm glad that we're thinking the same thing. I've recently committed myself to doubling down on my efforts. I think that we need to expand the tour, to have me visit more cities, perhaps Montreal & Vancouver."

Dennis sipped his coffee before putting it down on a coaster & sitting more squarely.

"Anita, I'm afraid that we're not necessarily thinking the same thing."

"What do you mean?"

"Well, it seems that as news of your impending visits has started to spread, there have been a number of... protests... against your visits."

"Protests?"

"Mayors, ministers & a few MPs such as I have been inundated with requests to cancel these visits, & a number of groups are setting up public demonstrations against the events that we wish for you to speak at."

"I see. Which cities are seeing protests to my arrival?"

"Nearly all of them. Apparently, the protests that took place in Toronto in January were just a warmup for what's coming. We're already seeing public protests at the speaking venue for your engagement on Saturday in Edmonton."

"It's not for another five days, how can they already be protesting."

"It's not you, they're protesting the entire event, we may have to pull the plug if it escalates the way the police think that it might."

"Jesus. What about the next day in Winnipeg?"

"Yes, I was just on the phone with organizers of the Winnipeg event, it seems that the entire event has already been cancelled."

"Cancelled! Over a few protesters?"

"It's not a few Anita. Just like in Toronto, it's thousands. People have already started travelling from across Alberta & Manitoba to protest these events & to counterprotest groups that are angry about the direction that Pierre Trudeau has taken our country in."

Anita sat there stunned. She couldn't believe what she was hearing.

"It's seriously that bad?"

Dennis sipped his coffee again.

"It seriously is. Apparently, the Prime Minister's message that the government shouldn't get to dictate what happens in the bedrooms of private Canadian citizens is resonating with the public. Between these sorts of protests to protect gay rights & polls showing growing concerns over the quality of life for the next generation, it's reshaping the entire Canadian political landscape. There's a federal election next year & apparently, standing for traditional values of marriage & sexuality is quickly becoming political suicide."

"Aren't those what you stand for?"

"They are, & my polling numbers have taken a massive hit. If the election were today, my seat would be almost a three-way tie between my Progressive Conservatives, the Liberals & the NDP with the winner only succeeding by one or two points."

"Jesus."

"I'm sorry Anita, but it looks like a lot of your stops in Canada might not end up happening. After long discussions between the tour organizers & a few like-minded conservative leaders, we've decided that we have to be… cautious with where we apply you & a few other speakers."

"I… I understand."

After a few more pleasantries, Dennis thanked her for the coffee & took his leave. After he was gone, Anita wondered what was happening to the world & what was going to become of her if she kept losing & having her events cancelled.

June 25th, 1978
San Francisco, California

Ronnie was barreling down the I-40. For the last thirty hours, he had been travelling almost non-stop down the highway from Alabama in the hopes that nobody recognized him along the way. The whole way there, he had been cursing himself for thinking that Gregory could be trusted to listen to him. The truth was that he wanted to demote Gregory after the trial, but of course, as he knew back then, he couldn't, not without losing the Huntsville contingent & a large chunk of the Sons of Adam.

Ronnie had spent the last two years trying to move people into positions of authority & access so that he could find the proof that he needed to show that the secret world government was responsible for the birth anomalies. It hadn't been easy & it wasn't going quickly, but the people that he had managed to position were finally getting some access to things the public couldn't see.

Unfortunately, they were finding nothing. Ronnie had then announced his plan to get a member of their group elected to office. Surely, members of congress or the senate knew what was happening. If abducting one of them wouldn't work, they would just have to infiltrate the higher levels of government. Gregory had disagreed.

Gregory, ever the righteous firebrand, wasn't happy with stealth & infiltration & the lack of progress. He wanted to do something big to set America back onto the path of righteousness. He proclaimed that the organizers of the gay pride parade must be in on the conspiracy. He pointed to the fact that from the time the anomaly began, it only took them five years to get the parades going & to start winning political battles for queers. He proposed that they attack the pride parade, abduct its leaders & force them to tell them the truth.

Ronnie didn't like the idea. It was too public; Gregory hadn't really spent any time planning it out & there were too many things that could go wrong. When they had tried to abduct the Lieutenant Governor of Alabama, they had spent weeks planning it out & observing him only for their plan to fall apart because they made a move on the one day there would be bodyguards around him.

Ronnie argued that they didn't have enough time to plan for a frontal attack like that & that it was too dangerous.

He should have realized that it was weird that Gregory didn't push against him. Two days before the pride parade was set to begin, Ronnie had tried calling some of the folks from Huntsville & realized that he couldn't raise any of them. It was almost sunset when he finally got in touch with somebody that could tell him what was happening. Gregory had rounded up his loyalists, which consisted of all of their Huntsville members & a hundred more from all over Alabama, & he had led them to San Francisco.

Rounding up the dozen men that were available to him at the moment, they got into half a dozen cars & hauled ass down the highway. Ronnie figured that if they drove day & night in shifts, they could get to San Francisco just before the parade started & hopefully talk Gregory or his men at least out of this foolishness.

When they got to Bakersfield, Ronnie pulled over at a payphone Before beginning his shift in the driver's seat, he called his home base to see if there was any news. There was. It wasn't good.

His asset in the Birmingham PD had heard that somehow, Gregory's plan had been leaked to the authorities. Some FBI informant had made a call & California authorities were getting ready to pounce. Authorities all over the country were being put on high alert as the word got out that some two hundred & fifty anti-government conspiracy theorists were on the move & that there was going to be a massive police presence at the parade.

Ronnie cursed. He had a moment to consider what he should do. Should he risk everything & charge towards the parade & hope that he could warn Gregory's forces before they struck that they were charging into a trap, or should he cut his losses & run home? It would be a heavy loss. He would lose almost everything in Huntsville & a good number of the Sons of Adam wouldn't appreciate him abandoning Gregory. Still, if he got caught, how much longer until the sons fizzled out?

"Ronnie. What do you want to do?"

Ronnie looked to the man that had been driving in shifts with him. Ronnie wanted to cut his losses. Even if he lost Huntsville, it might be worth it to not have to deal with the self-righteous Gregory & his crusade followers.

"We haul ass to San Francisco & hope that we can get to Gregory before he does something stupid."

"Yes sir."

The man handed Ronnie the keys & four hours later, they were driving through San Jose when it happened. Ronnie's partner tuned the radio to a news show & they heard the bad news.

"This just in, an anti-government group of radicals that call themselves the Sons of Adam just attacked the sight of the gay pride parade. Reports are coming in of at least two hundred assailants charging in to where the parade was supposed to be held. Fortunately, law enforcement was warned of this attack late last night. Delaying the parade until next week, police & FBI forces set a trap for the men that has resulted in a massive confrontation."

"Fuck!" Ronnie shouted as he pulled the car over.

"Early reports are that after a series of brief, but intense exchanges of gunfire, almost a hundred members of the Sons of Adam have surrendered or been taken into custody. At least twenty are dead with dozens being wounded as police, state & federal officers have sustained relatively few casualties. At least fifty members of this group are still free & are believed to be trying to flee the state. Checkpoints are being set up around San Francisco & at ports & state crossings. At this time, it is believed that the leader of the insurgent attack, Gregory Parker, has been apprehended by police. We'll have more on this story as it develops."

"Fuck! Fuck! Fucking Hell!"

"What should we do Ronnie?"

"San Francisco is already crawling with law enforcement. Soon all of Southern California will be on high alert. We can't stay. We have to cut & run."

"Are we going to head back East? I think that they'll be expecting us to make straight for Arizona, fastest way home & what not."

"You're right. They're probably already locking down the border with Arizona & Nevada. Grab the map, we're going to haul ass to Oregon & we have to avoid the major cities. We'll head all the way up to Washington, then head East through Montana & North Dakota. We'll figure out the rest of the way from there."

"Won't that take forever?"

"Yeah, but they'll never expect us to circle around the country. But first thing is first, once we're out of the city, we have to find a payphone & tell the folks back home to go into code black. After an attack like that, it won't be long before Gregory's captured men start spilling secrets. Most of what they know is about Huntsville, but they still know enough about the rest of the setup to make deals with the feds."

"Shit. Alright, fastest way out of the city… … Uhm… take a right at the next light."

As Ronnie turned & started heading out of the city as fast as he could to warn home base about their impending raids, he saw something strange. A car driving by with a flag that looked like a rainbow. He had no idea what it meant as he drove by & hauled ass.

July 30th, 1978
University of Manchester, United Kingdom

"Unbelievable."

Doctor Edward Swanson put down the report that he was reading. He, along with the heads of several national research projects from Europe & Australia & Japan, had been invited to one of the main birth anomaly research facilities in the United Kingdom to learn about this new medical breakthrough.

The Royal Commission of Birth Ratio Research, the UK's organization doing research into the birth ratio anomaly had partnered with a team of scientists working on a new form of reproductive technology in the hopes of using it as a way to cheat the anomaly. Edward was stunned as he read the report.

"Invitro fertilization. Hendrix, you actually figured out how to make test tube babies."

"We prefer to call them artificially conceived infants, but yes. With the help of doctors Steptoe & Edwards who pioneered the process, we were able to successfully impregnate ten women who were having trouble conceiving with embryos that started their existence in petri dishes. Over the last few weeks, each of them gave birth to a healthy baby."

"Fantastic."

"C'est très bien."

"Fantastisch."

The leaders of the various research programs from around the world were duly impressed. This could be a work around for women with reproductive issues all over the world. This was game changing. This was one of the most incredible scientific advancements of the twentieth century, up there with splitting the atom & landing on the Moon. As the head of the Japanese research team was congratulating them in his broken English, it was the leader of the French program that asked the inevitable question.

"Quels sont leurs sexes? Sorry, pardon, what is the gender of the babies?"

Hendrix's shoulders visibly slumped. They all knew what the answer was going to be before he said it.

"Nine girls, one boy. The new normal."

Edward raised his glass as everyone's mood dropped a bit.

"To invitro fertilization, not only is it going to help women all over the world get pregnant, but it's also going to open up all kinds of research into reproductive medicine."

Everyone in the room lifted their glasses & cheered to the success of artificial conception & impregnation. Many of them could already here various churches lamenting that this would lead to a flood of bastards as women would no longer need to marry or even meet a man to have children. The news was going to hit the media in a few hours & the world was never going to be the same again as news anchors, journalists, experts & talk show hosts discussed the hot new topic over the coming weeks.

August 27th, 1978
The Vatican

The world had been rocked by the death of Pope Paul the Sixth. The leader of the church had passed a few weeks earlier from a heart attack. After the mourning period had come to an end & the college of cardinals had gathered, the papal conclave had begun on the twenty-fifth day of August to elect the 263rd Pope. The world now waited with anticipation as the process continued into its third day.

As the conclave went on, only sending up signals of black smoke to announce that a decision had not yet been reached, the people watched on as famous news presenters commented on why it was taking so long.

Some were proclaiming that the church needed to buckle down & take a hard line against the progressive surges occurring all over the world in the wake of an unprecedented & prolonged crisis. They called for one of the more conservative cardinals to be called upon to renew the traditions of the church & restore normalcy.

Others cried out for a more liberal Pope, one who would realize that the church needed to change with the new reality of the world. Someone who could modernize one of the oldest institutions in the world.

Just as the media couldn't agree, it seemed that the cardinals couldn't either. Cardinals Siri, Luciani, Pignedoli, Baggio & Lorscheider were clearly the favourite choices among the cardinals, but after eight ballots, none of them had the seventy-four votes needed to meet the requirement of a two-thirds majority.

After seeing black smoke for the eight time & seeing how late in the day it was, many were convinced that a new Pope would not be chosen on this day. Most camera crews were packing up for the night, preparing to switch over to junior reporters that would cover the relative lack of events over the night. A young reporter from Ireland had taken over from the normal reporter for the BBC. He had headed back to the hotel after a long day standing around, telling the people of the United Kingdom that a new Pope had not yet been chosen.

With sound checks finished, she waited around as the sun set, waiting on the off chance that something happened. She wasn't very hopeful as the cardinals had probably already gone to bed. She was prepared for another night of making minor comments on the crowds & gauging the expectations of random people. After a while, just to have something to do, she looked to her camera operator.

"Everything looking good Harold?"

"Yeah, everything is still fine. You've just got a fluff on your left shoulder."

"Thanks."

She grabbed the piece of fluff & blew it off into the breeze. She wouldn't want a fluff on her shoulder as television channels played their normally scheduled programming, ready to switch back at a moments notice if something happened.

"How do I look Harold?"

Harold simply starred past her.

"Harold! Earth to Harold, are you all right?"

Harold pointed past her to the Vatican where a cloud of white smoke lifted into the evening air.

"Jesus Christ, Harold, roll the fucking camera!"

Harold snapped out of it & positioned the camera as their aid woke up & called the production department in London to tell them that they had thirty seconds to be ready to go live. All over the UK, people watching the BBC or listening to it on the radio suddenly found their show interrupted with an announcement that they were going live to Rome. Harold signalled that he was rolling in 3, 2, 1.

"This is Faye O'Hanly, live from the Vatican, where, as you can see behind me, a cloud of white smoke is rising into the sky & the people still gathered are cheering at the selection of a new Pope. It's been three long days that the conclave has been deciding who to appoint to the highest position in the holy see & at last, long after everyone believed that it would be wrapping up for the night, a choice has been made."

The young Irish woman reported the news in her heavy accent. Since this was her first time on television, the BBC tried to get the daytime reporter that they had sent to get back to the Vatican & relieve her. Unfortunately, he had made himself unreachable by going to someone else's room & not telling anyone who he was spending the night with. As such, they had no choice but to let this rookie with her thick Irish accent spend the next few hours making announcements.

She reported to the people of the English commonwealth that it was Cardinal Sergio Pignedoli, the progressive candidate & closest ally to the late Pope Paul the Sixth that had been chosen to lead the

Catholic church. Shortly thereafter, as the veteran reporter still couldn't be located, she was the one to announce on the BBC that Pignedoli had chosen to take the papal name of Pope Peter the Second.

While several people were analyzing the choice of name & deciding if it was blasphemous to name himself after the apostle appointed Pope by Jesus himself, or if it was a sign that the church was going to be rebuilt to meet the needs of the new world that everyone lived in, the man was being prepared to stand before the public.

Shortly after the debate of his name began, Faye pointed Harold to the papal balcony where the newly minted Pope Peter the Second greeted the people of Rome in the full papal regalia as the world celebrated a new Pope.

October 9th, 1978
New York City

Lena tried to focus on the biography that she was writing for the new lady astronaut that had graduated flight training. The young woman had surprised everyone as nobody had thought that she was going to be able to pass the tests. She had been the only woman allowed to apply to that class, a token to women's rights so that nobody would try to sue NASA through the ERA or call them sexists. Yet she had passed the training & was now a NASA certified astronaut.

Lena was supposed to be doing a piece on her, but instead, she kept thinking back exactly a month, to the night that she heard the news out of Miami. The news that Janis Joplin had died of an apparent overdose. Lena was shocked. After the close calls in seventy, & seventy-three & seventy-five, a lot of people had started to think that she was indestructible. She may have looked like a walking skeleton at a few points, but she seemed to keep bouncing back.

Now here she was, thirty-five & not bouncing back. All over the country, singers that she had inspired had spent the last few weeks holding vigils for her.

Lena knew that she only had another day to write up & proof three more pieces or Wednesday's paper was going to be thin. Even with Sarah writing segments, she still had a tight deadline to meet & barely enough time to meet it. Still, instead of buckling down, she went to her record player. Pulling out a joint, she lit it up as she put Joplin's latest album, Twenty-Seven Years, on to play. As her classic style played throughout the office, Lena listened to the last album of one of the greats & felt her herbal remedy relaxing her. As Janis said in her song, sometimes you've got to tell the world to wait for a minute so you can catch up.

As the new age of women running the world continued to approach, Lena, like many women, said goodbye to a star from the old world.

November 27th, 1978
San Francisco, California

Harvey Milk lay bleeding on the ground. The freshman supervisor had been shot twice, once in the shoulder & once in the chest. He saw Dan White standing over him, leveling the gun. Parts of his life started flashing before his eyes. The hardships that he had gone through as a gay man. Winning the election last year for supervisor over more then a dozen other people. Seeing the Briggs initiative fail five to two, losing by over three million votes as the man that pushed for it & a small number of republicans lost re-election.

He closed his eyes. He had been so full of hope that he was going to get to see a future free of the kind of suffering men & women like him had to endure. Now he was certain that if he heard a bang, it would be the last thing he heard.

The bang came. He felt nothing. What felt like both a fraction of a second & an eternity later, he heard a thud as something fell against the wall. Opening his eyes, he saw Dan White slumped against the wall, red spreading from his shoulder. One of the new security guards that had been added after the Sons of Adam attack was standing in the doorway, his hands were trembling on his revolver as he pointed it at White.

"Put the gun down & surrender!"

White looked around confused.

"Now!"

The nervous guard cocked his gun. White dropped the gun & slid down the wall, clutching at the new hole in his shoulder.

"Shooter down! I repeat, shooter down! Man down, I need some help in here!"

Everything went fuzzy for Harvey as he heard the sound of sirens in the distance.

The next day, he woke up in the hospital to see a young nurse changing his IV bag. She wore a pin on her scrubs that read Milk for Supervisor. He smiled.

"What happened?"

The young woman jumped about a foot in the air before running off to get the doctor. A minute later, the doctor, an old man whose hair had long since turned snow white, walked into the room.

"Glad to see you awake Mr. Milk. You had us all worried for a while there. Tell me, do you know where you are?"

"A hospital..., & call me Harvey. What happened, I was... shot... by Dan..."

"Yes, I'm not sure of the specifics of how he managed to get into the building..."

"He snuck in through a basement window."

The doctor gave the nurse a look & she quieted down.

"As I was saying, you were shot twice, once in the shoulder & once in the chest. It was a miracle you survived; you lost a lot of blood before we could close you up. You're still not entirely out of the woods, but it looks like you'll survive."

"That's good. Was anyone else hurt?"

The doctor turned to the nurse who seemed to have all the answers.

"Mayor Moscone. He didn't make it."

"Goddamn. I knew Dan had issues, but this..."

Harvey took a deep breath before he continued, he could already feel himself getting sleepy again.

"That means... Dianne Feinstein.... Is the acting mayor."

The doctor watched as his patient began slipping back into sleep.

"It's going to be a little while before you really wake up. Rest up for now. We'll call Ms. Feinstein & inform the acting mayor that you're recovering."

Harvey then fell asleep before the doctor checked his meds & told the nurse to call up city hall. As news of Harvey Milk's recovery spread to the city, it quickly reached the small group of people gathered outside the hospital, waiting for news about his recovery.

December 17th, 1978
Church of the Lord's Son, Fort Worth, Texas

Reverend Thomas Edwards was not blind, nor was he particularly stupid. Over the last year, it had been getting harder & harder to recruit new congregants, particularly young women. He also noticed the fact that there were relatively few women in their late twenties & early thirties among his flock. He also noticed that a large number of families seemed to stop having children after their third daughter in a row. It was clear what was happening.

His church's policy of banishing women after having four daughters in a row was backfiring on him. Most of the women that kept trying until they had a son ending up getting banished. He couldn't understand why until he pulled aside a member of his flock after last week's service.

The young man was good with numbers. He could do in his head what most people would need a calculator to work out. He asked the young man what the odds were of a woman having a son after four attempts. The man didn't question why Thomas was only asking this now, after five years, he just sort of looked off into the distance & did the math in his head.

"At one in ten odds per pregnancy, after four pregnancies, she would have a... one in three chances of having a son."

Thomas had been shocked. In his mind, he mentally kicked himself for not asking this question years ago. If the man was right, it explained why so many of his followers stopped at three daughters. If they tried again, it was a two in three chance that they would be banished. He had figured that four tries would be enough for the odds to be in a woman's favor, but the growing number of parents in society with four, five, even six young daughters was a growing testament to the problem he now faced. Math.

"One in three. Okay, what would be the odds after five attempts?"

The kid looked off again & ran the numbers.

"About forty-one percent, or two out of five."

"That's still a bit unforgiving. How many attempts would it take to get even odds?"

"Hmm, that would take… … seven attempts to have better than even odds."

Thomas almost cursed. Seven tries just to have even odds of having a boy. Seven. Just for a flip of the coin chance of having a boy.

He spent the next several days considering what he could do about it. The obvious solution was to increase the number of daughters that his congregation could have to seven or eight. But it wouldn't look good if he just came out & doubled the limit. There were already people calling him a fraud & a charlatan full of empty promises. This would make him look like a huckster, trying to sell salvation.

He considered ending the policy of banishing women, but that could create all kinds of problems for him. Some of the women that he banished would want back in, which would be awkward at the very least, but what right would he have to turn them away? Even with the policy, it was getting harder & harder to justify banishment. Not to mention, a number of men had divorced their wives rather than be banished. If he ended the policy, many of those women would sue their former husbands or the church itself. He couldn't end the policy; he also couldn't just jack up the limit to seven. He only had one option & he would have to play it carefully.

A week before his Christmas Eve sermon, it was time. He had wanted to wait another week, announce the news on Christmas Eve, but one of the women in his congregation was already overdue to go into labor & he didn't want it to look like he was changing the rules for her. Just changing the rules was risky enough.

He stood before his congregation. As per usual, pregnant women were in the front being tended to by altar boys & handmaidens while families with sons sat behind them & families without sat at the back. He ran his hand through the grey & copper mess that was his hair & cleared his throat & raised his hand before he began.

"My children! This is a momentous day; I can feel it in the air. Raise your hands & feel it for yourselves!"

Almost everyone among the thousands before him in his massive church raised their hands.

"Feel the righteousness, feel the virtue of Heaven in this place! Our years of effort have born fruit my children! While the world outside slips into depravity with our leaders giving up on fighting the daughter curse, in this place, the lord shines his light on his faithful children, Hallelujah!"

"Hallelujah!" The people before him cried out.

"Over the years, we have cast out witches & whores & wicked women, cleansing our flock of the corruption in the world! Hallelujah!"

"Hallelujah!"

"We here who hold our hands up in the Lord's light are the righteous few! The virtuous & the vigilant! The uncorrupted! We who reject Satan & his ill works! Hallelujah!"

"Hallelujah!"

His congregants were cheering with him. They could feel their Lord smiling down on them & they were opening their hearts to him.

"So righteous we have been that God almighty has seen fit to reward us alone over the heathens & pagans & false followers out there! Hallelujah!"

"Hallelujah!" They all shouted like an unpracticed chorus.

"Here, in the house of the Lord on high, we, his most righteous children who have cast out the devil's whores, we shall have a fifth chance at sons! Hallelujah!"

"Hallelujah!" They all screamed.

"Yes my children! Rejoice! For so clean we have made his holy house that the wickedness of the feminists & the lesbians & the liberals outside cannot penetrate into our house! Hallelujah!"

"Hallelujah!"

"We may still be cursed, & so we may still need to bear as many as five to have a promised son, but we are clean in the eyes of the Lord! We are righteous, we are worthy of his mercy! Hallelujah my children! Hallelujah!"

"Hallelujah!"

The sounds of the congregation was drowned out when one of the pregnant women in the front, the one that was almost dangerously overdue screamed out in pain. As every altar boy & handmaiden in the large church rushed to her, she fell to her knees & screamed out at the top of her lungs.

"The baby is coming!!!"

Her husband & their three daughters rushed to her as one of the other priests called for an ambulance.

"You see my children, the Lord on high blesses his chosen flock with new life! Keep the aisle clear, the paramedics are only a few minutes away from here!"

It was perfect. He had riled the congregation up into a religious fervor that had them enthusiastic about the rule change & just as he finished updating the rule to five daughters, a woman up front gave birth to her fourth child. He couldn't have timed it better if he had tried to make it perfect.

He had intended to visit her the next day in the hospital, but labor was prolonged & after twenty-two hours, the doctors determined that an emergency caesarean was needed.

It was Thursday before she was fit to receive visitors. Reverend Thomas Edwards walked into her room full of cheer about the miracle baby. He was happy to congratulate the young couple on their success & to let them know that if they weren't yet recovered enough to attend Christmas mass, he would come back & bless them himself.

He walked through the door to her room & his smile instantly vanished. As her husband kept their three older daughters entertained, she was carefully nursing her newborn twin girls with help from a pair of nurses.

Three plus twins. Five daughters in a row. It was as if God was punishing him for thinking that he could change the rules. The miracle pregnancy that had lasted just long enough to not violate the old rule, now violated the new rule. Now, in just three days, on Christmas Eve no less, he was going to have to banish a woman who had just undergone a C-section & was resting in the hospital before going home to her five daughters.

1979

January 22nd, 1979
Queens, New York

It wasn't often that Elizabeth would rather sit through a normal math class. Normally, the only math that she liked to do in those classes was to count the minutes until she could get out. Today was another story, however. Instead of learning about algebra, the class was instead sitting there & listening to some man talk about his work as an engineer.

He was in the class as part of a program where people come in & tell students about some of the jobs they can get if they keep their grades up & go to university. Back in September, it had been a pilot, he talked about all the places that he got to travel to. In October, they had met an electrician who was actually very interesting once they realized how dangerous his job could be. In November, they had talked to a lawyer, the uncle of one of the students. Just before the holidays, they had listened to a firefighter talk about how hard the job was & how rewarding it was to help save lives.

Elizabeth had to admit to herself that it was kind of interesting, listening to the engineer talk about figuring out to make buildings stand & adapting to the challenges posed by some overly creative architects. Something about figuring out how something worked spoke to her a bit for a moment.

Still, when she got a note passed to her from Sarah, she couldn't help but agree with the fact that the engineer had only answered questions from the boys. The clock on the wall claimed that an hour had gone by, but Elizabeth was certain that it had been at least three years. When the class was finally over, the teacher thanked the engineer for taking some time out of his day to come & talk to his class. As everyone was getting ready to go to recess, the teacher called Elizabeth & Sarah to his desk.

"You wanted to see us sir?" Sarah asked.

"Yes, don't think that I didn't catch you two passing notes between each other while our guest was talking."

"Sorry sir."

"Mind telling me what was so important that you risked interrupting the man that was taking time from his job to be here today?"

"Sarah was just pointing out to me the fact that he only answered questions from the boys."

Their teacher looked at Elizabeth incredulously.

"I assure you; he didn't do that."

"I assure you, he did. We have four boys in this class, more than I've ever had to share a class with before, & every answered question came from one of them."

"Miss, Robinson, questions were answered, maybe not to your satisfaction, but they were answered."

"No, they weren't. By the end of the class, he knew the four boys on a first name basis, never even acknowledged the girls."

"Which is impressive since there's thirty of us." Sarah added.

"Watch, tomorrow in class, ask everyone who got an answer for their question to raise their hands. You'll see the four boys from our class raise their hands & nobody else."

Seeing their united front & intensity, he wondered for a moment if he hadn't noticed what was happening in his own class. Pushing the thought from his mind, he refocused on the issue at hand.

"Regardless of who's questions got answered, you shouldn't be passing notes around in class, especially when we have a guest who's got a busy schedule that he rearranged for us. Do I make myself clear?"

"Yes sir." They both said together.

"Good, now I won't keep you from recess any longer."

As Sarah started walking out, Elizabeth stuck around for a minute.

"Yes Ms. Robinson?"

"Sir, when is the school going to invite some women to talk to us?"

"Excuse me?"

"All the people that have come to inspire us have been men that usually ignore most of the girls. When are we going to get to meet a woman with a cool job?"

He blanked. He had no answer to this one. She was right about it. A grade of young girls & they were bringing in these men that mostly ignore girls to talk about cool jobs the students can get if they apply themselves.

"I admit, that might be a bit of an issue. I'm certain the school is working on it. In the meantime, I'll talk to them about it. Now go, you don't want to spend all recess here & be late to your next class."

Sarah grabbed Elizabeth's hand & pulled her to the door so they could get to their neighbouring lockers. As they left, he thought about whether or not he could recall any girl in his class getting a question answered today.

February 13th, 1979
CBS News desk

Around the country, Americans watched the Tuesday news with some interest. Whether it was to see if the weather was going to ruin plans for the next day or an actual interest in the news, millions watched as Walter Cronkite, the wise old sage that America loved, took a second to rearrange the papers on his desk before looking into the camera to address the nation with the final story of the hour.

"As all of you with a significant other hopefully know, tomorrow is Valentines Day, the annual celebration of love & romance when we all try to get out of work a little early to spend some time with the one that we love. Valentine's Day is a time-honoured tradition in this country dating back centuries. However, this tradition it seems is due for a few changes. For well over a decade now, many in America & around the world have worried about what love will look like for the XX generation, a popular term to describe children born after 1965."

"Many people have spent countless years wondering how love, marriage & romantic relationships would work once a generation that was ninety percent female was old enough for it to matter. We'll, it seems that we may be getting a bit of a preview."

Flipping a sheet of paper on his desk purely for show as he was reading off of the teleprompter, Cronkite continued.

"While many schools are getting into trouble with parents & rights groups for trying to force the old normalcy onto their students, many schools have been more lenient of the new reality their students face. At thirteen years old, many members of the XX generation have begun the age-old quest of looking for love & going to school dances. In many middle schools & junior high schools, the last year before beginning high school is when many students go to a school dance for the very first time. For many of these students, that first dance is the Valentine's dance. However, with some schools having less than a dozen boys in any one grade, the question arises of just who will the girls be going with this year?"

"Over the last two weeks, with permission from parents & a promise of anonymity, CBS sent out reporters to conduct surveys at schools. Now while it should be noted that these children are only thirteen years old, we can sort of get an idea of what direction this new generation might be going in."

Cronkite glanced at the card on his desk with the statistics on it.

"Of those girls aged thirteen who are attending Valentine's dances this year, a full half have reported that they are either going alone, or with a group of friends. About a quarter have reported that they are taking another girl as a friend so that they can have a date. Of the remaining quarter, fifteen percent are going with a boy as their date with just over half of them going with a slightly older boy, eight percent are going with a girl as their date, & two percent are going to be sharing a boy on their date, being one of two girls going with the same boy."

Across America, those numbers brought relief to some, anger to others & fear to more than a few. Many were happy that the vast majority of girls were either going with boys, friends or not at all. Some were concerned that at thirteen years old, almost a tenth of girls were already going to dances with other girls as their dates & many were dumbstruck when they heard that some girls were sharing a boy.

"Ever since we first announced the anomaly in the birth rates, this issue has been entirely theoretical, an issue for tomorrow. It seems that tomorrow has now arrived. While some of the reported statistics no doubt brought some comfort to those who support traditional styles of romance, the simple fact is that it is time to find new ways as this new generation continues to age & figure out how they're going to love."

March 14th, 1979
Los Angeles, California

Govind Dayal sat cross-legged in his studio as people & couples slowly walked in. A lot of the more conservative people walking in were a bit nervous at the sight of him mediating at the head of the room wearing what looked like a saffron colored sheet around his lower body & a vibrant red turban. The rest of his lean body with his flawless dark caramel skin was on full display. A lot of people sat down very awkwardly as they had not sat cross-legged on a carpet since they were children.

The room, decorated with old tapestries & books of religious scripture opened to pages concerning fertility, had a funny sort of smell to it. At one moment, it smelt like the incense in church, in the next moment, it smelled like something the police might be concerned about. After everyone was sitting there for a few minutes, a small chime sounded & Govind opened his eyes.

He was happy to see that after a month, one of his sessions almost had a full studio. He saw many young couples & a number of men & women who were here alone, all with a singular goal in common. He put his hands together as if in prayer & bowed his head to his customers before greeting them in his thick Indian accent.

"Good evening to all of you. It is a privilege to welcome you into the first iteration of my temple. I am here tonight to teach you all the ways of Nine Sons Tantric Fertility. If learning this is not why you are here, you are as free to stay & learn with us as you are free to leave."

When nobody left, he smiled.

"Excellent. As many of you know, tonight, in orbit around the Moon, a woman named Marilyn Addams is bidding farewell to her colleagues as she becomes the first woman command module pilot. She will remain up there alone while her colleagues explore the Moon for a record breaking seven days. Truly, Western science has achieved many incredible, fabulous & wonderous things that up until a decade ago, were nothing more than the fictions of the raving mad. However, as you yourselves well know, Western science has not solved the issue of having sons."

Govind stood straight up in a graceful motion that few could do from sitting cross-legged.

"For the last fourteen years, scientists have been working tirelessly to find a solution to this problem. But what many do not realize is that spiritualist, such as myself have also been working tirelessly to achieve success in restoring the birthing of sons to the world. I am now joyous to tell you that the tantric fertility rights that I have studied have worked. I know that they work because three of my first four children are sons as you can see on the picture to your left."

The entire room looked over to their left & sat there confused for a moment.

"Sorry, my English is still not entirely perfect, your right, my left."

Turning again, they saw the picture that he was pointing too of himself & his four young children, three of whom were boys. These people, hopefully his future disciples, were all impressed. Couples clutched together with hope for a son or three. Govind sat back down in the lotus position.

"I & a few of my most trusted colleagues from the temples of India, have studied the fertility rights & mediations of over a dozen cultures, including the teachings & prayers of your own catholic Saint Colette. Through this research, we have devised the methods of spirituality & conception that will grant you the sons you crave."

At the mention of a catholic saint, many of the people in the room felt surer that this would work for them. They sat there as he went on.

"Men, place a hand over your testicles, feel the feminine energy that has infected every man's testicles on Earth. Know that through our meditations & the herbal remedies of nature, we shall expel this feminine corruption from your manhood's."

The men all sat there, cross-legged & covering their crotches, many of them convinced that they could feel something wrong stirring within them.

"Women, place a hand over your womb, just below your navel. Feel the masculine energy that has corrupted you & fights off any manly essence that would infuse you. With the meditations & remedies that we will have for you, you shall be able to expel this unwanted manliness from your uterus & accept the life-giving gift for newborn boys as easily as you can for newborn girls."

The women before this spiritual healer from the mysterious Eastern half the world placed a hand over their bellies & felt the masculine energies fighting their chance at a newborn son.

"It will not be easy my children. But I, Guru Govind Dayal, will work tirelessly to teach you how to rectify the spiritual energy in your body through my special combination of mediations, herbs, exercises, prayers & tantric sexual positions."

As everyone in attendance perked up, Govind laughed.

"I will not be showing you the sex positions this week. First of all, my wife is not here this week. She is preparing her own body so that in time, she will be able to conceive a fourth son for me. Second of all, without the mediations, teaching you the positions will only lead to more daughters for you. While there is nothing wrong with having a daughter, I have one of my own after all, that is not the goal here. Tonight I shall teach you the first basics of meditation, for quieting the mind so that you may access your soul. Then next week, my wife & I will teach you the first position."

The people in his class nodded their heads as they wondered if he & his wife would be simply showing them the position, or actually stripping down & preforming it in front of them.

"For the next week, I want you to practice the meditation I'm going to teach you for at least half an hour every day. I also want you to do your best to abstain from sex for this week. I know that it may seem counterintuitive, but the more powerful orgasms that you will have next week will help to push out the corrupted energies. Now please, try to sit in this lotus position as I am if you can. Do not worry if you cannot, I simply wish to see how much I will have to teach some of you."

As all of the people in the room struggled to get into something that loosely resembled the lotus position, Govind could see himself getting rather wealthy from his followers & all that he would have to teach them.

May 9th, 1979
BBC Nine O'clock News

Richard Baxter, one of the BBC news presenters went over the information carefully one more time before cleaning his glasses as the studio prepared to go on. As the producer counted down, he looked into the camera.

"Good evening, this is the BBC Nine O'clock News, I'm Richard Baxter. Tonight's main story, after her historic win in the election six days ago, Margaret Thatcher, the nation's first lady prime minister & her new cabinet entered ten downing street today to begin leading the new minority conservative government."

"Falling just two seats short of a majority in Parliament, Thatcher may find it more difficult than she had imagined to enact her vision for the nation's economy & values. Many people were stunned six days ago to find that she had not won a majority government. All expectations had been that she would easily sweep up a major victory until she was caught making a number of statements that were labeled as anti-feminist. Many analysists are pointing to these statements in the face of the ongoing birth crisis as a major cause of her falling short of the expected mark."

"A similar situation has occurred in the Canadian elections held today where Liberal leader Pierre Trudeau managed to overcome the odds against him by winning re-election, albeit with a minority government of his own."

Millions all over the United Kingdom & around the world watched & listened as Richard continued, confused as to why he was bringing Canadian politics into the conversation.

"These two elections seem to be part of a larger global trend away from conservative governments. A conservative minority in the UK, a liberal victory in Canada, the United States have not elected a republican since Eisenhower & despite many conservative efforts, most early indicators are saying that Jimmy Carter will win re-election next year. All over the world, calls for a return to more traditional ways of life are going unanswered. In Iran, Reza Pahlavi II's second white revolution to empower women is proving more than a match for conservative rebels looking to return the nation to an Islamic theocracy. It seems that all over the world, from parliamentary elections in India, to state elections in Australia, from general elections in Botswana to local elections in Ireland. It seems that conservative candidates & advocates are struggling against parties & groups that intend to prepare for the new incoming generation."

"Even the new Pope was considered to be the more progressive choice among the cardinals that were favorited to win the Vatican's conclave. This is leaving many people wondering what the future of politics will look like & whether or not conservatism can survive."

June 22nd, 1979
Kennedy Space Center, Florida

Dawn was still a few hours away from happening. Nevertheless, the stands a few miles away were packed with spectators braving the pre-dawn to witness this moment. At first glance, the rocket looked exactly like a regular Saturn V that had already carried over twenty missions to space & several to the Moon. At closer inspection, it was a bit different from the ones that came before.

This rocket, the Saturn V-a, used new materials & assemblies that had been developed over the last decade so that it could squeeze even more raw power out of its fuel & engines. Its predecessor, with its missions stripped down to the bare essentials & pushed to its limit, could send two people to the Moon for a weeklong stay. This new version could send them for ten days with ease.

The news of this more incredible mechanical beast was not the only reason that Americans were tuning back into the space race though. Just two days ago, news had broken that there was new activity being seen at the launch complex that the Soviets had used to send to cosmonauts to the Moon. With the Soviets making another push & America's new version of their super heavy lift rocket, people all over the country were tuning into the launch.

Tightly strapped into the command capsule was Myrtle Cagle, commanding the mission with Deke Slayton as her lunar module pilot on his first trip to the Moon & Karl Gordon as the command module pilot on his first mission beyond low earth orbit. As the countdown resumed with just a few minutes left on the clock, mission control let them know that everything looked good to go. Myrtle looked at her two crewmates.

"You boys remember to pack everything, toys, swim trunks, sunscreen, because once we leave, we're not turning back if you forgot something."

Deke & Karl laughed as Myrtle mothered them.

"Ten days on the Moon boys. Who knows, they might schedule in some time for us to actually just enjoy being up there for once."

Deke chuckled & looked over.

"I doubt it. You've been there twice, you know that if they find space in the schedule, they'll find something for you to do."

"Probably but let a girl dream that she'll actually be able to appreciate being on the Moon while she's there."

"Fair enough. Here's hoping."

As the last few seconds ticked down, the five powerful engines at the base of the ship kicked into life. When the timer hit zero, the umbilical & the clamps disengaged & the most powerful version of the most powerful rocket ever built by humanity burned into the sky to kick off a series of new, longer missions that would change the game as the Soviets struggled just to get to the Moon.

August 11th, 1979
Ferris Barracks, Bavaria, West Germany

The triple chevron insignia felt heavy on Sergeant Debra Foster's arm. The feeling was completely in her mind, it was just a simple patch that she had sewn into her uniform. The weight that she was feeling was from the responsibilities that it represented.

Debra was surprised when her promotion was announced. Unlike most others that either never got promoted or had to wait years once they qualified, Debra had been promoted pretty much the moment that she met all of the requirements for the job.

Her rapid promotion led to a number of men complaining that she was being promoted so that the army could say they had a new lady Sergeant. Many of these men were told by their superiors that if they wanted to get a promotion, they should get off their asses like Debra did.

Back home, even her parents were thrilled when she called them up to let them know the news. She had expected her grandfather to be proud, especially now that she outranked him, but when her parents were happy for her, she had to check to make sure she had called the right number. Her mother kept going on about how she was the talk of the town. Little Debra Foster, the Sergeant in the army.

Of course, all of this new praise & status also came with new a bunch of new responsibilities. As a Sergeant, she wasn't just going to be in charge of a small four-person unit. With her promotion, she now found herself in charge of a newly formed mechanized infantry squad. Thirteen people now answered directly to her. She now commanded nine riflemen, & four vehicle operators that worked both in & on the M113 armored personnel carrier under her command. Where just days earlier she had been a Corporal, she now commanded three of them in her squad. Unfortunately, her squad was suffering from a malcontent.

A riflemen named Susie Ambers from Oregon, who after a piss poor performance in their first training exercises under Sergeant Foster, now found herself in the base's jail. As Susie sat there, head in hands, Debra walked up to the cell.

"Private Ambers, care to explain just what in the hell you're doing in here tonight?"

"Oh, good evening, Sergeant. Isn't it obvious, I'm under arrest."

"Yes Ambers, I can see that. I also saw your record when I was put in charge of the squad. Insubordination, gambling, reporting for duty drunk, a streaking incident."

"To be fair, most of those are just me having some fun."

"Right, well now it seems that in your quest for fun, you've added picking fights to a record that is impressively long for such a short career so far."

"Asshole had it coming. He kept siding up next to me & asking me if we could go streaking together. Didn't seem to hear the word no."

"So, you decided to break his jaw?"

"What else was I supposed to do?"

"Come to me. You could have come to me, or you could have gone to Lieutenant Mends, or Captain Harris. Then he'd be the only one in trouble. Instead, you're the one sitting in here while Colonel LeBeau considers disciplinary actions."

"Whatever. It doesn't matter."

"Doesn't matter! Dammit Susie, the way you're going, you're heading for a dishonorable discharge. Is that what you want?"

"No… I might not get my benefits that way."

Debra sighed.

"I see. You're one of *those* girls."

"Those girls?"

"Enlist for two or three years, half ass your way through your contract, then head home with some military bonus like housing benefits or a college scholarship."

"That, or enough money to get myself out of a tiny little town that only exists because someone went & built a post office at the intersection of two highways for some reason."

"I see. So, for you, the army is just a paycheck."

"Sorry Sergeant, but a way out is a way out. I don't want to spend the rest of my life as some alfalfa farmer's wife."

"I see."

"Don't get me wrong, I have nothing against alfalfa farmers. A lot of my friends are alfalfa farmers. I just don't want to be a farmer's wife that lives in a town that exists to service an intersection. The army seemed like a great option. See some of the world, I mean look at us, we're in Bavaria. Plus, I can get paid enough that I can save up for a house in a town big enough to exist on a map."

"Okay Susie, so the army is a paycheck, that doesn't explain why you're picking fights & breaking rules."

"Sorry Sergeant, but my enlistment is almost over & in these last few weeks, I just… I don't know, it feels like it doesn't matter. It's not like we're in an active war zone, we're next to the iron curtain in case the reds decide they want to start World War three. They're not going to make a move on a NATO country."

Debra looked at the young woman in front of her & sympathized. She understood wanting to get away from a farming community & her hometown was about three hundred times bigger than Susie's.

"So, I guess that means that you don't intend to reenlist."

"No mam. Gonna go home, find me a nice little city to live in, find my prince charming before we run out of those & settle down."

"Sounds nice, but I can't have a member of my squad picking fights because she's bored & she's running out the clock. You don't have to excel if you're just going to quit on us, but it would be nice to get a minimum effort from you. The military actually means something to the rest of us. Some of us have been working our tits off to make a place for ourselves here & it's disrespectful to those of us who care when you can't even be bothered to try."

Susie leaned back against the wall.

"Sorry Sergeant. I'll try to do better for my last few weeks. But if one of the men tries to get handsy, he'll be eating through a straw."

"Fair enough private."

Susie saluted weakly. Debra turned on her heels & walked out the door hoping that this incident didn't reflect poorly on herself. A week in charge of a squad & one of her riflemen was already in the cooler.

September 18th, 1979
Manhattan, New York

Lena sat on the couch, wearing nothing but a thin sheet made of Egyptian cotton as she flipped through the channels on the small television with the bulky remote control in her hand. Finding ABC, she turned the volume up & sat there for a few minutes, watching the headline news before it got to the story that she was waiting to hear. As the presenter was talking about the next Apollo mission & its first ever all-female surface crew that would be descending on the Moon in a few weeks, Cassie O'Dowd walked into the living room wearing nothing but a grin.

"There you are. Usually when you come over, I can't get you out of my bed, not that I'm complaining. Now I take one phone call, & here you are, having absconded with my favorite sheets to watch the television."

"Sorry Cassie, I got a call earlier from a friend of mine that works at ABC. He called me up just before I came over & told me I would really want to see one of the stories in the middle of the broadcast tonight."

"Is that so? Did you not tell him that you would be busy staring at a pair of Irish hills?"

Lena laughed.

"Not in so many words, no. But he said that it was something that I was going to want to see, so I said that I would catch if I could."

"So that's why you're watching a story about two women that'll be playing around on the Moon when you could be giving me a new reason to sing your praises into the night."

"I'll be just a minute, if the next story isn't whatever it is that I'm supposed to see, then I've got better things to be doing with my time."

Cassie sat down next to Lena & wrapped her arm around her sheet wearing lover.

"This had better be a good story, your thighs could be wrapped around my ears right now, instead we're here."

Before Lena could reply, the story about the two women who would be walking on the Moon came to an end. Tempted to simply march her sometimes lover with her thick Irish accent back to her bed, she kept listening to the man on the late news.

"About six to eight years ago, elementary schools all over the country started creating sports teams for girls as many schools could not get enough boys on their teams to keep the teams going. While every elementary school in the country has since started focusing on girls' sports, it seems that one school in a small town in Idaho has changed their mind & has decided to just not have any school sports whatsoever."

Lena stared at the television in disbelief.

"I don't believe it. That's my story."

"What?"

"The elementary school in Idaho. Just before the school year started, they cancelled all the girls' sports. I wrote about it in Sunday's issue of Lavender Press."

"Hang on."

Cassie searched around her apartment for a moment before finding the paper. Flipping through the pages, she found the article.

"Here it is."

Cassie held up the Sunday edition so Lena could see her story. Turning back to the television, she watched on.

"… school in Idaho cancelled all girls sports a week before classes started & mandated that all boys in the school must play on a grade appropriate football team. The truly surprising part of this story is how it was able to fly under the radar. Even now, most news sources in Idaho have yet to report on this story. In fact, the story was originally reported in a regional women's newspaper, the Lavender Press, in Manhattan this past Sunday…"

"Oh… my… God… ABC news just name dropped my newspaper as the source of their story. Oh my god."

"That's incredible, but how did you get the story if papers in Idaho don't even have it yet?"

"One of my truck drivers has a cousin in Idaho. He heard a rumor from his niece that they weren't going to get to play against one of the other schools because they had gotten rid of the girls' team. So, I got her to call up her cousin who called his niece & asked her which school, I then called the school & pretended to be a concerned parent."

"Wow. Talk about luck. How do the papers & news stations in Idaho not know about it?"

"It's a very small, very conservative town. I guess nobody cared enough about it to call a reporter."

"Yet you were able to figure it all out. That's incredible Lena."

"It is pretty incredible, isn't it."

"I'll say, your driver just happens to casually mention a rumor she heard from, what was it, her cousin's niece on the other side of the country."

"It was lucky for me."

"That couldn't have been easy."

"Honestly, the hardest part was getting the phone number for the school. I'm sure there's a very confused operator in Idaho who's hearing this story & wondering if the woman from New York who asked for the number was a reporter."

Cassie chucked before holding out her hand.

"Come on Lena, while we wait for your Pulitzer, I've got another prize for my nationally recognized reporter."

Lena smiled, took Cassie's hand, & followed her into the bedroom.

October 28th, 1979
Pallas Crater, the Moon

Jerrie Cobb & Sandra Cohen were taking careful notes of the small boxes that were sitting under a small lamp. Normally the lunar lander would have been too small to bring & store these boxes, but with the new rocket, NASA had a new lunar lander that was larger than the ones that they had been using since Neil & Buzz took one small step.

Aside from being the first all-woman surface crew, they were now also the first two people to try to grow plants on the Moon. While Sandra took pictures & video that was being broadcast back to Earth, Jerrie carefully measured each of the radishes that had sprouted in the three small boxes.

Each box had different soil in it. One was soil brought from Earth. One was filled with lunar regolith & the third was a mix of the two. With every leaf that sprouted, the two of them were growing more convinced that it was only a matter of time before the President announced a push to build a permanent base up here. Why else would they be testing to see how well radishes sprout & grow in a lunar environment? Sandra got a picture of one of the freakishly tall radish leaves.

"Got it. Say, did I ever tell you about how hard my father worked so that he could get out of the family business of growing root vegetables."

Jerrie laughed.

"Look at you now. What would your father say about you doing this?"

"He's definitely not thrilled about it. I told my family about it at my grandmother's birthday, that one of the things that we'd be doing up here was sprouting radishes & he just put his face in his hands."

"Sometimes there's just no escape. How did the rest of the family take it?"

"My grandfather doubled over laughing. I haven't heard him have a good belly laugh like that since I was a kid. You know he gave me the seeds that we're using here."

"Really? I thought that NASA would have picked some agricultural company to supply them."

"Same, but I brought them in, the scientists checked… whatever it is they check & they approved the seeds. It was also good for the press, you know, astronaut from a family of small farmers bringing in the heirloom seeds that her family has been cultivating for generations."

"Yeah, that would probably play very well in the press & to conservatives. So, these are Cohen family radishes that we're growing on the Moon."

"Growing quite well. My grandfather showed me some freshly sprouted radishes before I left. They weren't this tall & the leaves sure weren't this big. Everything that isn't in pure regolith is thriving & huge."

"Remember what Janet said, the low gravity might make the plants grow taller. I guess she was right on that one."

"I guess."

As the two of them talked about their experiment to sprout radishes on the Moon, the video & pictures that they took were being transmitted back to Houston where they were then sent to a lab in Florida at the Kennedy Space Center. There, amid stacks of reports & control boxes filled with Earth soil & simulated Lunar regolith, was Janet Hill & the team that she was on.

They watched each incoming picture with fascination & read over every data point, working to figure out how lunar gravity & soil would affect the plant's growth. Janet wished they could watch the full life cycle of the plants on the Moon, but the mission was only going to last a few more days before the plants were blasted into space, spent two days in zero G & went through reentry into Earth gravity. Still, there would be a lot that they could learn from the plants, even if they were only growing for nine days on the Moon.

For several hours, they poured over the data which seemed to indicate that while the lunar regolith made poor soil, it seemed to make a great fertilizer when mixed with Earth soil.

At the end of the day, Janet was left wondering how she had managed to end up doing some of the most incredible science in the world. Just a closeted lesbian from Canada & here she was, investigating plant growth occurring on the Moon. That was when one of her coworkers got her attention.

"Hey, a bunch of us are heading out for a bite, you wanna join us?"

"Sorry James, I've got plans tonight."

"That's too bad, I hope your plans aren't in Orlando."

"Why not?"

"You know those equality marches that have been going on for months all over the country?"

"Yeah, the one in South Carolina turned into a full-blown riot."

"Yeah, well there's a coordinated one going on that started today. It's happening in DC, New York, Houston, L.A., a few other cities & here, in Orlando."

"Well James, it's a good thing my plans aren't in Orlando. Is it a women's rights march or a gay rights march?"

"Both from what I've heard. Apparently the one in DC already has over a quarter of a million people protesting for rights."

"Wow. What about the one here in Orlando."

"Last I heard, it was about fifty thousand or so."

"Wow. Thanks for the heads up."

"No problem, see ya tomorrow."

"Tomorrow James."

When Janet got into her car & started heading home to Rebecca, she thought back to all of the times she joined demonstrations in Montreal & almost got caught by the police. She remembered the night that she was caught. She remembered how great it felt fighting the laws that tried to keep her & Rebecca apart. A part of her was tempted to grab Rebecca & make their way to the protests to join in. Sadly, she couldn't risk getting caught. This was Florida. If they got caught, Rebecca would be fired from the school she taught at & she might be fired from NASA. She was certain that many of her coworkers knew, but there's a difference between them knowing & them knowing.

December 3rd, 1979
Rural Alabama

Ronnie watched the news as the verdict was read aloud. Guilty on all charges. Gregory Parker stood up in his orange jumpsuit as the judge handed down his sentence for the attack on the gay pride parade in San Francisco & the people who lost their lives. Life in Prison. Gregory then spit at the judge & began quoting scripture as he was dragged out of the courthouse.

Ronnie felt his worries lessen. After spending five days driving around the country so that he could get home, he had been burdened with the task of trying to rebuild the Sons of Adam out of what was left now that nearly a third of them were dead or in prison for the next few decades. It hadn't been easy. Several members of the group gave up the cause, taking almost a fifth of what they had left. It would be a long time before their numbers were back up.

Still, Ronnie wasn't upset. After thinking about the events that had happened over the last few months, he saw all of this as a good thing. The wild firebrand was gone & those who weren't completely committed to the cause had left. All that was left of them now were the devoted & the levelheaded, exactly the kind of people he needed right now.

They would listen to his orders to not make any noise for a while. They would go along with his quieter, more long-term plans. No more hot heads that wanted to launch attacks & take hostages. Now they could take the time to infiltrate into higher levels of law enforcement & maybe even government. Somewhere in all of the bureaucracy, there had to be a level where people were being read into the truth about the new world order that was using the birth ratio crisis to take over.

"Ronnie, we're ready for you now."

The man was one of the twelve patriarchs. With Gregory gone, his seat had been filled by a calmer, more rational man. As Ronnie went into the four-year leadership challenge, he was certain that with Gregory serving as an example of what happened when they went off half-cocked, he would easily get another four years as Shepard with the plan for long-term infiltration he was about to propose.

December 23rd, 1979
Oval Office

President Carter walked into the oval office despite how late in the night it was. So late in fact that some would call it early. He didn't appreciate being woken up & dragged to the Resolute Desk so early in the morning. It was bad enough that he & his family weren't going home to Georgia for the holidays this year, but to be roused to work this early was not something he appreciated. Still, when the director of Central Intelligence & a few four-star generals request an emergency meeting concerning news from the USSR, a President wakes up, fast.

With strong coffee in hand, President Carter sat down at the Resolute Desk, drank some more of the industrial strength brew & turned to the Director of Central Intelligence sitting across from him in front of a pair of generals.

"What seems to be the trouble Stansfield?"

"The trouble is that about two hours ago, the USSR's minister of Health announced a new major breakthrough in combating the birth ratio anomaly."

The President suddenly got nervous. This was the nightmare scenario that Presidents had been worrying about since 1965. If the Soviets could come up with a cure before the Western world, it would be bigger than if the Soviets had beat the Americans to the Moon. He would have hordes of protestors demanding that America negotiate &, if necessary, capitulate to the demands of the Soviets for access to the cure.

"Do they have a cure?"

"Not as of yet, they don't claim that they've cured it. They claim that they've developed a treatment for women that would reduce the imbalance in the birth ratio. The claim is that with this treatment, instead of nine girls for each boy, it has been reduced to six girls for each boy. Still a problem, but a significant improvement."

Not as bad as an outright cure, but still not good news for the President.

"Do we have any idea of what this treatment is?"

"No sir, however, there seems to be a number of… oddities."

"What kind of oddities?"

"Well, according to their announcement, it's something so simple that Russian women won't need a doctor. They'll be able to do it at home. The other thing is that they aren't mentioning the doctors that led the effort for this cure, they're just saying that they've done it."

President Carter looked at the translated announcement that the director handed him.

"Are you saying… that this is fake?"

"We believe so sir. We think that this is a desperate attempt by the Soviet leadership to pacify the population & convince them that it's better under the communists than it is in the West."

"But won't people notice that nothing has changed?"

"Not right away sir. They'll probably spend the next few months reminding people that the first results of the treatment will only appear in nine months, when more boys are being born. They're probably hoping that nobody will be able to tell that boys still make up ten percent of newborn children instead of fourteen percent. It's not a very noticeable difference."

"So, they're going to spend a few months convincing everyone that they've begun rectifying the problem, then they're just going to hope that nobody notices that the small difference they've proclaimed hasn't actually occurred?"

"Essentially sir."

"What if they do notice? Wouldn't that infuriate the Soviet people?"

"Sir, the Soviet people are already furious. The party has refused to begin transitioning society to a female majority culture & all along the way, there's been propaganda & promises that have proved false. Birth ratio riots have been breaking out all over the USSR & its sphere of influence with growing intensity & frequency."

"So, this is a hail Mary."

"Exactly sir. They're hoping that this will pacify the population for at least the next few years, giving them a chance to reinforce their control."

"Seems risky."

"It is sir. That's one of the two reasons that we woke you up so late, or early as the case may be. Soviet leadership is getting desperate. Their economic growth has been slowing over the last few years, there are rumors going around that in 1983, they're going to make mandatory conscription of all men on their eighteenth birthday the law, & the people no longer believe a lot of the Soviet propaganda concerning efforts to fix the lack of newborn boys. If they're playing a story like this, & it is a lie like we think it is, they must be very desperate."

"Desperate people do desperate things."

"Exactly sir. If they're going to this kind of length to maintain control, then the situation must be more delicate & fragile then we believed."

The President leaned back in his chair.

"Something so simple that women can do it at home. Would Soviet women actually believe this?"

"It's hard to say sir. They know that a lot of what their government says is just propaganda, but they may be desperate enough to believe it. In any case, if they don't believe it, protests could get worse."

"Which would make the leadership more desperate. Keep an eye on those protests & find out what this treatment is. Coordinate with the Department of Health, Education and Welfare... sorry, the Department of Health & Human Services to find out if this treatment actually works. So early in the morning that I forgot we renamed it a few months ago. I don't know what would be worse; if this treatment works or if it doesn't."

1980

Jan 16th, 1980
Greensboro, North Carolina

Tom Beasley worked on his math homework. The work was easy for him as it usually was, which made both of his parents happy. So far, he wasn't finding fifth grade math to be any more difficult than fourth grade, which also made his parents happy because they loved it when he brought home A's. Finishing up his work, he went into the kitchen to get a snack when he heard his father on the phone. His father wasn't happy.

"What do you mean he's off of the team! I thought that he loved playing football?"

Tom's father listened to the coach's response.

"Come on... it barely slowed him down."

Tom listened as his father listened.

"Alright, I'll ask."

Tom's father thanked the coach for the call & hung up. Tom's mother, who was cooking supper looked over to him.

"What's wrong hon?"

"You know Mark, the kid from the Green Beans team that can just mad dash across the field?"

"No hon, you're the only one in the house that has the teams memorized."

"He's the boy that took that mild tackle last week."

"Mild tackle... mild tackle... you don't mean Cassandra's Mark? The way she told it, you would think that he was hit by a bus. Didn't he leave the field crying?"

"Not at all, he finished his team's play & then walked it off to sit out the rest of the game. Impressive for a ten-year-old."

"Okay, well what about it?"

"Well apparently, he quit the team today, which means that they don't have enough players for proper games. So now the coach is calling up the parents of other boys to try & see if anyone's boys want to play."

"Seriously, we've been through this, you know that Tom will say no. He doesn't like sports."

"I've got to try. I made some of my best friends playing football at his age. It'll be good for him to get some friends."

"He has friends."

"I mean proper friends, not just the other two boys in his class. He needs some guy friends that are little bit more… manly."

"This again, they're ten."

"Even at ten, his friends are a bit… let's just say that's it good for them the girls won't have many options."

Tom's father then noticed him standing there.

"Hey Tom, that was the Green Beans coach on the phone, how would you like to play? You wouldn't even have to sign up for it."

"No thanks dad."

His father slumped. One of the few parents fortunate enough to have a boy on the first go & he didn't want to play sports. He turned around back to his wife as Tom took a cookie.

"I knew that we should have sent him to that private school."

"We can't afford private school."

"Girls' families can't afford it. The school in High Point that Bob & Charlie mentioned offers cheaper tuition for boys. We could afford to send him there."

"Not if the supreme court says otherwise."

"What?"

Tom's mother pointed to the tv in the living room.

"It was on the news; a group of people are suing all the way up to the supreme court. They say that offering lower tuition for boys violates the ERA. They said that it's depriving young girls of a fair chance at accessing educational institutions & is giving preferential treatment to the boys."

"Well shit. Guess the private schools aren't an option."

The next morning in class, Tom was sitting in the corner as students filed into the classroom. As he sat there, his father's words about private school replayed in his head. He didn't want to leave his school. Fortunately, it seemed that his father couldn't send him somewhere else, but still, Tom didn't like the idea.

"Hi Tom."

Tom looked up to see Leo getting into his seat in front of him.

"Hi Leo."

"Tom, did your dad ask if you want to play football last night?"

"Yeah, I said no. Why?"

"My dad asked me too. He said that you were probably going to be playing now, so I should switch out of baseball so we can play together."

"Well, I'm not playing football."

"Yeah, I didn't believe my dad. He thinks baseball is boring."

"Not as boring as reading is."

Leo screwed up his face.

"I like reading."

Before Tom could reply, they heard the excitement from some of the girls that could only mean that Paxton had shown up. Turning to look, they saw Paxton sitting on one of the girls' desks as he & a small group of them gossiped about… something. When the teacher walked in, Paxton headed for his seat next to Tom.

"Hi guys."

"Hi Pax." Tom & Leo said in unison. While Leo faced forward to avoid getting in trouble, Tom leaned over to Paxton.

"Hey Pax, did your dad ask you if you wanted to play football last night?"

"No, he was too busy trying to explain to me that there's an important difference between dolls & action figures."

"There is a difference Pax."

"No Leo, there isn't, not really."

"That's enough chattering at the back!"

They all focused on the class as the teacher started going on about something that happened a hundred years ago. The three boys sat together in the corner as they had since kindergarten when they had been grouped together & became best friends because they were always the only boys in their class.

February 8th, 1980

Presidential Debate in Iowa

The republican primaries were turning into a circus. People from Alaska to Florida, from Maine to California & even the Apollo

28 crew on the Moon had just watched or listened to a stage full of men quietly debating turn into a borderline grudge match. While the first Canadian on the Moon made a comment about how at least in Canada, elections don't drag on forever & remain somewhat civil, the moderator moved on.

"Alright, some passionate arguments concerning women in the military. Gentlemen, I appreciate that this issue is important & has many of you impassioned, but please try to remain civil."

He readjusted his tie & took a breath before continuing.

"What is your opinion not only on women in the workplace, but in being completely independent & fully supporting themselves?"

Before he could even choose the first person to answer the question, three of the republican candidates were interrupting each other to get their view on the matter out. One candidate tried to reason that times have changed & that the new reality meant that most women would have to support themselves entirely. Another proclaimed that decency needed to be restored & that aside from being schoolteachers, waitresses or librarians, women shouldn't be working at all, they should be taking care of their husband's home. While the first man tried to point out that that wasn't going to be a viable strategy for much longer, another candidate was blaming democrats for not finding a cure despite the ample time & resources that they had at their disposal.

With every question that was asked, the results seemed to be the same. Some candidates demanded a return to tradition while others begrudgingly admitted that the democrat's failure meant that things were going to have to change.

When asked about allowing women to marry each other, hardliners responded by proclaiming that it was a sin while others tried to argue that it shouldn't be allowed because marriage was about having children & two women couldn't do that. When asked about allowing polygamy or the idea of men being allowed to cheat for reproductive purposes, the rage was palpable. They made it very clear that they had no intention of changing the foundation of marriage or the nuclear family because it would be inconvenient for some.

Some candidates, in an attempt to draw attention away from themselves, tried to point out that under the democrats, NASA would be spending billions of dollars just on the Apollo program, or that a lot of investment seemed to be heading to Iran & foreign countries instead of being spent here at home.

However, the issues always returned to the topic of the XX generation. The simple fact that this was the last federal election that this generation of ninety percent women wouldn't be voting in at all had a lot of people on edge. People on both sides of the political isle were giving up on the idea that everything would be able to carry on as normal & predictions of the election in nine months were all over the map.

Some people were claiming that the democrats would win enough support that they'd be able to rewrite the constitution if they wanted to. Other were predicting that the failure of the commission would lead to the republicans taking over. Some were predicting record high turnout while others predicted record low turnout as people abandoned hope. The future was impossible to predict & as candidates like Reagan, Bush, Dole & others argued in circles, more than one person in the audience considered not voting at all this year.

March 18th, 1980
Oval Office

Soviets return to the Moon! That was the headline in every major newspaper in the country. President Carter walked into the Oval Office & sat down on one of the two couches opposite the administrator of NASA & his campaign advisor & the secretary of defense.

"So, David, where did they land in the end?"

David Gomez, the administrator of NASA sat forward a bit.

"Posidonius crater sir. It's to the Northeast of the sea of serenity where Apollo 17 landed back in seventy-two."

"Is it any different from the one they launched a few years back?"

"The LK-1, not as far as we can see sir. They probably just spent the last three years working out the bugs & kinks. Other than that, it's most likely the same as before, two cosmonauts crammed into a space barely big enough for one."

"Is there anything special about this crater?"

"Posidonius, not as far as we know. Aside from being fifty-nine miles across & filled with ancient lava flows, as far as we know, there's nothing interesting. They most likely chose it because it's massive & relatively easy terrain."

"Makes sense. First launch in three years, you want it to go off without a hitch, you pick an easy spot to land."

"Exactly sir."

Taking a moment to consider this information, Carter turned to his Secretary of Defense.

"Harold, is there any indication that this lander is more than just a quick exploration mission?"

Harold Brown readjusted his glasses for a second.

"No sir. While our intelligence on the Soviet's space program is limited, there's no indication that the mission is carrying weapons or base building capabilities. Like the first Apollo missions, it's just a scientific sortie. A mission of exploration & being able to brag that they're at least as great as we are."

"I don't suppose that we have any idea of future Soviet missions?"

"It's hard to be sure sir, but based on what intel we've managed to acquire, we think that they might be able to send another mission sometime next year. It'll probably be the same design as this mission. Then after that, we think that they may be working on new designs."

"Probably trying to give their cosmonauts some elbow room."

The others all looked at David Gomez.

"The ah, the LK lander is uhm, it's very tight. Basically, a broom closet with the brooms."

"I see."

President Carter contemplated this new information for a long minute as he weighed what he could do with it.

"David, a few years ago, I directed NASA to start drawing up plans for a Moon base, have we made any progress on that?"

"Some progress has been made. Once we get the Saturn VI going, it should take twelve launches a year to sustain a continuous two-person crew on the Moon, or eighteen launches a year to sustain a continuous three-person crew. Estimates on the cost are about four billion dollars a year for a two-person crew or six billion dollars a year for a three-person crew."

"That would be about one percent of the entire budget."

"Unfortunately, we've yet to find the kind of resources that we need to sustain a crew, like water or oxygen. We're working on some ideas for oxygen extraction, but it's going to take some time. As for water, so far, the Moon appears to be bone dry I'm afraid."

"So, we have to take everything there. We can't save on costs with local resources."

"Not yet sir."

"Hmm. Harold, how sure are we that the Soviets are planning more trips to the Moon?"

"It's a very high probability. They can't afford to be embarrassed by us, especially with the birth ratio riots. They've calmed down a bit in the last few months. But with the economic troubles that the Soviets are starting to deal with, mostly from people having so many children, it's getting harder & harder for them to keep the people in line. They need big wins & they need to at least create an illusion that they can still go as far as we can."

"I see. Larry."

Larry Kraft, the President's campaign manager snapped up.

"Yes Jimmy?"

"How well do you think a massive expansion of the Apollo program would fly with the American people?"

"If you had asked me a few days ago, I'd say that it would be an expensive albatross around your neck. But with how well the economy has been doing the last few years & the Soviets on the Moon again... I think that we could sell it to them. It would definitely help that this would be a permanent presence instead of a few days a few times a year."

"Even with a clear majority in congress, getting it through will be a challenge."

"Not if the people are thrilled about it in an election year."

"True."

The President thought on it for a moment.

"David, do we have the technical ability to actually do this?"

"Yes. It'll be easier & more cost effective once the Saturn VI is up & going, but we can do this."

"Good. Harold, what do you think the Soviet response will be if we announce a proper Moon base by the end of the decade?"

"They won't be happy, that's for sure. They'll probably need to increase their manned lunar space program, which is very expensive to them & which they're already struggling with. If we have a permanent base before they do, it could lead to escalation in our defensive postures if they think that we're putting IPBMs on the base."

"IPBMs?"

"Inter-planetary ballistic missiles. Like ICBMs but fired from one planet or moon to another."

"I see. Do we have any IPBMs?"

"Not yet sir & God willing, nobody ever will."

President Carter sat there in deep thought weighing everything that the three men had just told him about the situation.

"Alright. Tomorrow, I'm going to announce that I'm continuing Apollo up through Apollo thirty-nine & that one of the main goals of our efforts will be to find an ideal location for a permanent base."

With that, the meeting was over. David Gomez left with news for NASA that they were to draw up plans for nine new Apollo missions & that the top-secret plan for the Artemis program of building a base on the Moon was about to go public. Timothy Kraft left the meeting considering the implications for Carter's reelection & what fires he would have to try to smother before they ignited. Harold Brown left the meeting contemplating all of the possible ways that this could even hypothetically lead to World War three.

May 8th, 1980
National Institute of Health, Bethesda, Maryland

Doctor Edward Swanson cursed. This wasn't the small, quiet curse he let out whenever he stubbed his toe or had to talk to the media. This was a wall shaking, echoing, profanity. People halfway across the floor heard it. With most of the younger researchers a bit nervous about seeing what was wrong with the old man, they let Doctor Fekete find out what was going on.

"Ed? Is it safe to come in?"

"What, oh, Todor, yeah, come in."

"You have a lot of folks out there nervous, spitting fire like that."

"Sorry about that."

"No need to apologize. I am curious about what has you so upset?"

"Smallpox was eradicated."

"This is a bad thing?"

Edward though for a moment about how to explain it to his Hungarian friend.

"It's not that it's a bad thing, it's just the timing of the announcement."

"The timing? Oh."

"Yeah. I just filed the fifteen-year report on our efforts & next week, I have to stand in front of a senate committee hearing to explain why we still haven't even figured out what's causing the birth ratios & now, they're going to know about the success of a handful of NPOs at eradicating a disease like smallpox from the Earth. Meanwhile, we've made zero progress in even identifying a cause."

"That's not true, we eliminated thousands of possibilities."

"That's not going to help. They think they've asked us what's four plus four, & fifteen years later, we come back & say it's probably less than seven hundred. Also, it feels like we've had this conversation before."

"We probably have, more than once. You get like this every few years when major reports are sent in."

"I suppose I do. I don't suppose that the genetics department has developed anything that could impress senators?"

"Not yet I'm afraid, but we're getting closer to being able to map out the entire Y chromosome. Another year or two & we should be able to do it."

"Y chromosome, that's the male chromosome, right?"

"Yes, it's also the smallest in the body, only about a hundred & fifty genes. Still, once we can map it, we can compare the Y chromosomes of men born recently to those who are later in life to see if there's been some sort of a change that is causing the birth ratios."

"That would be great."

"Yes, it would. Also, we're going to need some more computer power to process & compare those Y chromosomes."

"What about the Cray? We've only had it for about five years, last I checked, it was still one of the best super computers in the world."

"It's fantastic, but each Y chromosome has somewhere around sixty million base pair combinations. The cray only has enough memory to hold four, maybe five Y chromosomes. We don't need it just yet, but if we're going to be comparing entire chromosomes, we'll need more computer memory at least."

"I see. Thank you for giving me some advanced notice on this. You would think that an eight-million-dollar computer would still be useful after what, five or seven years?"

"I would think that, & for most things, it is still very good. It just won't be for this specific task."

"Well, that's good to know. Now I don't suppose that you know how to keep a bunch of senators happy with the idea of funding a program that after fifteen years, has achieved next to nothing, & wants a bigger a supercomputer?"

"If I figure something out, I'll tell you."

July 16th, 1980
Detroit, Michigan

"My fellow citizens of this great nation..."
Everyone outside of the convention was stunned. Even a few people inside the convention were stunned. The fact was that six months ago, nobody could have suspected that the former one term governor from California who had returned to acting for the last decade would be able to win the republican nomination for President. Yet with twenty-eight state contests won & just over half the popular vote from registered republicans, He now stood before the republican national convention, having received just over half of the delegates votes & was now the nominee.

With such a narrow win, everyone watched & listened to his acceptance speech in the hopes that he wouldn't alienate any voters since with such little support, they would have to carefully woo the independents to their cause.

"… our problems, are both acute & chronic, but all we hear from those in positions of leadership are the same tired proposals for more government tinkering, more meddling & more control, all of which led us to this sorry state in the first place. Can anyone look at the record of this administration & say well done?"

The crowd shouted out a resounding No.

"Can anyone say that they are happy with the state of the economy?"

Again, the crowd shouted no.

"Can anyone say that they are happy with the democrat's response to the birth crisis?"

Another resounding No echoed throughout the convention.

"I believe that come the first week of November, the majority of Americans will answer these questions the way that you have. That they will tell Carter & the democrats that we've had enough!"

The crowd cheered & roared.

"Come November, we will tell them that while we need to safeguard our environment, that we need to remember that a well-functioning economy is part of our environment!"

Businessmen & industrialists all over the country smiled.

"We need to tell them that we won the space race eleven years ago & that we don't need to order another ten Moon missions & lunar base every time that the Soviets barely manage to get there without crashing!"

Those few people that saw no value in reaching the Moon cheered.

"We need to tell the democrats that left wing social policies of letting women into the army, & new forms of marriage are not the way!"

A few people in the convention stopped clapping as they registered what he said.

"Under proper republican leadership, we will strengthen our economy, we will rebuild our failing military & we will renew the traditional values of this great nation!"

In the convention & all over the country, conservatives suddenly started getting nervous. As much as people were upset about the lack of solutions or cures from the democrats, & as much as they hated the idea that something like polygamy or lesbian marriage might be legalized, they knew that simply saying we're going to go back to how we used to do things wasn't going to work. Just because Americans didn't like the changes that were coming didn't mean that they believed they could just go back to the old ways of doing things.

While evangelicals & far right voters cheered, a lot of moderate republicans & independents started questioning their allegiance.

"Over the last two decades, the democrats have used these unprecedented events in history, from the Moon landing to the birth crisis to advances in technology, to push through radical left policies & legislation. As a result of this, we now have battalions of women standing guard against the communists. We have the ERA, which will be used to expand Roe v. Wade, to draft more women into the armed forces, & to open the door for lesbianism amongst our children. We cannot have four more years of this!"

As most of the crowd cheered, several campaign aides started panicking as Reagan attacked a number of very popular pieces of legislation & policy in his drive to renew American traditions in defiance of the new reality that most of America was bracing for. Eight years ago, or even four years ago, this might have worked, but now, everyone can see that the traditional ways weren't going to work for much longer, no matter how much some wished they would.

As his campaign manager worried that he was committing political suicide, over four hundred miles away, Carter's campaign manager worried that all signs were pointing to low turnout for the democrats as after fifteen years, the people were starting to lose faith that they would be able to fix the population crisis.

August 14, 1980
Mare Fecundities

Jerri Cobb looked out over the surface of the Moon once again. Unlike the brighter highland areas, the region that she was now in was several shades darker since the regolith here was basaltic & potentially full of minerals. As she & her partner collected samples from far & wide across the vast lunar mare, Cobb looked up to the Earth & took a moment to appreciate her unique situation.

Twenty years ago, she had been part of a program to see if women could go to space. When that was cancelled, she believed that her chances of getting to the Moon were completely lost. Then in seventy-one, a new chance to reach the Moon presented itself & now she was standing on the Moon for a fourth time.

"I don't think that this could ever get old."

Cobb smiled & turned around to see her partner on this mission leaping over to her in slow motion.

"It sure doesn't kid. Every time I leave, it feels like my time here was so short & I start counting the days until I can come back."

"I believe it."

"What do you think, is there anything here that looks more interesting than over there?"

Veora West landed next to Cobb & after taking a second to steady herself, she looked around the dusty plain.

"Nothing at first glance, but if we're just going to do first glances, they could have sent a rover. Let's get looking."

Cobb smiled. She had been surprised when NASA had paired her up with a black woman. It had only really been in the last few years that NASA had been willing to admit they even employed black women. She hadn't expected to live long enough to see a black astronaut, let alone a black woman astronaut. Judging by the reaction from Americans when Veora was announced to be the first black woman in space & on the Moon, the rest of America was taken by storm as well. Yet here Veora was, geologist extraordinaire, looking for anything that could be useful or valuable to them.

Republicans had instantly started accusing the Carter administration of pulling this stunt in order to pander to black voters. Veora had admitted to Cobb & Sandra Cohen who was flying the command module in lunar orbit that she had been stunned when the mission planner had come out swinging in her defense. Everyone at NASA had been impressed to see it, that old southern boy going to bat & setting the media straight about how Veora had been chosen because she was one of the best damn geologists that NASA, nay, that America had.

Once they were done claiming that Veora was a giveaway to black voters, several republican candidates started claiming that the whole mission was a giveaway to feminists & that that was the only reason to run the risk of having an all-woman team. That was when John Young, the Chief of the astronaut office & former Apollo astronaut himself faced them to remind them that there was no risk as Cobb & Cohen were two of the most experienced astronauts in all of NASA & that Cobb alone was a three-time lunar veteran before Apollo thirty even launched.

All that drama & politics so that the two of them could be up here, sifting through dusty regolith looking for anything that might be useful to them.

"Find anything over there Cobb?"

"Nope, just dirt. You?"

"Same. Got a sample of it, but I don't know why I bother, I could just give the boys in the lab this suit. I know you said that this dust clings, but this is ridiculous."

"Yes, it is, but think of how happy the lab boys will be when you walk in, covered in their samples & strip it off for them."

Veora started laughing hysterically as she pictured herself in full pressure suit gear trying to do a striptease for the lab & most of them being more interested in the dust than in her.

"They'd probably be upset… they'd probably be upset that the dust… wasn't in a sealed sample bag. Give me a second Cobb, I teared up a bit here."

Unable to wipe the tears away, Veora had to stand there for a minute for her vision to clear. As she did that, Cobb grinned & drove her rock hammer into the dust soil where it hit something hard. Tapping whatever she had just hit, she scooped some of the regolith away & dug out a small rock about the size of her fist.

"Hey, West, I think that I found something here."

"Veora, her vision cleared up, made her way over."

"What have you got?"

Cobb pointed to the hard, shiny black rock that almost looked like a lump of rough & chipped black steel. Bending down, Veora was grateful that the newer space suits were more flexible in the knees.

"That's interesting alright. Solid black, almost looks metallic, no discernable sign of cleavage."

"Not everyone shows cleavage on a first date."

Veora chuckled.

"You know, there aren't too many kinds of rocks that look like this. We should definitely bag it."

"Just the one, or should we take a few of them?"

Veora looked at where Cobb was pointing & saw that there were a bunch of these rocks sticking out of the regolith where Cobb had dug. Looking at a few of them, Veora could almost feel her heart race. Looking at the faint brownish tints being reflected by their lights; she recalled the course she had taken in university in identifying mineral ores for this mission & put one of the small rocks next to the joint in her glove. She could feel an ever so slight magnetic pull between the rock & her suit, which she also confirmed by the way that the dust was sticking to the rock.

"Jerri, plant a flag here, make sure we have an exact location, we're bagging a bunch of these."

"What did we find?"

"I can't be certain until we get these back to the lab, but I think this could be Ilmenite."

"Yeah, my geology crash course was a bit more limited than your years of training."

"Ilmenite is a mineral of Titanium, iron & Oxygen. On Earth, it's one of the most valuable sources of Titanium on the planet."

"Are you saying that we just found Titanium & Iron ore?"

"Yes. If I'm right, that's exactly what we found & we might be able to get oxygen from it as well."

The two of them quickly got out a bunch of their sample bags & very carefully filled them with the metallic looking black rocks. They planted a small flag & even called up Sandra Cohen on the command module to confirm their coordinates as accurately as possible. Then they called NASA with the news.

As soon as the news reached NASA that they may have found a very valuable mineral ore, the mission planners went crazy. Sure, if they ever wanted to get project Artemis off the ground & build a base, they would need a water source. Still, they would also need to find mineral deposits & they may have just stumbled on one. If they could find water nearby…

By the time that Cobb & West got back to the lunar module, plans for the next few missions were already being redrawn.

September 2nd, 1980
New York City

Sarah finished reading the article. With the air conditioner failing to condition the air, the article felt particularly impactful. Still, she had her concerns.

"I don't know Lena. I mean, sure, it's relevant to the world right now, but the Lavender Press has never really talked about the environment."

Lena stood by the open window, barely getting any relief from the air outside as it was only a degree cooler.

"I Know Sarah, we focus on feminist, women's & queer issues, but we sometimes do stories about big things that affect everyone. Elections, wars, big stories. This is going to affect everyone."

"Yeah, I get that climate change is going to be a big deal, eventually, but we've got more pressing issues that we can fill our columns with. Reagan is talking about repealing the ERA, Iceland just elected the first female President in the world, an all-female team of astronauts just found titanium ore on the Moon. I don't think that it's going to be good for us to devote so much space in our paper to a topic that half the country doesn't believe in."

"Isn't getting people to understand & accept the truth what newspapers are for?"

"True... But we don't really do these science type stories. This is a whole human race problem, not something that's limited to women or lesbians."

"I disagree. The scientists are saying that we'll really start feeling the effects of this in thirty or forty years, by that point, women will be three-quarters of the population of the world. That means that this will be a massive mess, created by male dominated governments & industry, that a woman led world will have to contend with."

Sarah thought about it for a moment.

"Sort of like... mankind is going out & leaving us one last massive mess to clean up."

"Sort of, yeah."

"It's interesting, I'm just worried that we're going to alienate a large chunk of our readership. I mean, we've only just started expanding into new territories. You just got your foot in the door with that one distributor in Connecticut, they're not exactly going to like that one of the large stories in one of the first issues we give them is us declaring ourselves as environmentalists."

Lena thought about that one. Ever since her story had been picked up by ABC, she had found new doors opening up for her in Pennsylvania, Massachusetts & Connecticut. It was starting to look like she was going to have to expand, move to a bigger space & get more presses to meet the demand. This could very well be the first massive step towards going national. She thought about it carefully.

"My mind's made-up Sarah. We're running the article."

"Alright."

Sarah turned to start looking into which stories would be ready for Sunday when she thought of something.

"Lena, how in the Hell are you going to get all the copies printed for tomorrow morning? We have to start sending them out in eighteen hours."

"The issues that are going out of state show up in stands on Mondays & Thursdays. A day later than in New York."

"So you'll be running the presses for almost two days twice a week? How are you supposed to keep that up & report stories?"

"Well, for the next few weeks, I plan on giving up sleep. Once we start making money from our new distributors, I intend to expand. Hire a woman who knows how to work the presses, maybe buy the office next door & tear down the walls."

"I suppose that makes sense. If we're expanding readership by leaps & bounds, we should expand production."

"Exactly. This might just be the beginning of us becoming one of the big names in the newspaper game."

"Here's hoping."

October 20th, 1980
Niavaran Palace, Iran

Shah Reza Pahlavi II looked over the police reports. Over the last few months, matchmaking services all over Iran had shut down as protests & furious customers grew in number & intensity. This latest demonstration had seen just over a thousand men & women outside a rather expensive & successful matchmaker demanding men for their daughters to marry.

"Are we seriously running out of unmarried men?"

In the ornately decorated office, the Shah looked across his desk to one of his advisors, a man tasked with keeping an eye on issues of marriage & marriage law in Iran as the second white revolution progressed.

"Not yet, however the preferable matches seem to be lacking."

"Amin, how is this happening?"

The older man sipped his tea.

"It's to do with the birth ratios sir."

"This is because the new people now old enough to marry are mostly girls."

"Precisely sir. Starting in March, the number of men available to marry dropped off rather sharply as the few men in this new generation are being quickly married off with parental consent to women with wealthy families, leaving only older & less desirable matches for young women."

"So, it's not that we're running out of men, it's that we're running out of fifteen-year-old men."

Amin took a deep breath before continuing with the bad news.

"Actually sir, we're running out of young men aged fifteen to twenty-five."

"Twenty-five? How?"

"Well sir, once these mostly female children turned thirteen, their parents started marrying them off while men were still available, depleting the supply of young men. Now that these people are fifteen, the girls are old enough to marry without parental consent. Since there's twice as many of them as there normally would be, many are working to marry men as old as twenty-five so that they don't end up with an old man or an undesirable."

Reza looked over the police reports once more & paid attention to the description of the damage & chaos.

"So, boys are being married off by their parents as soon as they are fifteen & the girls that are fifteen, that weren't married off at thirteen, are doing everything that they can to get a husband that isn't too much older than they are."

"That is the basic situation sir. It also seems that many parents have been using the courts to circumvent age restrictions. Since children can be married off at any age with permission from the court, there's apparently been a growing number of parents over the last few years that have been marrying their young sons to the young daughters of family friends. This is further depleting the availability of young men now that the new generation of boys is old enough to marry with parental consent."

Reza sat back in his chair. His second white revolution to help empower women in the workplace had done a lot to fend off the ambitions of conservative extremists that wanted to overthrow him & have a return to a strict authoritarian theocracy. But parents still wanted husbands for their daughters.

"Amin, do you have any recommendations for how to deal with these issues?"

"I do, but some might see them as... extreme."

"These are extreme situations Amin. We need to act if we're to protect our country & our institutions."

Amin noticeably gulped. He took a deep breath before he proceeded to calm his nerves.

"Very well, the first suggestion is stripping the courts of the ability to grant marriages at any age. They should be bound by the same minimum age laws as everyone else."

"The judges won't like that."

"No sir, they won't. The second suggestion is that we should increase the minimum age of marriage for both men & women to eighteen."

"Are you mad? I'm trying to prevent a mass revolt from happening, not cause one!"

"Sir, the growing problem is that the handful of boys available to be married are being married off so quickly that there are none left by the time that women are old enough to marry. Raising the minimum age of marriage in all circumstances would alleviate that issue & buy us another three years to prepare for when these children are old enough to marry again."

"This will not go over well with the people. Any other ideas, something that won't have me leading this country in exile?"

"There is one sir. Harems."

"Harems?"

"Yes sir. As it stands, a man can take four permanent wives as long as all previous wives consent. What if we were to increase this value for men born starting in 1965? Larger harems would allow for more of the women to find husbands & allow these younger men to wait a few years before taking a second or third wife."

"Larger harems. That's..."

"An idea that might work."

"Are there any other options?"

"The only other options are things so radical that you would have to announce them & then immediately flee the country to live in exile."

"I see."

Amin took another deep breath.

"Sir, if I may offer my advice."

"You are my advisor, so I hope that you can."

"Right. Whatever options you choose, I recommend that you choose quickly. Even if every man in the country gets to take four wives, that will still eventually leave more than half of the women in this country without a husband & that is not a situation that any administration can survive."

"I understand."

"Also, you may want to consult with the minister of defense. There are a number of revolutionary forces that are using this to spread propaganda."

"Understood."

Amin then took his leave as Reza went over his options. After about an hour, he called for his minister of defense who arrived promptly.

"Sir! You called for me."

"Yes, Ehsan, please have a seat."

Ehsan Hajar, without relaxing, took a seat opposite the Shah, placing his briefcase on the floor next to him.

"How can I help you sir?"

"Obviously, you know about the matchmaker riots."

"Yes sir."

"Well, Amin has proposed some solutions to me to consider to help mitigate the long-term situation. I believe that you're aware of these proposals."

"I am sir."

"Excellent. I was wondering your opinion about how certain elements of our country will react if I implement some of these proposals."

"The conservative extremists. Yes, they could pose problems sir."

"Yes, so please, tell me what you think of these solutions."

"Very well sir. Obviously, the best solution would be to increase the maximum size of harems. Neither liberals, nor conservatives will be happy about it, but a simple expansion of an old tradition shouldn't do too much to anger the conservatives, & as long as you maintain the requirement for consent from previous wives, liberals should be willing to go along with it."

"That's good to hear. Would your office be able to provide me with a report on how high I should increase the maximum number of wives a man can have?"

"I'll have it for you by the end of the week sir."

"Excellent."

"As for the other proposals sir, taking away the court's ability to grant marriages despite age restrictions is dangerous. There are a number of conservative friendly judges that will not look too kindly on this. However, if you make it so that the judicial system can grant marriages at the same ages that parents can, that will go a long way to soften the blow."

"What about the proposal to raise the minimum age of marriage for everyone to eighteen?"

"That would be a mistake sir."

"Should we at least consider it?"

"No. As it is, there are many parents of teenage children that are eager to marry off their children. If we tell them that they have to wait another two or three or five years, they will not take kindly to it, especially the parents of children that are near the minimum age."

"According to Amin, it would go a long way to solving the issue & postponing the problem."

"It would, I agree. But there would be a revolt if you tried. As it is, there are still many that think the minimum age of marriage should be lowered, not raised. Through the second white revolution, we've only just begun spreading the idea that it's safe to wait until women are a bit older to marry, but progress has been slow & will continue to be slow for some time."

"I see."

"Sir, I understand that we need to implement drastic solutions, but we need to balance these needs with the stability of the country. We have a large conservative movement that is already working to undermine us by telling people that we are moving too far too quickly, & that we need to put Allah back in the daily lives of the Iranian people. We can't risk giving them much more to work with. Perhaps in the future, we'll be able to implement these changes, after the second white revolution has had more time to prepare our society."

The Shah considered these words.

"The future. First, we have to get there. If we do too little, the people revolt. If we do too much, they revolt. It seems that we reach too far before we can overcome not doing enough."

"It won't be easy sir, but something must be done soon."

"The question is what?"

November 16th, 1980
Republican National Committee

Spencer King was still in a state of total shock. As chairman of the Republican National Committee & with his last name, everyone had been calling him the kingmaker since he won the vote to become chairman in seventy-seven. Under his leadership, conservative organizations had spent the last three & a half years laying the groundwork to push America to the right. Carter's landslide win in seventy-six had been a wakeup call for the GOP. They needed a new playbook in a world that had new concerns.

They had silenced a number of conservative activists, people like Anita Bryant who were loudly beating the drums against homosexuality & women in the workplace & women in the military. Under his leadership, they had also doubled down on spreading fears of encroaching socialism & talking endlessly about the billions being wasted on the Moon when the Soviets could barely even get there. One of their favorite arguments had been that there was no need for a Moon base when the Soviets could barely reach the Moon at all. It had all been working.

Poll after poll had shown that the country was pulling to the right. Through their tireless work, America was getting tired of Carter pushing radical liberal amendments like the ERA, & new policies like putting battalions of women on the front lines against the red menace. Seeing that this was their last chance to get a strong conservative into the white house before the XX generation started voting, the kingmaker had led his troops through a valiant effort that every poll & survey said would have Carter dethroned. Spencer, like many in America, wished that he had paid attention to the margins of error in those polls.

The first indication of a minor problem came when three of Maine's split electoral votes went to Carter instead of two along with Vermont & Delaware. Spencer wasn't worried about it at the time. They were leading thirty-seven to eighteen, but still, Vermont & Delaware had been polling in their favor for months.

The first indication of a major problem came when Louisiana was called for Carter, sending carter into a seven-point lead over Reagan. Looking at the map on their wall, he was stunned to see that every state called in the bible belt had gone to Carter. This had left him dumbfounded. Reagan had the backing of the evangelical church; how could he be losing the bible belt. The margins were narrow, but he was losing them.

Spencer flashed back to a rally in Alabama back in August. Reagan had promised the crowd that he would reign in NASA & several of the campaign workers had noted that a lot of the cheers from the crowd seemed to die down. Could it be that NASA was employing more people in the bible belt then he had realized & promising to cut NASA funding was an attack on jobs is the Southern states? A Moon base would mean a lot of jobs created by NASA.

He calmed himself down as best as he could. With over three hundred electoral votes to count & tally, a seven-point lead was meaningless.

By the time Massachusetts was called for Carter, Spencer was freaking out. Virginia was so far the only Southern state that had voted for Reagan. The entire Southeast of the country, except Florida, which was still counting, had turned blue. Even with the Western half of the country voting for Reagan, he was still behind by forty-four points & Spencer wasn't sure which way Texas was going to vote anymore. Sure, California would vote for their homegrown celebrity candidate, but based off of their polls from yesterday, they should already have secured a victory.

Spencer flashed back to all of the times that Reagan had proclaimed that he would bar new women from joining the army & that he would work to put women back into the comfort of the home. Embracing the traditional ways of America had seemed like a good way to bring people home to the right, but what if he had been wrong? Were voters ready to give up on women's roles in the house? Was the promise of the traditional housewife an albatross around Reagan's neck?

Spencer started to calm down when he saw that New Jersey & Florida both voted for Reagan, closing Carter's lead down to ten points. He breathed deeply & calmed himself. The bible belt was a fluke. A large fluke, the bible belt was just beholden to NASA, which explained that. Reagan would get New York & California & Texas & Pennsylvania & Ohio & Michigan & everything would work out fine.

Ohio voted for Reagan. Michigan didn't, & Spencer was freaking out. He practically had to bite his tongue to sound calm on the phone when George Bush called him to talk about Michigan. He had done a lot of campaigning there with Reagan & according to the polls, Michigan should have been in their hands with a ten-point lead, but it had completely flipped on that & gone to Carter.

Calming several people by reminding them that a six-point lead with a hundred & sixty-eight electoral votes still to be called was nothing, Spencer walked into his office & screamed in his closed office as most of everything East of the Mississippi river had gone to Carter so far.

When Texas chose Reagan as their next President, Spencer calmed down as Reagan momentarily took the lead. Then Illinois & Philadelphia chose Carter & he damn near had a coronary. Everyone was freaking out as all that was left was California & New York. The biggest states with over forty electoral votes each. At only twenty-nine votes short of a majority, Carter only needed one of them to go his way to win.

When California was called for Reagan, he breathed deep & calm. Everyone went into celebrations. California was locked down for their homegrown candidate & New York was a sure thing. A sure thing that was taking a while to be called.

By the time that the sun rose, New York still hadn't been called. Sure, it was a massive state, but when noon rolled around with no result, calls were made by both parties. It seemed that a number of official counters who were new to the job had made a number of mistakes in favor of both parties, mixing up several counts & forcing half the state to need a recount. Hours passed as counts were verified & reassigned to the correct parties. Both parties saw vote totals go up & down as corrections were made. Finally, almost a full day after the polls had closed, the result came in. New York had voted for Carter.

Carter had won a second term by twelve points. Over the next few days, quiet audits & recounts mandated by narrow victories confirmed the results.

Now, just over a week later, Spencer was sitting in a top-level meeting with GOP leadership. They had lost the Presidency again & while they had made gains in the senate & congress, they hadn't managed to flip either. So, they now gathered to do an autopsy of the election they had just lost to look at what they obviously needed to change before the eighty-two midterms & eighty-four.

The first agreement, which was universal, was that Reagan was not going to be the candidate in eighty-four. If he was crazy enough to run again, they would use all of their resources to make sure that he didn't win a single primary. Secretly, they had all been concerned when Reagan came out against women's rights & involvement in the workforce. That had not been a smart move.

As the meeting progressed, they kept talking about new ideas, new positions, new strategies, all of which would have sounded like a call for new leadership if Spencer had been paying attention to any of it. Instead, he was thinking about how every subsequent election from here on out would be harder for conservatives & traditionalists to win. Maybe they could make some ground in eighty-two, but after that, an ever-growing percentage of the electorate would be mostly women who saw little to no prospects for a conventional life in their future.

1981

January 20th, 1981
New York City

There was a loud thud, followed by the sound of a wall breaking. Lena watched with some interest as the contractor swung her sledgehammer, & began knocking out the wall between Lavender Press, & the office next door that was now also Lavender Press. As Lena watched the young woman that Cassie had recommended, she saw more than just a tight ass on a strong woman. She saw the results of the last three months of her work coming together.

Sleepless nights spent writing up stories about everything happening in the world. A story about Carter winning reelection despite the odds. A story about how somebody tried to assassinate John Lennon & almost succeeded, leading to the Beatles coming back together & talking about a reunion tour. A story about NASA choosing the Apollo thirty landing site to start building a base after Apollo thirty-one confirmed some findings.

At a time when she was playing journalist, press operator, negotiator, business owner & expanding titan of industry, 1981 was shaping up to be a busy year.

The reason that she wasn't dead from exhaustion or caffeine overdose was because just after the new year, she had hired someone to operate the presses for her. A young woman named Mila Merkel that had immigrated from West Germany. She had learned from her grandfather & with things getting a little tense between the Germanies, she decided that it was best to put a continent & an ocean between her & the issues. With riots in East Germany as people realize that the USSR's claims about reducing the birth ratios was a lie & rises in far-right activity in West Germany capitalizing on the ongoing gender imbalance to promote the policies of Germany before the end of World War 2, it was getting rough.

With Mila handling the presses like an old pro, Lena was free to focus on the stories in her paper & expanding her office. The landlord hadn't been happy about the idea of tearing down the walls between two of his offices, but in the end, he saw the wisdom in having a thriving newspaper remain in his building, even if it meant more lesbians coming & going, which after over a decade, was no longer much of an issue for him. It helped that Lena was the only tenant that was never late on rent.

With the vacant office secured, she then had to find somebody to do the work. It had been just a few days ago, after she had been wrapped up in Cassie's embrace, legs a tangled mess as they brought each other to a much-needed release, that she started talking to her lover about the expansion.

With Cassie's pale arms wrapped around her as she played the little spoon, she had been going on & on about trying to find a quality contractor that wasn't going to treat her like an idiot or a mark just because she was a woman & wouldn't hate her because she ran a lesbian newspaper. That was when Cassie, with her firm breasts pressed against Lena's back, spoke the most unexpected words Lena hadn't been expecting to hear.

"I know a woman who can help you."

"You know a woman with a good contactor?"

"No, I know a woman who works as a contractor."

Lena turned around so that they were face to face.

"A woman contractor? There's such a thing?"

"Yeah, she's been doing it for a few years. I met her when the club I was working at back in May needed repairs. She's good, & hot in a pair of jeans with those tools in her hand. I don't remember her name, but I've got her card around here somewhere, I could dig it out for you before you leave."

Lena leaned forward & kissed Cassie deeply.

"That's the second time tonight that you've saved me."

"The second? When was the first time?"

"When you rocked my world with your goddess like body & these magic fingers of yours. I was about to go crazy before you fucked me senseless."

Cassie grinned.

"Well then get ready to be saved a third time, cause I'm going to kiss you until you quiver."

Cassie then climbed under the blankets to apply her lips & tongue to Lena who was soon grabbing the sheets with her fists.

Now Lena stood in her office. Someone else was running the presses for tomorrow's issue, the Beatles might be getting back together after almost losing one of their own, women were kicking ass on the Moon, a ridiculously beautiful woman was expanding her office & the anti-feminist Reagan was back home in California looking for work as an actor where he belonged.
Life was good.

February 14th, 1981
Queens, New York

Mary Robinson fussed over her daughter's hair. She was upset when Elizabeth cut her hair short on New Year's Day. It was all part of some new fashion where a bunch of the girls were cutting their hair short & dressing like boys. Mary didn't get it; she was just glad that Elizabeth didn't get her hair cut short again after that. She didn't like the idea of Elizabeth cutting her hair short so close to the first big dance that she wasn't just going to with friends.
"Your first dance with a sort of date & all that we have to work with is a bob cut. Why would you do this Elizabeth? Every other dance you ever went to, you had your hair nice & long. Now you're going with a bare neck."
"It'll be fine Mom, a lot of the girls in school have shortish hair."
"I don't see why you have to be one of them."
"Because I lost January's coin toss."
"You kids & your coin toss hair. At least you're wearing a dress."
"You like the dress, right Mom?"
"The dress is beautiful. I just wish that you had some longer hair to go with it. Okay, let's see."
Mary backed up & watched as her daughter stood up in front of her vanity. The strapless, plum colored dress hugged Elizabeth's torso, ruffling a bit around her chest. It flared out around her waist before draping down her legs. The dark color of the dress

contrasted against her pale skin, causing her bare shoulders & arms to stand out.

"How do I look?"

"You look like a beautiful young woman."

Mary tried to hold back the tears.

"Mom? Are you okay?"

"It seems like just yesterday that you were taking Sarah's hand & walking off to first grade together. Now my baby girl is almost all grown up & going to a dance on a date. Who told you that you were allowed to grow up so fast?"

Elizabeth laughed & hugged her mother.

"I'm not grown up yet Mom, we've still got some time."

The two of them hugged for a moment longer until David knocked on the door.

"Elizabeth, there's a young man waiting for you in the living room."

Mary broke the hug & looked confused for a moment.

"Thanks Dad, tell her I'll be out in a minute."

"Can do. Crazy kids."

Mary realized what David had meant. A lot of the girls that were dating or pretending to be dating each other were flipping a coin every month or so & the loser had to be the 'boy' in the relationship; cutting her hair, ditching her makeup & wearing boys' clothes. A lot of schools weren't happy about it, but it did hide the growing lesbianism amongst the young generation a bit, so most were willing to tolerate it, especially since most thought that it was just a temporary thing, like bell bottoms.

"If you had lost the last coin toss, you wouldn't be wearing a suit right now, would you?"

"I sure would. I'd also be picking up my date."

"Only thing between my daughter & wearing a suit to the winter formal was a coin toss. The things that you girls get away with sometimes. If I had ever come home at fifteen with hair like this or a rented tux, my mother would have had me in stitches."

"Guess I'm lucky that you're a better Mom then grandma was."

Mary smiled & almost teared up again.

"You have... no idea... no idea at all, how much that means to me Elizabeth. Thank you."

"I'm just being honest, you're a great Mom."

"Thank you, Elizabeth. Your curfew is still eleven."

"Just my luck having a great mother."

"Alright, let's not keep your 'man' waiting."

Elizabeth smiled & let her mother lead her out of the room so that she could get pictures of her daughter coming down the stairs. As she descended the steps, she saw Sarah standing there next to David. Her formally long brunette hair was cut down to a short fade haircut. Wearing next to no makeup & just a bit of lip balm, she stood there in light navy-blue dress pants, with a light navy-blue vest over a light blue shirt. The vest left enough open at her neck to reveal the black tie she was wearing. Mary was surprised that she actually looked kind of nice in the getup. Mostly she was just thankful that Elizabeth was wearing a dress. She couldn't imagine what Sarah's parents' reactions were.

"Well don't you look… handsome."

"Thanks Mrs. Robinson."

"Is everything going alright down here?"

"Everything is fine Mary; I'm just making sure this young buck here doesn't have any inappropriate intentions towards our daughter."

"He was just explaining that he has a shotgun if a wedding is needed."

David & Sarah both laughed as Mary shook her head & took their picture.

"Got the camera ready, Mom?"

Mary did an about face & started taking pictures as Elizabeth walked down the stairs, one hand lifting her dress & the other on the railing as she descended. Sarah stood there in stunned disbelief. David put his hand on her shoulder.

"Remember young man, shotgun at the ready if she comes back pregnant."

They all burst into laughter as Elizabeth neared the main floor. After a minute, they managed to regain their composure before Mary finished getting her pictures. After a few more minutes of reminding them to drive safe & to be home before eleven & to not get into any trouble & to be home before eleven & to not drink any alcohol & to be home by eleven, Sarah was able to escort her maybe date to her father's Toyota Starlet which she had been allowed to borrow for the night.

The ballroom was like something out of a fairytale. Balloons, streamers, an ice sculpture, a dance floor, waiters. This wasn't just a simple dance in a gymnasium, this was a proper function. As Sophomores, they were thrilled to be there as most of the students were juniors or seniors. Still, it was easy enough to find the other sophomores, they were a group of ten boys & about fifty girls, half of whom were in suits.

Soon enough, they were with their friends, laughing & talking about everything & nothing. Couples danced, groups of friends danced, & when the sophomore dance came on, the older grades watched in fascination as ten boys & fifty girls took to the floor & danced to Abba's dancing queen, a song that seemed particularly appropriate when they sang *see that girl*, or *anybody can be that guy.*

The older students, the teachers chaperoning the dance & the staff at the hall all watched as girls danced with girls, as girls danced with girls in suits & as one boy danced with two girls in matching dresses. Some of the people watching were amazed, some were stunned, some were upset & more than a few were jealous.

Eventually, a slow song that none of the students could name came on & Elizabeth & Sarah were slow dancing together. Up close & with their arms wrapped around each other, this was not a dance for friends. As the song played, Sarah was the one to ask the question that they had both been thinking about for weeks.

"So... is this a dance..., or a date?"

"I... I don't know, I thought this would be weird. Us slow dancing like this, you in your suit, that hand of yours getting a bit low."

"Sorry."

"Don't be sorry."

Elizabeth smiled as Sarah let her hand rest just a little lower than was safe for two friends at a dance together.

"This isn't a dance, is it Elizabeth?"

"Well, there is dancing, but no, I think this really is a date."

"So, you won't be upset if I kiss you at the end of the song?"

"Nope."

"Not even in front of all of these people, it could become a scene?"

"Then man up & make a scene."

They both laughed. It had been hilarious over the last few months listening to their friends telling each other to man up. The boys had certainly gotten a few kicks out of it, encouraging the girls dressing as guys to man up so that they wouldn't be as outnumbered.

The teachers & the administration & even the guidance counselor had tried to discourage this game saying that it wasn't right for girls to be telling each other to man up & that this game was inappropriate, which only made more of them participate. It had been something else when the younger cheerleaders for the football team had shown up with buzz cuts.

As much fun as these games had been, it wasn't as much fun as the two of them slow dancing together. Elizabeth found she didn't care whether Sarah was in a dress or a suit. She wanted her best friend to make a scene & take them to a new dynamic, a new level.

When the song reached its end, Elizabeth wasn't disappointed as a number of students around them gasped at the sight of their kiss. There was a second round of gasps when some of the students finally realized that the dude in the navy-blue suit wasn't a dude.

March 6th, 1981
CBS Newsroom

Walter Cronkite sat behind the CBS evening news desk for the last time as the anchor of the evening news. For the last nineteen years, he had been delivering the news to America & had slowly become known as the most trusted man in America. Now he was delivering his final broadcast as an anchorman & it seemed that he wouldn't be retiring from this post on a quiet news night.

"We now turn to two stories from NASA. The first it seems is that Mrytle Cagle, the first woman to set foot on the Moon, is retiring at the age of fifty-six from spaceflight. Having recently returned from the Apollo 31 mission in January where NASA returned to Mare Fecunditatis to confirm geological results from last year, Myrtle was originally scheduled to fly on one more mission, Apollo 35, early next year. Neither NASA nor Cagle are commenting on why her retirement from spaceflight has been pushed up. Both released statements earlier this year that while Mrs. Cagle is now grounded, she will continue to work with NASA as part of the astronaut training program & as a mission coordinator."

Taking a moment to shuffle the papers on his desk, he took a deep breath before beginning his final story of the evening & his career as an anchorman.

"In 1969, on the twentieth of July, I watched with the rest of the world as Neil Armstrong took those first steps onto the Moon, changing a world that was already being gripped by countless changes. I, like many people, imagined forward to a day when we would begin colonizing the Moon & truly reaching out into the universe. Over the years, there were times when it looked as if that dream was in peril as setbacks both in NASA & in the world threatened to derail the Apollo program. Throughout multiple elections, prominent politicians have threatened to cut funding for the Moon program & our attempts to reach beyond the Earth. But now it seems that NASA is ready to change the world again.

After confirming geological reports of extractable resources at the landing sites of Apollo 30 & Apollo 31, NASA has announced that Apollos 32, 34, 36 & 38 will be redirected from simple exploration missions to further explore Mare Fecunditatis & to test out the equipment needed for a base. Then, starting in 1983, the Apollo program will continue to focus on exploring the Moon as NASA's new Artemis program begins construction of humanity's first off world base. The base, which is scheduled to be permanently manned by 1990 will be called Fertility Base after the region that it's being constructed in."

Cronkite gave America a moment to digest that news story before he continued.

"Now, finally, my final send off. What a story to leave you all with. Yes, this is my final broadcast as the anchorman of the CBS evening news. For me, it's a moment for which I have long planned, but which, nevertheless, comes with some sadness. For almost two decades after all, we have been meeting like this in the evenings & on this time. But those who have made anything of this departure

I'm afraid have made too much. This is but a transition, a passing of the baton, the great broadcaster & gentleman Doug Edwards preceded me in this job & another, Dan Rather, will follow & anyway, the person who sits here is but the most conspicuous member of a superb team of journalists, writers, reporters, editors, producers & none of that will change. Furthermore, I'm not even going away, I'll be back from time to time with special news reports, documentaries, & beginning in June, every week with our science program Universe. Old anchormen you see, don't just fade away, they just keep coming back for more & that's the way it is, Friday, March 6th, 1981. I'll be away on assignment & Dan Rather will be sitting in here for the next few years. Goodnight."

As the news went to the commercials in between shows, viewers across the country & around the world felt another era ending as one of the most trusted voices in the world retired from nineteen years of service.

Apr 27th, 1981
American Embassy , Moscow, USSR

Madison Eaton enjoyed the rolled bliny that she had been served for breakfast. She wasn't normally a fan of Russian cuisine, but she was quickly coming to like some morning bliny. As she ate & went over her morning briefings, she wondered for a moment how in the hell a nurse from Boston had managed to find her way to Moscow where she was leading negotiations to stop the production of nuclear weapons as the Secretary of State.

Just ten years ago, she had been leading nurses in a strike demanding the hospital hire more nurses & orderlies as the nurses were being forced to work too many double shifts & extended shifts. After being elected to congress in seventy-six with three quarters of the vote in her district, she led a failed bill to introduce single payer healthcare into the US. After winning reelection in seventy-eight, she fought for & advocated for health-care reform & made a name for herself as a tough negotiator.

She had been dumbfounded when Carter asked her just ahead of the election in eighty to bring her negotiating prowess to the white house & to be her new Secretary of State. In the last year, she had been involved in negotiations all over the world & now she was here in Russia, trying to convince the Soviets to go along with a plan to reduce the number of intermediate range nuclear weapons & to agree not to position them within ten kilometers of the border between the USSR & NATO.

The talks had been going on for years with progress & setbacks in almost equal numbers. But at long last, it looked like some progress was being made. Over the last few days, it seemed as if the Soviets were warming up to the idea of both sides keeping intermediate range & fast strike nuclear weapons away from the border.

This was something that NATO & the US had been working towards for years as it would make first strikes less likely to succeed by giving the attacked country more time to react & retaliate, making first strikes less likely to work without heavy consequences & making them less desirable.

As she was reviewing her briefing & finishing the last of her bliny, a Soviet official was escorted to the secretaries' room. One of the American soldiers was the first to enter the room after knocking & getting permission.

"Madam Secretary, Mr. Frolov is here to see you."

"Let him in."

The soldier stepped out & let the official in.

"Madison, it's good to see you, I'm sorry if I've interrupted your breakfast. Are those bliny?"

"That they are Nikita, & it's no interruption, I'm nearly finished anyway. What can I help you with?"

"The Kremlin has asked me to inform you that today's meetings have been pushed back to tomorrow."

Madison couldn't hide her concern.

"Is there a problem with the negotiations?"

"No, no, nothing of the sort. It's just that some of the people involved in the talks are required today to deal with an unforeseen event that requires their involvement. The talks will resume as normal tomorrow."

"Alright, as long as negotiations are continuing. Can I ask what exactly it is that they're being called away for?"

"You can ask, Madam Secretary, but I'm not at liberty to answer."

"Does it have anything to do with that protest that passed by the embassy this morning?"

"Not at all, the minor protests outside are nothing more than a few misguided people that don't understand the complexities of certain situations."

"Like the birth ratios?"

"I don't know what you mean."

Madison stood up & walked to her window.

"Nikita, as you can see, I have a decent view of the street from here, as do a number of my colleagues. My Russian might only be passable, but our translators were able to read the signs. They seemed to show variations on a theme of You Promised us SONS!"

Nikita looked around for a moment.

"Nikita, there are no microphones in here."

Nikita went over to the table in her room & sat down.

"There have been a number of… groups… that believe that the Soviet solution is not as effective as we've said it is. Of course, they are mistaken, the Soviet Union would never mislead its people like that."

"Of course, Nikita."

"Still, these groups are growing in number & have been giving our police some trouble. In truth, they've calmed down significantly over the last few weeks as most want these negotiations to accomplish something."

"I'm guessing that you're worried that once the negotiations are over, they'll go back to protesting in full force."

"It is a concern. I hear that there have also been birth ratio protests in the states."

"A few, yes. They got a bit bigger a month or two ago when XX's started going to winter formals & getting driver's licenses & after school jobs."

"Reminders that the great problem is still going strong."

"Yep. Fortunately, they've died down in the last few weeks."

"You are fortunate, but I fear that we will all be in trouble in a few more years when the birth rates drop. I'm not sure that either of our countries can handle shrinking populations."

Another group of protestors passed by the embassy outside as the two negotiators contemplated the future. Eventually, Nikita had to report back for some other business, leaving Madison to report their conversation & to hope that they were successful here as the added stress of shrinking populations in the future could lead to leaders desperate enough to try something.

May 28th, 1981
Oval Office

Shirley Hufstedler, the secretary of education, sat on one of the couches in the Oval Office. Sitting next to her was Ray Marshall, the secretary of labor. They were both there to report some troubling findings to President Carter. Walking into his office, Carter saw the two of them sitting there & when he saw the looks on their faces, he braced himself for bad news.

"I'm guessing that you don't have any good news for me."

They looked at each other & shook their heads. Shirley was the first one to start telling him what the issue was.

"Sir, now that the XX generation is turning sixteen, they're at the point where they're starting to enter the job market, after school jobs, part time jobs, that sort of thing. They're thinking about what they want to do with their lives."

"Sounds about right. What's the problem."

"Well, sir, the problem is what they want to do with their lives. We conducted a number of nationwide surveys & it seems that while we have made some great progress in convincing girls to enter non-traditional fields such as economics & the military, it seems that few to none of them are interested in things like industrial jobs or certain public service jobs."

"What kind of public service jobs?"

"Well, for example, we have many young women interested in being paramedics, but almost none who are interested in becoming firefighters or policemen... policewomen... police. We've also got a number of industrial & manufacturing jobs that they don't seem interested in."

Ray then took over & reached into his briefcase to pull out some charts & figures & spreadsheets.

"All kinds of vocational jobs that require significant manual labor are not drawing any sort of enthusiasm from these girls. Carpentry, metalwork, welding, trucking, construction, electricians, plumbers, etc. According to our surveys, only a small percentage are interested in these jobs. As for the majority, not only are they not interested in these jobs, but most of them also marked down that they wouldn't even consider these kinds of jobs."

"That doesn't sound good."

"No, it doesn't. Now, if one or two graduating classes have this issue, it's not a problem, but if this goes on for too many years, eventually these fields will start running out of new employees to replace those who retire or leave the profession."

"Then half the economy grinds to a halt. How did this happen? Haven't we spent the last decade trying to prepare the girls for the economy that they'll have to be a part of?"

Shirley took over from Ray.

"We have been sir, but there are a lot of employment fields that nobody thought to promote for girls, I think the psychologists are calling it unconscious bias. Even with the directive to push girls towards traditional male jobs, there were some jobs that nobody thought to push them towards, like firefighting. Some jobs are still being seen as the province of men & some people just don't seem to realize how severe the transition will be when it hits."

"Ray, how long until this becomes a problem?"

"A number of years, but we need to get on it. Shirley has come up with some great ideas for national job fairs geared towards girls to convince them that it would be fun, cool, or empowering to be a plumber or a welder."

"That's right sir. I'd also like to start a program to incentivize the few women in these fields to help us push girls in these directions by helping out at these job fairs & career days. It's not going to help girls too much if they only see a bunch of men talking about it."

"That's some good thinking."

"Also, we intend to put out a number of public service announcements to remind parents that they need to help by encouraging their daughters to go into trade & manufacturing jobs as well as other currently male dominated areas. According to some psychologists, a large part of the problem is families encouraging their daughters to either double down on getting a husband, or to go into more traditionally feminine jobs."

"Why do I get the feeling that no matter how hard we work at this, the economy is going to be rocked."

Ray took his glasses off.

"Because you're a smart man sir. No matter how hard we try, there's going to be a disruption. It'll go smoothly at first, there will just be a few more women in certain parts of the economy, but eventually the lack of men in certain areas that we're probably not even thinking of will result in consequences as nobody is thinking to train women for these jobs. We could see a major recession by the end of the decade."

"Of course, conservatives are going to fight us every single step of the way."

"That they are sir. Even during the election, they had that one ad where the government was putting wrenches into the hands of girls & sending them to a factory that mysteriously started failing."

"I remember that one, vote Reagan or vote for your daughter in a factory."

"Shirley & I have started coordinating on this issue more intensely. We've set up a survey to try & figure out which jobs are being overlooked, then we intend to do everything that we can to prepare both the girls & the professions for the transition."

"Good. Keep me posted. Don't forget to check if these girls are interested in farming. Last thing that we need is food shortages because we forgot to encourage women to become farmers."

Both Shirley & Ray made a note of the President's suggestion.

July 4th, 1981
Lodz, Poland

The television in the store showed an image of Nazar Vashchenko setting foot in Mare Fecundities, the pride of the Soviet space program showing that the USSR could go anywhere that the Americans could go. Outside, on the street, a screaming woman, one of tens of thousands, held up a sign that proclaimed that her daughter was hungry.

Police had tried to disperse the crowds when they started forming. They had started to get worried when the people broke the principle of not leaving the factories & taking to the streets. It had started with just a few hundred protestors. Manageable.

The resentment had been growing for months. Years some would say. Over the last few years, fields & factories had been filling with young women. It had been hard for the people to believe the propaganda in the beginning that the birth ratios were four to one in the USSR when the people could count the boys & girls & see for themselves that it was nine to one.

It was now hard for them to believe the Soviet government about their home remedy for Soviet women when damn near every woman in the city had tried & there still seemed to be no difference in the number of families that had sons with fewer than five sisters.

Then the food shortages began. A combination of lousy weather, poor record keeping, lousy farming techniques & so many families that just kept having babies until they got a boy had resulted in massive food shortages. Food rationing became tight, in some places, people had to wait in line for days at a time to get a monthly allotment of three pounds of meat. Some people would wait in line all week long, get their food, take it home, & get back into line to wait again for another week. It seemed that everything was running out. Meat, coffee, detergents, sugar, cigarettes, soap, spare tires for the buses. Even butter & flour were starting to run low.

When the government tried to blame the shortages on the people who were protesting instead of working, hundreds of protestors grew to thousands. Still manageable. Women, mothers, grandmothers, daughters & young sons, with men & war veterans surrounding them to protect them. They demanded food. Someone in the local government started making a big fuss of the Soviet LK-3 landing on the Moon, hoping that it would inspire the people to get back to work for the glory of the Polish People's Republic. They were wrong.

Between the time that the Soviet lunar lander touched down & Nazar took his first steps on the Moon, thousands had quickly swollen to tens of thousands. It was no longer manageable. Women, young, old & pregnant were banging empty pots & pans, shouting that their daughters couldn't eat glory & pride. It didn't help that many of them knew that the Americans were gorging themselves fat & stupid in their Independence Day celebrations where they would probably be eating more meat than Soviets got in a month in one meal.

By the afternoon, the local government was trying to call up reservists to quell the situation as the police were completely overwhelmed. Few were coming though. Many of the reservists were among the protestors or were themselves starving or had families that were starving. On top of that, many more reservists were being called upon all over Poland to quell other protests.

As an estimated seventy to eighty thousand people protested in the street, a number that continued to grow, a call was made requesting military intervention. They faced a similar problem, protests all over Poland were raging.

Ludwika had been one of the women to join the protests in the morning. A mother of six daughters, she had been hopeful when she heard in the first years that it wasn't as bad for the communists countries. A lie that she had believed until the truth slipped out. She hadn't minded working long hours in fields in the summer & factories in the winter. She was providing for her family. Then she heard stories from people that had seen the West, stories about how they work half as hard & have twice as much. How nobody ever has to wait hours for a loaf of bread, how there's so much that people were dying from eating too much. She had grown to hate needing to work so hard to get so little, but what could she do but work?

When the food started running short, & bus routes were cancelled because there weren't enough parts to fix the buses. When everyone's clothes were falling apart because they couldn't get enough fabric or thread to replace & mend everyone's clothes. When her brother had to wait in line for almost two weeks to get enough food for three days, she was silently cursing. It was when they tried to blame the people that were leaving the factories & taking to the streets that she couldn't swallow the injustice of it anymore.

She & her two oldest daughters marched all day, demanding food, demanding buses, demanding fabric, demanding coffee &

cigarettes & medicine & everything else that was in short supply which was everything else. With dreams of the hunger being brought to an end, she marched into the night until shots could be heard. The military had arrived & they were taking shots into the crowd. Ludwika grabbed her daughters who didn't seem to care about the bullets & dragged them away. They complained the whole way home.

The next day, martial law was in place & descent was being put down violently. Still, she could see the looks of some of the other women in the field that day. This wasn't over. It was only getting started.

August 25th, 1981
Just Outside Chicago, Illinois

"As you can see, the property has plenty of space."
The realtor stood on the back porch of the old farmhouse. He had been selling farmland for over twenty years & in his time, he had seen a few odd customers. Still, something struck him as odd about these two ladies. Sure, they were probably what country folk sometimes called *special friends*, or *roommates,* but it wouldn't be the first time that he sold land to those kinds of ladies, nor the last. Hell, in a few years, they might be a very large chunk of his business. It was something else about them, they just didn't feel like they were interested in farming, at least not just farming anyway.
"Like I said, it's five hundred acres, that's almost four fifths of a square mile. Plenty of land to grow whatever you want."
Virginia smiled as she looked out across the landscape.
"This will be perfect for growing & tending to our flock."
"Flock huh, looking to raise cows? Pigs?"
"Some would call our flock sheep."
"Right…"
He had no idea what she meant by that answer, but he didn't much care. This Virginia woman might be some pinup model that suddenly thinks she can raise cattle & would likely be selling the lot again in a few months, but the credit report said that her money was good, so he wasn't asking too many questions.

"What kind of privacy does the property have?"

He knew it. These lady lovers were looking for an out of the way place where they could have some privacy & do whatever it is that ladies that like each other do away from prying eyes.

"Well, aside from your nearest neighbours being three quarters of a mile away, there's also a farm fence around the property similar to the fence you saw at the end of the driveway. Simple four-foot-high wood posts, with a few horizontal slats between them. Although if you're planning on raising livestock, you might want to upgrade the fence. There's a section of the fence in the Northwest corner that is more designed for privacy, more of a six-foot-high wooden wall then a fence."

"We'll definitely need to upgrade the fences. Do we need permits for that sort of thing?"

"You'll have to look into the permits, I do know that if you're going to be making major alterations to the fence, you might have to inform the neighbors that you share the fence with."

"Makes sense."

The other one came out of the old house. She was shorter & chubbier with her cute brunette hair.

"The house looks like it's in pretty good shape. Only really needs one or two small fixes & a good coat of paint & it'll be good."

"What do you think Hope, looks like a great place."

"It sure does. We'll have a lot of work ahead of us, but I think that it'll work."

"We'll take it."

"Great, I'll go & draw up the paperwork."

As he left them alone to go back to his truck & get the papers that they would need to sign, Virginia wrapped her arm around Hope's shoulders.

"Look at it Hope. Our future sanctuary. We'll raise up some proper fences to keep the prying eyes of men out. We'll build a great big church in the center; we'll build houses & apartments for those that live here & visit. We can even grow our own food & sell some of the extra to help cover things like property taxes & expenses."

Hope looked out on the mostly empty land.

"It'll be incredible. A place where women can just be free without needing to worry about any men. A place where women won't be judged for not wearing makeup or bras."

"Or clothes."

Hope looked at Virginia.

"We're talking clothing optional, right Virginia?"

"Of course. We're not some sex cult. Just because this is going to be the new garden of Eden doesn't mean that we have to be naked. We're writing our own rules here. In the same way that we don't have an Adam, we won't have to be naked."

"Good. Just to be clear, I have no problem with everyone being naked, I just don't want people thinking that we're luring young women into a lesbian sex cult. We've already got enough grief from the former husbands of some of our members."

"Tell me about it. But that won't be a problem here. Here, we'll all be free & safe."

"No more former husbands picketing outside."

"Or forcing their way in to demand that their wife come back home where she belongs."

Virginia pinched the bridge of her nose.

"God, remember the guy last month who barged in & demanded that we stop witching his wife & let her come back home & get back to her cooking & cleaning."

"Not as bad as the time last year that the cops showed up in the middle of Sunday service with a warrant to search our basement because some idiot told them that we had his wife locked up in the basement where we were brainwashing her."

"Remember when they found out that we didn't have a basement."

"Yeah, he kept saying that we must have a hidden passage."

They both chuckled as they remembered the police rolling their eyes at him. Hope wrapped her arm around Virginia's lower back.

"Are you sure that we can afford to do this? Buying 500 acres of land, building a sanctuary & apartments, fencing off most of a square mile. It's going to be expensive."

"We'll be alright. After all, attendance is at record high levels, as are our donations, & Rome wasn't built in a day. It's alright if takes two or three years or even longer. We don't even have to

have the whole place up & running before we start using it. Once
we get the church up, we can host major events here instead of
cramming everyone into the current church like sardines."

"That'll be nice."

As the realtor brought them the papers, they filled out the
forms & imagined their first service here when the church was built.

September 10th, 1981
Bavaria, West Germany

The members of Debra Foster's mechanized infantry squad
groaned as they packed up their equipment. As excited as they had
been to find themselves only two clicks away from the Iron Curtain,
the thrill of being this close to the enemy was wearing thin on their
fifth day in the woods. As they complained about living in the
woods for a week, again, Debra reminded them that just because
they were a mechanized squad didn't mean that they might not end
up needing to travel through the woods if the Soviets turned the
cold war hot.

Standing in the middle of their camp, she drank some industrial
strength coffee as the thirteen women under her command got to
work breaking down their camp. Once again, they were going to be
spending the day marching through the woods along the border.
While this was officially a survival & capabilities exercise, they were
all armed in case they came across anything.

With the camp broken down once again & everyone getting
their packs on their backs, one of the women came up to her as she
did every morning.

"Mam! Camp packed & squad is ready to move out!"

"Well done, Corporal. Make sure everyone is ready, we're
heading South Southeast out of Flossenburg & into Eslam."

"Yes mam."

The Corporal didn't leave, instead she simply stood at
attention.

"Yes Corporal?"

"Some of the women were wandering if we had to stick to the
forest route today."

"Where else would they like to go?"

"They were wondering if we could use some of the minor roads & farms. Their argument is that if we invade the USSR or if they invade us, the dense forests are only along the border. We'd be able to mostly travel freely on both sides of the border."

"I see."

Debra put her fingers to her lips & whistled to get everyone' attention.

"Listen ladies, I get that you don't want to be out here in the woods. I don't want to be here either, but the whole point of this is that if there ever is an invasion, we may have to spend weeks at a time in the woods, hiding from Soviet snipers & artillery. So, we need to be able to move along winding paths in a forest."

The women groaned again.

"I know, it sucks, but it's only for two more days, then we get to go home to nice warm beds. In the meantime, no roads, no farms, stick to the route & no more groaning about it or we're doing this again in December."

With yet another day of hiking through the slightly mountainous woods ahead of them, they marched along the winding path that would take them to a camp site just South of Eslam where they would build camp & get some rest before returning to their current position the next day.

The hours dragged on as they slowly made their way through the Bavarian Forest. Each woman in the unit like every man & woman back at the barracks were glad that they only had to do this once a year & that they weren't part of the regular patrols. Near the end of the day, they were all grateful as they reached the one part of their route that wasn't in the woods, a four-hundred-meter stretch of dirt path between two farms. As they were about to enter the woods, they each waved to a young couple that was having a picnic.

Back in the woods, they kept marching, occasionally crossing small paths as they navigated their way back to their campsite for the night. Just one & a half kilometers from the border with Czechoslovakia, they went through the same process that they had gone through five times already. They swept the area, then set up a watch & began building their camp for the night.

As they were setting up their pup tents, tired from a day's hike & joking about which pair shouldn't make too much noise tonight, they heard something over their radios that they hadn't been expecting.

"Command, Watch two, Charlie inbound, possible civilian, over."

Debra felt a moment of panic. Watch two was to their East, looking for things coming from the border with Czechoslovakia, from Soviet territory. Debra grabbed her handheld radio.

"Watch two, command, confirm Charlie, over."

"Charlie confirmed. Two hundred meters & closing, civilian, one woman, one adolescent, two children, over."

"Leave them be unless they come right at you, do not engage, repeat, do not engage, over."

There was no answer.

"Watch two, confirm orders, over."

Again silence. Just as Debra was about to answer, watch two came back on over the radio.

"Command, we have more Charlie's inbound, non-civilian, potentially hostile, count four, over."

All of them felt their blood run cold for a moment. Military contacts coming from the East, this close to the border could only mean one thing.

"Secure civilian contacts if they come to you, prepare to defend against hostile forces, we're coming to you. Out."

Debra then turned to her squad.

"Harriet, Alice, you two stay here & help break down the camp, we might have to bug out fast. Jayda, call command, tell them that we might be engaging with hostiles, Yasmin, Miranda, Eloise, Tegan, Liz, grab your rifles, with me, now!"

In what seemed a matter of seconds, most of the riflemen in the squad were armed & charging East while soldiers that normally operated vehicles were packing up the camp as quickly as possible, in case they needed to bug out fast. Over the hundred-meter dash to Watch two, Debra mentally kicked herself for taking the time to call out her riflemen by name. After calling out the two to stay behind & guard the camp, she should have just called for her riflemen to follow.

Once they got to the watch location, they found that the two women there had secured the civilians who had come right at them. The mother was trying to calm her children in what sounded like Polish while the older daughter was trying to talk in Czech & broken German. They managed to convey that they were being chased, something that Debra's team already knew.

"Eloise, you speak some Polish, you & Ester take the civilians back to camp."

"Yes mam."

The two women then began escorting the terrified family back to the camp while Debra & her five other riflemen prepared to ambush the quickly approaching soldiers.

"Do not fire unless they engage. We don't want to start World War three because they lost track of where the border is."

"Yes mam." They all said.

Debra then had them spread out a bit as she stayed close to Yasmin who had some training in speaking Russian.

As the soldiers got close, it was clear that they were not some sort of forest patrol. They looked like the regular army that you'd find at a border crossing with their beige uniforms & blue shoulder boards. Debra seriously considered that they were lost & didn't realize they were in West Germany.

As the four soldiers stumbled through the forest, struggling to move quickly, Debra tapped Yasmin on her shoulder, Yasmin called out in rough Russian, telling the four men to halt & surrender. They pulled their guns up & grouped together. Yasmin continued by informing them that they had illegally crossed the border & entered into West Germany & that if they didn't surrender immediately, they would be treated as a hostile invasion force.

As they talked among themselves, Debra could see from the CA on three of their shoulder insignia & the CA with a single horizontal line on the other that they were three privates & a private first class. Low level grunts that were probably younger than she was. After a tense moment, one of the privates raised his hand off of his gun & took a tentative step forward.

"We surrender."

His accent was very thick, but he wasn't lying. The three privates & the private first class slowly & carefully put their guns down & got onto their knees.

"Is there anyone else with you?"

"No sir, mam. Just us."

Debra gave a signal & Tegan cautiously moved forward to collect their guns while Liz checked each of them for any hidden weapons. Once they were cleared, Debra instructed them to stand with their hands up. When the one that spoke English relayed the orders, they obeyed.

"No funny business, my Corporal will lead you back to our camp, you will follow with us right behind you. Try anything, & you go home in a pine box."

The translator relayed the message & they all nodded their heads.

Twenty minutes later they were back at a fully packed camp, where the family was relieved to see the Soviet soldiers disarmed. Jayda then approached Debra.

"I got through to command, they're sending extraction vehicles to a road about two hundred meters North of us. ETA is fifteen minutes."

"Good, get them back on the horn & make sure they know that we have four Soviet prisoners captured on our side of the border just over a click from Czechoslovakia."

"Yes mam."

"Everyone, we're moving North in one minute, be ready to go."

"Yes Mam!"

A minute later, they were moving North with three American soldiers up front, the Soviet soldiers following with their hands cuffed behind their backs & everyone else bringing up the rear. Five minutes later, they reached the road, more of a wide dirt path. About ten minutes later, a bunch of jeeps showed up with more soldiers jumping out of them.

In less than a minute, the civilians, a family of defectors that lost their father when he tried to slow down the soldiers were in a jeep & on their way to freedom while the soldiers were split into two other jeeps & escorted to holding cells at a nearby base. Debra

& her squad rode back to Ferris barracks with a hell of a story to
tell.

October 11th, 1981
Los Angeles, California

Govind Dayal was relaxing after a long day. Teaching Americans
the way of tantric meditations was a rewarding job with all kinds of
benefits, but it was also exhausting. Resting in his living room over
his studio, he relaxed & watched the news talk about the new space
shuttle program. He had to admit, he was surprised by how brilliant
& simple the concept of a reusable space vehicle seemed. After all,
you don't build a whole new train for each trip, that would be
insanely expensive.

Just as the news was switching to a story about how Apollo 32
had left supplies behind to extend 34's mission, he heard his
doorbell ringing. Getting up, he walked over to his front door &
pressed the button for the intercom.

"Hello, it is very late, who is this?"

"Govind, it's Charlotte, I need to talk to you now. It's an
emergency."

Charlotte. One of the benefits of his school had been the
private lessons with some of his pupils. There were few feelings in
the world as good as expanding his pupils' minds & filling them with
wisdom, knowledge & other things.

"Charlotte, can it wait until morning? I have had a long day."

"No, we need to talk now!"

"Fine, I'll buzz you into my studio, I'll be down in a minute."

Checking that his turban was still on properly, he checked that
his wife was already in bed, pregnant with their next child. Seeing
that she was already out, he carefully slipped out of his apartment
& went downstairs to where Charlotte was pacing in the studio with
her new daughter in her arms.

Charlotte's soft features, her brown hair & her million-dollar
smile had caught the eye of every man in the class, including
Govind. She & her husband had started attending the class about a
year earlier when they were having trouble conceiving, let alone
conceiving a boy. They had come to Govind because Western

medicine had failed them & couldn't explain why Charlotte wasn't conceiving. After just a few months, it had worked & just three weeks ago, Charlotte had given birth to a healthy baby girl.

"Hello Charlotte, what's the problem?"

"It's Rachel."

"Rachel? Oh, your daughter. If she's sick, you should take her to her pediatrician or a hospital."

"No, that's not the problem, she's not sick."

"Then what's the issue?"

"Look!"

Charlotte turned around so that Govind could see Rachel in the light & all of a sudden, the problem became clear. Rachel's skin had developed a deep tan, almost honey complexion. This would be fine if Charlotte or her husband were Indian, but since they were both white, this was an issue.

"Oh deary."

"You see! She was pale when she was born, but over the last few days, she started to darken. I took her to the pediatrician & he told me that most children are born paler than their parents & then darken after a few days or weeks unless both their parents are white. I've only ever been with you & Oliver & Rachel can't be Oliver's."

Govind was dumbfounded.

"But we only completed inside once. I know that my techniques are powerful, but one time after just three months should not be enough to impregnate someone with... your... condition. What was your condition again?"

"I don't know, the doctors could never figure out what was wrong with me."

Just as Govind was about to respond, a thought occurred.

"Charlotte, did Oliver ever get tested by the doctor?"

"No, he said that he was fine."

"Oh Gods."

"What?"

"Charlotte, you are not barren, your husband is sterile. He must be one of those men that just can't emit... sorry, my English, he can't... admit that he's shooting blanks."

"But the doctor..."

"Must have assumed that he had been tested & simply believed him when he said that he is fine. This is why they can't find anything wrong with you Charlotte, there is nothing wrong."

"So… the meds that the doctor gave me for my fertility…"

"They probably made you excessively fertile, which is how we got pregnant with one internal event."

"Oh God. What do I tell Oliver? He's going to notice soon that Rachel is darker than she should be."

Govind wondered if that was true but decided to air on the side of caution.

"Tell him that… the doctor said it was a side effect…. Of your fertility medications &… your unidentified fertility issue."

"But you just said that I don't have fertility issues."

"Yes, well, I'm thinking that Oliver does not need to know this."

"Right. Sorry, I'm just freaking out."

"Understandable."

"What do I do now?"

"Now, you let me hold Rachel, & you calm yourself down with some meditation."

"Okay… okay."

Charlotte handed Rachel over to Govind & went to sit down on one of the cushions where she started doing breathing exercises to calm herself down while Govind held his daughter.

"Hello Rachel. I have good news for you & I have bad news for you."

Rachel giggled.

"Good news is first; you will be raised by a mommy & daddy that care for you very much. The bad news is that your daddy will be a fool who will think that a daughter that is very much darker than him & his wife is his."

He then kissed Rachel on her forehead & held her until Charlotte calmed down.

"Thank you, Govind. I feel a lot better."

"No problem. Out of curiosity, does your husband want to have any more children?"

"I don't know. Why?"

"If you ever have more children that come out white, remember to tell him that you changed fertility medications, or he may grow suspicious that only one of his children *had side effects*."

"Right. Thank you again Govind."

"My pleasure."

The two of them hugged & Charlotte left to head home to tell her husband about the doctor telling her about the side effects. Govind pinched the bridge of his nose.

"Another daughter. That's... five... six... seven... eight since the anomaly began. My goodness."

November 12th, 1981

St Patrick's Cathedral, Northern Ireland

Faye O'Hanly stood in front of the massive twin spired, white-grey, roman catholic cathedral. With her hair perfect & the wind having died down, she turned to her cameraman as the they started recording, hoping to get a complete take this time without the wind picking up too much.

"I'm Faye O'Hanly with the BBC & I'm reporting to you from outside of St Patrick's Cathedral in Armagh."

The cameraman gave her a quick thumbs up to let her know that she looked great, & her thickly accented voice sounded great.

"This church, like many Catholic churches, has seen many great men leading its congregation in prayer. A fact that it has in common with churches & cathedrals all over the world. However, it will soon no longer share something with the Anglican church."

Clinging tightly to her hat as the wind picked up a bit, she waited for the cameraman to give her another thumbs up before she continued. Confident that they'd be able to edit that pause out, she went on.

"Since the dawn of Christianity, there has been an ironclad rule of all churches. Only men can be priests. However, it seems that some parts of Christianity are ready to abandon this rule in view of the new situation we find ourselves in. The Archbishop of Canterberry, leader of the Anglican church, announced this morning that starting in January of 1984, the Anglican church will allow women to take holy orders & become priests. While a number of

Christian churches have wrestled with whether or not allowing women into the clergy would be necessary, to date, only a handful of minor denominations or cults have started allowing women to reach the level of priest. With today's announcement, the Anglican church becomes the first major denomination of Christianity to allow women to take holy orders."

Turning around to look at the church behind her for a second, Faye continued with her story for the evening news.

"The Vatican, like many church heads, has been contemplating whether or not to make this monumental change as many experts worry that by 1995, there could be a massive shortage of new priests to lead us into the next millennium if women are not allowed to lead congregations. When asked for comments, catholic officials didn't respond. While the Vatican's view has long been that only men can be ordained, there are some who wonder if Pope Peter the Second might overturn this policy. In his short time as Pope so far, he has certainly demonstrated that he is significantly more progressive than his peers, but will this translate into a change in the organization of the largest branch of Christianity, only time will tell."

The cameraman signaled that that was it & he wasn't recording anymore. Faye walked over to him just as the wind started picking up again.

"How does it look?"

"It's perfect."

"Good, it's getting a bit chilly for another take, not to mention a bit breezy."

"Do you think the Catholics will actually allow women to become priests?"

Faye looked at him incredulously.

"I think that a snowball would have a better chance in Hell. The Vatican isn't exactly big on change."

"Yeah, you're probably right."

December 24th, 1981
Mare Fecundities, The Moon

"Hey, Mayflower, are we busting out the champagne yet?"

Cornelia Chambers waived off Eric's joke as she stared into the microscope's eyepiece. The champagne in question had been a surprise that had been left behind for them. Apollo 32, the last mission to visit this site, had left behind a small care package for them that had enough food, water & air filters to last them for two days, extending their mission from the standard ten-day mission to a twelve-day mission that would span Christmas. Unbeknown to them or most of NASA, included in the care package was a bottle of champagne with a note wishing them a happy holiday from Jerrie Cobb & Guion Bluford. A bottle that they had decided to save for Christmas Eve.

"See something interesting there, Mayflower?"

"First up, you don't always have to call me Mayflower."

"Sorry Cornelia, but it's a good nickname."

"No, it isn't. Just because my family came to America on the Mayflower, doesn't make it a good nickname."

"Okay, fine, Cornelia it is, no more Mayflower. Now, what has you so interested in that microscope that you're about to miss your call home to your family?"

Cornelia looked up.

"My call home... shit! Lost track of time."

"Well don't worry, you still have two hours."

"Asshole!"

She gave Eric a small shove.

"Seriously, what has you so interested in that sample?"

"Do you remember the little glass bead that came back in thirty-two's samples?"

"Yeah, like half of its mass was water. I remember them telling us to keep an eye out for more. Did you find one?"

"I found nine, from two different sites. NSAA will have to confirm when we bring them home, but they look to be the same as the last one that was found."

"Really?"

Cornelia offered up the microscope & Eric took a look at it. Under slight magnification, he could see one of the round, translucent beads sitting there in the microscope's light.

"That's definitely one of them. You say that you found nine nearby?"

"So far. I haven't completely combed through the samples yet."

"Do you think that means we're near a water source?"

"More likely just near a large deposit of these."

"Still, if the regolith nearby is loaded with these, we might be able to process it & get some water out of it."

"Sure Eric, but we'd have to process a shit ton of regolith. You'd need about a dozen of these beads just for a drop of water."

"You're probably right. So, champagne with supper?"

"That's the plan."

"Great. Now, have you seen my sock puppet? I've got a video call to my family in a few minutes & the nieces love Lunar Luna."

"No idea where she is. Just remember to record those videos so that in ten years, you can embarrass your nieces in front of their friends."

"Two steps ahead of you. I've got a buddy in Houston that records the footage where you can see both feeds side by side, so I'll be able to have a copy of them smiling & giggling while I bust Luna out."

"Fond memories to show at their weddings."

Eric laughed as he went hunting for the most ridiculous sock puppet on the Moon.

1982

January 17th, 1982
Shenzhen, China

In all of his years as a doctor, Tan Zhen had never seen anything like it. The closest that he had seen to it was the rush of panicked prospective parents when the anomaly began. He had been fresh out of school in those days & had found himself thrown into the deep end of dealing with terrified young couples demanding to know if their pregnancy would produce a son or a daughter & demanding to know if their child was a daughter because of this phenomenon.

Many young couples begged & pleaded with him to ensure they had a son. He found himself inundated with offers & bribes if he could fix them & give them a son. He also found himself threatened & complained about when he informed them that he had no way to do such things.

Naturally, being forced to spend so much time dealing with panicking parents that nobody else wanted to deal with ended up paving the way for him to specialize in reproductive medicine. Now he was cursing that specialty.

A billion. There are now a billion more girls in the world than there were boys. That was what they had said over the news, that in the last seventeen years, almost one point two billion girls had been born verses just over a hundred & forty million boys. A difference of just over a billion.

That was the story two weeks ago. Then there were new stories & one of them was jamming his office. The People's Republic of China, under the direction of the Communist Chinese Party, was implementing a new two child policy. To stop the practice of families simply continuing to have children until they had a son, the new policy limited families to just two children.

Naturally, many people freaked out. Doctors, lawyers & government officials had to keep reminding people that the limit would only take effect in nine months & that any child born before the first of December would not be counted against the couple.

Couples that had only given birth to daughters had flooded his office demanding to know how long they had to conceive a son so that he could be born before the deadline. Every day was a surge of couples that had either just gotten pregnant in the nick of time or who were looking to get pregnant just in the nick of time.

Everyday had been worse than the day before with more & more people panicking as pregnancy tests came back negative & he had to deliver the news that if they tried again in a few weeks, there was a sizeable chance that the child would be born after the deadline. He could almost see the cockeyed hope in men's eyes as they weighed the odds & decided in their heads that a son was worth the risk. At the end of the day, Tan liked to imagine half of them being hit with massive fines & nine tenths of them having another daughter.

After another long day, he went home where his wife poured him a stiff drink & fussed over him as he sat down in his living room. She turned on the tv & switched on the news so that he could see what was going on in the world. After watching a story about radical protestors in the USSR that had been influenced by Western propaganda into attacking communism, another story came on that he had not been expecting.

"In domestic news, the government of the People's Republic of China has announced a new policy concerning marriage laws in China. Starting in the new year, women born after 1965 will be allowed to marry other women."

Tan's wife was shocked by the news. Tan wasn't. If the world had hit a billion more girls than boys, then that would have to mean that China had at least two hundred million more girls than boys. People would not like that eight out of every nine women would become spinsters who might consider traveling overseas to foreign or even Western nations for a husband. That could make it look like there was a problem or even a failure in Chinese communism & that couldn't ever be allowed.

Tan understood that all that mattered was that the nation & the party continue to look strong in the eyes of the people & the world. A solution had to be found & without the Western nation's belief systems to hinder them, China was able to find a solution that would work that Western nations would struggle to implement. A solution that would make it look like they were able to adapt to the new reality in ways that the West couldn't. If these girls couldn't have husbands, they could have wives.

February 25th, 1982
Norfolk, Virginia

When the first IVF clinic opened in the US, doctors, employees, & members of the commission had warned the public that children born in this manner were subject to the very same nine to one birth ratio that the general public was subject to. They had worked very hard to make it clear that this was a way to help people who were infertile, not a way around the anomaly. But desperate people rarely listen to warnings.

The clinic had opened back in seventy-nine & in the intervening three years, had very quickly taken in as many clients as they could. In just three short years, just over four hundred children were born in this first clinic & only about forty or so had been born as boys.

Sam Chambers had spent nine long years working with the commission. Seeing that they were making essentially zero actual progress in even figuring out what was going on, let alone how to fix it, he had gotten himself transferred. He had gone to a department where they were conducting research into how to keep the birthrate up when these new children were old enough to be the ones making babies.

They had a bunch of projects that they were working on there, IVF, cloning, ectogenesis. They even had a few projects that seemed wild & out there, like research into the possibility of two women conceiving a child together.

When IVF had become an option, he got together with a bunch of commission employees working on it & they applied for grants & government loans to open IVF facilities around the country. The argument was that these facilities would need a few years to start churning out large numbers & that multiple dedicated facilities would accelerate research in real world conditions.

Sam had been thrilled when the clinic opened. He was helping couples conceive & doing vital research. He also made sure that each of the clinic's clients knew that once it worked, nine out ten children born would still be girls. It didn't stop clients from complaining that they were only having girls.

Almost every week, he received complaints about how much money people were spending & still not having sons. He tried reminding them that he had told them from the beginning that was probably going to be the case, but they didn't care.

A few months ago, he had been served with a class action lawsuit from over a dozen couples & a conman of a lawyer looking to make a quick buck. They accused him of promising sons. The lawsuit failed when he was able to show that at every step of the way, they had informed people that their ratios were nine to one, just like everyone else's.

Now Sam showed up to work only to find a mob outside of his clinic. Some of them were saying that IVF was unnatural, or that there was something inhuman about test tube babies. Some were accusing him of doing experiments on the babies being born & some were saying that commission men like him had orchestrated the birth ratios so that they could open clinics like this just in time to meet the demand for babies in an almost fatherless world.

With police called in to manage the crowd, Sam spent a good part of his morning responding to requests for comment from the media. Sensing that he would have to make another appearance on a number of news shows that night, he called home to tell his wife he'd be late & then wondered how in the hell they were going to get enough clinics going to meet the need for newborns by the end of the decade. Once again, the numbers came up short.

"At least it's not another lawsuit this time."

"I'd rather be dealing with a lawsuit. People don't try to attack you when they're in the middle of suing you. These people are crazy."

"Do you think that you're in any danger?"

"No darling, the police are here & we have our own security. The crowd will disperse in a few hours & I'll just be home a bit late."

"Alright, just be careful Sam."

Looking out at the baying crowd, he wondered if he was lying when he said that he'd be fine.

March 21st, 1982

Church of the Wives of Christ, Illinois

The church was barely half built. Outside the main hall of worship, it was all scaffolding & half-built structure. Even in the main hall, most of the architectural finishes hadn't been put in yet. Still, this church which had been built entirely by female contractors, with a capacity for five thousand attendants. Even though it was far from finished, the simple fact that they could gather for Sunday mass after just six months of construction was damn near miraculous.

Virginia Green stood on the stage before her congregation. They were starting over an hour later than normal since most of the congregation had never been to this place & they needed time to organize the parking. With everything finally coordinated & everyone seated, Virginia came out on stage wearing only her white robes, very loosely tied up in the front.

Hope stood to the side with the things that would be needed later on in the service, watching Virginia begin her first sermon in their new hallowed place.

"Welcome daughters, to the Church of the Wives of Christ!"

The women throughout the audience clapped & cheered.

"I have to admit to you all, sixteen years ago, when a young brunette looking for something to believe in stopped & listened to me preaching in the park, a part of me didn't believe that we'd get here. I had hoped, but I could scarcely imagine actually achieving all of this. That was because I hadn't started realizing that no one woman could do this. It was only on that day sixteen years ago when Hope put her faith in me & I put my faith in Hope, that this began to happen. That's how we all got here, by putting our faith in each other & working together to build this temple to the Lord, the only man worthy of our love & admiration."

The women in the audience cheered. Hope stood dumbfounded by the praise & gratitude that Virginia gave her.

"It is through you all, the faithful, those who recognize the wickedness of men, that we were able to build this church, that we shall build this sanctuary, & that we shall cleanse this world when Christ returns!"

More cheering from her followers.

"Now, I've seen that many of you have noticed the incompleteness of our church & you're probably wondering why we're preaching in a construction project. It's because today is a special day. Today is exactly seventeen years since the first doctors started to notice that almost all the newborns in their nurseries were girls. Today, the oldest of the XX generation celebrates their seventeenth birthday. This means that the last days are nearly at an end!"

The congregation murmured among themselves. Virginia wasn't the only preacher that had been proclaiming that everything since 1965 was this time called the last days. A time where this ninety percent female generation was still growing up & before the massive consequences of their gender balance would upheave society. Several preachers all over the world had been proclaiming it. But to say that it was coming to an end implied something big was about to start.

"One year from today, some of these children will be grown women. As soon as this happens, Christ can return at any moment. It may be years or even decades, for even I cannot know how the Lord intends to return his son to us, but it could be a matter of days. Starting on this day next year, the one worthy man can return at any moment!"

Women throughout the assembly nodded their heads, believing that the end truly was coming, that they would see Christ return with their own eyes.

"His time of arrival is approaching us. The sanctuary for him & the apostles that he chooses from his virgins will have home & sanctuary here. Our church will be ready for him when he comes. But that will not be enough."

She paused for dramatic effect.

"It is not enough to simply have a place for him to stay. We need to be ready to receive him."

Quick as a whip, she unbound her robe, & shrugged it off. With her robe on the floor, Virginia Green stood before the thousands of women in her congregation wearing only a small gold crucifix around her neck.

"To be ready for the return of our Lord, we must be as Eve was in the garden. Eve could walk naked in front of Adam, for Adam was hand made by God almighty, the only mortal man that was not corrupt. His son began the corruption when he smote his own brother. As Eve was without fear before Adam, we must be without fear before the Lord. I stand here now, adorned only in his symbol, ready. I am untouched & unbound by men; I have no fear or shame of the form that God has given me. I am ready."

Mothers tried to cover their daughter's eyes, some women looked away in embarrassment or modesty, some women cheered & celebrated.

"I see many of you looking away from me. Why do you hide your eyes? Have the men of this world made you so afraid of the female form that you cannot bear to look upon one of your own? Fear not the work of the Lord, for he crafted your body. As Eve stood before Adam, as I stand before you now, so will you need to be ready when the Lord comes & that time approaches."

Several of the women looking away started glancing towards the stage, astounded by how unafraid Virginia was to just be exposed in front of thousands.

"You shall see that there is nothing about our bodies to be ashamed about. That gut wrench that you feel that makes many of you look away is simply the conditioning of men to submit us to their devilish corruption."

As the initial shock wore off, many more women were now looking to her.

"Be not afraid, especially since every sermon that I give in here will be as I am now, ready to meet the Lord. Do not worry, none among you have to bear yourselves every Sunday, I understand that such a thing would be a great burden for many of you. I will neither force you, nor stop you from being so ready as I."

Women through the hall calmed down as they had been afraid that a crucifix was the new dress code.

"Now that I've woken you all up, let us truly begin our first sermon in this newly hallowed hall. Hope, our bible please."

Another robe hit the ground. Everyone, Virginia included was stunned as Hope walked onto the stage, carrying Virginia's personal bible to the waist high lectern as naked as Virginia.

Hope certainly hadn't been planning on it. She had never felt bold enough to stand naked before other people before. It was one thing when Virginia & her perfect body showed off, but Hope had always been afraid to show off her rounder body. She was no blonde goddess. Yet, as Virginia stood there, bear & brave & talking of being ready, Hope had felt herself compelled to be braver than she ever had before, & so off had come the robe & her clothes beneath it. Now, she walked onto the stage to hand Virginia her bible & to stand next to her, naked before thousands of eyes with her heart hammering in her chest.

"I see that I'm not the only one here who's ready to meet the Lord. Now, let us begin."

By the time that Virginia was done preaching, a dozen more women had either stripped down partly or completely. That day, in this new church, She & Hope preformed twenty unbinding ceremonies as women who had recently divorced their husbands discarded their wedding rings.

Redressing as the congregation left, Hope felt alive in a new way & she knew that she would do this again & again without fear.

May 14th, 1982
Mare Fecundities, The Moon

Olivia Woods took her helmet off as she finished cycling through the airlock & made her way into the base. Even the new magnetic ring around the vacuum hose hadn't been able to get all of the lunar dust off of her knee or her gloves.

"Hey, Kendrich, the starboard porch light went out. It's pitch dark out there & apparently falling on your knee can still hurt in lunar gravity. Kendrich?"

"Sorry Olivia, need a hand?"

"Just getting out of these pants. Mind?"

"No problem."

Kendrich turned down the small television screen & grabbed the first aid kit just in case they needed it. He then helped Olivia wiggle out of her spacesuit, which proved a little more challenging when it got to getting her sore knee out.

"Jeez, what happened out there?"

"Told you, the porch light went out. Even with the flashlight, keeping track of every little dip & nook in the landscape gets tricky."

"That's weird, an exterior lamp went out on thirty-four as well. Thirty-five also had some flickering that they reported. Might be something for the engineers back home to look into."

"Yeah, especially if we're going to be doing these night missions. PhD from an ivy league school, top of my class in astronaut training & they've got me doing nighttime yardwork."

"Someone's gotta do it. If we're going to have a permanent base up here, we need to be able to work in the dark. Hang on, this might sting a little bit."

Kendrich rolled Olivia's pant leg up to check her knee. She winced a bit as he rolled the pant leg up.

"How does it look?"

"Not too bad, just a bruise. We'll tell the flight surgeon & he'll tell you to stay off your leg for a day or two."

Olivia sighed & looked out the window. Everything outside was completely dark. What little light that they had was either coming from their lamps or was being reflected off of the crescent Earth in the sky. While Kendrich rolled her pant leg back down & then helped her out of the inner part of her suit, Olivia looked to the television that he had been watching.

"So, anything interesting happening on Earth?"

"Oh, you have no idea. Shit's going a bit crazy down there."

"Let me guess, they still haven't picked a new pope?"

"Nope. It's been three weeks & they're all still trying to decide between the more progressive archbishop & the more traditional one. The more traditional one almost got enough votes this morning apparently, but he was still a few short."

"Three weeks. Has there ever been a conclave that long?"

"Not in this century, but apparently a few weeks is nothing. They said that the longest one in history lasted for almost three years."

"Damn. So, everyone's going crazy over the conclave."

"Not just the conclave. The prom."

"The prom, like the high school dance?"

"Yep. Apparently, after the last few dances where XX's showed up with a lot of... what did they call it... non-traditional dates, a bunch of the schools & schoolboards dropped some last-minute rule changes for the prom."

"They banned lesbian couples again, didn't they?"

"Lesbian couples, polygamy couples, basically any couple that isn't a guy & a girl."

"Didn't they do that last year?"

"Not like this. Not in this many places, not with this many rules, & not a week before the prom. Students all over the states & all over Europe are protesting in the streets."

On the screen, they could see a lot of high school students, almost entirely women, dancing in the streets to popular music while wearing their prom outfits. Olivia stared at the tiny screen in the hopes that she might be able to make out some better detail as some of the boys looked a bit odd.

"What's up with some of the guys? It looks like they've never worn a suit before."

"Most of them aren't guys. Apparently, it's some new trend that's going around, some of the girl & girl couples, or maybe I should say woman & woman couples. They do this thing where they flip a coin, or play rock paper scissors or something, & the one that loses has to be the boy in the relationship. They cut their hair, stop wearing makeup & where boy's clothes."

"Really?"

"I guess they're finding a way to make do without."

"I guess."

"Alright Olivia, up on your feet, let's see how you move around without a spacesuit on."

Olivia stood up carefully. Grateful for the reduced gravity, she took an uneasy step before finding her stride in the cramped module. Taking the few steps that she could take in her underwear, she turned to Kendrich.

"What do you think Kendrich? Am I gonna get to keep the leg?"
He chuckled.

"Yeah, I think that you'll be fine. But I still gotta tell the flight surgeon about this."

"Fine, but I'm putting on some clothes first. Just because he made us all drop our pants for every little examination doesn't mean that I'm gonna do it a quarter of a million miles away."

Kendrich looked at her with a confused look.

"What do you mean?"

"You know, every time he needs to check you it's please drop your pants. Check your ears, drop your pants. Check your blood pressure, drop your pants. Check your eyesight, drop your pants."

"I don't know. The only time that he ever asked me to drop my pants was to check my prostate."

"What? No, he always asks patients to drop their pants, that's what Alice & Veora & I talked about when we would get drinks after."

"Right... well, as far as I know, he doesn't do that with any of the guys. At least not with me."

There was an awkward silence in the module.

"I think that I'm going to make a call to the director."

"Good idea Olivia."

June 21st, 1982
New York City

Lena threw the article down on the table. This was not what she needed right now. Between trying to find printers in other states so that she could get the Lavender Press out on the same day as in New York, covering the issues going into the midterms & wondering if she & Cassie were becoming more than just casual lovers, competing headlines was the last thing that she needed.

That was when Sarah walked in.

"Hey Lena, good news, I scored us an interview with Anton Domna, the guy running for state senator that's pushing for gay marriage to be legalized."

"Great."

Sarah looked over to Lena & recognized the look of Lena being far away in a distant train of thought.

"Then he took his face off & revealed himself to be a purple lizard living in exile."

"Nice."

"Naturally he proposed."

"Sounds good."

"Long story short, I'm pregnant with purple lizard babies & I'm running off to Saturn to live with him & you're completely not paying any attention at all."

Sarah snapped her fingers in front of Lena's face.

"Sorry, I'm paying... purple lizard? Sorry, I guess I'm distracted."

"I figured as much."

"Sorry Sarah. What were you saying?"

"I scored us an interview with Anton Domna."

"You did! How?"

"Turns out he's heard of us through his daughter, so when I mentioned that I work for the Lavender Press, he jumped at the chance to be interviewed by New York's premier queer newspaper. His words."

"Holy shit! When's the interview?"

"Friday afternoon, so we can put it in Sunday's issue."

"Thank goodness, I don't think I could have fit that into Wednesday's issue as well."

Looking at the piles of paper on Lena's desk, Sarah quickly figured out what was happening.

"Did something happen to knock the Beatles survival tour out of the headlines?"

"Yes."

"Must be big, if it knocked them off the headlines."

"It is."

"The Beatles all getting back together to do one more tour. I heard that they're going to include some songs that the label dropped from previous albums because they promoted women in power."

"That's why I was going to put them as the headline of Wednesday's issue."

"So, what the hell could knock Beatlemania out of the headline?"

"This."

Lena held up the article from the New York Times. On the cover was a picture of Prince Charles & Princess Diana.

"What's this?"

"Princess Diana gave birth last night."

"Ah."

"Yeah. Even the Beatles doing a tour together can't top the birth of Prince Charles' heir."

Sarah opened the article up to read the story.

"Early last night, Princess Diana went into labor… no significant complications… early this morning, she gave birth to Princess Elenor of Wales, heir presumptive to the throne after her father. Wow, the future Queen of England."

"Maybe."

"What do you mean, maybe?"

"She's the heir presumptive, not the heir apparent. If Prince Charles has a son, that son will supersede his older sister. & become the King."

"Wait, I thought that it goes to the first born?"

"Apparently not. It goes to the first-born son. Daughters only inherit the English crown if they have no brothers."

"Well fortunately for Elenor, that's not to likely."

"But it's possible. I tuned into the BBC a little while ago & there's already a debate about whether or not that rule should be overturned since from here on, princes will be few & far between."

"I bet. I heard a few weeks ago that there's a small movement in the UK demanding that they change the order of succession & make Princess Anne the next in line. I think that they call themselves No More Kings."

Lena waived it off, not wasting time thinking about them.

"Yeah, so now, instead of a retrospective on how the Beatles have helped push a few progressive movements forward, I have to defer to British Royalty, & wade into the hot mess that is an actual patriarchal line of succession when male heirs might only pop up every few generations."

Looking over to the counter in the new break room, Sarah knew what to do for her boss.

"I'll put some coffee on."

July 25th, 1982
Kennedy Space Center

Janet Hill was making a mad dash for her office. Of all the days to be late, today was not one of them. Nobody is supposed to be late between launch & splashdown, not even the botany department. Didn't matter that the Moon was a barren & lifeless rock, Apollo thirty-seven was in lunar orbit & getting ready to land.

To be fair, she had tried to be on time. It wasn't her fault that Rebecca had decided to cook breakfast naked, something that she hadn't done in years. Janet had known that she should get to work. She had known that for the next ten or eleven days, everyone at work would be a little more stressed out than normal since they were going to have boots on the ground. But how do you say no to the woman you love, in her birthday suit, making you French toast?

"I really shouldn't. I've told you how the directors get when someone is late on a mission day."

"What I know is that when those three get back to Earth, I'm not going to see you for two weeks because you'll be sorting through all of those samples looking for organics, & nutrient levels. If they're getting you for all of that, I'm getting you this morning. Now undress, sit down, & have some French toast with the maple syrup that your parents sent from back home."

Janet relented, she put her briefcase down & quickly started unbuttoning her blouse.

"I really don't have time for this."

"I know."

"Rebecca you little minx."

Feeling like she was in her twenties again, Janet laughed as she ate breakfast with the love of her life, in the buff, like they had all the time in the world & not a care in it.

But the world doesn't pause. So now she's somewhere between walking & jogging to get to her office before anyone noticed that she was late. Her secretary had a cup of coffee waiting for her.

"Thanks. Did anyone notice that I was late?"

"Nope. Everyone's busy with thirty-seven, nobody has time for the plant department today."

"Thank goodness."

"One of your buttons is undone."

"What, oh, thanks."

Janet quickly did up the loose button on her blouse.

"Been a while since you were this late & hurried getting in. New boyfriend maybe?"

"No, no boyfriend."

"One night stand then?"

"I haven't done a one-night stand since my freshman year."

"Alright, don't tell me. Mr. Harmon called a little while ago, he said that he'd be down in half an hour to talk to you about something. I think that you've got about two minutes left."

"Thanks."

Janet rushed into her office & tried to make it look like she'd been there for nearly an hour already. When Francis Harmon walked into the office, he didn't suspect a thing as he took a seat.

"Good morning, Janet."

"Morning Francis. What can I do for you today?"

"I'm looking for your help on a project of ours."

"What can the plant science department do for the Artemis program?"

"Well, the goal is to have a permanent presence up there by the end of the decade."

"Right, I still don't see where we come in."

"Well Janet, simply put, food is heavy. It would be really nice for us if we didn't have to carry a few tones of it up to the Moon a few times each year."

"You want to grow crops on the Moon?"

"I want to see if it's an option. We know from your previous experiment that plants can sprout in the lunar soil, now the question is, can they grow & produce food?"

"Why do I think that it'll be a little more complicated than just waiting until we have a continuous presence & then trying to farm up there?"

"Cause you're not some dumb broad. We'd like to have some idea of what we'll be working with before we actually have to start trying to grow crops for astronaut consumption. Not to mention that crop yields would need to be reliable. We want to set up a small, controlled experiment that can run on its own with nobody there."

"A self-contained agricultural experiment with nobody there to tend to it, on the Moon?"

"Exactly. We'll fly it up next year on Artemis two, then we'll set it up & leave it running. We'll have a camera that sends us back regular pictures of its progress, then seven months later, when Artemis three shows up, we can see how it worked out."

"Seven months! You want to leave vegetables growing on the Moon, unattended, for seven months?"

"Yes."

"That's insane! First there's the water issue, there's next to none to be had, which means that we need to either supply it with a ton of water or find a way to recycle its water. Then there's the daylight issue, a lunar day night cycle is over twenty-eight days long, no vegetable plant can survive two weeks of perpetual day followed by two weeks of perpetual night over & over again. So, this experiment would need lights & shades. Then there's the temperature, gets damn cold on the Moon. Plus, who knows what the radiation & the low gravity will do to it."

"Sounds like just the kind of challenge up NASA's alley. We'll have you coordinate with one of our engineering teams & the astronauts on the two missions. You can be part of the first serious attempt to grow crops on the Moon. What do you say?"

"Yes. What else can I say? Yes"

August 23rd, 1982
Greensboro, North Carolina

"It's fucking outrageous! What in the Hell were they thinking!?"

Pax didn't know why his father was blowing up like this. He just knew that it was embarrassing, especially in front of Leo who was hanging out at his place until his mom got back from work. Pax's mother wasn't sure why his father was so upset either.

"What's wrong William? It's not the first time that Paxton has taken a class & been the only boy in there. It happens."

"Not for home economics it doesn't. I'm sorry Jewel, I know that everyone takes home economics in schools these days, but my boy will not be the only boy in a class that until very fucking recently was considered a class on women's work!"

Jewel Tillman gave her husband a death glare.

"Language!"

Remembering that Pax & Leo were both there, he calmed himself down a bit & cleared his throat.

"Pardon my French boys. Don't go around talking like that. That's language for grownups."

He then fished around in his wallet for a pair of quarters to put in the swear jar.

"Right, now, as I was saying. I don't want my boy learning about sewing & cooking & whatever else they teach girls about in those classes if he's the only boy."

"What difference does it make?"

"Look at the boy Jewel! He hates sports, he loves literature, he fights tooth & nail when it comes time to get a haircut. I'm just worried that if he has to take home economics as the only boy in class, it might just push him over the edge."

"This again. William, we've been over this, not every boy that hates sports is going to... go into musical theater. Paxton, Leo's mom must be nearly home, why don't you walk him home while mom & dad talk."

Leo got his things together & they walked out the door to the sounds of Pax's parents still arguing.

"He's at that age Jewel, he's at that age where if he's completely surrounded by girls..."

When they got to the end of the driveway & out of earshot, Leo finally spoke up.

"Your dad is really pissed that you're going to be the only guy in that class."

"Yeah. I don't know why; he's always going on about how I'm going to have a bunch of girlfriends."

"You'd think that he'd be happy."

"But he isn't."

They walked along for a moment in silence.

"Hey Pax."

"Yeah Leo?"

"What's wrong with musical theater?"

"I don't know. I think it's one of those grown-up words that means something else that they don't want us to know about yet."

"Ah. Do you think that your dad is going to call the school? Jeremy's dad called the school when they tried to make him take shop with no other boys."

"What happened after his dad called?"

"They put him in a different shop class with another boy."

"I hope my dad doesn't call. It's embarrassing when he yells about not having enough boys in my classes."

"That does sound bad."

"Does your dad ever yell at the school like that?"

Leo thought about it for a moment.

"No. I think that he doesn't mind because I play baseball."

"Lucky."

Once again, they walked in an awkward silence for a moment as they thought about their fathers.

"Do you want to see my new baseball cards when we get back to my house?"

"Sure Leo, got any good ones?"

"Would you know if they were good?"

"No."

They both laughed as they approached Leo's house.

September 24th, 1982
Cedar Rapids, Iowa

Debra sipped her coffee as she watched the sunrise. Having been on military time for the last eight years, she had already been up for about an hour. Marcel was still in bed, sleeping off the previous night. As boring as home could sometimes be, there were some perks to coming back when she was on leave & Marcel was a big perk, in more ways than one.

Standing in his bedroom, she hadn't bothered putting anything on. Last night wasn't the first time that he had gotten to see everything, not to mention that modesty was not always an option in the military. Looking around, she found her service jacket hanging off the back of a new chair in his room. She admired the triple chevron with the rounded bottom denoting her new rank as a staff sergeant on its shoulders & the medal for her performance in dealing with the stray Soviets on its chest. It was all rumbled up & tossed in such a way that if she caught one of her subordinates doing it, she'd have them running laps & doing pushups until they gave out.

She laughed at how unprofessional she was being, standing in a man's room, naked & admiring her tossed service uniform.

"There's my amazon."

Turning around, she saw Marcel sitting up.

"I can't think of a better sight to wake up to then this."

Debra smiled.

"You wouldn't rather have some skinny thing with big jugs?"

"Over you, never."

"Really?"

"Damn straight. I want a girl whose body ripples when she flexes."

"Like this?"

Debra posed as if she was in a miss universe competition, flexing her muscles. After eight years of training & working out, her muscles weren't exactly lean anymore.

"Fuck yeah. I don't trust women that can't bench-press me."

"Biceps over B cups?"

"Every day of the week my amazon."

Debra grinned a bit wickedly.

"Is that why your soldier is standing at attention."

Looking down for a second, he noticed the bulge forming in his sheets.

"Just respecting a superior officer, you can hear him say yes mam if you get close enough."

Debra burst out laughing at the cheesy attempt to get her closer to his member. After a moment, when she calmed down, she lay across the foot of the bed as he pulled the sheets off of himself & sat up.

"So, when are you going to quit the army & let me make an honest woman out of you?"

"When will you let me make an honest man out of you?"

"Yeah, that's going to be a while."

They both laughed.

"Seriously Debra, you ever consider quitting uncle Sam, or are you an army girl for life. Will I be getting blown by a brigadier general in a few more years?"

For a second, she imagined him saluting her & calling her general, then she told him that it was major general to him before pushing him back onto this very bed to teach him some respect.

"I don't know. I kind of like life in the army, but sometimes I do think about raising a family."

"Is it an either-or situation, can't you do both?"

"Well, having women in the army is still relatively new, so I don't know. I heard about a new policy that the upper brass is considering where women soldiers can go on maternity leave for a year or two to have a kid. I think they're worried that the birth rate in a few years will be low enough without women going childless to serve."

"So, they're going to allow women to take time off for baby-making?"

"Something like that."

"You gonna keep more medals fighting the Soviet menace while I'm here raising our daughters?"

"You think that you're going to be the father of my babies?"

Marcel maneuvered himself so that he was on all fours on top of Debra, his impressive member pointing at her small chest.

"I think that I'd like a whole lot of trying to get you on maternity leave while you show me what the staff in staff sergeant refers to."

Debra grinned wickedly. Grabbing his hip with one hand, he was surprised when he found himself looking up at the ceiling as she straddled his thighs.

"You want to see what this sergeant does to staffs, alright, I'll teach you a bit of respect for my rank while I'm at it."

"Yes mam."

As she wrapped her fingers around him, they both grinned knowing that Debra was going to be late for whatever she had planned with her family while she was home.

October 31st, 1982
Church of the Lord's Son, Fort Worth, Texas

The day was a bit warm for the last day of October. The summer heat had long since passed, but it sure did not feel like tomorrow was going to be all saint's day. Reverend Thomas Edwards looked out over his assembled congregation, & he couldn't help but notice that almost nine tenths of the adults in his congregation were men. He noted the peculiarity of the sight, a perfect mirror to the world outside. It drove home the urgency of his message on this day that society gave over to the pagans & the devil. Running a hand through his grey hair, he had wondered that morning where the copper red had gone.

Accepting that he was now sixty-two years old, he had started asking himself if he should start slowing down & grooming his replacement. Looking out onto his congregation, he knew that he couldn't retire just yet, not as long as the fire burned in his veins. His hair may have gone grey, but his blood was still red.

"Ireland."

The people in his congregation, from the expecting women up front, to the families with sons behind them, to the families with only daughters at the back, all looked at him in confusion for a moment.

"For the last seventeen years & some change, I have from time to time brought you news of the world beyond America's shores. Today, I bring you news of Ireland."

The congregation murmured at what could have been so big in Ireland that he had to tell them about it in Sunday mass.

"Since the beginning of the Lord's last test of mankind & man's worthiness, Ireland has held fast as a most righteous country. Catholics, Protestants, Presbyterians, Methodists, even the Eastern Orthodoxy called the country home. They're different from us, yes, but they're good, God-fearing men & women. I truly believed that Ireland could go the distance. That they would be one of the righteous nations that would resist the temptation of liberal damnation. That they'd be ready for the true test that begins in four & a half months when the cursed children are grown adults. But it seems that even they have fallen by the wayside."

More murmurs from the congregation.

"Just four days ago, they violated God's almighty law & did the unthinkable. They legalized homosexuality for those over the age of fifteen."

Gasps & murmurs ran throughout the crowd.

"I know my children. I too was shocked. If Ireland could give in to this corruption & allow for homosexuals among both women & men, then truly, any nation could fall. At the very least, they had the good sense to protect the children from it. However, that will not save them from ruination! Soon these XX children will be grown & will start to marry! They will demand queer marriage, but we must not let them have it!"

The congregation loudly shouted out Amen to his proclamation of what they needed to do.

"The XX generation. A grave insult to all boys. Have they forgotten that a tenth of this generation is still male? Do these liberals intend to pretend that boys don't exist & just label the entire generation as lesbians? Do not use this name for these children! It is another liberal trap! An attempt to subtly put the idea of a new world order run by women into your head by making it sound natural & normal! Do not fall for it my children!"

"Amen!" They proclaimed.

"Now I'm certain that a good many of you have probably noticed that over the last five years, our numbers have shrunk just a bit, especially among the women folk."

Everyone looked around as if only really noticing for the first time.

"It is because through our vigilance, righteousness & heeding of the word of the Lord & his Son, we've cast out the wicked & the vile within us. We have banished the witches that hid among us like weeds in the garden. On this day devoted to witches & the devil's pagans, we can proclaim to the Lord & all that we are clean, we are true & we are righteous! Amen!"

"Amen!" A thousand voices shouted out as one.

"We now prove our righteousness with a new blessing from the Lord. Another child with which to try & bear a son! Sonless wives, take your husband's seed once more that your sixth born might be born a man to defend his five sisters from the lesbians out there that'll try to corrupt them!"

There was cheering amongst the congregation. Several of the women in the back where thrilled that they could have one more chance to become one of the good families. They had stopped having children after giving birth to four, just to be sure they weren't banished, but now they could try for another one & many of them subtly indicated to their husbands that they would start trying tonight while the demons roamed the streets disguised at children in costumes.

"Know my children, that this gift granted onto us by the Lord almighty & his mercy requires that we maintain our vigilance. Hollie Dawson, Maisy Hawkins, please stand before the congregation."

The two girls, one seventeen & one fourteen, stood up in front of the congregation after their father's brought them up to the front. The congregation gasped as they wore short hair & not a trace of makeup. Hollie stood there in a suit & Maisy stood there in jeans & a dress shirt.

"For those of you who have not heard, there is a new trend going around among teenage girls. Many of them like to pair off. Then they play a game of chance & the loser has to get a haircut, cross-dress & act like a boy in their pretend relationship."

Gasps & murmurs as the two girls stood there.

"These two girls were engaging in false relations with two other girls. They lost their contest & have been pretending to be the boys."

Maisy & Hollie stood there, embarrassed as all Hell in front of their congregation.

"Now, before we pass judgement on these two poor souls, let us have compassion as the Lord's Son would. They are young girls, not yet mature, not yet able to fully fend off the devil's influence. Let us remember, there are not enough boys for them. It's easy to understand how some may want to pretend that wasn't the case. The same sort of thing happens in prison. People have needs & wants & when there are no real options, some try to make do."

The assembled flock thought about this for a moment. It did make sense that some of the girls in this generation would be desperate.

"We must have understanding for these girls. They've been led astray, but there is still hope for them. Let us open our arms to these lost sheep, & remind them that God made them as women, & that they must be true to how God made them. Let us pray for their souls in Jesus sweet name."

The entire congregation then began praying for them as they stood there, embarrassed. When mass ended, the two of them were held back so that Reverend Thomas could talk to their parents about how to lead them back to God's plan. As they sat on the pews normally reserved for pregnant women, Maisy, fourteen & humiliated, stared at her feet.

"Guess it was fun while it lasted, at least I don't have to pretend to be a boy anymore."

Hollie was not so accepting.

"I like being the boy. If that old preacher thinks he's going to stop me, he's sorely mistaken."

"Hollie, you'll get in trouble, didn't you hear, they're trying to lure us into becoming lesbians."

"Maisy, have you seen the boys in this church. I'd rather pretend to be a boy for my girlfriend then to actually end up with one of them."

"Don't say that."

"I said it & I mean it."

While Maisy shook her head, Hollie didn't tell her about the Halloween party that she & her girlfriend were going to sneak into because they were almost old enough. She also didn't tell Maisy that she intended to take her girlfriend into the closet for seven minutes of heaven like boys & girls do at these parties.

November 8th, 1982
Baikonur Cosmodrome, Kazakhstan, Soviet Union

Balakin Nikodim & Balashova Verka sat strapped into the tight confines of the Soviet lunar lander. Some political officer from Moscow droned on about how they were the pride of the Soviet Union & that they needed to complete their mission with valor & glory. He droned on so long & loud that they could barely hear the last-minute instructions coming in from the technicians. As a result, when Balakin was instructed to flip a switch to the ready position, he misheard & flipped the switch next to it to the ready position.

As the political officer continued on far beyond what was expected of him in an attempt to impress his bosses, the flight director had to cut him off. The launch window was soon too close. Feeling offended that his speech about glory & duty had been interrupted, he stepped back as the people around him worked to begin the mission.

After the last checks were confirmed, they began. As a deep voice counted down from ten, the whole rocket shook as the engines lit. As fire tore out of the outer ring of rocket engines, the directors quickly noticed that the inner ring was dead. With the inner ring of their rocket's first stage not responding, they went to call for an abort as one of the technicians called out to the cosmonauts to flip a switch. Before the flight director could ask what was happening, there was a flash of light on the large screen followed several seconds later by the entire facility shaking as if in an earthquake.

The wrong switch that had been flipped had been the switch to prime the second stage engines. The switch to prime the inner ring of the first stage engines had been left off. So, when they began firing the engines, instead of the two rings of the first stage engines firing, it was the outer ring of first stage engines & the second stage engines that fired. With the second stage engines going, it only took a few seconds to heat up & rupture the liquid oxygen fuel tank that they were pointed at. This turned the first stage of the rocket, the most powerful stage, into a bomb & set it off.

Once the building finished shaking a moment later, the flight director picked up the red phone that would connect him to the Kremlin. Expecting to be put straight through to Leonid Brezhnev, the General Secretary of the Communist Party & the leader of the Soviet Union, he was surprised when he was instead connected to Yuri Andropov, the chairman of the KGB.

"Comrade Radoslav, the general secretary is unavailable, you'll speak with me."

"Comrade Andropov, I am sorry, but I must speak with the secretary. It's a matter of the utmost importance."

"Comrade Brezhnev is unavailable. You will talk to me & I will handle the situation."

With the urgency of the situation & the fact that he was talking to the head of the KGB, probably the most secure man in the union, he decided to talk.

"Sir, the LK-4 mission to the Moon has failed catastrophically. While attempting to launch, the inner ring of engines failed to ignite, this was followed by an explosion seconds later."

"How large of an explosion?"

"Massive sir. Over a thousand tons of rocket fuel & it all went up at once. The rocket is gone, the cosmonauts are gone, it's possible that the launch pad is gone as well."

Yuri Andropov stood there for a moment at the secretary's desk. After fifteen years of leading the KGB, his instinct was that it couldn't be a coincidence that that their next manned mission to the Moon blew up on the launch pad on the same day that Secretary Brezhnev suffered a heart attack.

"Lock down the launch complex, I assume that you're already implementing emergency services to secure the wreckage & preserve it for investigation."

"Yes comrade."

"Good. Make sure that nobody leaves. Make sure that the press discovers nothing. As soon as your people are able, I want you to find out what happened & if this was sabotage."

"Yes sir."

As Andropov reeled from these two cataclysmic events happening on the same day, he hoped that Brezhnev would recover soon or expire quickly. They needed a secretary that would be ready to do what needed to be done. If this was an attack, they needed to be ready for anything.

A few hours later
The Oval Office

President Carter sat in the oval office going over the surprise results of the midterms with his chief of staff.

"Ethan, please explain to me how a group calling themselves the Matriarch Party managed to get someone elected to the US senate? How does a party that makes itself sound like a would-be monarchy win a US election?"

"I don't know Jimmy. In the last few elections, they've been able to hold a few seats in the California legislature & on a few city councils. Nobody ever predicted that they would actually win a race for US senator."

"Aren't they the party that almost costs us races in California?"

"Yes, they are."

"Any idea how this Kathleen Howard is going to vote when she gets sworn in next year?"

"There I have some good news for you Jimmy. It seems that for the most part at least, their political agenda lines up fairly well with ours. Their primary goals are to push for women's rights & lesbian rights. They're in favor of fighting global warming & fighting for more social reform. They support unions, especially ones that fight for gender equality in the workplace. I think it's safe to say that we can work with them."

"So, if the case in the supreme court doesn't go through, she'll definitely be in favor of our proposal to legalize homosexuality across the country?"

"In favor, she probably thinks that we aren't going far enough. One of things that her party is pushing for is the legalization of lesbian marriage. They think that it should be legalized across the union before April so that it's accessible to the XX generation the very day that they turn eighteen next year."

"Lesbian marriage, by April. They're certainly ambitious, we're still trying to get eighteen states to repeal their sodomy laws. Okay, tell me about this guy from…"

They were interrupted as Harold Brown, the Secretary of Defense rushed into the room with a rather hurried pair of aides behind him. It was clear that he was in a rush.

"Mr. President, we have a situation in the USSR."

"Harold, is this about Brezhnev's heart attack?"

"No sir, this is a new situation."

"What now?"

"The Soviet lunar lander, LK-4."

"I guess they launched it this morning, well we knew that they were going to launch soon."

"No sir. They tried to launch it about four hours ago. It exploded on the launch pad."

"Dammit."

The President collected himself for a second.

"Harold, how bad is it?"

"It's bad sir. With Brezhnev in the hospital, the Soviet Union is officially being run by a trust composed of Foreign Minister Andrei Gromyko, the Defense Minister, Marshal Dmitry Ustinov & the head of the KGB, Yuri Andropov. However, unofficial reports show that the others are just falling in line with Andropov."

"So, the KGB is basically in charge of the Soviet Union on the day that their leader has a heart attack & their Moon mission blows up on the launch pad."

"Exactly sir. They seem to be moving a number of forces into a high alert stance. We believe that they think we're up to something or that we'll take advantage to launch a first strike while their leader is indisposed & they might not be able to retaliate with a full nuclear strike."

"Jesus."

"Sir, should we mobilize our forces?"

Carter thought about it for a moment.

"No."

"Sir?"

"If we start moving forces around, that could scare them, & we need them calm right now. Don't raise the Defcon level, don't start redirecting forces. For now, we keep an eye on the situation at hand & try to deescalate. I assume that you have a proper briefing prepared."

"Yes sir. Relevant personnel are being gathered in the situation room as we speak. Good. Ethan, we'll have to continue our discussion tomorrow."

"Yes sir."

The President then followed his Secretary of Defense to the situation room to begin their more detailed briefing on the situation.

Dec 7th, 1982
Washington D.C.

The relatively young reporter quickly read over the announcement before he began speaking into the radio to report the national news.

"In the supreme court decision of Rose vs the State of Utah, after two months of back & forth & impassioned arguments on both sides, the judges have ruled eight to one against the state of Utah by declaring that sodomy laws banning sexual acts between members of the same sex are unconstitutional. The ruling…"

Space Coast, Florida

Rebecca dropped the wooden spoon that she had been stirring with into the sauce as she heard the news over the radio. She stood there slack jawed as Janet walked into the room with a tear in her eye & a smile. While their jobs might still be in danger, they finally didn't have to live in fear that they might be arrested if anyone found out about them while they were living in Florida.

Just outside Chicago, Illinois

Virginnia looked up from the updated plans of the new sanctuary that was beginning construction outside their new church as Hope walked into the room.
"Virginnia…"
"What's up Hope?"
"The supreme court just struck down all sodomy laws in the country."
Virginnia looked up.
"Say that again."
"The supreme court just struck down all sodomy laws. No police in the country can arrest anyone for having gay sex anymore."
"Jesus Christ. With four months to spare."

Manhattan, New York

Stunned by what she heard on the radio, Lena was glad that she had listened to Sarah. Even after running the Lavender Press for twelve years, she could still be surprised. She hadn't expected Rose vs Utah to work. She had expected that poor girl & her girlfriend to go to prison for a year. She hadn't wanted to write a front-page article for the case succeeding, but still, she had listened to Sarah & started a layout of it. Heading into the pressroom where Mila was printing up everything but the front page, she tapped on Mila's shoulder & Mila stopped the presses.

"What's up Lena?"

"Did you print up the front pages?"

"Nope. You said to wait on those."

"Good, Rose vs Utah won, I've got to finish writing the front page."

"Wow. Well, I can hold off for a few more hours, but at some point, we need a front page."

"I'll have it. Wow."

As Lena walked away from the pressroom, she was tempted to call up Cassie.

Rural Alabama

Ronnie turned off the television & turned to the assembled crowds of the sons of Adam.

"You see brothers. As I predicted all those years ago, so has it come to be. Months to go before the first victims of the government's gender control turn eighteen & what do you know, gay sex has been fully legalized by the ultra-liberal supreme court that Kennedy, Johnson, Humphrey & Carter appointed. Watch, you'll see, in a month or two they'll legalize queer marriage, then by the end of next year, they'll start mandating that all men born after 1965 have to give sperm at the new clinics they opened up where the government is taking control of impregnating women."

Ronnie took a breath as his brothers in arms watched him with rapt attention.

"It's no coincidence that this ruling came as Apollo thirty-nine is on the Moon, installing the final components that'll get past any signal jammer that we can come up with. The court made this ruling just as the project was completed in space with a few months to spare. It's also no coincidence that the Soviet Moon mission exploded on the launch pad; Carter doesn't want the communists to be able to interfere with their plans. Remember how that didn't turn into an international incident? The liberals have been gaming this since the end of Worl War II & it's all coming together for them."

One of the newer recruits from Mobile raised his hand.

"Yes Floyd."

"If the gender satellites have been working for decades, what did they just finish building on the Moon?"

"Good question my boy. All that stuff about a Moon base was a lie, it's actually going to be the control center for the queer field. Now that nine tenths of people under eighteen are girls, & they've legalized queer sex, in a few months, they'll turn on the queer field. That'll make all of these people born from the satellites queer. They'll then have no choice but to go to these invitro clinics where the commission's new genetic technology will allow them to engineer a race of ultra obedient, ultra-liberal lesbian patriots!"

"They can do that?"

"Of course they can boy. Do you really think that the commission has been researching the birth anomaly for nearly eighteen years & that all they could accomplish was to learn how to read a whole chromosome? That was just to justify themselves to the public. They've been working on genetic engineering. These liberals are taking control."

"What do we do?"

"We have to step up recruitment even more & increase our infiltration. We need to get deeper into the police, we need to get into political office, we lost this time, but we still have time. We need to get into NASA. We need to find the proof & bring it to the people. Today begins our last chance. The majority of the population is still unaffected men & women born before sixty-five. We've got maybe another fifteen years before those of us who are unaffected are still the majority. We have to succeed before we're the minority. If the new generations are the majority, then we won't be able to stop them."

Taking a moment to chug some water before he continued, he watched as the men talked among themselves.

"We need to stop them before their ultimate plan takes effect. Its manifest destiny done by the government. Around 1990, when the birth rate all over the world is collapsing, America will show off its invitro clinics, & they will offer the technology to any nation that joins the United States of America. By the time the Soviets catch up, half the world will already be under an American flag with over a hundred stars on it. We have to…"

"RAID!!!"

A man known as Junior burst into the barn where Ronnie had been talking to the various leaders of various groups within the Sons of Adam. Behind him, they could hear the sounds of men in heavy boots running.

"Shit figures they'd make a move today. Everyone scatter, evacuation plan Alpha. Run!"

Ronnie had been worried that with so many new recruits joining over the last few weeks & months, it might be easy for an informant to slip in. He had asked his informants in the police stations throughout Alabama if they'd known about anything, but they had all said no. Ronnie didn't know if they had been kept in the dark, or if they had been compromised or if they had been captured themselves or some combination of these possibilities, all he knew was that he had to haul ass once again.

Slipping out of the back of the barn with about twenty other men, he & six others barely got passed the police. Seeing them up close, he saw that these were Alabama state troopers & ATF agents. Seeing the ATF, he figured that the raid was more to do with the materials that Wayne, Lester & Cal had been gathering in a nearby barn. A nearby barn shook the Earth as it went up in a fireball.

Using the distraction, Ronnie & several of his men fled into the woods. With the explosion & the commotion back at the barns, it seemed the authorities had their hands full. He didn't know if they had been there specifically for him, but he knew that he would be able to use the timing of this event as proof to potential new recruits into the Sons of Adam that this was all part of a grand conspiracy.

1983

January 8th, 1983
Church of the Lord's Son, Fort Worth, Texas

Reverend Thomas Edwards new assistant was reading a local newspaper when the Reverend entered his office. The young man seemed rather engrossed in the article he was reading.
"Anything interesting Marcos?"
Marcos jumped in his seat.
"Sorry sir, I didn't hear you come in."
"That's alright, anything interesting happening in the world?"
"A few things sir. These are happening times."
"That they are. Hit me with some of the highlights."
Marcos was surprised by the Reverend being so friendly, but he didn't want to risk upsetting him.
"Well, the big story was about a commission report. Apparently, now that high school students are ninety percent girls, the teen pregnancy rate has dropped to almost zero, but the venereal disease rate has only dropped by three-quarters."
"I suppose that's mostly a good thing, although the lesser drop in diseases of premarital sex would show that we've failed as a nation to instill our children with proper conservative values."
It took Marcos a second to catch onto what Edwards was saying.
"Right, well, there's also an article in here about the protests going on in Poland."
"What are the commies upset about now?"
"Communism apparently."
"What?"
"Yeah, apparently, they're protesting because food is running out, the government lied to them about their efforts in dealing with the birth ratios, & apparently they've started mandatory conscription of all men when they hit eighteen."
"Not an ideal scenario, although I prefer it to our solution of letting women serve."
"Well apparently the people in Poland aren't too happy about it."

"I can imagine. Anyway, time to set up for today's sermon. We've got our own demons to fight."

"Yes sir."

An hour later, Reverend Thomas Edwards stood before his congregation. He knew that among the congregants, there were a few dozen women that would be sitting up front with their pregnancies on full display as dozens of couples got to work on having a fifth child. This was great news for him as the front rows were getting a little thin as families stopped having kids just before the limit so that they wouldn't be cast out.

With his congregation gathered, he began.

"Matriarchs! We've all heard the term recently. Women elevated by divine right to rule over men as if that were their place in the world. I'm not talking about Queen Elizabeth over in England, although perhaps they should have done like the French & found some uncle or cousin to rule after her father died. No, I'm talking about the other Matriarchs that have been in the news. The ones in California!"

Several of the congregants booed.

"It's good to see that we still have our heads on right. For many years, these misguided women who think themselves American Queens, have tried to obtain power over the men of California! They've taken places on city councils & in town halls. Then they started working their way into state government, claiming positions in the California legislature. But now, that's not enough for these witches!"

Thousands of eyes watched him in fear.

"These harlots have now convinced the state of California to send one of them to the United States Senate! That's right! One of this great nation's senators is a woman that thinks herself the Queen of California! What's worse, she has proclaimed her desire to fight for women's rights, for more women in the military & NASA, & for lesbian marriage!"

Gasps erupted from the crowd as he shouted.

"Yes. This Matriarch Party is the serpent in the garden. They seek to turn your daughters away from men, to turn them queer!

They seek the end of decency & to lead us astray from the Lord in this trying time!"

Taking a moment to drink from the water bottle that he now kept at his podium, he chose his next words carefully before continuing.

"They are the serpent & they are not happy just having California. In the past weeks, I heard tale of a candidate of theirs that lost in Nevada, & another in Oregon! These serpent women failed for now, but this coven of Californian witches is growing & they are spreading. They're infiltrating more states. Just last night, I read a report that they are setting up an office in Arizona for the next election. How long until they try to come to Texas! How long until they try to come for us!"

Gasps & murmurs broke out among the flock.

"We must be resolute! Now, when these cursed children are on the verge of adulthood & about to begin voting & demanding unholy things like queer marriage & banning men from the army, we must say NO! We must not let them put these matriarchs in charge, we must not allow them to shatter the very concept of marriage & we must not allow them to spread their corruption & filth to our homes!"

As the congregation cheered the Reverend & proclaimed that they would be vigilant, a young man named Jacob King, fresh off of his sixteenth birthday, took Reverend Thomas Edwards' words to heart.

February 12th, 1983
Lahore, Pakistan

The police were struggling to keep the mob of women out of the civil secretariat & the civil courts. It had started with just a few schoolgirls holding up a poster that proclaimed that there weren't enough men.

Dealing with them had been simple enough, a few police & a bit of time in the city jail & they had been taken care of. But then more showed up with the same message. Then more. Then even more. Every time they gathered; the police would arrest them & they would spend more time in jail.

Then one day, hundreds showed up, all girls, all screaming the same thing, that there weren't enough men. As President Muhammad Zia-ul-Haq watched on, he understood what they were screaming about. Many of the new laws that he was pushing weren't exactly popular with the female generation. From making a woman's testimony in court worth half a man's, to mandating conservative dress codes for women, to his efforts to ban women from leaving the country without a man to escort them. These policies had drawn the ire of women all over Pakistan & from the West, but these schoolgirls were incensed.

Breaking up those protests had been challenging, but eventually they were dispersed. Now, on the day that he had been set to announce the updates to the zina laws, thousands of women. Schoolgirls & adults both, were flooding the streets & surrounding important government buildings. They waved signs & banners proclaiming that they were a whole person, or that they were the victims, not the men that had attacked them. Of course, there were also the signs proclaiming that there were not enough men.

The signs were an attack of the new changes to zina laws that he had intended to announce that would impose harsh punishments on fornicating outside of marriage. Even some of his conservative advisors had warned him that this policy might not work to well with the deficit of men for this new generation. He had waived off their concerns. Now he wondered if that had been a mistake.

As military forces began moving in to reinforce the police & to try & disperse the growing crowds, Zia decided to delay the implementation of these changes until the situation cooled down.

"Sir!"

Turning around, Zia saw one of his assistants standing before him.

"Sir, we've received a new report from the police, they're making progress in dispersing much of the crowd around the courts."

"Excellent."

"Yes, but some of the dispersed women are now creating smaller protests throughout the city around universities, stores, mosques, wherever they can be heard by many people."

"I see. What are the police doing?"

"They're relocating what few forces they can spare, but this protest is growing sir. The military is considering bringing in a helicopter to get you out."

"Not yet. That would only give the impression that I'm afraid of them. Have faith that the police will turn this around."

"Yes sir."

The President looked out on the hoard of women with the new realization of their determination. A part of him blamed the West for inspiring such radical notions in women. Another part of him was beginning to realize that restricting women when women would be nine tenths of the population was always going to result in this scene before him.

February 28th, 1983
Supreme Court of the United States

Esther Levenberg sat on a bench in the halls of the highest court in all the land, waiting for a decision that could not be appealed or denied. It had been just a year since she had walked into a military recruitment office in Kentucky. Eager to serve her country & to fight the red menace, she, like a number of patriotic women, had decided to enlist. She & three of her friends had gone down to enlist together. Her friends were able to enlist, but she had been denied by that one little box next to one line of text on the application form.

Are you a homosexual?

She hadn't known at the time that ticking off that box & being honest would automatically disqualify her from serving. She was shocked to find that out from the enlistment officer.

"What do you mean it's illegal?"

"Mam, it's always been illegal for queers to serve in the armed forces. I'm sorry, but the moment that you ticked off that box, you were automatically barred from serving."

"Seriously?"

"Yes mam."

"What if I hadn't ticked it off?"

"Then you would have had to live in secret because if you are homosexual & you don't tick off that box, you can be court marshaled & dishonorably discharged for lying on military forms & being homosexual in the armed forces."

"Dishonorably discharged. Are you serious?"

"Yes mam."

"There's got to be a way."

"I'm sorry mam, but I've already filed the paperwork on the computer here."

Ester looked at the commodore 64 sitting on his desk.

"Can you take it off of the computer?"

"No mam. This computer is connected to a military recruitment office somewhere & they already have the forms. I'm afraid that there's no way to change them now."

"This isn't fair! I have a right to serve my country! We're all supposed to be equal!"

"I agree mam, but there's nothing that I can do about it."

"Well, someone is going to fix this."

That had been a year ago. A week later, she had found a law firm in New York that specialized in minority rights. They normally served racial minorities in civil cases, but they decided to take her on as well, a number of major law firms were dipping into lesbian & gay rights & this could be the landmark case of the century.

The lawsuit quickly surged into the spotlight. The whole country knew her name. Resistance to her demands was fierce. Conservative leaders & talk shows hosts proclaimed that women shouldn't be serving in the army let alone lesbians. Some proclaimed that the other women serving wouldn't be able to focus on their jobs if they were constantly worrying that the soldier next to them was eyeing them up. Some of them even brought women soldiers onto their shows to talk about what they thought about it. This strategy quickly backfired.

"I didn't mind at all. There were two of them in my unit & they never caused any trouble for us."

The host had been speechless for a moment by what the first soldier there that day had said.

"They... they didn't... they didn't distract from your duties?"

"No, because the us army does a damn good job of training its troops to focus on the job at hand. When we're on the job, we're on the job. When we're on patrol, we're on patrol. When we're training, we're training. Unless the person next to you turns purple, they're just another soldier."

"I... see... What about when you're not on duty? What about when you're in the showers or the locker rooms?"

The other soldier who had been mostly silent spoke up.

"Listen son, I know that you like to imagine that boys & girls always have separate facilities, but that's not always the case. We spend our free time with men, we often sleep in the same dorms as men & yes, sometimes necessity dictates that we shower with them. If we can handle men, we can handle lesbians. Besides, the lesbians in the army give us a lot less trouble than the men do."

The host's response to that had been to cut too commercial. Some General in the Army had seen that one & had ordered up an anonymous survey to try & figure out how many gay men & women were serving. The partial survey with a guarantee of anonymity had produced staggering results. Almost one percent had admitted to being queer on the anonymous survey. If that statistic was representative, that would mean almost seven thousand queers in the Army & over five thousand in the Navy. Enough soldiers to easily form a dozen battalions.

When that news broke, the country was shocked, especially when they realized that many wouldn't have admitted it even on an anonymous survey. Some demanded a purge of the armed forces. One senator from Kansas called for every soldier to be strapped to a polygraph & tested to root them all out. Some demanded the military policy of no homosexuals be revoked as it clearly was just getting in the way of America loving patriots who wanted to serve. One congressman from South Carolina suggested that a solution could be to put queers into all queer units, that way there would be no mixing of straight & gay soldiers.

As all of this raged on, the trial moved forward with the justices of the court hearing arguments about the issue from both sides. Conservatives brought up the issues of tradition & Christian morality & begged the court to think about the poor straight soldiers who would have to work shoulder to shoulder with queers.

Liberals argued that traditional procedures weren't going to be viable for much longer & that denying gays & lesbians at a time when recruitment of men was about to take a nosedive was ludicrous. They argued by bringing forth an endless parade of soldiers that proclaimed they had no problem serving with queers. They also argued that the ERA prevented the army from discriminating against women of any kind, lesbians included.

For endless months, the arguments raged on in the supreme court & in the court of public opinion. At the beginning of the month, the court finished hearing testimony & began the process of reviewing the evidence. Weeks went by while they contemplated their decisions. When word of a decision on the matter reached Ester, she made her way to the court & waited with one of her lawyers to find out if she would finally be allowed to serve. It was almost noon when her lawyer got hold of a copy of the decision.

"What does it say?"

"It says a lot, but if we skip to the conclusion… seven of the nine justices agree that the overwhelming evidence from serving & formerly serving soldiers, as well as surveys of existing soldiers, & the issue of real-world concerns, means that denying homosexuals the right to serve is foolish. It then goes on to say that such bans on homosexuals serving in the armed forces violate the equal protections guaranteed by the fourteenth amendment & the equal rights guaranteed by the twenty-seventh, also known as the ERA. Therefore, it is the opinion of the court that military homosexual bans are unconstitutional."

Esther read the decision three times before it sank in. She had won. The bans on homosexuals serving in the armed forces would be struck down in a few months & she would finally be allowed to serve. After hugging her lawyer, the two of them walked out of the court to a barrage of press who had also found out about the ruling & had heard that she was there.

Across the country, military recruitment officers had been prepared for this ruling & began taking a heavy black marker to their recruitment forms. Instead of going through the cost of printing up millions of new forms, someone had deemed it cheaper to just black out that one question on the form that would soon no longer be able to disqualify someone from serving.

March 21ˢᵗ, 1983
National Institute of Health, Bethesda, Maryland

Dr. Edward Swanson watched the news. Today was the day. Eighteen years since the birth ratios changed. Six thousand five hundred & seventy-four days had passed & in that time, he had made basically zero progress whatsoever despite heading one of the largest research programs in American history & often having a blank check to work with.

Looking at a picture taken of the staff in the early days, he wondered what had happened to the younger & more hopeful Edward. Even at forty-five, he still had a good long career ahead of him & many considered him a great success at the time. He remembered when his old boss had chosen him over doctor Harris because Doctor Harris was close to retirement & they were worried this project could go on for longer than he had left.

Now he was the one approaching retirement fast. The hope of the nation had been placed on his shoulders & in just two years' time, he was going to hand in the twenty-year report & then promptly retire in failure. At least he would finally have some time to spend with his daughter & granddaughter at long last.

For the time being, he downed a finger of brandy & began looking over some of the most fringe grant requests he had ever seen to look into the birth ratios. Although he was certain he'd end his career in failure, he'd be happy to not have to sort through this crap anymore. No more reading hypothesis about a pyramid in antarctica, or how liberalism had feminized the world.

Queens, New York

Elizabeth was glad that Sarah had pulled her away from her AP anatomy homework & dragged her to Fernando's birthday party. They weren't really friends with Fernando, but he had invited pretty much the entire school to his eighteenth birthday party.

About a quarter of the girls at the party were shamelessly draping themselves over Fernando in a desperate attempt to be one of the one in nine women that got a man. About half the women there were just hanging out & partying with friends while the rest were with their girlfriends.

That was where Elizabeth was, in a corner near a speaker, listening to Janis Joplin's last album as they made out. As per usual, when their hands started wandering to intimate areas, they pulled back. Having been friends since they were three, it was still a bit weird going to second base with each other, but they were slowly getting more comfortable with it.

"Glad that I pulled you away from your AP anatomy homework?"

"What are you talking about, you just gave me a crash course."

Sarah laughed as Nolan, one of Fernando's friends, came around with a camera.

"Want your picture taken to remember the first ninety to hit eighteen?"

They both posed for the camera, making stupid kissy faces as Nolan laughed & snapped the picture. After he left, Elizabeth kissed Sarah's cheek.

"Seriously, thank you for dragging me out here."

"Anytime Elizabeth."

"Are you always going to be there to make me take a break when I need it?"

"Always. Even when you're a big fancy doctor, I'll still make sure you're getting enough of all this."

Elizabeth laughed.

"Well, I seem to be running a little low of all this."

As Sarah grinned & leaned in for another make out session, Elizabeth believed through & through that they might just end up as the annoying high school couple that live happily ever after.

Just outside Chicago, Illinois

Hope knelt on a small pillow in front of the altar in the new sanctuary. Construction was finished & the building had just been opened & sanctified in Sunday mass the day before. It was always still a thrill to see Virginia preaching in the nude. It was always thrilling to stand next to her in the same way. But over the last month or so, Hope had noticed that more & more of the women in the congregation were starting to dress down a bit, sometimes even during the sermon as they became more comfortable.

A number of women had stayed at the sanctuary overnight to celebrate it's opening & a few had even requested to stay so that they wouldn't have to go back home. Now, on the great day when the first of the blessed children turned eighteen, Hope, along with a number of congregants, kneeled before the altar in the new church, naked, praying to God to communicate that they were ready to receive the second coming of his holy son.

Just before noon, Virginnia & another congregant, both nude, walked into the church to join them. Kneeling next to Hope, she leaned over & whispered in her ear.

"Sorry I'm late, I was moved by the spirit."

"I see, I didn't realize that the spirit was in Matilda."

"I don't have… Matilda, shit, I was calling her Madalynn."

"God, Virginnia."

"I'm sorry Hope, I really tried to be here on time, you know that I'm not perfect."

"I know."

"I really tried Hope, I really did."

"I know & since you made it here to lead the afternoon prayers, I forgive you."

"Thank you Hope. You have no idea how grateful I am that God sent a paragon of abstinence to help guide me. One of these days, you'll have to teach me how to resist temptation the way you do."

As Virginnia began praying at the head of the congregants, Hope wondered how she'd be able to explain to Virginnia that she had never once in all of her days felt tempted by lust.

Sacramento, California

Patricia Torres & her husband Hank watched as Senator Kathleen Howard brought the Matriarch Party into the national spotlight once again. A part of her had never imagined that the political party she & some other housewives had started all those years ago would now be a part of the US senate. Yet as she watched, Kathleen stood before the steps of the senate &

proclaimed that she was putting forward a bill to legalize lesbian & gay marriage in the United States.

"We've certainly come a long way since the days when you had me handing out pamphlets to the guys at work."

Patricia smiled as she held hank's hand.

"That we have. Not entirely sure how we managed it, but here we are. A senator of our own in the government & calls for us to open chapters all over the Southwest. Not bad for some housewives."

"Not bad all hon."

April 13th, 1983
Fertility Base, The Moon

She couldn't believe that she had been chosen for the Artemis one mission. NASA had almost two-dozen women that could've been chosen for this mission with previous experience not just on the Moon, but at this site. Sally had expected to be considered for one of the first shuttle flights. She had even pictured herself on the maiden flight of the Challenger shuttle that had just gone up a week or so ago. Instead, when she was given her assignment, she was stunned to find herself training for Artemis one. It would be her & the legendary Jerrie Cobb setting up the first actual permanent structure of Fertility Base. Cobb & Ride.

Officially, it was the Semi Cylindrical Universal Habitat A model or SCUHA for short. Of course, nobody actually called it that. They just called it the Quonset hut, because that's what it looked like, a reinforced, airtight, Quonset hut. The truly impressive thing about it was the simple fact that they could actually fit it into the storage capacity for their mission. It might have been the definition of minimalist construction, but it was still a thirty-two-foot long & sixteen-foot-wide semicylinder.

Having spent their first day unpacking the components in sheer amazement at the Tetris-like perfection with which they had been packed in, they had then begun to build the damn thing. With the arches of the building standing upright like the ribs of a fallen beast, Jerrie & Sally sat in the lunar module, eating their supper, exhausted.

"God, even with all those months of practicing, my fingers still feel like I stomped on them."

Sally put down her spaghetti & cracked her knuckles as Cobb grinned.

"Yeah, working in those gloves all day long is like working with boxing gloves on. One of the many things they leave out of the brochure."

"Do you ever get used to it?"

"Probably only when the arthritis sets in."

Sally laughed as she picked up her supper.

"On the bright side, at least when we're done building, we'll have enough space to actually stretch out a bit."

"Yeah, that'd be nice. As much as I love it up here, some of these missions are a bit to close quarters. It would be nice to be able to sleep & eat & not be up in each other's business like this. Not that I have anything against you."

"I get it Jerrie, even between good friends, this is intimate for two weeks."

"Exactly. It's even worse when you have one of the guys here. They've been decent & polite so far, but men were clearly built to shower more frequently than our water budget allows for."

Sally almost choked on her spaghetti as she laughed.

"Well, if that isn't something to look forward to, I don't what is."

"Artemis missions are going to be better than Apollo. It'll be great. We'll be able to actually spread out without going outside, in a year or two, we'll have the Saturn six with a bigger ship to take us here."

"No more sardine missions."

Cobb smiled.

"Nope. No more sardine missions. Honestly, I didn't get this close to some of my boyfriends."

Sally quickly swallowed a bite of food.

"Yes! Like look how close we are. We're practically eating supper in each other's laps! I never ate this close to my first girlfriend."

Cobb went silent for a second.

"What's up Cobb?"

"Girlfriend?"

Sally's eyes went wide when she realized that she had blurted out her first girlfriend.

"I..."

"Just a second."

Cobb went to the radio controls.

"Shit. Did anyone fucking hear that?"

Two & a half seconds later, a man's voice came on over the radio.

"This is capcom, I just had a bunch of static on my end, probably some solar interference like we get all the time. Nothing worth noting down."

"Alright, you get that cleaned up, we're going off mic for a minute."

"Understood."

Sally sat there in a full panic as the damn mic had just caught her slip & sent it to Houston where most of what they said was recorded for later analysis.

"Goddammit."

"We've got a few minutes before they start to worry about us. So... girlfriend."

"Yeah."

"Okay... okay... wait, aren't you & what's his name a thing?"

"No, no... no. He's interested, so I let him sniff around a bit. I figure that eventually he'll give up on me & move on when he doesn't get anything."

"Okay Sally, why not just tell him..."

"That I'm gay, no. I'm not telling anyone, except for you & mission control apparently. I know that it's legal nationwide now & half the kids these days are lesbians, but a lot of conservatives still work at NASA."

"Okay, that makes sense. Still, you could have told me when we started working together. How many times have we changed in front of each other or been in cramped quarters like this."

"Sorry. I couldn't run the risk of you freaking out & telling anyone."

Cobb sat there for a moment & thought about it.

"Well, I guess I can't stay mad at anyone for wanting to come here in a tin can with too few air fresheners so they can ruin their fingers by building a Quonset hut while wearing space gloves."

They both chuckled.

"I guess that you have to turn the mic back on now."

"Yeah, NASA isn't happy about astronauts going quiet for too long."

"How bad do you think it'll be?"

Cobb thought about it.

"Well, I would bet that until we get back, they're just going to pretend that they heard nothing. Then when we splash down, they'll have a few questions for you. Then everyone else will have many, many questions."

"Dammit."

Cobb flipped the switch.

"Houston, this is Fertility Base."

"Fertility Base, Houston. It looks like we had a bit of space weather there for a second. It looks good now, just don't forget about comms issues."

April 24th, 1983
Capital Building, Washington DC

"The shocking revelations about astronaut Sally Ride's sexual orientation continues to rock the country. This morning, when astronaut Jerrie Cobb was ambushed by tabloid reporters & asked what it was like to fly a mission with a lesbian, her response was that it was no different than the missions that she's flown with men, except that the smell in the capsule was more tolerable. Senators & congressmen from red states all over the country are calling for Ride to be removed from NASA. At the same time, lesbian rights groups all over the country are embracing her as an icon. She's quickly becoming the face of a growing push to legalize lesbian marriage. Governors & elected officials from the states of New York, Michigan, Wisconsin, & Illinois are calling for their legislatures to push through emergency measures to legalize these same sex unions."

Kathleen Howard turned off the radio in her office. She was trying to go over the bill that she was trying to put forward to the senate to legalize same sex marriage. She had intended to put the bill forward a week ago, but the world had started going a bit mad.

All over the country, starting on March twenty-first, lesbian couples all over the country were putting in marriage license requests. Some people were spreading rumors that some states had legalized it already & couples who heard these rumors were rushing there to try. Some people were just trying to see if they could get a license in their state. Some people were heading to Vegas to elope & a number of people were getting scammed by charlatans & conmen who were promising that they could perform a legal ceremony.

If all of that weren't enough, every single day, tens of thousands of people from the XX generation were suddenly old enough to marry & a significant fraction of them either wanted to marry another woman or knew that they would want to in a few years. Protests were popping up all over the world & countries around the globe were dropping their sodomy laws as this new generation of grown adults didn't want their government telling them who they could love or sleep with.

As Kathleen was going over one of the last items in the bill that she was going to propose, one of the senators from Louisiana knocked on her door.

"Hey there Vincent, what's up?"

"There's been another one. The Bahamas this time."

"The Bahamas?"

"Yes mam. Their prime minister just announced that their parliament has voted to repeal all of their sodomy laws."

"Wow, that's the second country this week & it's only Monday. Are they going to legalize same sex marriage?"

"No. At least not yet. I think that the commonwealth countries are waiting to see what the UK is going to do."

"When in doubt, refer to the crown."

"Something like that. How's the bill coming along?"

"It's as ready as it's ever going to be. The question is, will anyone vote for it?"

"Two months ago, probably not too many, but since they started turning eighteen, I think that we'll get a few more votes than we expect. Heck, a few states are trying to beat us to the goal."

"God, that's going to be a mess. We're still trying to convince a quarter of the states that legalizing being gay was a good idea, & now a quarter of them want to legalize gay marriage."

"Imagine what it'll be like next year with a presidential election in the mix."

"Jesus. It's going to be chaos."

"Just between you & me, a friend of a friend of a friend of mine may have heard something interesting."

"Nothing like third hand gossip. What did they hear?"

"Apparently, Carter is considering putting an initiative on the ballots for the country to vote for legalizing gay marriage."

"Not a chance in Hell. With how narrowly democrats won last time, he wouldn't put that on your shoulders next year. There are a lot of states that very nearly flipped to the Republicans & would have if Reagan hadn't been their nominee."

"You never know Kathleen. Stanger things have happened."

"Yeah, & we're dealing with the consequences of them."

May 12th, 1983
10 Downing Street, United Kingdom

Margaret Thatcher watched on in abject horror as parliamentary seats that she had won in seventy-nine were now going to the Labour party & the even to the Liberal party & the Social Democratic Party. Nobody in her campaign could understand what they were seeing. Chunks of the Labour & the Liberal parties had broken off in the last few years to form new groups like the Social Democratic Party who seemed to value some form of socialism, & the Queens party that seemed to be an ultra-feminist, royalist party that wanted Princess Anne to succeed the Queen.

Every poll, every survey, every appeal to reason said that she should be sailing to a majority of at least thirty seats. Instead, she was losing ground to leftists, socialists & feminists, three groups of which she was not fond. As the fledgling Queens party actually managed to win a seat from Manchester, Thatcher remembered the advice of from the campaign manger that she had let go.

"You're going to lose the country with your unwillingness to promote women's rights. This is the last year where the electorate will be split fifty-fifty between the sexes & the younger demographics see you refusing to promote a single woman to your cabinet. People under fifty deeply care about women's rights & you've ignored them."

Thatcher had waived him off. The swift & decisive victory in the Falklands War had earned some significant support along with an economy that was slowly improving. With the Soviets continuing to push to the Moon & building bigger rockets, her stance on defense had also brough her some significant support. Yet still, she sat there watching as her lead slowly evaporated.

Even the Soviets launching their fifth manned mission to the Moon the day before the polls opened didn't seem to be securing her the win. Districts that were normally concerned about defense weren't rallying to her as they should have been. She turned to one of the men who had been making calls as he put the phone down.

"Marshall, what' happening in Liverpool?"

"Nothing good. The Liberals just picked up one of our seats."

"You mean Labour?"

"No mam, I mean the Liberals. It seems that their stance on lesbian & gay rights has won over a lot of parents with teenage children who are worried about their daughter's ability to find a spouse."

"Dammit, has the whole country gone mad? These things don't matter!"

"They do matter mam."

Thatcher glared at the man who had dared to contradict her on this of all issues.

"I assure you Mr. Bennett, a person's sex has no importance on their place in the world."

"All due respect mam, it seems the country disagrees. The fact of the matter is that a person's sex does play a role in their lives, now more than ever as every subsequent election will have a greater majority of women voting."

Thatcher stood there silently as she debated in her mind whether or not she should replace the man with someone more sensible. Deciding to wait & see if she would still be Prime Minister by the weekend, she returned to watching the election play out before her.

All through the night, the labour party seemed to be nipping at her heels, overtaking her momentarily on multiple occasions. By the time the sun rose, a number of presenters were forecasting a Labour win while many more could not make a prediction. Finally, in the early hours of the morning, the results were in. With the last reports being confirmed, the last man on a phone hung up & tallied the numbers.

"Well Mr. Andrews, what's the damage?"

"It seems that we've lost twenty-two seats, bringing us down to two hundred & ninety-four seats in parliament, putting us just four seats ahead of Labour's two hundred & ninety seats. We've won by a rather narrow margin."

As the men in the room celebrated their win, Thatcher sat down as stern as ever. This was not a victory. Barely outnumbering the Labour party, any legislation that they tried to pass would be even harder than it had been over the last four years. Now they would have to convince thirty-two MPs from other parties to vote in their favour instead of two. Her ability to lead would be tenuous at best & in any confidence vote, even if her party was united behind her, she would need at least thirty-two MPs from other parties to vote in her favour or she'd be removed as Prime Minister.

July 16th, 1983
Ferris Barracks, Bavaria, West Germany

"To Eva!"

Debra's squad toasted the young corporal with glasses of sparkling water. None of them had been expecting her to end up pregnant. None of them knew that she had been meeting up with a local guy who owned a shop in town. They had all been clueless until a week ago when she asked Debra if she could talk to her for a minute for a personal issue.

"What's up Corporal?"

"I'm pregnant."

"Pregnant. I didn't even know that you were seeing anyone. Are you seeing someone or was this a one-time thing with one of the boys?"

"No, I'm seeing someone. His name is Jannick, he works at his father's fabric store in town."

"You've been dating someone in town? How long has this been going on & I didn't know about it?"

"Six months."

"Six months. Jesus. Have you told him yet?"

"He was the first person I told. He was so happy that he cried. He called his parents right away & they were thrilled; I think that he's going to propose any day now."

"Wow. Congratulations."

"Thanks. The thing is, this means that I'm going to have to use the new program, for pregnant soldiers."

"Of course. Patrolling the iron curtain is no place for a pregnant woman. I'll get the paperwork going on that right away."

"Thank you Sergent Foster."

Everyone had expected the new protocol for maternity leave in the military to take years to iron out & implement. But as soon as the new generation started hitting eighteen in March, recruitment centers started reporting massive changes. By April, it had become apparent that several new protocols for women serving in the armed forces would be needed immediately.

As militaries around the world rushed to implement new policies for women in their armed forces, other militaries that hadn't been preparing saw their recruitment & conscription numbers plummet as the number of men turning eighteen dropped by eighty percent overnight.

Grateful to be in one of the few militaries that had spent years preparing & working towards this time, the squad celebrated Eva's last night before she shipped out on maternity leave.

"Speech! Speech! Speech!"

With everyone calling for it, Eva stood up to give a farewell speech.

"Ladies, it's been an honor to serve with you over the last three years. You're some of the closest friends that I've ever had & I'm going to miss you all dearly."

"Aww."

"But the good news is that Jannick & I have decided that even though America is further from the red menace than West Germany is, we're going to stay here & raise little Tobias in West Germany."

As everyone celebrated the fact that Eva would be in town just a few miles away, it clicked in their heads that Tobias was a boy's name.

"Wait, you're having a boy?"

"That's right Sergent, we're having a bouncing baby boy! Jannick's father is so happy that we're giving him a grandson that he's buying us a house!"

The entire squad congratulated her as they realized that that probably played a factor into why they were staying. As Eva sat down, Debra stood up.

"Eva, we're glad to hear that you'll be just down the road after you come back from visiting your family to give them the news that you're staying here. We originally got this as a gag gift for Jannick since his English is so good. But I guess you'll be able to use it here if you're staying."

Debra reached for the bag under the table & pulled out the English German dictionary.

"Thank you everyone. Make sure you come & visit when you're not in the woods arresting stray Soviets."

Everyone laughed & raised a glass to cheer their friend once again.

August 3rd, 1983
Space Coast, Florida

Janet Hill walked into the apartment that she had been sharing with Rebecca ever since they moved to Florida in Seventy-four. Having just been at work for another fourteen-hour day, she was exhausted & just plumped herself down on the couch. Hearing her walk in Rebecca went to the fridge as she called out.

"Welcome home babe, how was your day?"

"I hate this state!"

Grabbing a beer from the fridge, Rebecca headed to the living room & handed it to Janet. Twisting off the top & sipping it, she looked to Rebecca & laughed.

"God, I've become a husband from a fifties sitcom, greeted at the door by my wife with a beer."

Rebecca chuckled.

"I don't mind if I get to be your wife who welcomes you home."

"That's so sweet, to bad we've got conservative democrats running the show here."

"Yeah I heard about that. Can't believe that they signed that into law. Not even going to recognize lesbian marriages from other states. I really hope that they get voted out next year."

Janet sipped her beer.

"That's not even the worst of it, some guy from the governor's office showed up today."

"God, what did he want?"

"Well, first it was more of the same with Ride, the Florida legislature is demanding that she be fired & that NASA make a public statement that we do not approve of sexual deviants in our ranks."

"Jesus, what happened?"

"The director reminded him that NASA is a federal agency & that the Florida legislature has no right to tell them to take Sally Ride off of Artemis three."

"Damn."

"That's not the end of it."

"It's not? Jesus Christ Janet, what else happened while he was there?"

"Once the guy found out that Ride is going to be on next year's Artemis three mission, he pulled some official Florida document out of some pocket & informed the director that the state of Florida had directed him to investigate the facility for any sexual perverts. That was when the director reminded him once again that NASA was a federal agency & that only the FBI had the authority to investigate their personnel."

Rebecca sat there in disbelief as Janet continued.

"The guy then actually tried to order the director to set up a conference room or two for his investigation. Story has it that the director then called security & had the guy & his cronies thrown out on their asses."

"Jesus. Can they actually do anything like that? Launch an investigation?"

"No. NASA is a federal agency, on top of that, the launch complex & the building around it are on federal land. Florida can't do anything about it."

"Thank goodness because they're really cracking down. They're sending police & swat teams into the protests & things are getting violent. I saw one woman on the news, she was being dragged away unconscious by guys in full riot gear."

"Christ."

Janet sipped her beer for a moment.

"You know Rebecca, there's a part of me that has spent all day wishing that I was in the protests. Even hearing what you just said, I'd still go if it wouldn't cost me my job."

"Same here. I'd love to be marching in the crowd, screaming for what was right. But then the cops might get us, or someone might recognize us. Then the school would have questions about why the unmarried teacher who lives with another woman is protesting in favour of lesbian rights. A lot of people in this state don't like the idea of a lesbian teaching high school students anything, let alone about literature. They'll accuse me of trying to make their kids gay by confusing them with propaganda."

"Don't you use school approved books?"

"Doesn't matter. Accusations will fly, complaints will be made & I'll be fired & black-listed. The way the governor is going, I wouldn't be surprised if he started organizing book burnings."

"I think that's a bit extreme Rebecca, we're a long way from that."

"No, Janet, we aren't. I've been to school board & PTA meetings, trust me, there are some people in this country that are just looking for an excuse to burn anything that they don't like. It could happen so easily."

Seeing that she had chilled Janet to the bone, Rebecca quickly changed the conversation.

"So how's Artemis two going? Did anything in your experiment sprout yet?"

"Not yet, but we can see some soil shift where one of the carrots is about to push through."

Rebecca listened intently to Janet telling her about the experiment that she had helped to organize before warming up some supper for her lover & dreaming of the day that they could be wives instead of just being lovers.

August 28th, 1983
Queens, New York

Columbia University was only a day away. Having graduated top of her class with honors & a few AP courses under her belt, Elizabeth had gotten into Columbia with ease. The best part was that with the campus being in Morning Heights, Elizabeth would be able to commute from home. She had thought that staying at home for her first few semesters at least would make things easier for her mother. She was wrong.

"God, my little girl is going to university. Where did the years go?"

Running her hand through her fresh pixie cut, she turned to her mother who was sitting on the edge of her bed & had pulled a photo album seemingly out of thin air.

"Where the hell did you pull that out of?"

"These are from your first day of kindergarten. God, the chaos that day. The whole morning was a circus."

"Doesn't answer my question."

Elizabeth sat down on her bed next to her mother.

"Look, Mom, it's not like I'm going off to war or Europe or something. It'll be like high school, but with a longer commute."

"You're still going to leave one day."

"I give up."

Elizabeth went to turn on the radio in the hope that a bit of music would help to snap her mother out of it while she picked an outfit for her first day in university. As the tail end of total eclipse of the heart finished, the afternoon host stopped playing any music at all.

"Hi there folks, I know that you're all expecting Prince's little red corvette to be playing right now, but I just got word from the studio about a major news event & the studio has decided not to wait until five to share this with you. It seems that about twenty minutes ago, the Governor of New York signed into law the New York marriage equality act. The new law which will take effect sometime early next year will legalize same-sex marriage in the state of New York, making New York the first state in the nation to legalize it. We'll have more for you on the matter at five when we go to our Sunday evening news. For now, as promised, we have little red corvette by Prince."

As the song started playing, Mary started crying.

"Mom? What's wrong?"

"Now not only are you going off to university, but now you & Sarah can get married & you'll move out & what will I have then?"

"Dad?"

"Don't be ridiculous Elizabeth, a husband & a child are not quite the same thing."

"Would it help if I told you that Sarah & I aren't going to tie the knot just because it's legal in one state?"

"You're not?"

"No. We just turned eighteen, I've got university & med school ahead of me, Sarah is taking a year off of school to work & save up some money. We're nowhere near ready to get married."

Mary wrapped her arms around Elizabeth & breathed a little easier.

"Still my little girl."

"Sure Mom."

Elizabeth was certain that when the day came for her to move out or get married, that her mother was going to be the biggest issue.

September 26th, 1983
Warsaw, Poland

As buildings burned & bricks flew at them, the members of the Polish People's Army retreated from the protestors to form a stronger defensive line around the Sejm, where the parliament of

Poland operated. The people had been raging for days all over the country & military reinforcements weren't having the pacifying effect that the Polish United Worker's Party was hoping that it would have.

Over the last several years, the protests had been getting bigger & more frequent. At first, it had been demanded that the government stop lying about the birth ratios. Everyone knew that Poland was being hit just as hard as the West & that the Soviet home remedy didn't work.

The government's response had been too double, triple & quadruple down on their propaganda in a futile attempt to discredit the protestors & journalists who refused to get in line with the government's version of the facts.

A year ago, when women approaching adulthood had started demanding that the government relax its sodomy laws, the government's response had been to reinforce those laws with stricter punishments, & to proclaim that these teenage lesbians were being corrupted by Western & American influences. Influences that were trying to wipe out their population by making them all queer.

When the teenagers refused to back down, the government went as far as to bring self-proclaimed experts onto television & radio interviews to talk about the possibility of instituting a breeding program where women whose first or second child was a son might be required to have many children in order to populate the next generation with those that could have more sons.

Every time that food ran out or that people couldn't get new clothing because of fabric shortages, they would march & demand that the government stop forcing them to use farm & factory policies that weren't working. The government's response was to bring in workers from other regions in Poland or even from the USSR & arrest the protestors. They were then sent to labor camps & made to work in misery.

More & more problems kept coming up as the country continued to struggle to meet basic needs while the reality of having a nine-tenths generation settled in. The stories of abundance in the West certainly didn't help as the communist party failed to crush these stories.

Then came the bag of bricks that would break the camel's back. The government announced that in order to maintain the capabilities of the Polish People's Army, it would follow the Soviet example & that effective almost immediately, all men upon their eighteenth birthday would be required to serve in the armed forces for at least two years.

This was it. If it had just been that, then they could probably have gotten away with it, but the people of Poland had had enough. As military recruiters started showing up to pick up the small number of young men that were now turning eighteen, they found themselves under attack.

It started with a woman in Poznan who came home from waiting in line for a full day for a loaf of bread. She saw three men in uniform escorting her son towards a military truck. With his father having already died in Afghanistan a few years earlier, he was the only man left in her household & she decided the military couldn't have him.

Grabbing a broken brick from a pile of garbage next to her, she ran up to the soldiers & without thinking, she cracked one of them over the head. The middle-aged woman attacking the soldiers drew on stares from the onlookers around them who had been half watching another son be dragged off to fight in the army. When the two soldiers turned on her & drew their sidearms to threaten her, the onlookers decided that they had had enough as well.

If they were going to threaten sweet little old Kaja like that, it was time for things to change. The two men found themselves surrounded by a mob of almost a hundred people. Realizing that they didn't have enough bullets, they grabbed their third man who was coming round & retreated without their new recruit.

The recruiters fled back to their base to file a report & demand police action, but by the time they had gotten there, word was already starting to spread that they had been driven back. People started talking about how they had so few sons & that they didn't want to see them dragged off to the army to protect a government that was forcing them to suffer.

By the time that the police started showing up to arrest Kaja, her son & the others that had intimidated the recruiters, a mob was already forming. They were demanding that the government keep their hands off their sons. The police tried to call for reinforcements, but news of the protest was spreading fast, more & more people were ready to stand up.

The government tried locking down the city & even cutting phone lines in & out to contain the situation, but it was worthless. Somehow, news spread to neighboring towns & cities. Within a day, protests were popping up all over the country.

Police tried to disperse the crowds & arrest troublemakers & convince society to return to order. But too many people had been pushed too far, & now they had their few sons to protect.

Wherever the police went, there were protesters with bricks, rocks & rotten vegetables to throw at them. When they tried to divide the crowds into smaller, more manageable groups, more crowds just seemed to appear from nowhere. The cops were outnumbered & a third of them were sympathetic to the people as they were in the same boat.

As the cops struggled to make any headway, the propaganda department went all out. Over radio & tv & on billboards, they proclaimed the virtues of the Polish United Workers Party & the Polish People's Army. They tried to convince people that other protests that had been much larger had already failed & that those who weren't arrested were already going back to work. They tried to convince people that the army was a great place to be & that the young men being conscripted were happy to be serving their country.

It didn't work.

Whether or not people believed that other protests had failed didn't seem to make much difference. They were tired of the struggle of communist life. They were tired of being hungry. They were tired of never having enough & they were angry that the government kept taking & taking from them while giving them next to nothing back. Most of all, the few people who had sons in the new generation didn't want to lose their boys.

By the beginning of the second day, it seemed that entire towns were rebelling & the police could no longer wrangle the crowds. The police surrounded important areas of government & finance. Forming defensive lines against the angry mobs. It was clear that all that they could do was to protect the vital parts of major cities from the chaos.

At the beginning of the third day, the police & the government were convinced that the people would soon run out of steam as they made little progress, & that sanity would be restored. By the end of the day, many police lines had to pull back as several officers had to be pulled away as a result of injuries. In the dead of the night, the government called in the military to help resolve the situation.

The military quickly rolled in with weapons & tanks. At first, they made inroads against the crowds, securing parts of cities & reinforcing the exhausted police. But the army suffered from the same problem that the police had. A lot of them were sympathetic with the people. Many of the soldiers were freshly conscripted recruits that seemed to disappear into the crowd. The crowds then seemed to miraculously have military grade weapons that they pointed at the soldiers & the police.

Many of the younger men in the army had only joined for a paycheck & had barely gotten that much. As such, they were in no mood to fight their own countrymen & people from their own neighborhoods. As for the older soldiers, while many of them were willing to do as they were told, many had no desire to stand against their own, especially when they saw the conditions that the people were living in.

As colonels & generals demanded that they open fire, many would intentionally aim high, pretend that they were shooting, pretend that their guns were jammed or pretend that they were busy with something else. Among the soldiers that had signed up to protect the people of Poland, they couldn't believe that they were being ordered to fire on their own.

It took the people & the mobs the better part of the fourth day to realize that there was little motivation in the army to actually attack their own people. This became the people's advantage & they pressed it for all it was worth.

Over the fifth day, in every major city, the protesters came at the authorities in waves, hurling whatever projectiles they could throw & overwhelming them with numbers beyond counting.

Meter by meter, their defensive lines pulled back, forcing them to evacuate some buildings that they could no longer defend.

In Warsaw, the police were evacuating a radio station used by the propaganda department to discourage the rebellion. The crowds were close enough that rocks & garbage being thrown were hitting the windows. A few of the more hardcore promoters of communism refused to leave, demanding that the police do everything in their power even as the crowds were mere meters from the front doors.

As people in the safety of their homes & among the crowds listened to the station. They heard the muffled sounds of propaganda specialists arguing with the police. They couldn't see the police throw up their hands & rush out of the office. They didn't know that the police that left the room were evacuating themselves, leaving these political officers with more balls than brains to the mob.

As the broadcast continued, the last line of police defense pulled back into the building & ran for the back doors as the mob rushed into the building. A moment later, the people could only listen as they broke into the studio.

"Know this comrades, these traitors that have been poisoned by the West & the American spies among them will be captured & they will be… Who are you, what are you doing…"

A thunderous crack could be heard over the radio. A gunshot that silenced the officer permanently. For a moment, there was silence & muffled sounds on the radio as people argued in the studio. Then a new voice came on.

"People of Poland, this is Wiktor Oleski. We have pushed back the police & military protecting this place & we have taken it from the ministry of propaganda. Hear us, the police are exhausted & demoralized, many within the army are not actually fighting us & we are gaining ground every hour. Soon we will reach the Sejm & we will liberate Poland from the Polish United Workers Party. Stand strong comrades, soon we will be free! Soon we will throw the communists out of Poland!"

All over Poland, the protests & rebellions seemed to find a second wind. As officials sought to jam the broadcast coming from Warsaw & downplay it, movements that were beginning to wane found themselves surging as people who had been staying home to remain safe joined the movement. Hearing that a prominent propaganda station had already been captured, many police & a few members of the army ducked out & slipped into the crowd, discarding their uniform & abandoning their posts as only the most dedicated officers & soldiers continued to protect the government.

As officials in the Sejm called Moscow for support, the leaders of the USSR debated whether they should send in units from the Soviet Army to retake Poland. In the end, seeing how quickly the situation was deteriorating there & considering the protests that they were dealing with themselves, the Soviet leadership decided not to intervene & instead, offered asylum to any member of the government that could get out of Poland.

As soon as the Polish United Workers Party got word that they were on their own, many of them started trying to get out of the country. As helicopters came in & took them out, they could only watch as the ring of police around the last few government buildings struggled to hold out the massive crowds of people trying to overthrow them.

As party members began to leave, so did the police who saw the writing on the wall. Even devoted members of the police began to disappear into the crowds.

As the crowds got closer & closer to the seat of government, they became even more emboldened. When half the party had been evacuated by helicopter, it reached the point that more helicopters could no longer land as the last ground was lost & the police had retreated to the entrances of the building.

Seeing that their escape route had been cut off, many party members tried to either surrender or escape. It didn't work for some of the more famous ones who had become the public face of some program or agency. After that, it wasn't much longer until the rebellion pushed into the Sejm.

The last members of the party were dragged outside by police that had defected early & ripped off their communist insignias. They would await trial in prison while a new government was formed. As cities all over the country realized that the capital had fallen to the rebel forces, many organizations abandoned the party & either surrendered or fled the country. As the people jamming the airways gave up, the new voice of the movement could be heard as Wiktor spoke on what had once been a propaganda station.

"The Polish United Workers Party has fallen! We've taken the Sejm & we've discovered that the Soviet Union is not coming to take Poland back. All that they've offered is sanctuary to the party members that escaped Poland. We are free brothers & sisters! We are free from the communists! Poland is free!"

October 14th, 1983
Manhattan, New York

Lena walked through Manhattan with a fresh interview recorded on a tape in her pocket & her notes in her bag. The interview was going to be for a new segment in the Lavender Press called interviews with the ten percent. In this rather experimental segment, she would find a man born after 1965, a man who grew up surrounded by women & outnumbered nine to one. She'd then interview him about his life & growing up & his opinion on several issues.

She had had her reservations about trying this segment. After all, Lavender Press was a newspaper written by lesbians, for lesbians. It was the last paper in the country that you would expect to care about the opinions of men. Still, it was worth a shot.

As she walked down the street, she came across the now familiar sight of the line of people waiting at the courthouse. Within hours of legalizing lesbian & gay marriage, countless people had proposed to their significant other & the courthouses had been inundated. People from all over the state & beyond wanted to tie the knot with their beloved. So many people were flooding the courthouses that many had posted signs to remind them that while they could get a marriage license, they wouldn't be able to tie the knot until January.

Over the last month, Lena had gone to churches all over the city to enquire about their position on performing same-sex weddings so that she could create a sort of map of the city that her readers could use to find a church that would be willing to marry them. However, finding a church wasn't the hard part in the end, getting a straight answer was. While many were adamant that they would not perform such marriages, a surprising number of them were willing to do it.

It had taken her a week to find a priest that would give her an honest answer as to why he was willing to preform lesbian weddings. He had figured that if only one out of every nine women could get married, the other eight wouldn't be too happy about how the church operated. It was a move of desperation to keep the new XX generation coming to church & filling both pews & collection plates.

As she had written about in her story that week, it seemed that the churches in New York were being divided along these new marriage lines. Some of them wanted to pander to the new generation & so they were rolling out the red carpet to these queer couples that wanted to live together as wives. The other churches seemed to be aligning themselves with older generations & more conservative folks who didn't care about the effects on society, they wanted marriage to stay between one man & one woman.

Walking back into her office, Lena found Sarah typing away at the new IBM personal computer. Lena had no idea how the hell it worked, but after Sarah had taken a class on how to use these things, she had convinced Lena to buy one. Lena had to admit that it did make things easier than using a typewriter. It was easier to fix mistakes & it was easier to keep track of everything since Sarah could save several stories on the hard drive at a time. If they ever ruined a copy, instead of needing to type it up again, they could just hit print & make as many copies as they wanted to.

Sitting next to the computer was something that Lena had never thought that she would ever see in all of her days. A newspaper typewriter gathering dust. It almost seemed wrong somehow. Society had been running on typewriters since long before she was born & now it was being pushed aside. Shaking the thought from her head, she turned to her intrepid young reporter.

"How's the story going?"

"Why would you let me write a story about something happening in China? Why would you let me do that to myself, I thought that we were friends?"

Lena laughed. Sarah's idea had been a good one. With same-sex marriage months away, she had wanted to talk to people about how lesbian marriage was going in China. The idea was to hopefully get a preview of what they might expect to see. Unfortunately, they didn't really know anyone in China.

"Do you have any idea how hard it is to get a Chinese newspaper in English? I had to call about a dozen domestic Chinese newspaper distributers to find issues that talked about lesbian marriage in China. Then I had to find people who could translate it into English. Then I had to find fresh immigrants who might know a bit about how it's affecting society in China, but it's so new that many of them didn't even know it was legal because they came from some small village that doesn't get all the news."

"Learn anything useful?"

"You mean besides how to curse in Cantonese? Yeah, I've learned a thing or two, like if you're going to legalize something, legalize it for everyone, not just the women born after 1965."

"Sounds like things are getting rough over there."

"Protests, demonstrations, lawsuits, imprisonments. Then there's the fact that their society is more geared towards family obligations, which means having babies."

"So, it's a bit chaotic."

"It's really chaotic & it's going to be like that everywhere. Most of the world works on the idea of a man & a woman, & now, there aren't enough men to go around. It's chaos everywhere & it's going to get worse before it gets better in most places."

"I know the feeling. Not only is there a bit of a civil war going on between churches in New York, but it seems battle lines are being drawn between states."

"What do you mean?"

"One of my friends in congress just told me that by the end of the year, a number of red states are not only going to reinforce their same-sex marriage bans, but they're also going to refuse to recognize same-sex marriages performed here in New York."

"Jesus. I can just picture the lawsuits flying."

"Yep. We're not going to be short of news for the next few months."

"If that's the case, maybe we should reconsider your ten percent interviews."

"Nope. Just got the first one & it's gold."

"If you say so. I'll have this story finished tomorrow morning. If you come in & hear Cantonese, it's me at the end of my rope."

November 29th, 1983
Topeka, Kansas

Dexter Simpson sat alone in the small restaurant. The last few days had been a bit of a roller-coaster. Of all the times for a special senate election, now was not the time for it. Over the last few days, he had wished that senator Hayden could have held out for a few more months, just long enough so that they could keep his seat empty until the general election next year. Sadly, the cancer had spread fast & now Shawnee county was in an uproar over who the republican candidate for the state senate was going to be.

Half the county was supporting Hector Green, a younger, more dynamic man who while extolling family values & the sanctity of traditional marriage & the nuclear family, also acknowledged that uncomfortable exceptions might have to be made in light of the new reality. The other half of the county was staunchly favoring Garvin Foster, an older & much more religious man who was doubling, tripling & quadrupling down on the traditional family, circumstances be damned.

For days, both candidates had been downright harassing members of the Kansas senate for endorsements. Like many of his colleagues, Dexter was struggling with which side to pick. On the one hand, like most republicans, he was a traditionalist & wanted to maintain the same kind of family & social structure that he grew up in. But on the other hand, reality wouldn't be denied. Much like with his party, it was an issue that was dividing him.

"Mind if I join you?"

Snapping out of it, Dexter looked up to see Luke Kaur, a freshmen senator that he sometimes gave advice to about some of the older members & rules.

"Have a seat."

"Mind if I pick your brain for a minute?"

"Let me guess, it's about who to endorse."

"You guessed it, Dexter."

"I honestly don't know. The back to God crowd & the traditionalists make some valid points. No matter how our country has changed over the last two centuries, the basics of marriage & family have been more or less constant. Radically changing something so fundamental just seems… dangerous."

"So, we should go with Foster?"

"Then again, one man & one woman doesn't really work out to well when there's nine women to every man. We've got a few more years before it gets bad as women from the new generation go after men a few years older than them. But it won't be long before that stops working. As much as I don't want to make drastic changes, the old way of doing things just won't work for much longer."

"So, we should go with Green?"

"I don't know. Green is probably the right choice, but Foster feels right to me."

"I know that feeling. Half the senate has that feeling."

Dexter took another bite of his lunch while he thought it over.

"You know, sometimes I think that the party might one day split over this issue."

"You can't be serious. It's just one issue."

"One issue that punches the very heart of being a conservative. The democrats were lucky, the birth anomaly is giving them an excuse to do a bunch of the things that half of them wanted to do anyway. Half of our party is pulling towards the center while the other half is pulling to the right. How much longer will it be before we can't bridge the gap."

"Maybe I'll just stay out of this fight."

"Probably the best idea Luke, although it's not going to work next year."

"Right, the general election."

"Yeah. Once we're done spending months ripping ourselves apart over this issue in this county, our party gets to do it on the national scale as we try & pick a candidate to represent us that both halves of the party will agree to."

"That's not going to go well at all, is it?"

"Nope. Either way, a large part of our base won't be motivated to vote. So, unless the democrats royally screw up in the next eleven months, we're probably going to lose the presidential election again. You realize that we haven't had the white house since Eisenhower left in sixty-one?"

"I'm aware."

"Progressive rights, a Moon base, this upsurge in environmentalism just because we've had a few warm years. The democrats have been in power for so long that they're getting to play some long games & I honestly don't think that we can stop them."

"It does seem a bit hopeless, but we've got to try."

Dexter went back to his lunch a bit more depressed than he had been before.

December 17th, 1983
Church of the Lord's Son, Fort Worth, Texas

For all thirty-four of the young women, it felt strange to be in church on a Saturday. It felt even stranger to be competing against each other. Reverend Thomas Edwards had declared that since the three young men watching the proceedings had turned eighteen, that it was time for them to start choosing wives from the similarly aged women of the congregation.

However, he did not want the men to simply date the eligible women. He had declared that dating was evil, it led to premarital sex & was a way for witches hidden among the womenfolk to trick & seduce their way into a marriage with a righteous man. He would not allow these wanton witches to lead the few young men they had off the path of righteousness. Nor could he allow for the men to simply choose a bride from the available women as the same problem would present itself.

To help the new men choose righteous women who would remain loyal to the church, he set up a series of tests that he would hold twice a year to weed out the wicked. He had proclaimed that witches would struggle with the duties of a wife to keep a home, & so the women would be tested in the womanly duties of housekeeping. Every Saturday, for a month, the eighteen-year-old men & women would gather in the church basement so that the women may compete against each other.

For this first week, the women were tasked with an age-old duty of all wives, sewing. Many of the families in the congregation had kindly donated old clothing that was ripped & torn so that the young women could demonstrate their skills under the eyes of the Reverend & the three men that they were competing over.

Some of the young women, like Eliza or Madilyn, knew that their parents were smiling as they found that they either had a natural talent for sewing or that the years they had spent practicing with their mothers & aunts & grandmothers were paying off.

Standing behind Zoe, Reverend Edwards smiled.

"Very well done, Zoe. Such nimble fingers. The Lord has clearly gifted you with a talent for this wifely duty."

"Thank you Reverend. I'm so fortunate to be so blessed."

Thomas looked into the audience behind the three eligible men to Zoe's father who smiled knowingly. The Reverend had long ago determined that his family was most righteous as they were large donors to the church & its many improvements over the years. So, the night after he had announced the competitions, he had informed Zoe's father & a few other true believers, about exactly what this first set of competitions would entail, giving their daughters a chance to practice at the exact tasks that would be required of them.

As Zoe's father beamed with pride, Lexie's father sat there fuming & turning red with anger. His printing company had been printing the churches' expensive bibles & literature for free for the last decade. A small fortune in lost revenue for his business so that he could be in the inner circle of righteous families & his daughter was just sitting there. Lexie was flat out refusing to take part in the contest. She & one other girl simply sat there with their arms crossed, refusing to even touch the needle & thread. Rumors swirled around that the two of them were witches or lesbians & that they had been corrupted by the government or the communists or the devil or the democrats or some combination of the evils in the world.

Seeing the anger of one of the large donors, Reverend Edwards sought to intervene.

"Lexie, my dear child, how are you going to win the heart of a righteous man if you're not even willing to try & show him that you too are righteous?"

"I don't sew father. I also don't cook or clean & if you have a problem with that, maybe I can tell the other girls how I know that next week's challenge is to cook roast pork with Carolina gravy."

"Carry on in your own time then."

Lexie's father was going to be furious with him. The rules said that if one of the young women refused to compete, she was supposed to be disqualified. He couldn't break the rules on the first contest, but he didn't want to upset his donors.

With over an hour left, he decided to circle back around to the problem child with a penchant for blackmail a little later, after he could think. Walking past Sienna, Amelia, & Carlee, he saw them struggling.

"Keep calm ladies, there are three more categories & if worse comes to worse, you can compete in the next competition in six months when some more boys come of age."

Amelia calmed down. The other two went into a panic & tried to rush it, resulting in poking themselves a few more times. Walking past Victoria & Leah, Reverend Edwards saw a curious sight. They had each sewed up a single rip in a single piece of clothing. They had done a fairly good job, but now they were just making themselves look busy. He knew why Victoria was aiming for a low score. She had been getting a little close with a boy who would only turn eighteen in time for the next competition. She was trying to fail this contest so she could win the next one. A clever girl, which made him nervous for the boy.

But as he ran his hand through his grey hair, he couldn't understand why Leah was doing the same thing. Based off of what he knew about the bonds between the younger members of his church, she wasn't interested in anyone. It was as if she didn't want to participate, but she didn't want to get in trouble, so she was doing the bare minimum.

Looking up, she winked at him. This threw him off. The young brunette had done that a few times over the last two months since she turned eighteen. He was going to have to have a talk with her about it. He decided against bringing in her mother on the conversation, just in case it was something innocent or unconscious. No need to worry the single mother unnecessarily.

Finally, he walked by Barbara & once again, he knew that she was going to be a problem. The three bachelors were basically just staring at her & it was not to do with her admittedly impressive sewing skills. He had reminded her to dress modestly, & she had dressed in accordance with the dress code. However, like her mother, she was… overdeveloped in one pair of aspects that men noticed & she knew it. She was the only one that he had hoped would fail badly enough to be disqualified. If a woman who was that shapely & seductive at eighteen wasn't a witch, then he didn't know who was.

"First hour is over ladies, only one more to go. While it's wise to take your time & get it right, I'd recommend that some of you also hurry up."

Several of the women, realizing that half their time was up & that they were behind, started going faster. Lexie glared at him.

1984

January 22nd, 1984
Church of the Wives of Christ, Illinois

New York City was chaos. Pure chaos as once the year began, it was the only state in the union where same-sex marriages could be legally performed. Hordes of couples started showing up just after Christmas. Parts of Dick Clark's New Year's Rocking Eve wasn't showed in certain states because Time Square was packed with queer couples.

The next morning, before the sun even rose, courtrooms all over the city & state had lines out the door & around the block of men paired off in suits & women paired off in dresses or white suits as they waited in line to tie a knot that many had thought could never be tied. Two of the women waiting in line in the first days of the new year had been Lexie & Bridget.

Lexie had joined the Church of the Wives of Christ in seventy-one, back when they were renting space in a strip mall. Attending that first service had been a transformation in her. A place where she could worship God & not feel guilty about her desires for women. While it had cost her dearly to leave the Catholic church & her family had cut her out of their lives, she had found a community that welcomed her in as is, no changes or hiding needed.

Bridget had joined just a few years ago. After fourteen years of marriage to her high school "sweetheart," she had been silently grateful when he left her for his secretary like a lame stereotype of a middle-aged corporate man. Saturday, he moved out. Sunday, she left the kids with her brother's family & went to church for the first time since middle school.

In eighty-one, they met by chance as they sorted out donations for the wives of disabled veterans. They were both proud of the charity that the church ran to help the women taking care of wounded soldiers. A simple compliment led to a conversation. A conversation led to a date. A date led to two years of happiness & the meeting of children & family. The day that New York signed a bill into law legalizing same-sex marriage, they both went to a jewelry store to buy a ring to propose with.

Bridget's husband tried to sue for full custody of their kids, calling her a sexually deviant cult member. In what had been a landmark ruling for the state of Illinois, he ended up losing custody when it was revealed that he had a serious drinking problem & was struggling to hold down a job.

Only one of Lexie's cousins even responded to her invitation, a polite refusal. Lexie didn't mind, she only invited them because they were related.

On New Year's Eve, they had been one of the couples crowded in Times Square, kissing each other passionately as the ball dropped to ring in the year.

Four days later, they stood in a clerk's office. Like many of the women behind them, they wore simple white suits as the clerk, his normal duties greatly delayed, stamped the document that they had just signed. Handing them their marriage license & a copy of their marriage record, he proclaimed them wives & as they kissed before rushing out the door, they could hear him calling out,

"Next! Number 147!"

With wedding bands on their fingers, they were one of the many couples jumping with joy in the big apple. With the legal aspect of their union out of the way, it was now time for the ceremony.

In the Church of the Wives of Christ, nobody gave them away. Instead, both of them, in beautiful, flowing white gowns that hugged their bodies & showed off their middle-aged womanly curves, marched down the aisle. Surrounded by the women of their community, they faced each other at the altar as Mother Virginnia stood at the alter to officiate. Clad in only a rainbow stripped stole, the garment covered her bare breasts & the two lengths came together just below her waist to cover her womanhood as she prepared to perform the first marriage ceremony of the church of two people who were considered legally married in most of the country.

They were both glad that someone was recording the event, because neither of them could remember what Mother Virginnia was saying. Once their vows were read, Mother Virginnia turned to each of them for the big question.

"Lexie Baxter, do you take Bridget Dixon to be your lawfully wedded wife, for richer or poorer, in sickness as in health, for better or for worse, until death do you part, so help you God?"

"I do."

"Bridget Dixon, do you take Lexie Baxter to be your lawfully wedded wife, for richer or poorer, in sickness as in health, for better or for worse, until death do you part, so help you God?"

"God yes I do."

As the three of them smiled, Mother Virginnia raised her arms.

"Then by the divine grace of God almighty & the legal authority of the blessed state of New York, I hereby proclaim you to be lady & wife. You may both kiss the bride."

Cheers, applause & organ music erupted from everywhere as they kissed. Even Bridget's daughters were happy to see them kiss. Walking back down the aisle, they walked into a barrage of photos before heading to the newly built community hall for their reception & dance & double bouquet toss before retreating to one of the commune's houses for their honeymoon.

February 14th, 1984
Harlem, New York

Grateful that her first class the next day was in the afternoon, Elizabeth waited in a booth as Sarah finished up her shift. As she waited, she continued studying her textbook to the point where her vision was about to go blurry. That was when she felt a tap on her shoulder. Sarah was standing there in jeans & Elizabeth's favorite sweater. No trace of the red & white pinstripe uniform that she had to wear for work.

"Ready to get out of here?"

"Just waiting on you."

After sharing a quick kiss, they headed out the door with Elizabeth leading the way.

"So where are we going tonight?"

"Well, at first I thought we could go dancing at a club, but then I figured that after eight hours on your feet, dancing isn't an option."

"Thank God, I couldn't catch a break today. I always heard that men are complete idiots, but you would be amazed at how many of them think they're going to get laid tonight because they took their girlfriend out to a greasy diner & sprung for lunch."

Elizabeth almost bent over laughing.

"So, no dancing. Then I thought that you might like to go out to eat, but I figure that you've probably had enough of restaurants & we don't need another night of being gawked at by older couples who are still surprised that women are dating each other out in the open."

"Sounds positively wretched."

"Yeah, so then I figured…"

Elizabeth pointed to the movie theater that they had just come up to with a poster of Arnold Schwarzenegger in a black leather coat holding a gun up.

"Terminator again? Look, I admit it's a great movie, watching Sigourney Weaver come back in time to save Linda Hamilton, all while Arnold hunts down every man that donated sperm at a specific clinic in a specific month is great. But we've seen it three times."

Elizabeth chuckled.

"No, I was thinking that we should see the new movie that just started last week, Police Academy."

"That's the one where the mayor changes the recruitment requirements & women from all walks of life enroll with the police."

"That's the one. It's supposed to be hilarious. No love scene between Weaver & Hamilton unfortunately."

"Well, you can't have everything, I guess. Still sounds good."

Paying for their tickets, they made their way in & found a cozy little pair of seats off to the side. As the movie began, they watched as the uncomfortable police lieutenant & commander looked over their new recruits consisting of nine women & two men.

Laughs ensued as endless comedy hijinks left the audience in stitches. Like many of the people in the theater, Elizabeth & Sarah only got about two-thirds of what was happening in the movie as they were constantly sneaking kisses.

At one point, they broke their kiss just in time to see one of the men trying to sneak into the women's dorm to be caught by the Sergeant who dragged him into her room & convinced him to say Yes Ma'am instead of Yes Sir, then had him walking back to his dorm at dawn. As they both got ideas, Sarah leaned over & whispered Yes Sir in Elizabeth's ear. Elizabeth turned to her & whispered Yes Ma'am before leaning over & kissing Sarah while she snaked her arm around Sarah's shoulder.

When the movie ended, they made their way outside to catch the bus to head home. As they were waiting, a guy got pulled over near them. When a women climbed out of the police car to ask him for his license & registration, he said Yes Sir right away & they burst out laughing.

The cop looked at them & then looked over to the movie posters on the theater & got the joke. Shaking her head, she took the guy's license & said,

"Yes Ma'am."

Elizabeth & Sarah couldn't stop laughing as the young cop played along.

March 17th, 1984
Rural, Alabama

Ronnie sat in the old barn, slowly drinking a cold beer. After being in hiding for over a year, the remnants of the Sons of Adam were finally coming out from whatever rocks they had been hiding under. Judging by the smell from some of them, they had literally been hiding under rocks.

The raid had left them devastated. Vast swaths of their organization had been arrested & most of the rest had quit & were now pretending that they had never even heard of the Sons of Adam. The twenty or so people in the barn were most of what was left. There were a few more still living out beyond the fringes of society. Ronnie honestly didn't know if there was even a point in trying to reach out to them.

The man that owned the barn was setting up the television so that they could all watch the news. It had taken the authorities some time to work their way through interviews & evidence & due process. After all of that time, the trial for the captured members had begun. Some were being tried individually, others in groups & watching the evening news was the only way that they had to know what was happening.

Flipping on the news, they watched a scene from inside NASA's mission control in Texas. A young woman spoke into a microphone as a crowd gathered to watch the special guest at NASA.

"Welcome back to mission control where Democratic frontrunner & likely nominee Ted Kennedy is being given a tour of the facility. With Republicans complaining about this year's estimated federal deficit of approximately a hundred billion dollars, many have criticized the space agency as a waste of money that could be better spent elsewhere. In an attempt to justify the cost of the ongoing Apollo program & the newer Artemis program, Senator Kennedy, a supporter of the space agency in recent years, was allowed to watch as astronauts Sally Ride & Darwin Ward tested a device named the… Lunar Ilmenite Processing Smelter, or LIPS for short. The device, a proof-of-concept project, proved its metal when it successfully produced enough titanium from the Ilmenite ore to make a one-gram ingot. Astronaut Ward spent several months training with titanium manufacturers brought in to help design LIPS. Senator Kennedy then had a few words to say."

The scene switched to the Massachusetts Senator standing in front of the large screen that showed the astronauts admiring the ingot they had produced. Ronnie & the boys half watched while waiting for the story concerning their brothers in arms.

"I'm not going to lie, there were times when I wondered what value there could possibly be in these field trips to the Moon other than some interesting science that might benefit our grandchildren. But now, as Apollo continues to explore our heavenly neighbour, & Artemis brings us one step closer to being able to settle a new frontier for the first time in generations, I see the value as America pushes forward. This ingot is proof that there's a place for American industry not just on our world, but others as well. As the Soviets struggle to keep up with American greatness, we cannot let up. A new world & it's riches, both material & societal are now within our grasp & if elected President, I will strive to make sure that NASA & one day, private enterprise can carry on the work of extending our reach to the Moon & beyond."

As the remaining Sons of Adam booed & proclaimed him a liar, the scene went back to the studio.

"Thank you, Lydia, in more terrestrial news, the trial of Sons of Adam member Lester Andrews concluded today. Lester Andrews is of course one of the members of the terrorist group who came to the attention of the ATF & the FBI when he began purchasing large quantities of materials needed to make large fertilizer bombs. The jury came back after a quick session with a verdict of guilty on all charges."

Ronnie wasn't surprised as the others groaned. After a moment, they kept watching.

"The judge then sentenced Mr. Andrews to twenty-five to life. His cohorts in the bomb making process will continue their trials next week. In the meantime, while police & authorities are certain that they've dealt a crippling blow to the Sons of Adam, it's worth noting that their leader, Ronald Adams, also knowns as Ronnie or Shepard, is still at large with a number of his men. If you have any information at all, you're encouraged to contact the police immediately."

Ronnie turned off the TV. As questions about what they were going to do next were asked by his remaining men, he seriously considered disappearing into the wilderness himself, like some of the members of the Sons of Adam that still hadn't resurfaced.

April 23rd, 1984
Oval Office

As President Carter read through the latest reports on the interim government being set up in Poland & the situation on the ground, he was considering the latest request from the country for humanitarian assistance. After decades of authoritarianism & communism, it was going to take more than a change in leadership & possibly ideology to fix the country's problems. He was reading about a new political party that was forming that seemed to want to embrace European style socialism & hardcore feminism when he heard a knock at the door.

"Cecil, come in."

Cecil Andrus, the Secretary of the Interior, walked into the oval office with a thick report held under his arm.

"Thanks for seeing me on such short notice Jimmy."

"No problem, I assume that worryingly thick stack of paper that you have there is for me."

"It is."

"One thing that I'm not going to miss about this job is the tons of papers being handed to me every day."

"I can imagine."

Carter took the stack of papers that Cecil handed him.

"Nine more months to go, so what's this report concerning?"

"Everyone's favorite topic. How the birth ratios are continuing to cause problems for us."

"Great. What is it now?"

"What isn't it. Power plants, fire departments, garbage removal, plumbers, welders, construction, pretty much every area of employment that typically involves men doing hard labor or highly specialized technical work is throwing up red flags."

"Let me guess, shortly after this generation turned eighteen, the number of people applying to be educated & trained in these fields went down."

"Indeed sir, like a rock in some cases."

"Haven't we spent the last fifteen years or so preparing for exactly this event?"

"We have sir, & that has helped. Instead of an eighty to ninety percent drop in people applying to these programs, it's more of a forty percent drop on average."

"That still seems high."

"It is. The reports do note that in more liberal regions of the country, there isn't too much of an issue. The drops in eighteen-year-old applicants are minimal. Much of the problem seems to be coming from more conservative areas where school boards & politicians refused to change how girls are educated."

Carter pinched the bridge of his nose.

"How bad is it going to get Cecil?"

"Well, we've still got a few years before the shortages of personnel hit since it takes time to go through training & there are still older men applying to these jobs."

"What happens when those few years run out?"

"Well, in some states, like battleground states, it won't be as bad. They haven't embraced the idea of women making up the bulk of the workplace like other areas have, but they have done some preparation. So, once they start running low on people for these jobs, they should be able to address the problem relatively easily."

"Plenty of overtime work for their technicians while they sort things out & reach out to women."

"Exactly."

"What about the more conservative areas? The ones that haven't been preparing & have been educating girls to be housewives to men that don't exist?"

"It's going to be bad. Even now that the numbers of applicants to these programs is starting to drop off, most of them are still refusing to admit there's going to be a problem. They don't want to see women working on powerlines, replacing sewage pipes, or bending rebar."

"You can explain the problem, but you can't change a culture that doesn't want to change."

Carter sat there for a moment contemplating everything that he had just heard.

"So, Cecil, what can we do about this?"

"Not much I'm afraid. We can run more ads & public service announcements to try & convince girls & women in these areas to reach for traditional manly jobs. However, that's not going to have much of an effect on them if their families & schools & pastors are all telling them to just focus on more womanly traditions."

"An uphill battle that sounds like it'll end in disaster for a lot of people."

"That about sums it up."

Carter leaned back & thought about it some more. Looking at a newspaper that had been left on his desk that morning, he shook his head.

"You know Cecil, just two days ago, I read a story about a group of people setting up a new basketball league. They want to call it the WNBA."

"The Women's National Basketball Association. I heard about it."

"There are also people floating the ideas of women's football leagues & bringing women's sports into the mainstream."

"Makes sense. With women making up more & more of the population, women's sports should become more popular."

"Yeah, funny how even a few red states can see that logic, but they can't understand that we'll need women as firefighters & plumbers & garbage collectors."

June 20th, 1984
Kennedy Space Center, Florida

Janet sat in her office with Gavin, the only other Canadian in the department that was working that day. Instead of doing what he should have been doing, which was analyzing some minor readouts from some experiment for Apollo forty-one, he was here, listening to the radio with Janet.

"While the progressive conservatives are still somewhat hopeful that they can get one or two more seats as the last votes are being counted, they have admitted that they have failed to dethrone the Liberals. Many in Canada were worried that after Trudeau's resignation, the Liberals wouldn't be able to recover. Yet it seems that Josephine Altman was the right woman for the job. Falling seven seats short of a majority government, she has nonetheless brought the Liberal party to victory, leaving the Progressive Conservatives stumped as she has become the first female Prime Minister of Canada. A historic moment on par with Margaret Thatcher's victory to become Prime Minister of the UK. Might it be that these two women mark the beginning of a new era in commonwealth politics..."

"Gavin!"

The two of them quickly turned around as one of the flight directors of Apollo forty-one ending his shift called for Gavin's attention.

"Yes sir?"

"Any progress on those readings?"

"Not yet sir."

"Then get to it, Commander Sullivan is going to need those results at some point. Janet, Elliot Hamilton wants to see in his office."

"Hamilton? What does the director of the Artemis Program want to see me about?"

"No idea."

Following Gavin out of her office, she made her way across the complex until she reached the Artemis division. Making her way to the director's office, his secretary indicated that she should walk right in. Naturally, he was on the phone, so she took a seat & waited for him to finish.

"Sorry about that Janet."

"No problem."

"Yes, well, thank you for coming in. I'm certain that you're wondering why I asked you in here today."

"The question had crossed my mind."

"Janet, you were the one who designed the agricultural experiment on Artemis two. I've just been going over the results again & it was amazing."

"I'm glad that I was able to help."

"As are we. Now you know quite well that we're now moving towards a permanent manned presence at Fertility Base, obviously."

"Everyone knows that. The President announced it on television."

"Right. Well, it's been determined that to help make this slightly less catastrophically expensive to the taxpayer, we want to be able to grow crops on site by the time that we're there permanently."

"Makes sense, less food to haul up would mean more room for other things which would make it all more cost effective. Do you need me to help design another experiment?"

"Well, yes, but that's more of the smaller ask. We're going to need someone up there, a highly qualified botanist that has both an understanding of growing plants in Lunar regolith & an in-depth understanding of the experiment itself.”

“That’s not a huge pool of people, People on Artemis Two might... Wait, what are you asking me?”

“I’m asking if you would like to go up on Artemis Nine?”

“Artemis Nine! Like, to the Moon?”

“Yes. You would go up with Olivia Woods who was on Artemis Two. It’ll also be the first ever Twenty-Eight-day mission, a full four weeks including a Lunar night.”

“Holy crap. When would this happen?”

“For now, Artemis Nine is slated to go up in October of eighty-six, so you would have about two years of astronaut & mission training.”

“Holy crap!”

“We don’t need an answer right away, the training would only start in September.”

“I’m in.”

“Well, alright then. Once Apollo Forty-one splashes down, we’ll start working on having you transferred to the Artemis program.”

“I’m going to the Moon.”

“That you are.”

“Not too bad for a girl from Montreal.”

“Not too bad at all Janet.”

“Wow, I... thank you.”

After saying goodbye in stunned disbelief, Janet made her way out of Hamilton’s office & slowly made her way back to her office. Artemis Nine. She was going to spend a month on the Moon. She had to tell..., well, she had to tell everyone. Her mother was going to freak out. Her father & her sister were going to be impressed & Rebecca...

That was the moment when Janet realized that she had just agreed to go to the Moon for a month without even discussing it with her girlfriend of seventeen years. Realizing that there was going to be an awkward conversation with Rebecca where she would be both proud & furious, she wished that there was someone she could talk to, but that would mean outing herself & she was still in Florida.

Peter Evan Fatouros

July 16th, 1984
Warsaw, Poland

Paulina Dulska stood before the assembled crowds in victory. The last few months had been chaotic for Poland. Now that the Polish United Workers Party had been removed from power, there was technically nobody in charge. The remnants of the police & the military worked together to try & maintain order as a transitional government was set up. As soon as there was someone that could be said to be in charge, the first thing that they did was to turn to the West & vigorously request humanitarian aid to help with the massive supply shortages.

Aid had come in droves as western nations welcomed Poland in from the cold of the Soviet sphere of influence & intended for them to not fall back to the USSR. The aid was never enough, but it was far more than what the Polish people had had for the last decade.

While the Soviets reorganized their defenses around the fact that their neighbor's nuclear weapons were now being pointed at them, political parties of every imaginable variation began to emerge. From parties that wanted to make Catholicism the state religion, to parties that wanted to return to communism, to parties that wanted Poland to split into smaller countries. Most of these parties didn't last long & eventually only about a dozen were left.

After almost a year, nationwide elections were finally held & after two rounds of voting, Paulina Dulska, the leader of the Free Future Party, had been elected as President of Poland. Now she stood before a crowd cheering for her & cameras ready to broadcast her message to Poland & the world.

"People of Poland, ten months ago, we told the communists that enough was enough. We had had enough of being fed just barely enough to keep us alive. We were sick of our clothes being held together by nothing but hope & rotten thread because there was never enough material to make more. We were tired of there never being enough of anything except for cruelty & hunger. The Polish United Workers Party didn't care for our plight, nor did the Soviet Union, so we threw them from our backs!"

The people cheered. Even people who had voted against her cheered.

"Now, today, we take the next step toward a future where we can all be free, where we can all be fed & where we can all live without fear!"

More cheers from the people around her erupted.

"I am honored to have been chosen by the people of Poland to lead us into this future. I wish that I could just snap my fingers & bring it here to you, but as we're all aware, it will take some time. We have a country to rebuild, different ideas about how our country should be & hungry wolves to the East that would love to devour us once again. But we are Poland, we've stood for a thousand years, & we will stand through the challenges to come!"

Everyone from hardcore liberals to ardent nationalists cheered her on as she spoke.

"As we rebuild our nation, we will seek to join NATO & form alliances with the free countries of the West to help protect us from the Soviet wolves. We will wholeheartedly embrace the elements of capitalism & socialism that are clearly working for other European nations. We will in time build a nation where we can live as well as the Americans do."

Another round of cheers disrupted her speech, giving her a moment to go over the next lines in her head.

"Many of my opponents over these last few months have criticized my intention to give lesbian couples any sort of legal recognition. I understand where they are coming from. While we got rid of our short lived & never enforced sodomy laws in 1932, I am just as Catholic as many of you. I understand why so many dislike the idea, but we cannot be like the Soviets, who are sticking their heads in the sand as young women come of age & ask who shall I marry? We must address the reality that we are living in. This is why I intend to grant lesbian couples the right to form civil unions."

Throughout the deeply religious country, few people cheered. Many were unhappy with this aspect of how their country was about to change. Still, a quick glance at the young & the lack of boys among them reminded them that sometimes, the solution to a problem is something that you might not like.

"The times ahead will be trying, & unlike anything we've ever been through before. But we will see this transformation through. We will stand tall, & we will live free!"

The cheers returned, not as enthusiastic as before, but loud enough. In Moscow, the party looked to find ways to discourage NATO from accepting Poland as a member. In the states, President Carter interrupted his review of the NASA budget to take a call from the Secretary General of NATO.

August 5th, 1984
London, England

Frederick Bailey barged into the cabinet room of 10 Downing Street, interrupting the Prime Minister's conversation with the Secretary of State for Defense.

"Ma'am, pardon the intrusion, but we have a situation developing in Trafalgar Square."

Annoyed, she turned to the Secretary of State for Defense.

"Sorry Philip, I'm afraid that if Frederick interrupts so brazenly, it must be an urgent matter."

"No worries, our situation isn't overly urgent, we can resume later on. Madam Prime Minister. Mr. Bailey."

The Secretary of State for Defense gathered his things & walked out the door, leaving them to their matter.

"Apologies again Ma'am."

"What's the situation Frederick?"

"It seems that we have a large protest brewing in Trafalgar Square."

"Frederick, there are protests in Trafalgar Square all the time these days. Just leave it to the police to make sure that nobody is hurt."

"No Ma'am, this is not like the normal protests. The police are being overwhelmed & are calling in reinforcements."

"Reinforcements? How large is this protest?"

"It's hard to say, it started gathering this morning & quickly swelled. Reports to the Commissioner of Police estimate the size of the demonstration at between forty & fifty thousand people & continuing to grow. That report is from an hour ago."

"Fifty thousand people! What are they protesting about?"

"It seems that they're not happy with Parliament voting against the bill to legalize same-sex marriage."

"That was over a week ago, why are they only protesting now?"

"Because of news from America."

"God, what have those liberals done now?"

"It seems that there's a celebration going on in the state of Michigan because they've become the second US state to legalize same-sex marriage."

"How does that create a protest of fifty thousand here?"

"Because multiple stories about the event included details of other states & other countries that are considering legalization in order to get ahead of what some are calling the looming marriage crisis. Countries all over the world are considering everything from decriminalizing homosexuality for women to allowing for same-sex marriage or civil unions, & many people in the UK now see us as a stick in the mud."

"Frederick, correct me if I'm wrong, but if memory serves, technically, lesbianism has never been a crime in the United Kingdom."

"You are correct ma'am, a fact that has been of great benefit to us over the last few years as girls & now young women are becoming the clear majority of the population."

"So, what is the problem?"

"The problem, ma'am, is that there's a difference between dating & marriage. Most people in this generation want to settle down with a spouse, not a lover. On top of that, there's the issue of gay men, & older lesbians. They want to be able to marry as well."

"For God's sake. Is there no end to this."

"It certainly doesn't help us that Canada just legalized same-sex civil unions a few weeks ago & that several of our neighbours are considering doing the same."

Thatcher pinched the bridge of her nose.

"There has to be a way to make these people see reason."

"I'm sorry ma'am, but with every month that passes, it's getting harder & harder to convince people that traditional marriage is a viable option on its own. If we want to maintain order & a conservative government, we are going to have to compromise at some point & give some form of legal recognition to homosexual couples. At the very least, we'll have to give some form of legal recognition to lesbian couples."

"No."

"No? ma'am?"

"Mr. Bailey, it is bad enough that these children have had to grow up in an environment where there were almost no boys. We cannot allow these people to further confuse the youth by compromising with them. Parliament voted against legalization & that's the end of the issue."

"Then I fear that it may be the end of this Parliament."

"We will persevere Mr. Bailey."

"I hope so ma'am."

"Keep me appraised of the protests Mr. Bailey."

"Yes Ma'am."

August 27th, 1984
Greensboro, North Carolina

Pax walked into the living room of his house to find his father still at home & watching the morning news.

"That was democratic Presidential nominee Ted Kennedy promising that under his administration, he would move NASA to both lower the costs of manned Moon missions & promising to continue Carter's directive for America to have a permanently manned base on the Moon by 1990. This speech comes ahead of the maiden flight of America's new space shuttle Discovery. In recent months, a number of..."

"Hey there Paxton, ready for your first day of high school?"

William stood up & turned off the TV.

"Sure. What are you still doing home?"

"Told my boss that I was coming in late today so that I could drive my boy to his first day of high school."

Pax stood there dumbfounded & worried.

"Don't worry Paxton, I'm not going to drive you up to the front gate & scream out I love you. I'll drop you off at the corner & you can walk the rest of the way."

Pax visibly relaxed.

"Thanks Dad."

"Had you scared there for a minute, didn't I?"

"A little bit, yeah."

William smiled.

"Come on Son, it's a big day for you. We don't want you to be late on your first day of high school."

"Alright."

Pax followed his father out to the car. When they got in & William got it running, the radio came on. As the morning news talked about traffic conditions on the I-40, they also reminded listeners that George H. W. Bush had won the republican nomination for President.

"I suppose he was their best choice."

"What do you mean Dad?"

"Oh, yeah, guess that you're still a bit young to be interested in politics."

"Yeah, but it's all over TV & the radio."

"I suppose. I meant that he's the best choice for the republicans because he's reasonable. He's willing to compromise & right now, that's exactly what they need in a candidate because the party is ripping itself apart."

"It is?"

"Yeah, you've got some people like congressman Elliot or Senator Doyle who realize that the country is changing & the party is going to have to adapt to the way things are now. Then you've got people like Hampton & Mills who are doubling down on the traditional way of doing things, even though it's not going to work for much longer."

"Because there aren't enough boys."

"That's right Paxton. How many boys are there in your homeroom this year?"

"Four, me, Tom, Leo & someone from another middle school."

"So, four out of thirty-four."

"Yeah."

"When I was in high school, boys were half the class. If there were thirty-four kids in a class, about seventeen of them would be boys."

"Wow."

"Yeah. So, when it comes times for school dances, if you have to do things the way that we did, then only four girls would get to have a date while the other… thirty-four minus four & minus four… the other twenty-six girls wouldn't be able to have a date for the dance."

"That would suck."

"Yes, it would. You think that you might like to take a girl to a school dance?"

Pax thought about it for a moment.

"Would I have to take just one?"

William laughed.

"In the old days, yes. These days, I hear that a boy going with a few girls might be an option in some schools."

"Sounds complicated."

"Get used to it Son, life loves to be complicated & it often finds new ways to do it."

As they turned onto the street that Pax's new school was on, they saw Leo walking up.

"Here's your stop Paxton. Looks like you we're just in time to catch Leo."

"Yeah. Thanks for the ride, Dad, & thanks for being cool & dropping me off here."

"No problem, Paxton. Have a good first day."

"Thanks dad!"

Like a shot, Pax was out the door & catching up to Leo. William watched his son head off to High school for the first time as Pax & Leo talked.

"Hey Pax."

"Hey Leo, any sign of Tom?"

"Yeah, I just saw his mom's car heading to the school."

"Here's hoping that she just drops him off."

September 4th, 1984

Houston, Texas

Hollie Dawson hung up her apron. It was annoying to have to wear an apron as part of her uniform, but at least it wasn't frilly like the ones she sometimes had to wear back home. This was just a simple dark green apron that she had to wear as she worked all day long, packing groceries. Still, at least she was allowed to wear pants. That had been one of the best parts of leaving the Church of the Lord's Son several months ago. She would never again have to wear a dress, a skirt, or a gown.

She remembered that December night last year. About a week before Christmas & the night before the ridiculous tests that the reverend had set up to prove their womanly virtue. Recently single from having been dumped by her boyfriend of three weeks & having recently turned eighteen, she decided that it was finally time to get out.

When her parents & her brother & her three sisters had all gone to sleep, she snuck out of her bed. Careful not to wake up her sister, she put on the one pair of pants that her father hadn't found. They were ripped in the knees & a bit dusty, but as she slipped into them, she knew she wasn't coming back. She packed a few things into a duffle bag, food, water, what little money she had been able to get her hands on & some underwear. Not one dress was packed.

She left a note for her sister. Her sister was the only family member that wouldn't rat her out for having pants or money. Mostly because they shared a room & she liked keeping secrets. The note didn't mention where she was going because she wasn't entirely sure herself.

Carefully slipping out of the house just before midnight, she then walked four miles to the nearest intercity bus stop. Her original plan had been to get a bus that led out of state. But when she got there, she saw that those wouldn't leave until morning. Not wanting to risk her parents waking up early to prepare her for the contest & coming to look for her, she changed tactics. She got a ticket on the next bus out of Fort Worth & figured that wherever she ended up, she'd regroup from there.

Twenty minutes later, she was on an all-night bus & six hours later, she found herself in Houston. The station that she was at could send her East to Georgia, or all the way West to California. But when she saw how little money she had to work with, she came up with a new plan again.

With the shortage of young men her age, there were plenty of companies, even in a red state like Texas, which were hiring young women. She figured that she could get a job for a few weeks, earn some money & then keep on moving away from Fort Worth.

A few weeks turned into several months.

Houston was unlike Fort Worth in just about every way. Sure, there were still conservative & traditionalists everywhere, but they clearly weren't running the show. Young lesbian couples walked around hand in hand everywhere. Countless women wore short hair & more masculine clothes like she did & she quickly found out that a woman alone could make a life for herself now that women were being hired to do all kinds of jobs, especially the jobs normally held by teenagers & young adults.

She had spent her first month in the city living in a run-down motel. Then the next several months living in a better motel. Now, after nearly ten months, she had realized that she had no interest in leaving Houston. She was certain that her family either couldn't find her or weren't looking for her. Houston was also a place where she wasn't constantly getting stares for dressing masculine & where she could easily find men & women to be with.

Having realized that it had been several months since she had even checked the bus routes, she realized that she was feeling at home. Then there had been this morning when her manager asked to see her in his office.

"You wanted to see me, Frank?"

"Yes, please close the door, Hollie."

"What's up?"

"Is everything going alright in your home life?"

"Why do you ask?"

"Well with the recent turnover in some of our departments, I've been reviewing the personnel files to look at who I can move around in the store & I noticed something odd about your home address."

"What's odd about it?"

"It's a motel."

"Yeah... I'm currently between homes."

"I see. Do you intend for your next home to be in the area?"

"I'm not sure, why?"

"Well, you do a good job; you seem to get along well with the others & you seem to be enjoying your work. So, I was contemplating promoting you to cashier. But if you're going to be moving away soon, I'm thinking that I should give the position to someone a little more permanent."

"I see."

"So, are you?"

"Am I what?"

"Moving anytime soon."

It took a second for Hollie to realize what her manager was saying. He wasn't telling her that she was being passed over for promotion because of her lack of a permanent address. He was offering her a promotion if she was intent on staying. Her plans to flee to some far-off blue state where her family wouldn't even think to look for her flashed before her eyes.

"No. I mean, I will be moving out of the motel at some point soon, but I think that I'll be staying in Houston."

"Well in that case, I'll tell Laura that she's got to train you on the cash register tomorrow."

The rest of the shift had gone by in a flash. That evening, instead of checking out bus routes & train schedules, Hollie found herself looking at apartment listings. This city was going to be her new home. Her sanctuary.

September 15th, 1984
Los Angeles, California

Govind Dayal sat before his Saturday morning class. Many of his students thought that the bright pink turban was an odd choice for someone trying to help couples have sons. Still, they were certain that where Western medicine had failed, some ancient Eastern practices would work. Once they were all seated in their best approximations of the lotus pose, Govind picked up a newspaper & read it out.

"Early this morning, Diana Princess of Wales, gave birth to Princess Harriot Charlot Anne Elizabeth. Princess Harriot is the second daughter & child of Charles Prince of Wales & Diana Princess of Wales. Many rumors had started to spread that their second child would be a boy & would therefore be made the heir presumptive over their older sister Princess Elenor. However, these unfounded rumors have been put to rest as Princess Harriot now sits as third in line for the throne."

Govind put down the newspaper page from the morning paper & faced his students.

"Even the royal family, with the Queen being the head of state of I believe eighteen nations, even they are not able to dispel this corruption. Even they can only give birth to daughters. Yet you have all seen with your own eyes the success of my practice. Just last week, Charlotte gave birth to a healthy baby boy & let us not forget Mariana who just last month welcomed her own son into the world. I know that many of you think that some of these practices are strange & that the teas taste funny. In all fairness, they do taste funny sometimes."

Most of the students chuckled.

"But as you can see, the process works. Let us not be distracted by how silly some of it may look. Whether it is a strange position, a strange sounding name, a funny tasting tea or a teacher wearing a pink turban..."

Many of them chuckled once again.

"Let us not let a little silliness distract you from your desire to have a son. Come, let us begin."

Over the next hour, Govind carefully guided them all through their meditation. As he occasionally walked among the crowd, he kept noticing that Aubree wasn't there. She had been a part of his Saturday morning class for three years & she never missed a class, except to give birth to her three daughters.

As soon as the ultrasound came back as another girl, he knew that he had to move her to another group. These classes worked on faith. Faith that he could remove the blockage that was preventing boys from being conceived. A woman in his practice with three straight daughters in a row would undermine that.

Having planned for such eventualities, he had ensured that some of his classes would be for those that he claimed were having trouble with the process. It was a great plan. When women kept having daughters, he simply put them in a class for those having difficulties & they accepted that the problem was with them.

Unfortunately for him, those classes were filling up faster than he had anticipated. He had figured that after a while, these students would give up & consign themselves to be the parents of daughters. But some, like Aubree, seemed hellbent on continuing to try & try until they succeeded. He was now running out of classes to put these women & couples in.

Taking a page from the way that many nations were feminizing to account for the growing lack of young men, he had been considering getting his wife to help him lead the classes instead of simply help out from time to time. They could have larger classes & accommodate more students. However, as Jessica walked past him & winked at him, he felt that bringing his wife in on this full time was a dangerous idea.

The pregnancy scare with Jessica a month ago had scared the crap out of him. She & her husband were as pale as snow & Leon was smart enough to figure out that his wife giving birth to a half Indian baby was not the result of intense meditation.

If he brought his wife in on this, then he would have to stop taking such foolish risks as sleeping with his students. Sure, it was fun, but if his wife found out that he now had two children outside of their marriage, she'd make sure they were the only two children that he had outside of their marriage. Even worse, if the students found out that most of his children were daughters & that he had lied to them, his practice was done for. He couldn't risk more daughters.

"I must be faithful; I must be faithful."

As he whispered to himself, Ireena walked past him & winked as well. As he continued whispering, he could feel his newfound will to resist her invitations fading.

November 6th, 1984
Columbia, South Carolina

Joel Thomson stood in front of the podium set up just outside the South Carolina Republican Headquarters. He stood before a cheering crowd of men & women waving American flags & bibles, many of them chanting his name. Smoothing back his blonde-tinged grey hair, he stood before his adoring crowd & spoke over the loudspeakers.

"My fellow South Carolinians! The verdict is in! While there are still a number of votes to count, the Democrats can no longer get enough to hold on to this state! Come January, I will be your new Governor!"

The crowd erupted in applause & cheers at having dethroned the progressives from the state.

"There is still a seat or two up for grabs in the state assembly, but we already have a majority in the general assembly! The liberal rain of Carter & the democrats comes to an end in South Carolina!"

A crowd lacking in young women roared in approval.

"We've won South Carolina & Virginnia & Connecticut tonight folks, & we're going to keep winning state after state & come the morning light, every newspaper, radio show, news show & talk show will be celebrating that for the first time since Dwight D. Eisenhower left office in sixty-one, a republican will sit in the white house!"

The applause was thunderous as young women all over South Carolina lamented & considered leaving.

"We'll reverse these liberal amendments, we'll force New York & Michigan to stop marrying queers & sodomites, & we'll make this country God's country once again!"

An almost religious fervor overtook the crowd as they cheered for their impending victory.

Frankfurt, Kentucky

Edgar Bolton had watched Joel Thomson's speech two hours earlier & had shaken his head. It had been far too early in the night to proclaim the new President. As much as he wanted George H. W. Bush to succeed over Ted Kennedy, declaring victory when only ten states had been called was a bit short sighted.

But now that North Carolina, Kentucky & Alabama had all come back into the fold & thrown off the democrats, he was feeling confident. In his head, he thanked the democrats for overstepping. Sure, people loved going to the Moon, but it was already ridiculously expensive & they wanted more & more. Sure, there were going to be some issues with finding husbands for these young women, but they still had time. They didn't need to start legalizing lesbian marriage. The dems had overstepped & the country was coming home.

"Mr. Bolton, ABC news, do you think that it's still too early in the night to be proclaiming victory for the republicans?"

Edgar snapped out of his moment of accepting that he was going to the US senate & returned to the cameras in front of him.

"Not at all. Seventeen states have been called & we already have a thirty-one-point lead. States that voted Carter in seventy-six & eighty are coming around to the party of God & country & I feel that we can now confidently say that America has gotten over its birth ratio panic & is willing to see reason again."

As the people behind him cheered, more reporters started clamoring to ask him questions.

Jackson, Mississippi

Salenna Berry toasted her win along with her fellow new US congressmen heading to DC when she found a microphone being shoved in her face.

"Ms. Berry, CBS news, not a lot of people had you picked to beat Kramer. How does it feel to be chosen to represent Mississippi's second district?"

"I've got to say, it feels great."

"Are you surprised that Mississippi didn't flip to the republicans?"

"Not at all. Sure, they made a few unexpected wins, like in Alabama, but the count is far from over & the night is young despite the hour."

"The republicans do seem to have an early lead in this election."

"True, but we're gaining on them. They're only ahead by seventeen points & most states haven't been counted yet."

"Do you think the democrats will win the election?"

"Sir, the democrats have not lost an election in twenty-four years, we're not starting tonight!"

As Salenna turned back to the party, the reporter turned to the camera.

"Well, there you have it. The democrats might have been slow to start tonight, but they are not out of the race as they continue to gain ground. We can only wait & see who will come out on top."

Columbus, Ohio

"Mr. Walsh! Mr. Walsh!"

Brandon Walsh quietly ignored the reporters calling out to him from the entrance. He was far too busy hugging his wife as they celebrated his victory.

"Looks like they haven't run me out of town like Horton said they would."

"I bet that he's fuming tonight from losing to you yet again."

"Definitely red as a lobster."

"Mr. Walsh!"

"Go be a leader; we've got all night to celebrate."

Brandon kissed his wife & walked towards the hungry press that was demanding his attention.

"Mr. Walsh!"

"Yes, what can I do for you?"

"Mr. Walsh, several polls had you & the democrats losing the state of Ohio, what do you have to say about your surprise win here tonight & what do you think it means?"

"Well, I have to say the same thing that I've been saying for months. You can't always trust the polls, especially when they're being done by a very biased company that's trying to write a narrative before it happens. They all predicted that Ohio would stay red & that I'd be one of the few blue representatives in the state. Instead, Michigan & Florida stayed blue while Pennsylvania & Ohio flipped to blue."

"What do you say to republicans who are saying they can still turn this around?"

"Before most states had closed their polls, the republicans had... what was it, a forty-point lead or so. Now we're ahead by fifty-one points. The momentum of this election is taking us to a new Kennedy administration."

"What do you say to Horton who's demanding a recount?"

"I say that we can count the votes of Ohio all he wants. Ohio, like many states, is rejecting a conservative party that is out of touch with reality & refuses to admit that their traditions aren't going to work anymore. Americans can see that they're stuck in 1964 & Americans are saying no to the delusion of a party that refuses to pull its head out of the sand."

"Was it a surprise for you when Florida remained with the democrats?"

"No surprise for me. Florida's legislature has been riddled with some of the most extreme traditionalists in the country. At one point, they even tried to conduct a lesbian witch hunt in NASA. I'm not at all surprised that their republican legislature lost their majority & I won't be surprised if their conservative democrat governor gets replaced in eighty-six with a progressive."

"What do you say to those that are claiming America is abandoning its traditions?"

"I would say that America's true tradition has always been that she is a nation of innovation, progress & change. We have always been the country that wasn't afraid to push forward, to test limits & push boundaries. That's why in just two-hundred years, we've gone from being farmers & settlers to the greatest nation on Earth!"

As Walsh turned to another reporter, midnight parties were breaking out all over several states as traditionalists were thrown out of office.

New Mexico

It was only when the coffee hit Felix's brain that the news sunk in. His party had won & he was going to be New Mexico's new republican us senator.

"Congratulations Felix."

Ethan, his predecessor who was leaving the job two years before the end of his term to run to run for governor, clapped him on the shoulder.

"Looks like we're both getting a promotion."

"We sure are boss."

"Think, in a few hours, they'll announce Bush as the President, & then we can start fixing this country."

Felix looked up at his mentor, the normally reasonable man that he had been working for over the last decade.

"Ah, sir, are you sure about that? Nationally, we're now sixty points behind the democrats."

Ethan waived it off.

"Don't forget, except for Illinois, everything East of the Mississippi has already been counted & called. It's just what's West of the Mississippi that's left to count & almost all of that went to us last time around."

"True, but what if..."

"What if what? What if Texas & California turn blue? Impossible. There might be... a hundred & fifty..."

"A hundred & fifty-Two electoral votes."

"Felix, there may be that many votes left, but we'll get just about all of them. The West will vote red, just like back in eighty & we'll take the white house."

"If you say so sir."

As the sky outside began to lighten ever so slightly, Felix wondered if they would really be able to hold everything West of the Mississippi river.

Springfield, Illinois

With the light of dawn threatening to appear within the next hour, democrats celebrated their reelection & gains in Illinois as republicans asked themselves what had gone wrong. As reporters that were fresh from a few hours of sleep & strong coffee arrived to relieve the ones about to keel over, tired politicians turned their heads as a newly elected progressive congressman spoke up.

"Congrats everyone. I'm going to bed. Somebody wake me up when Kennedy wins."

Everyone laughed as he sat back down & began preparing for interviews with reporters who had the audacity to have gotten some sleep. Only twenty-three points short of getting the white house for another four years, many wondered if Kennedy's efforts to flip the Western states had paid off.

Austin, Texas

As Senator James Harris celebrated his victory in becoming Governor of Texas, he welcomed the morning wave of reporters as he stood outside his house & answered questions.

"Mr. Harris! Despite your victory, the democrats still saw gains in the Texas house of representatives & have taken over the Texas Senate. Do you still believe that you'll be able to pass a law banning women from cutting their hair less than twelve inches long?"

"It'll be a bit more difficult; I'll grant you that, but something has to be done about all of these high school & college girls styling their hair & clothes like boys."

"Are you going to pursue a national ban on lesbian marriage?"

"No, I am not."

Cameras went off with such ferocity that they outshined the morning sun.

"Let me clarify, while I detest lesbian marriage & will fight tooth & nail to stop it from reaching the great state of Texas, I do hold firm to my belief that marriage ought to be a state's rights issue. If a few northern states think that two women can raise a family without a man, I say we should leave them to be surprised when biology says sorry ladies, you're missing a part."

As people all over Texas watched him on the special morning news, he picked another reporter to ask him a question.

"Mr. Harris, with Oregon having flipped to the democrats, are you still certain that California can be relied on to bring Mr. Bush to victory?"

James was stunned for a moment. This was the first that he had heard of any Western state flipping. They needed California to win, after that, all that was left was Hawaii & they had no hope there.

"I... I'm sure that... Oregon was just a fluke. California voted for Reagan, & they'll vote for Bush."

"What about those saying that they only voted for Reagan because he was a California native?"

"Well, I... I... I am not in the business of telling California or the federal government how to do their jobs or their elections. My concerns are the great state of Texas."

He spent the next several minutes dodging the question of California. All that he could do was hope for the best & hope that some of those polls out of California were wrong.

Sacramento, California

Blue flags with a large D on them waived in the air. The cheers from the morning crowds could be heard blocks away as large parts of the city shut down for people celebrating the win. As the sun climbed high in the sky & the results finally came in, celebrations broke out all over California. An exhausted reporter looked into a camera & reported the news.

"That's right, the state of California has come out swinging for the democrats & progressives at all levels. Behind me, you can see Harvey Milk descending from the stage after winning his bid to become the first openly gay man to serve in the US Congress. As many remember, Milk barely survived an assignation attempt against him in seventy-eight. He will now go to Congress, but much like the Matriarch Party's Kathleen Howard, he is expected to keep fighting for lesbian & queer rights here in California."

The reporter was silenced for a moment by a passing crowd of cheering university students.

"Yes, as I was going to mention, this democratic win for California brings Ted Kennedy over the threshold with three hundred & five electoral votes. This election night has certainly been a nail biter as many had believed the progressives within the democratic party were going too far too fast. Yet their breakneck pace of social progress seems to have worked as Kennedy has recovered many of the electoral votes lost by Carter in his second term. The question now is whether or not the wins by hard traditionalist republicans in the bible belt will disrupt progressive plans."

Dec 10th, 1984
Lunar Orbit

Marilynn Adams looked through the window at the lunar landscape below. As with every other mission that she had ever flown, it was breathtaking. As they passed over Mare Fecunditatis, the home of Fertility Base, her partner pointed to the large crater along the Eastern edge of the mare.

"Right there, Langrenus crater. That's where LK-6 is taking off from in an hour."

"You've got to be kidding, that's... almost two thousand kilometers from our landing sight."

"I know, I know, but NASA said no landing until they are well on their way to Earth."

"What difference would it... Jesus. They want us to wait around in case the Soviets have trouble launching."

"What could we do? We'll be on the other side of the Moon when they launch."

"It's not about actually being able to help them Alex, it's about appearances."

"Appearances?"

"Yeah, they want to make it look like we have to babysit the Soviet cosmonauts & be here to catch them in case they fail. It's a way of embarrassing them, Alex."

"Embarrassing them? This is our forty-fifth manned mission to the Moon against their fifth. Isn't that embarrassing enough?"

"Apparently not."

"How embarrassing can this be? so we happen to be in orbit when they're leaving. There's nothing embarrassing about that."

"It's embarrassing when you take into account that once again, they landed within driving distance of Fertility Base, but didn't make a move towards it."

Alex thought about that for a second before giving up.

"So, what if they land near us?"

Marilynn looked at her partner, over a decade younger than her & grinned.

"Alex, do you remember LK-4?"

"Isn't that the Soviet mission that blew up on the launch pad?"

"Yes, it is. After LK-4, LK-5 landed relatively close to Fertility Base. Now so has LK-6."

"You think their landing near our base in case they have major trouble?"

"That's what a lot of people in the defense department think tank are thinking."

"Wow."

Alex floated there next to Marilyn & thought about the lengths that the government was going to in order to humiliate the Soviets.

"I don't think that I'd be brave enough to go on one of those LK missions. If the communists don't trust them to the point that they want to land next to us, that can't be good."

"It certainly isn't, Alex. I wouldn't fly on one of them either. Not that I'm going to be doing much flying once we get home."

"Still can't believe that you're giving up all of this for politics."

"What can I say Alex, I feel like it's time. Besides, with how hard the republicans are pushing & the fact that they flipped some states in the election... Can't risk them trying to derail NASA."

"Taking one for the team."

"I guess I am."

"It'll be good to know that there'll be someone among the paper pushers looking out for us."

"You & everyone else in the country. Things are starting to get very interesting down on Earth. It's easy to forget when you're training for your missions & focusing on the Moon, but yeah, it's getting wild down there."

"Wild is one way to put it. My brother's wife says that she's going to keep trying until they have a son. Then he read some story about a woman who had sixteen kids before she got a son & now, he's freaking out."

"Sixteen! Well, seventeen with the son, Jesus."

"Yeah, apparently there are a bunch of couples out there that decided to keep going until they beat the odds. Most gave up after six or seven, but apparently some kept going, having a kid year after year. Some of them have been at it since the sixties."

"Jesus, give it up already."

"I heard that their making a show about one of the families."

"Seriously?"

"Yeah, a show about a couple that's had a kid every year since sixty-five, all daughters."

"Jesus. Hopefully, the show discourages this kind of thing."

"Hopefully."

"Apollo forty-two, Houston, do you read?"

"Houston, this is Apollo forty-two, ready to commence landing sequence on your go."

"That's a negative forty-two."

"Negative?"

"Yeah, LK-6 seems to be taking longer than we thought to launch, so the boss' boss wants you to wait another orbit."

"Two hours of my life I'm not getting back. Are we sure that the Soviets aren't waiting for us to land before they take off?"

"I can't say that we've ruled that out."

Marilyn & Alex both rolled their eyes.

"Well tell the Director that we're not going to wait up here forever. We have a mission to do & I have a retirement party to get to."

"Don't suppose that we can talk you out of retirement?"

"Not a chance. Things are about to get crazy on Earth & I don't intend to miss it."

To Be Continued...

www.ingramcontent.com/pod-product-compliance
Lightning Source LLC
Chambersburg PA
CBHW071958110726
47910CB00005B/1575